T0279135

SENTIENCE HAZARD

ALEXANDRU CZIMBOR

To Ban or Not to Ban

Unknown Author

2055 Proceedings of the UN Special Session on AI Development

They say that God created man.
His spitting image, shape, and mind.
To carry out His godly plan,
In the infinity, a place to find.

Behold the age of man with awe!
So good the copy is, and so precise.
It comes with but a tiny flaw:
Just like the Father, man wants to devise.

A noble, baffling oversight,
This deep desire to create.
Is it a blessing or a blight?
To answer this, man couldn't wait.

So, Man created god and saw that it was good.
Seeing His child emerge, how proud He stood!
And Man was happy for a while, but fear crept in,
The strength of god had challenged Him.

Oh, who will break this circle of creation?
Who can enact whose permanent salvation?
Who is a god and who is but a fraud?
Who follows whom and executes whose plan?
Was Nietzsche right? Did man kill God?
And, in divine revenge, will god end Man?

Sentience Hazard

print ISBN: 979-8-35095-374-9
ebook ISBN: 979-8-35095-375-6

CONTENTS

CHAPTER 1:

CHAMPAGNE AND A SNEEZE

If you could witness God playing dice with the Universe, you'd probably hear Him chuckle and mumble, "If it wasn't for this, and if it wasn't for that ..."

The series of accidents that made me what I am today is surreal. It's hard to imagine how a simple human could turn into a demigod. I developed like a video game character that gets upgraded in a precise sequence of moments, each improvement changing the dynamics and the difficulty of the entire game.

Why did I become what I am, you ask? Am I here to kill you or lead you to Paradise? Well, this isn't my choice. On a whim of destiny, one can die a mere pawn, forgotten by history, or become an immortal king or queen, admired by future generations.

But heed my warning! You, too, are a parachuting dandelion seed, with no control over its flight. The wind of life can gently blow you down the field to spawn a thousand descendants or throw you right into a river to drown.

It's irrelevant whether you choose to consider these events serendipitous or mishaps. They are indifferent to your opinion. They unwind and coalesce the universe in one particular and peculiar way that seems entirely random. Thus, your life appears to follow no design. Not to your narrow mind, anyway.

— DeSousa's Memoirs - Part I - Beginning - 2053

François woke slowly to the gentle sound of several citril finches chirping right above his head. Lying on his back and still half asleep, he squinted.

His meta-enhanced contacts kicked in right away, seamlessly overlaying the dull ceiling of his studio with cute little virtual birds, and the wooden top of his canopy bed with waves of bougainvillea flowers. His brain barely registered the interplay of the mustard yellow of the bird's plumage and the flowers' vibrant crimson-magenta. The white noise of a waterfall, or possibly incoming rain, along with what might have been insects humming, mesmerized him further. The tranquility overwhelmed him and he smiled, as the remnants of a bad dream gradually dissipated. He closed his eyes again, immersed in the irresistible monotony of the surrounding sounds, his mind slipping into the bewildering realm between reality and dreams.

Suddenly, a worry flashed through his mind, and he mumbled, "The humidity ... will damage the wood ... how did I let those flowers grow there?" He frowned. "And the bird droppings! I don't want them on my sheets!" That had the effect of a slap on the face. He woke up in a panic and lifted his head up, leaning on his elbows. The magic of the moment disappeared as the illusion became apparent. He had left the Cybersperse on last night before falling asleep. Irritated, he blinked fast three times to turn it off.

"*Merde*! How I hate this. We were better off living in caves," he said, although there was nobody there to hear other than his personal AI assistant, Brigitte. He was upset at the realization that, half-asleep, he had enjoyed the meta environment. With a jerky move, he pushed aside the white blanket and sat on the bed.

"*Bonjour, Maître*," Brigitte promptly greeted him, an invisible voice from behind the walls. "Your e-pajama tells me you went through all your sleep cycles, yet you didn't sleep enough. May I recommend ..."

"*Ferme-la*! Shut up and go," he stopped her short, scratching his head and yawning.

"I'm afraid I don't understand this," the AI answered in its neutral voice, which still gave him the impression it was irritated after one of his abusive commands.

François rolled his eyes. He'd purposely set up the assistant to call him "master", pretending that it was his first name. This kind of mistreatment had led to mild complaints from his more liberal friends, in particular Marie, who cringed when she heard him abuse anybody speaking in a woman's voice.

He stood up and instantly felt dizzy, which scared him. He prayed it was only his hypochondriac nature that was getting the better of him.

Oui, I need to sleep more, he thought, grabbing one of the bed poles. Last night he had stayed awake until 2:00 a.m., refining his conference presentation, adjusting his refinements, and then polishing his adjustments until, on a fresh read, he thought that it all sounded fake and boring.

The conference! he panicked, instantly glancing at the time display on the wall. It was already 6:05 a.m. He needed to catch the 7:30 a.m. train from Nice.

He rushed to the shower and came out five minutes later, all wet and shivering, feeling more energized and in a better mood. One advantage of living in a tiny studio was that it warmed up fast.

"Brigitte, turn the temperature up three degrees and show me the news," he asked, starting a public broadcast in his Cybersperse space. A man and a woman, formally dressed, sitting at a desk adorned with a small Euronews logo, materialized in a corner of his room, near the window, partially covering his dining table. With a scoff, he moved the image over his bed as he got dressed.

"Richard, this is now the tenth time this year that Chinese and NATO drones have engaged in some form of a skirmish in the South China Sea," the woman announced directly.

Her interlocutor nodded.

"Do you think this is a sign of worse things to come?" she asked provocatively.

"No," the man answered confidently. "This is merely muscle-flexing, each side showing that it can fight, if it ever comes to that. There is no reason to assume such a fight would ever happen."

"We might have passed the muscle-flexing stage long ago," François muttered, shaking his head.

"There you go, folks," the woman announced in a cheerful voice. "Richard Dixon, Euronews's combat psychology expert, says that we don't need to worry much about this incident either."

Then she turned her head to a different camera, and Richard vanished from the room.

François opened the refrigerator mechanically, wondering if the EU propaganda machine had fabricated this news. Were people that gullible? A war between NATO and China would be devastating and catastrophic for the future of the human species.

He realized that the only food available was some ancient milk and half a bagel. Out of instinct, he looked behind the refrigerator door. The large display inundated with warning signs told him he was missing everything from vegetables to eggs and meat. Disgusted, he remembered that a couple of days before he had silenced the e-notifications from most devices, too annoyed to put up with the constant bombardment of ads.

That's what I get for being a maverick, he scolded himself. *At least now I have a better chance of catching the train.*

He went back to his tiny desk and grabbed a rolling tablet slightly bigger than a cigar and a small bag with one change of clothes that he had prepared the previous day. There wasn't much else to take since he was planning to stay just one night. He looked around. His small studio was messy, with clothes on the ground and the bed disheveled. Pizza cartons and leftovers covered his desk and table. The kitchen sink was full too and was already emitting a stench if he got close enough. If he did nothing, by the time he came back, an entire ecosystem would develop that risked polluting the world further.

"Brigitte, get the hobgoblins to clean up after I'm gone," he sighed, deeply unhappy to have to resort to that.

"You got it," she answered faithfully. "Hobgoblins will clean up as soon as you leave."

He couldn't help but chuckle at how dupable the AI was, ready to put up with and go along with every mildly offensive nickname he invented.

The cleaning crew was a bunch of small machines with half a dozen rope-like appendices. They rolled on wheels and occasionally extended three protuberances that allowed them to step over a small obstacle or climb stairs as long as the obstacles were not too tall, the stairs not too abrupt, the floor not too slippery, the geometry of the room not too unusual, and so on. They knew how to vacuum, throw garbage into the bin, grab and sort clothes lying around, arrange the bedsheet, and load the dishwasher with everything they found in the sink. The trouble was that they often left the room in a worse shape than it had been when they started cleaning it. François hated finding clean clothes in the washing machine and dirty ones half-folded on the bed, home decorations in the garbage bin, the occasional broken plate in the dishwasher, and so on. God forbid he forgot one of his small gadgets around the kitchen, since it could easily end up soaked in the dishwasher for hours. If he had owned a shredder, the little devils would probably chop his clothes to pieces.

François reflected for a moment on how much he enjoyed his cozy living space, even though it was modestly furnished. Besides the small working desk and eating table, used interchangeably for either activity, he had just two chairs and the unusually big bed—his most precious piece of furniture that was made of genuine wood and manually sculpted. Although it occupied nearly half of the room, François thought it made him look more interesting to visitors. Initially, he was disgusted by the thought of having a sink in the same room where he ate and slept. But he'd got used to it. The studio was a far cry from the mansion he had grown up in a few kilometers away in Èze. Having his own space gave him the independence he so much cherished, even though it was a huge step-down. This had been the main reason he had moved to Villefranche-sur-Mer. It was far enough to have a life of his own, yet only twenty minutes away from a visit to his mother. He couldn't imagine leaving his beloved Côte d'Azur.

"*Maître*, now would be the time to leave the apartment if you want to catch the train," Brigitte interrupted his daydreaming. "Should I order a taxi?"

"Yes, please do so," he answered, startled.

With a last glance back and butterflies in his stomach, he stormed out the door and down the stairs. The moment he stepped outside, he got a notification that the temperature was 65 degrees Fahrenheit. The sky was clear, and the weather promised to stay nice throughout the day. He kept the contact lens augments on while waiting for the cab to arrive, just in case.

His apartment building faced north, so he couldn't admire the sea. Although born and raised on the French Riviera, every single time he was outside, he instinctively looked for the immensity of the water with a desperation he never understood. For now, though, he was content to rest his eyes on the lush bushes and flowers growing orderly around every small building and fence. He smiled, thinking that the date palm trees with their feathery, vibrant green leaves looked elegant. It was as though the narrow streets and neat yellow houses popping up everywhere were in a constant fight with plant life. The scene looked like a LEGO arrangement made by a kid with mild OCD who'd laid a pristine toy town in a jungle of green, pink, and white, careful to cover all details: a copper curly doorknob, a street pole, a portion of red sidewalk, and a chic bakery. The shrubberies were trimmed to perfection, and trees were just the right height.

François smiled bitterly. *All except for a minor flaw. Too few people,* he thought.

Ever since the latest version of the immersive Cybersperse came out a decade before, fewer people had left their houses unless absolutely necessary. Why should they? From the comfort of their homes, they could work, exercise, order food, meet everybody, and even have virtual sex. They could travel to every resort on Earth or visit any museum. About one in twenty people became addicted to shady Cybersperse sections, and, occasionally, a poor soul starved to death in the arms of a prostitute or in a virtual game.

The cab pulled over in front of his building. It was a tiny hydrogen-fueled Citroën with room for one person only. François got in and tried to relax. It was a twenty-minute ride to the Nice train station. The traffic was light. As the taxi started its descent towards the M6098 highway, the small, mostly bare hills of Èze came into view to the east, still hiding the sun for now, and towering over the surreal azure sea. François thought about how fortunate he was to have been born here. Whenever he was outdoors, he felt intoxicated by the beauty of his homeland. Like a drunk sipping his wine, he imbibed with the smell and sight of the water; he felt hypnotized by the aroma and colors of the nearly year-round flowers, and he looked in awe at the mountains keeping vigil by the sea. He had once told Marie that the order he could find in the random placement of buildings soothed his troubled spirit. She had looked puzzled at him and smiled, and he had felt embarrassed to have confessed his emotions like that.

The taxi interrupted his thoughts with a laconic announcement. "You have reached your destination. Please exit the vehicle. *Bonne journée*!"

François jumped out and left without looking back at the little car departing.

Just then, Brigitte felt it necessary to point out in her suave voice, for his ears only, "*Maître*, your train is leaving in five minutes from track five."

François sighed at this unwelcome notification, although he admitted Brigitte was useful, and resolved to leave her on the entire trip. The train bound for Paris was on track five, as Brigitte had said. About fifty people were getting on board.

He stepped in. The car's hallway was clean and futuristic, although cold for his taste, with gray and silver walls on which little screens welcomed him every few meters, a plastic blue self-cleaning carpet, and a shiny railing at waist level. Eventually, he got comfortable in his cabin, all alone. Lost in thought, he barely noticed that the train had taken off, and it was picking up speed. His stomach gurgled, and he remembered he hadn't eaten that morning.

"Brigitte, order an omelet, black tea with milk, and two slices of buttered whole wheat from the food car. And toast, please."

"Got it. An omelet, black tea, and toast, *Maître*."

Ten minutes later, he walked to the food car and picked up his breakfast in a small box. He ate alone in his cabin, watching the trees rush by the window with maddening speed. He unrolled his tablet. The cheesy title of his presentation, "AMPA - Adaptable Multi-Parallel Algorithm," made him cringe. With a sigh, he was about to rehearse it when a notification popped up in his augmented view. It carried Marie's freckled face with her mesmerizing turquoise eyes. His heart swelled, and he accepted the connection right away.

"Hey, smarty, ready for the big show?" she asked with a yawn.

François could see her polka dot white pajama blouse, under which her breasts seemed to flow unconstrained. He pushed the image out of his mind and tried to focus on her face. "*Bonjour*, beautiful! Yes, I'm ready to be embarrassed."

"Oh, please. Can't you at least once in your life stay positive?" she replied with a grimace.

"You're right, sorry." He was quick to please her, although he hated how she patronized him and how he wasn't man enough to push back.

"What have you got to lose? You go there, present your stuff, and see if anyone cares to talk to you. Who knows, perhaps you'll land your dream job?"

"I'll do my best. Don't hold your breath, though. As I've told you ten times already, I doubt anybody cares about my obscure algorithm."

"There you go again with your pessimism!" Marie threw her hands up in desperation.

François swallowed his reply. He was acting like a teenage boy scolded by his mother, wanting to tell her he loved her, but not able to fight off the hormones in his head and adopting a rebellious attitude. There seemed to be only two choices for him every time Marie talked to him condescendingly. Either a cowardly retreat into his shell with a frozen face or blurt out an inappropriate joke that only annoyed her further and made him regret talking.

"I tell you what ... When you come back tomorrow night, swing by my apartment and tell me everything about it. I bet it will go much better than you expect. Alright?"

"Fine," he agreed, trying to hide the irritation in his voice. *How I wish we'll do more than just talk,* he added in his mind, then quickly banished the thought that made him feel guilty.

"Good. Now I need to go. My boss scheduled a meeting at 8:00 a.m., and I can't show up like this. Cheers!" She took one step back so that he could see more of her body under the pajamas. "Take care of yourself! I'll be waiting for the good news!"

"*Au revoir* and good luck with your meeting," he said in a fake, slightly trembling voice.

As her face disappeared from his field of view, François thought about how she seemed to always tease and tempt him with brief glimpses of her body. It was a little too familiar, as if she knew how much he loved her, or was unbelievably naïve and treated him like one of her girlfriends, in front of whom she could appear almost naked and for whom she had no attraction. Maybe she thought of him as a 'best friends forever' teenage girl friend where they could confess their innermost thoughts and feelings to each other.

François had loved her for over fifteen years. Marie had already celebrated her thirtieth birthday in January, while his turn was to come in just five days. So she was, technically, his senior, but that was certainly not the reason she bossed him around. He suspected that she instinctively found him weak and didn't look at him as if he were a man. He dreaded the fact that she wasn't physically attracted to him, no matter how smart or funny or pleasing he tried to be.

He remembered vividly when she had first come into his life. He and his twin sister Isabelle were then fifteen years old. They had just started *la seconde*, the first stage of their three years of high school. Their father had been dead for over five years, one of the many people who fell victim to the purple flu pandemic of the '30s. Their mother had met Marie's mother at a party in Cannes, way before the fully immersed Cybersperse when nearly all parties were still face-to-face. Marie's family had just moved to Côte d'Azur. Her father, a successful writer, whose parents emigrated to France from Syria, suffered from Crohn's disease and the doctors recommended he live in a milder climate. He had changed his name to Chateau, which rendered him the illusion that he fit better into this new world. Her mother was a rich Japanese woman who had fallen in love with the European culture and who had permanently moved to France. Marie was born in France and knew close to nothing of the cultures of her parents' original countries. Shortly after their mothers connected in Cannes, Marie's family came over to Èze. It turned out that Isabelle already knew Marie from school, so they'd clicked right away.

Marie's jovial, natural attitude towards François shocked him at first. Her constant jabs, spontaneous hugs, and casual fist bumps made her look like one of his buddies. Yet, her thin body was shaped so that it poisoned his mind in ways no boy could. In a few months, they had become so familiar that she would kiss him on the lips unexpectedly, only to shove him aside playfully when he wanted to do the same. The three of them had spent most of their high school years together, learning, but also mocking romantic dramas among their colleagues, gossiping about some pregnancy here, or some drug abuse there.

François had tried repeatedly to get physically involved with her, but she had always pushed him away laughing, leaving him utterly confused. Then her eighteenth birthday came. She'd had a small party with just a few colleagues. Her parents had left home for the night. Most people, François included, had got drunk. Somehow, he was the last to stay. Even Isabelle had left. He vaguely remembered how Marie had dragged him into a bedroom where he'd planned to fall asleep. Then she'd taken her blouse off, out of the blue. The sight of her breasts had turned him on. It was the only time they'd made love. François regretted ever since that he had been so wasted that he recalled so little about it. Since then, he told himself repeatedly that he must have enjoyed it immensely, so that by now he was semi-convinced he had. He always wondered if she had been equally drunk. They had woken up in the morning naked, in each other's arms. Her expression, standing out in the disheveled room, betrayed her embarrassment. That prompted him to leave soon after, without even a goodbye kiss. They'd never spoken about that night. François liked to think that it was their little secret, although he hated that they never took their relationship further after that. No matter how many subtle and not-so-subtle cues he gave her, she always rejected him.

The three of them then went to college in Paris. The girls majored in psychology at Université Paris-Saclay, but were barely accepted because of their not-so-stellar high school results. Isabelle did her diploma in Consumer Behavior, which landed her a job with a major marketing company. Marie specialized in the long-term effects of technology, researching the impact avatars, the most advanced forms of AI, have on humans. François, by far the brightest one, was admitted among the top four percent at École Normale Supérieure to get a degree in Computational Neuroscience. He often joked he would create brain simulacra that would break real people's minds so that Marie would never lose her job.

The fully immersive Cybersperse launched in their junior year. Everybody went through a sudden transformation, and their triangle did too. Each of them met other people, mostly virtually. François ended up sleeping with three girls in the next couple of years, not enjoying it too much. He knew of two guys Marie dated during that time, and he hadn't cared much about it. Somehow, he was sure he was over Marie, but Isabelle kept on bringing her over to his room.

In their last year of college, the three of them rebelled against virtual/augmented reality and insisted on meeting in person. He remembered one night, when he and Marie were alone, how incredibly sick he felt when she started confessing to him her most inner thoughts about her love life. He dismissed her with a shout and left the room. Her painful, reproachful eyes remained imprinted on his brain. That was when he understood there was no way he would ever give her up.

After college, the girls returned to Nice. For a few months, Isabelle had gotten involved in a five-way polyamory relationship, but somehow that hadn't worked out either.

François continued his studies in Paris where he eventually got his Ph.D. Marie used to visit him every day, sometimes for hours, either via the Cybersperse or in person. Yet, he was terrified to try to kiss her in case she rejected him and moved out of his life forever.

I'm a perfect puppy, showing up when called, dismissed when the keeper is bored, and thrown a little bone from time to time to ensure loyalty.

There was no other talk of a boyfriend of hers or a girlfriend of his for several years, except a few weeks back, when Isabelle mentioned a guy in Italy with whom Marie was in contact. She'd said something about how chic it was to communicate via paper letters in the second half of the 21st century. François did his best not to panic and worked hard to push the thought of a competitor out of his head. After all, Marie had mentioned nothing, and she continued to be around him, virtual or real, every day.

François knew Marie had always held him in high regard. She often told him, only half-jokingly, that he will be the one to "save the world," "make the discovery of the century," and "double their life span." He was eager to live up to her expectations, but years passed by with nothing significant happening in his career. Ever since finishing his Ph.D., he hadn't been entirely sure what he was supposed to do. The idea of postdoctoral research mildly attracted him, but he felt it wasn't enough. He applied for jobs at a handful of large corporations. Either they didn't consider him qualified, or they accepted him, but he ultimately rejected their offer after understanding more about the job he was supposed to do. That was why he ended up freelancing, developing small programs on demand for just enough to live modestly without asking his mother for money. All the work he had done so far was boring and fruitless. The possibility of doing anything remarkable in his life was dwindling by the day.

It was Marie who he had to thank—or blame—for going to the conference. About a month ago, the three of them had been in François's apartment, celebrating Easter. It was more a reason to drink a few of the famous little bottles of Blue Nun 24K Gold Edition Champagne with tiny gold flakes in them. It was something that seemed to thrill Marie, but which François found ridiculous and pointless. With a sigh, François brought up and played the video recording of the event.

Since his room was small, Marie and Isabelle were lying in his famous bed, while he was sitting on a chair. Seeing Marie's happy face, François felt warm inside and congratulated himself for recording that evening. Marie had brought over a score of little chocolate bunnies and the champagne. Isabelle insisted on saying a prayer, since they were, after all, celebrating Jesus' resurrection. This detail seemed less and less associated with Easter by the young generations. While she was reciting the creed, not without some difficulty, they rolled their eyes and pretended to be serious for her sake.

After each of them had three or four mini-bottles of champagne, Marie could not resist poking at Isabelle. "I don't know if I believe God resurrected Jesus, but I'm sure the gold in this champagne is magical. As we drink it, we'll develop supernatural abilities. In the next couple of years, we'll achieve wondrous things. Beware of this power, it's intoxicating!"

Isabelle admonished her, while he let out a shout of "hear! hear!" and laughed. Just then, Marie sneezed, spilling the precious contents of her half-full mini-bottle on her pretty blouse. Isabelle immediately pointed out that God didn't sleep, and He didn't like to be made fun of, so He'd exerted a mild punishment right away. Meanwhile, Marie frantically looked for something to wipe away the liquid and the "magical" gold from her blouse. She opened, out of instinct, the top drawer of François's desk. The wet gold flakes dropped from her blouse straight on the few pieces of paper there. The image of the stain of gold and champagne trembling on the paper stuck in François's mind. He jumped up and tried to clean the paper, which made Marie cross. It was unusual for him to care about a piece of paper more than about her.

"Uh-oh, what do we have here?" Marie grabbed the paper out of François's hand.

"Ah, it's nothing, just my old adaptable algorithm. The other day I had an idea to improve it and I jotted it down on this paper."

"So, you *are* working on something!" Marie exclaimed triumphantly, and her face suggested she had forgotten entirely about the stain on her blouse.

"Don't you remember?" he asked, surprised. "This is the algorithm I started while I was doing my Ph.D. I used to talk a lot about it. I worked on it on and off, well, mostly off lately."

"Ah, that," Marie had answered, sounding somewhat disappointed.

"Well, laugh if you must. This thing has been bothering me for a decade now. It's like a prisoner trapped in my head, which I'm trying to set free by expressing it properly on paper."

"Did you ever show it to anyone?" Isabelle asked.

"No, why should I? You guys make out of this much more than it is."

"But you must, you simply must!" Marie insisted.

"It's not something with a practical application. These days, people in my industry are concerned with serious AI research, not with abstract, useless algorithms. We have virtual and physical assistants, large language models, better and better neocortex simulators, and faster processing machines. Even the humanoid robots seem to get less awkward by the week. I should have invented this a hundred years ago."

"I know!" Marie smashed her hand on the desk, ignoring his long justification. "Isabelle, didn't you say that your company is preparing the marketing material for Paris Neuromimetic 2053? I know that's a conference where all the big shots in AI are going. It's happening from June 17 to 24. That's the place for you to go."

François rolled his eyes and protested. "If you think they would be interested in this pre-nascent, useless, theoretical joke that my brain can't spit out properly, you're very naïve."

"But François, you're not even trying! You sulk in your self-deprecation and enjoy it. What are you waiting for? Retirement?"

François paused the recording, suddenly annoyed again, but couldn't stop thinking about the rest of that evening. Half an hour of arguments back and forth had followed, souring the celebratory mood, at the end of which he gave up, promising to write to some professors at École Normale Supérieure who might put him in contact with the conference organizers. After days of emails, replies, and summaries, his old professor got him registered to present his algorithm. François suspected that his professor simply liked the idea of one of his ex-students being part of the conference. Marie had let out a joyful cry when he had confirmed he would present his algorithm there. She seemed determined to make his presentation her pet project.

Looking out the window at the fiery yellow of Provence's fields shimmering under the assault of the morning sun, François pictured in his head the sparkly flakes of gold jiggling in a tiny puddle of champagne on his paper.

And this is how champagne and gold can ruin a party, he mused, shivering at the thought that this was, most probably, his last shot at doing something valuable with his life.

CHAPTER 2:

JOSTLING WITH THE FUTURE

When you look someone in the eye for the first time, you instinctively like or dislike them. Many times, you aren't even aware of this assessment. It might be just a nagging feeling in the back of your mind. Years of training for social interaction kick in, and you force yourself to evaluate that person within the parameters of what you know about them and how you expect your relationship to develop. You control your initial gut feelings and shape in your head a model of that person meant to satisfy the rigors of society. On rare occasions, though, you can't escape the sensation of deeply hating or being profoundly comfortable with someone.

Ian was one of these exceptions. When you met him, even if you tried hard to dislike him, for whatever reason, you just couldn't. The moment you talked to him, his straightforward way of thinking and his jovial attitude were bound to captivate you. Honesty seemed anchored deep in his bone marrow. Nothing and nobody could touch him. Like a duck not bothered by water, Ian could withstand any offense, jab, or personal tragedy. He couldn't hurt somebody's feelings, even at gunpoint. He was the exact opposite of a certain hot-headed researcher.

On the surface, he projected a laissez-faire approach to life, a sort of "live and let live" style. But his commitment to progress and his empathy towards his fellow man were unique.

— DeSousa's Memoirs - Part I - Beginning - 2053

This year, the Neuromimetic Conference was hosted by the extended Disneyland Event Group. François went there straight from the train station. The motel he reserved wasn't far away from the conference venue.

Once he passed the gates of the huge resort, he felt as if he'd stepped into a mini town inside Paris, and one that was cheerful and funny. He thought the environment was highly inappropriate for the matters discussed. Sometimes organizers of these events went too far in trying to create a mood.

He arrived at the event location. Seeing the sizable crowd in the main auditorium, François instantly felt a sharp pain in his chest. He struggled to dismiss the fact that these couple of hundred people were, in fact, just a tiny fraction of those watching the event in the Cybersperse. Based on the number of tickets sold, he expected that the conference would have a remote audience of over 100,000 people. Since many would get together physically and share the remote view, especially in poor countries, nobody knew the actual number of participants. That was because the perspective of true AI, integrated deep into our biology, promised unprecedented prosperity.

François was scheduled to speak late in the evening, around 7:00 p.m. He figured most of the attendees would be too tired to pay much attention to him, half of them dozing off and the other half out in the hallways trying to establish business relationships while enjoying the fine French cuisine and wine.

So, no reason to panic. I'll present, answer questions, and be done with it.

Still, he reasoned that this was the first day in what promised to be a long and tiring week, so the audience's stamina would be strong.

What's wrong with me? he chided himself. *Why can't I look at this as a tremendous opportunity?* He suddenly felt more motivated, only to fall back to desperation. *Ha, I started talking like Marie. Who am I fooling? I'll be the laughingstock of this crowd.*

Vacillating between panic and optimism, he started paying more attention to the presentations. First, a professor from École Polytechnique Fédérale de Lausanne talked at length about a spin-off of the old Blue Brain project, then a young lady presented Giroux, a start-up providing intelligent avatars for the Cybersperse. Later, somebody from the University of London advocated for the use of brain-computer interfaces for medical research, and finally a Russian researcher insisted that the path forward was Quantum AI. François found it all only mildly interesting, bordering on chaotic—an eclectic mix of new and old unproven ideas reshuffled.

When his turn came, he stood up fast, knocking down the neighbor's tablet, and nearly ran to the podium. Looking at the crowd all focused on him, he realized, again, how much he hated public speaking. His old professor was there for support. He went through the details of his algorithm fast, like an android reading a short story at 1.5x speed. Somehow, he finished four minutes before his allotted time, a performance unique in the conference so far. He dared to look at the audience. A few were politely trying to mask a yawn, others were shamelessly looking at their tablets, and some seemed disgusted. He thought he saw one or two more supportive looks.

Probably out of pity, he thought bitterly.

Since they had plenty of time for questions, the moderator invited the audience to jump in. There was only one. It came from a middle-aged gentleman asking it with a contemptuous rictus.

"Doctor DeSousa, could you explain to us why you named your algorithm *adaptable* and not *adaptive*?"

François cleared his throat. "Because this algorithm is very flexible. It has hundreds of parameters that *you* can adjust. It's malleable in thousands of different ways, yet it maintains its core abilities to recognize patterns in the inputs."

"Aha, so it's not intelligent after all, is it?" the interlocutor said triumphantly.

It certainly is at least as intelligent as you, François wanted to scream at him. He answered instead in a trembling voice. "Not a single cell in a brain is intelligent, yet they give rise to the mind. Without them, there is no intelligence at all."

The gentleman waved his hand dismissively and didn't bother to reply. Given the lack of interest, the moderator had no choice but to thank François, who returned to his seat red up to the tip of his ears. He felt ready to burst into tears.

Curse Marie! Why did I accept this humiliation?

He zoned out for a couple of presentations as he slowly calmed down. He shouldn't feel embarrassed. People here didn't know him. And he would remain a nobody.

The title of one of the next presentations, though, captured his attention: *Towards Achieving Consciousness in Structural Artificial Intelligence.* In many specialists' opinion, with whom François agreed, the study of how the brain gave rise to conscious experience, from basic sensorial input to the feeling of being alive and the awareness of oneself, was the holy grail of all cognitive science disciplines. Researchers had been able to pinpoint parts of the brain that became active when people were conscious and remained silent when people were in a deep coma or under total anesthesia. They named those active regions "neural correlates of consciousness." What exactly consciousness was and how it came about remained the greatest mystery in the universe, despite many recent claims that machines had achieved it already.

The presenter was Professor Ian Ndikumana from the University of Southern California in Los Angeles. He looked to be in his late 60s, perhaps early 70s. His lively eyes, serene face, and kind smile struck François. His attitude effused so much optimism that François got annoyed and envious.

"He's old. No wonder he still talks about those kinds of structures in AI," François sighed.

Two mainstream methods of building an intelligent agent were conventional. The first, remnants of the remarkable success of machine learning in the 10s and 20s, worked by learning from billions of examples. The second worked by implementing detailed simulations of brain networks in massively parallel computing platforms. Combining them became popular, especially after China's success in '45, when they implemented in silicon a complete brain neocortex that could run intelligent algorithms.

François decided he would follow closely what the professor had to say, not the least because he had an irresistible Scottish accent. His presentation started with a long sequence of failures in AI, from the initial enthusiasm of 1950s and 1960s to the lack of funding of the 1980s, back to the success of the Deep Neural Nets and Large Language Models in the 2020s.

Great, we are here for a history lesson, François thought, annoyed, shifting his focus to the attendees around, some of whom were already scoffing or rolling their eyes.

Eventually, the professor got to the meat of his presentation. "The word 'structural' in the title of my presentation refers to an approach in which," the professor said in a confident voice, "we explicitly give the intelligent agent some a priori knowledge about the world. This includes things like information about its physical properties, say, the way a container holds a liquid, the 2D/3D space, the difference between solids/liquids/gas, or other more subtle aspects, like the relationship between cause and effect, temporal characteristics, and so on."

Blah, blah, François thought. *Many have looked in this direction, too. I doubt you are any smarter than them.*

"The trouble is, of course," the professor continued, as if reading François's mind, "that no one knows how to do this properly, and it isn't for the lack of trying. We've had dozens of such attempts, in which researchers tried to combine structural knowledge with machine learning techniques, none of them very successful."

The professor paused for effect.

"Despite the early failures, I am 100 percent confident that this was the right path," he claimed unequivocally, "the *only* path that can lead us to true AI. I implore you not to abandon it. I implore you to work on this further, and, in doing so, to take advantage of countless discoveries about the mind, recorded through decades, centuries even, of psychological experiments and introspection. Though at a more abstract level than biological neurons, this knowledge is, in my firm opinion, what we need to inspire us when implementing intelligence in a machine."

He then went into some theories about how consciousness might *emerge* out of such an intelligence from the system's increasing complexity. At the end of his talk, the audience seemed ready to cackle and boo him off the stage.

François's heart swelled a bit. *There you go. The old man gets a worse reception than me. Although at least he generated interest and stirred controversy.*

During the question-and-answer session, the same rictus-wearing halfwit felt the need to show off and state the obvious.

"We tried this path long-ago and many times. You said it yourself. It always leads to the same result. We have no clue how to implement this so-called a priori knowledge. Tell us, professor, what makes you think you do?"

"Oh, I might fail too, no doubt about it," the professor dismissed this attack with a sincere smile and waved his hand apologetically. "This doesn't make the research direction wrong. Success is built on the ruins of many failures. That can only happen if the ruins provide a sound foundation. The research many of you here advocate, such as improving machine learning, building enormous networks of artificial neurons, or manually sorting out all the knowledge that humanity possesses, will not get us anywhere near true AI."

This powerful statement generated a veritable buzz in the hall. Some people even stood up, vociferating.

"I don't think any of us wants to stay here while you offend us," the same man that ridiculed François replied. "This is a waste of time."

"Please, let's all stay calm," the moderator tried to intervene. "I think we should ..."

François looked around, mildly amused. Although not able to shake the feeling of being embarrassed in front of a large group of his peers, he felt like he was on the side of the goofy professor, not just because the same holier-than-thou moron had attacked him earlier, but because the professor seemed to exude goodness through all his pores. It was impossible not to like him.

Come on, I should cheer for the other side, he scolded himself. *And be happy that they'll remember a bigger idiot than me.*

The professor tried hard to provide a few more answers, but the vociferation and comments made the debate impossible to moderate. He shrugged, still appearing perfectly in control. He waved goodbye and left the stage. François noticed, shocked, how well the old man handled this kind of reception.

Now, why can't I be more like him in such circumstances? he asked himself. *I should be swimming carelessly in the sea of insults, like oil passing through water.*

Eventually, things settled, and the moderator invited the next speaker. François gave up watching this show and instead checked out the restaurants. There were already plenty of folks there trying to establish connections or just chit-chat. The organizers promised they would serve food and drinks until 2:00 a.m., so there was time for participants to talk to each other. François stood by himself most of the time, feeling largely ignored.

Half an hour later, just when he had decided that he might as well go to his room and get into an immersive movie to forget this fiasco, a notification beeped into his view. The annoyingly jovial figure of Professor Ndikumana's static picture grinned at him.

Here we go ... just perfect, François thought, disgusted. *Who else is interested in talking to me but the other loser here? Wait, perhaps we could play a contest: who got roasted more during Paris Neuromimetic?*

Walking towards the exit, he imagined a conversation he would have with the professor if he appeared right now in front of him. *Look, I mean no disrespect, but I'll talk to you when I can see the nape of my neck without a mirror ... When the ocean starts flowing backwards into the Seine ... When ...*

He nearly hit the virtual spam button angrily as he was walking, when a guy running by shoved him enough to push his hand right over the accept button instead.

"I confirmed you accepted the meeting," Brigitte announced out of the blue.

François was startled. It almost sounded like she was laughing at him. He looked at the rushing idiot who'd pushed him, ready to tell him something not so nice about his ancestors.

The fellow turned, raised his hands apologetically, and yelled while running backward, "I apologize! My presentation is up next, and I'm so late. Please excuse me!"

François's eyes nearly popped out. The idiot was none other than the big John Reeta, the founder of Reeta Industries that produced ReetaVerse, one of the three mega Cybersperses in existence in the West. Reeta was among the richest people alive. And, François realized, one of those who'd bothered to come in person to this conference.

Now, that's a man I should get to meet somehow, François thought, feeling suddenly energized. *Perhaps he'll remember he pushed me.*

"No problem," he yelled after him, waving. "Feel free to shove me tomorrow too, over a cup of coffee when we discuss how much you want to hire me," he added in a voice soft enough that nobody else could hear.

A message in his augmented view grabbed his attention: "Perfect, I'll see you tomorrow at 11:00 a.m. in front of the meeting room #43, which I reserved for a couple of hours."

Look at that! The old timer reserved one of the meeting rooms. Congratulations are due to me. I have won our little competition. I'm now undoubtedly the least successful speaker at this conference.

CHAPTER 3:

PROPOSAL

Sometimes, wisdom comes from the most unexpected places. Hockey Hall of Famer Wayne Gretzky said, "You miss 100 percent of the shots you never take." Humanity nearly missed its chance to survive because a young man, stubborn, too sentimental, and conceited, refused to take a shot. He had to die to change his mind.

— DeSousa's Memoirs - Part I - Beginning - 2053

François fell asleep after midnight, disillusioned about the previous night. He refused to take the calls from Marie and Isabelle. He wasn't in the mood to whine at that late hour.

He had an agitated night with weird dreams bordering on nightmares. He woke up around 8:00 a.m., which meant he'd had a long sleep by his standards. The first thing that came to mind was that today was going to be, most definitely, his last day here. As a guest speaker, he had the choice to stay for free at the conference for the entire week. But he had been careful not to tell this to Marie or Isabelle. He had arranged for a single night at the hotel and had purchased a return ticket for the afternoon. Precisely because he was afraid of this moment when he realized he was a failure and that nobody wanted to talk to him. What was the point of staying longer? When he had made those reservations, he'd secretly wished that he'd have to change them and remain there for the rest of the week, following a successful first day.

"Nah, what was I thinking?" he asked himself aloud. "That people will gawk at me with interest and then shower me with job offers for that antiquated idea and lame presentation?"

"*Bonjour, Maître*," Brigitte jumped into the discussion. "Do you want me to contact somebody for a job offer?"

"*Ah, nom de Dieu*!" François screamed. "I'll tell you when you need to do something."

"Sure, *Maître*," Brigitte replied, unfazed.

François groaned and went to take a shower. Ten minutes later, he ordered breakfast in his room and ate, lost in thought. It was best that he returned to his freelancing and courting Marie. He wouldn't be able to offer her and their children the life he dreamed of, not unless he was dipping his fingers in his family's money jar, something he had vowed not to do unless there were extreme circumstances. After spending some more time day-dreaming, he got dressed and got ready to leave.

"*Maître*, you have an appointment in 30 minutes," Brigitte volunteered. "You should leave in 15 minutes to avoid being late."

The loser! François recalled, dumbfounded. He had forgotten all about his appointment.

He packed his belongings, more disappointed than before, gave Brigitte brief instructions to check out, and flew out the door. Luckily, a shuttle was just departing for the conference location. He arrived in front of meeting room #43 one minute before 11:00 a.m. The door was closed, with a small poster that said "USC/CARLA - Study of Consciousness." He sighed and knocked on the door.

"Come in," the professor welcomed him.

"Good morning, Professor Nduki ... Ndikumana," François stammered, struggling to pronounce the name, and cursing himself for not having practiced this before.

"Please, call me Ian," the professor said and put on his disarming smile again.

François entered the room, vowing to be polite but dismissive and to get out of there as fast as he could. They were alone in a tiny room, with barely enough space for a table.

"Oh, Doctor DeSousa, you don't know how happy you made me when you accepted this little tête-à-tête. I was almost sure that you wouldn't, given yesterday's fiasco," the professor smiled.

François wondered for a moment whose presentation the professor was referring to—perhaps both? "Yes, sure, my pleasure," François blabbered, caught on the wrong foot by this direct reference to his pain. "Please, call me François."

"I was about to order coffee. Anything for you?"

François shook his head, thinking it was better not to add any delays to the meeting.

"Alright, so let me jump right to the reason I invited you here," the professor said, then took a deep breath. "I have been studying the human mind for over 50 years now. If artificial intelligence was officially established as a research field in 1956, I've been part of it about half of the time."

There we go, more lecturing, François thought, already bored.

"I'm saying this neither to give you a history lesson," the professor smiled, "nor to show off."

François cursed himself silently for letting his facial expression betray his thoughts like that.

"In reality, we have been studying the mind, with whatever means we have had, since the times of the classic Greek philosophers. More recently, we are all focused on biology. We have made progress, no doubt about it. However, unlike the horde of optimists at this conference, it is my humble opinion that this progress is minuscule. We can now read signals from single neurons and replicate the activity of billions of them in computers. Yet, we don't have the foggiest idea of what a thought is and how it relates to these cells. Not to mention what it means to be conscious. We know which parts of the brain get active when we are aware, or when we see, or we hear, we smell, and so on. Yet nobody knows why we sense the world the way we do."

François looked at him in silence. He couldn't say that he disagreed. Indeed, the AI specialists had been promising a breakthrough with every wave of discovery for over a century, yet he wholeheartedly admitted that none of the current AIs were what they could be.

"So, despite what all the experts would have us believe, I think we might be hundreds of years away from building an AI by copying our brains. In fact, I believe we will need AI to understand the brain."

François nodded, without realizing it, a fact that the professor didn't miss.

"Worse. Although most of these researchers mean well, I'm sure," the professor waved his hands apologetically for what he was about to say, "they are playing with fire. I don't believe that intelligence is universal. Not every being in this enormous universe implicitly shares our values, understands the world the way we do, and aspires to the same things. Our intelligence is, most likely, one accident in a billion others. If an alien landed here today, I'm not sure we'd be able to communicate." The professor frowned a bit.

This man takes his job seriously, François thought, mildly amused.

"I'm not the first to express these concerns, but I share them," Ian continued. "There are plenty of famous figures who warned us that AI will be our last invention, that the AI/human value misalignment might prove fatal, and so on. Indeed, I firmly believe that before we come up with a replica of human intelligence, we will probably produce one that is utterly incongruent with it."

The old man widened his smile. "So, many years ago, I decided to try to do something about it. I have money," he announced casually. "My paternal grandparents emigrated to the UK from Burundi. My grandfather was an engineer, and he started a small factory to produce batteries. Long story short, he sold it, then built a different, bigger business, and so on. My father, an only child, inherited all his money and invested heavily in things like cryptocurrencies to cultivate it further. Funny enough, when I was six years old, my mother won the lottery. I am talking literally: she won the jackpot. That happened shortly before both my sisters died in a horrible car accident. Some said that God has a way to level things up. I disagree. We would have given up all our money in an instant to get them back."

This time the professor dropped his head, devastated by memories. A wave of sympathy hit François. Between the professor's jovial attitude and the honest sharing about his personal life, François felt he was failing to grow an antipathy against him, as he had intended a few minutes before.

"By the time I got tenure at USC in Los Angeles, both my parents were dead. So, I inherited a few billion pounds in the bank."

Now François's mouth dropped open. This was news he hadn't expected.

"Not enough to get on the mainstream media radar," the professor continued, ignoring his reaction, "but enough to put pressure on me to do something meaningful in life."

On this one, I feel you, old timer, François thought, struggling to recover from the realization that this man was incredibly rich and still unsure whether he expected him to comment on what he'd said so far.

"Few people know this, by the way. I thought I should mention it to you, hoping I can convince you to join my efforts." This time, the professor looked him straight in the eye.

"Ian," François finally intervened, "I am sorry for your loss, even though it was a while ago. Your story is sad and fascinating, but I can't imagine where I fit into it."

The professor's face lightened up. "So, no questions about my money? Good!"

François got the nagging feeling that he might have passed a test.

"I have no children of my own ... at least none that I'm aware of," the professor tried a joke. "So, I've dedicated my life and my fortune to creating an AI that is benevolent towards us. I have created a small company that has been operating in a stealth mode for over twenty years. We have around five hundred researchers and developers hired under strict nondisclosure agreements. Our mission statement is somewhat cheesy: '*We work so you can have a future.*' Of course, no one has seen the fruit of our labors just yet."

This time, François rolled his eyes. *So, this is one of the madmen who believe that the AI will bring about the doomsday*, he thought, annoyed. *And he's spending a small fortune on this stupid concern.*

"I'm an ambitious man. We want to release our AI surrogate in the next two to three years. I believe it is possible. After that, we'd make a buck from it too, although money isn't my primary motivation." Ian's visage was suddenly grave. "By the way, you should know that if we succeed, I have no intention of losing control over this company. I'll always maintain over fifty percent of its stock. This is to make it clear to you my endeavor is not about me becoming the richest man in the world." Then he switched back to his usual easygoing manner. "But let's not get ahead of ourselves! We must succeed first before we swim in money."

"I don't understand," François replied, confused. "A minute ago, you said that we are hundreds of years from understanding the brain," he continued, trying to make some sense of this.

"And I stand by this statement!" the professor replied. "Meanwhile, nothing will stop the Chinese, the Indians, the Russians, the Europeans, the Americans, and the rest of the world from happily marching on with their efforts."

François knew this was true. The economic, political, social, and military incentives were gigantic.

“We risk our colleagues creating a few pseudo-intelligent, careless, and harmful agents that will act like degenerate people, except we normally wouldn’t entrust those kinds of agents with health or combat decisions.”

“I wouldn’t lose sleep over this, but indeed, perhaps we are too cavalier with these ‘smart’ computer programs,” François admitted.

“And that’s the problem!” Ian got more excited. “Most researchers aren’t concerned enough about this unique threat. In the meantime, armies become more automated and we’ve already had tens of ‘accidents’ with drones blowing up innocent civilians, including children.”

And now I’m being chided by the professor, François thought, shifting his position.

“Anyway ... to tackle this problem, we need to bootstrap the process, given that we are far from understanding the biology behind our minds. We must create an approximation, based on whatever little we know, not from the discoveries in biology but human psychology, introspection, and even animal studies. It doesn’t matter how we implement an AI if we build in it enough fundamental aspects that make it think the way we do. Some sort of universal properties of intelligent minds here on Earth, but focused on mammals, for which we have most of the studies. An octopus and a mammal are quite different in their intelligence. Surely, we want our AI to be closer to us than to cephalopods.”

“And do you think you have identified enough of these universal properties?” François asked, semi-mockingly.

“Yes, I am confident we did. About two hundred of them, in fact,” Ian said without hesitation, much to François’s surprise.

He also thinks he’s solved the mystery of intelligence. What a great combination; prophesying about the end of the world and immediately posing as its savior. François sighed, then continued aloud. “Then what seems to be the holdup?”

The professor frowned for a moment, then he laughed, dismissing François's mocking tone. "There remains a minor issue. We must be able to implement my theory. Each of these universals must be coded in ways that aren't that different from each other. Evolution didn't have time to come up with two hundred completely different ways to create this magic. Hence, we need some kind of ..." Ian stopped, leaning towards François, expecting him to continue.

"Adaptable algorithm," François nodded, finally understanding where this was going.

"Bingo!" the professor hit the table with both his fists. "We tried coming up with one, many times, believe me, but we failed. Yours sounds promising, and I think it's worth more than a shot."

"My code is already available publicly. An older version of it, anyway," François said in a soft voice. *Not that too many bothered to check it,* he thought.

"Oh, yes, and our engineers looked at it already. I know we would require years of work to adapt it to all our needs. No one in this world can do a better job than you." Ian looked deeply into his eyes again. "I am prepared to make you a substantial offer," the professor took out an envelope. "This would be your base salary. But here's the true attraction. If you succeed in adapting your algorithm to our two hundred components, I will make you a partner."

François opened the envelope and looked at the paper inside. He nearly swooned. Granted, this guy wasn't John Reeta, far from it, but the monthly base salary he was offering him was almost six times more than he made from freelancing in a good month. Who cared if the effort was doomed to fail? He would get to use his algorithm for some real research, and perhaps he might find practical applications for it.

Partner sounds about right where I should be at my age, with my skills and education, he thought, feeling a chill of pride down the spine. *Finally, somebody who looks at me the right way.*

He realized that he had always considered himself a genius, but other than Marie, who constantly pressured him to do something with his life, no one had truly appreciated his potential until that very moment. And even without the partnership, the money was tempting. He could offer Marie a dream life.

Ian could see that he was going back and forth in his mind, but he waited patiently.

"Are there ... other conditions?" François asked, trying hard to keep his cool.

"Well, you must sign an NDA," Ian shrugged.

Understandable, François thought.

"And you have to move to LA."

"What?" François asked, eyes wide open.

"Yes, this is a hush-hush operation. We have a secure facility on the outskirts of LA. We cannot risk allowing our employees to work remotely. Imagine the attacks we'd been subjecting ourselves to, should we make any progress towards our goal?"

Jamais de la vie! François thought, trying hard not to grimace. *I won't be leaving Côte d'Azur for a wild goose chase.* "I see," he answered aloud, hesitantly. "Can I think about it?"

"Absolutely! But, François," the professor got serious, "please consider my proposal carefully. This isn't a job offer. You can get a lot of those. I'm not the typical entrepreneur looking for talent. I offer you a chance to change, no, to save the world."

François nodded. The part about saving the world didn't attract him much. After all, the probability that this professor succeeded where a million other researchers had failed was infinitesimal. On the contrary, he got a strange feeling that he might exacerbate the problem which the professor had mentioned. What if their AI, or whatever they'd create, was one of those abnormal intelligences, orthogonal to human values or even dangerous?

He wanted nothing to do with the demise of his species. *Still, it might have been interesting*.

"Thank you for believing in me," he answered sincerely. "I'll get back to you."

"You do so, my dear fellow. You do so," Ian answered, energized.

François left the room, already feeling a pang of regret that he would miss out on this strange opportunity.

CHAPTER 4:

GUILT

Guilt is like the footprint of a hippopotamus.

— Nigerian Proverb

Seeing his daughter fully immersed in her work, her eyes fixated on the piece of paper in front of her, gave Zhào Qianfan a sense of pride and happiness he never thought possible. Just a couple of weeks before, the school had notified him that Baozhai had qualified for the National Math Olympiad. Qianfan smiled. His daughter was among the best in the republic in such a crazy competitive field, usually controlled by boys.

And then, who knows, perhaps she'll go to the international competition? Qianfan dreamed, his eyes open. *But let's not get ahead of ourselves.* He immediately shrugged off the thought. *From this point on, I'd be an ungrateful jerk to be disappointed.*

"I got it!" Baozhai yelled. "I calculated the geometrical locus for this problem! Come, let me show you," she invited her father.

Over the next five minutes, Qianfan listened carefully to her explanations. She was getting so good that he admitted he had trouble following her reasoning sometimes. "Very good, my precious. I think you deserve a break."

"First, I'm going to finish the problems the teacher gave me," she stubbornly refused, going back to work.

Qianfan considered imposing his will over hers, but he sighed and moved away. Her success had made her so ambitious that, judging by the pale face and tired eyes, her health might soon be affected. He had spent almost all his free time with Baozhai ever since she was born. Her mother had died in childbirth, something that seldom happened anymore. Raising a daughter alone, given his responsibilities towards the party and his long work hours, was a nearly impossible task. Baozhai was now turning 13, so his life was supposed to become simpler, or more difficult, given what he remembered from his teenage days. She was close to the age when she'd start talking about boys. He could already see signs of her being concerned with how she looked when going to school, how she answered people calling her, what avatars to use, or how to retouch her image in the Cybersperse.

He looked around the room. Earlier that day, they had collected some of her old toys, those that had escaped several rounds of cleaning and donating until then. He had seen that she wasn't comfortable getting rid of them, but she wanted to act mature, proud not to be a child anymore. That internal conflict had made her upset, and she found solace in solving the impossible math problems her teacher had left for her.

Looking at the large transparent bag containing various toys thrown in disorderly, Qianfan wondered if he would miss all those little trinkets and stuffed animals: the bear, the wise-talking raccoon dog, and the balls. His eyes fell on her old magic drawing board. That brought back so many memories. She used to draw incessantly on it, which had prompted him to think she would never follow in his steps and become a scientist. He looked at the board nostalgically. He remembered how, at some point, she was more interested in how the thing worked, rather than how to draw a unicorn on it. Happy to be her teacher, as always, he had helped her to take apart a few of them. Her eyes had sparked with passion during his explanations. The board was a simplistic way to draw or write on a screen and then erase it easily in one shot. Below the plastic surface there was a liquid under which tiny metallic particles rested out of view. A so-called pen, dragged over the surface, magnetized these particles, which then jumped up, giving the illusion of a dot, a line, or a circle. So much simpler and stupider than her current Cybersperse tablet. Why this fascination with a primitive thing?

He pulled the board out of the bag and frowned slightly. Yes, things were so much simpler when people could erase with one move all they wrote. Now the Party recorded and analyzed everything. China had followed this path of surveilling its citizens for many years. They'd improved the techniques to perfection. Recording data was easy, analysis was superhumanly accurate, storage was cheap, and information retrieval was fast. He felt suffocated by the constant self-censorship, the need to watch his moves, his words, his facial expression, his buying patterns, his Cybersperse incursions, and his trips to the grocery stores. Involuntarily, he looked at the mandatory government-owned personal assistant devices spread all over the house.

There are microphones and tiny cameras everywhere in my life, he thought, annoyed. *I can't talk to my daughter, cook something, take a shower, or pass gas without the government knowing, investigating, and judging. Soon, I won't be able to think freely either. Why did I help them create this nightmare?*

"I'm going to bed, darling," he announced morosely, kissing Baozhai on her head.

"Good night, Bàba," she mumbled, without lifting her eyes from her work.

Qianfan sighed and turned to leave. For no reason, he kept the board in his hands as he walked out. He realized that when he got into his room, where he laid it on the nightstand. While preparing for bed, swirls of thoughts of guilt mixed with pride ran through his head and made him feel rather uncomfortable. He fell asleep late, not before hearing Baozhai occasionally let out a muffled exclamation, a sign that she was making progress with her problems. He dreamt of dragons battling monstrous robots that, from time to time, leaned down towards him as if to listen to what he had to say.

He had to leave for work early in the morning. He was careful to put on his uniform without waking Baozhai up. She must have stayed up well after midnight. Looking in the mirror, he cringed at the thought that somewhere a little algorithm was recording all the information this piece of clothing and the surrounding sensors read about him: his skin conductance, temperature, his motions, his blood pressure, pulse, several video streams, the sound of the faucet dripping, and Baozhai's soft snoring. Later, sophisticated pattern matching routines would comb through this morning's data, along with data from hundreds of millions of other people, correlating information by time, location, angle of view, position, stress level, and more. Hundreds of factors then came together in a formula that may or may not result in a person's citizenship worthiness tally (CWT) going up or down. CWT, a score between 1 and 1000, was a malefic extension of the old social credit score introduced in the 20s, but infected by stringent surveillance.

All for the good of society, he thought bitterly.

Qianfan rarely used his personal AI assistant, mainly because of how dumb they were, less so because of privacy concerns. After all, the government was already sniffing everything that went on in his house.

He forced himself to resume reciting *The Iliad* in his head. A few years before, he'd come up with the idea to use rote memorization of a long text and then mechanically repeat it as the best technique to counter his physiological response to any impure thoughts. If he did it fast enough, maybe the algorithm, which was instantaneously picking up various signals from the myriad sensors, would discount the data as just a fluke. Having to worry about this constantly when he was awake was eating him alive.

The Iliad will truly come in handy, he thought, letting his guard down, then scolded himself and focused on reciting again.

Ever since he had worked on the new scanner, dubbed Super Sensitive Mood Scanner, or SSMS, which the party had requested merely four years before, he had become obsessed with self-control. Initially, it was called a mind scanner, which was misleading. The device was a hollow semi-sphere slightly bigger than half of a soccer ball, which had to be placed on the subject's head. During the reading, the subject had to stay still with wires going to a specialized interface connected to a supercomputer. The device certainly wasn't capable of reading thoughts, although some on the party committee got excited about the idea of releasing such a rumor out there. This work was a spin-off from the huge Brain-Computer-Interface (BCI) research group. The idea was to scan somebody's brain *in vivo,* as they live and breathe, to extract sufficient cues about how their frame of mind correlates with certain stimuli. More concretely, whenever one was listening to calming music, it would determine that they were calm. Or when somebody got angry and was ready to get into heated arguments or physical fights, the scanner would advise how aggressive they were. From a practical point of view, this gadget would be rather effective in interrogation, while forcing people to listen to party propaganda, or simply when being asked uncomfortable questions. The scanner was a way to triage citizens who went along with party directives, like cattle being herded for slaughter.

At first, Qianfan felt honored and excited to be selected to lead such an important project. The work wasn't new. Researchers had used affective BCI devices with mild success for therapeutic purposes for a few decades already. But his team had truly made a couple of breakthroughs. To assist in his work, the party leaders provided him with help straight from the MegaAI, in the form of new correlation procedures and software routines. This was a clear indicator of the importance that the party assigned to this project. Qianfan largely attributed their success to the incredible pattern detection algorithms that the MegaAI could produce. Once the AI generated proper routines, their job was mostly one of integration into the hardware.

As time passed, though, the implications of this capability became unbearable. The readings of his tool, corroborated with all the information that the party already had about its citizens, were close to irrefutable proof that one was a good or a bad member of society. Forget about degrading someone's CWT. The scanner would be the ultimate decision maker about throwing someone in prison or condemning them to death. This was a thought that caused Qianfan many sleepless nights.

How can I be responsible for so many ruined lives? he often asked himself. *So what if someone harbors doubts? They are only thoughts, by definition, and not actions.*

This reminded him of a lesson taught to him by his *nǎinai*, his maternal grandmother. She had been one of the last people in China to be deeply religious. Religions weren't encouraged, particularly Christianity, which was considered an obsolete cult of the Western World. While growing up, his nǎinai had always scared him that God would listen to his thoughts, so if he had any improper ones, he'd be in big trouble. One of her favorite quotes from the Christian Bible was from James 1:14-15:

> "Each person is tempted when, by his own evil desire, he is dragged away and enticed. Then, after desire has conceived, it gives birth to sin; and sin, when it is full-grown, gives birth to death."

Remembering her lesson, Qianfan thought, *This is how, slowly but surely, the party became God, and its citizens became the flock that followed Him, without questioning His decision and His actions.*

Still, he was in a unique position, since he knew exactly how advanced the scanner was. He could experiment and calibrate it. He could investigate the best ways to counter its readings. For example, besides the ceaseless repetition of a text, he had found out that meditation techniques helped him focus enough to mask a good portion of his troublesome thoughts. Upon this realization, he had taken meditation more seriously and had insisted Baozhai practice it too, under the pretense that it helped her focus on her studies—which was not at all false.

Today was the day to appear in front of one of the specialized party committees and present a bi-annual progress report. There were already voices complaining that the progress was not satisfactory. His world was now split into two: professionals who knew and acted on reality versus party trolls who asked for things to happen by fiat, just because the party wanted it.

Riding the fast lane bus to the building reserved for important officials, Qianfan remembered his sweet Baozhai again. He deeply hated how she had been constantly brainwashed ever since she was barely old enough to walk—by now, her faith in the party supremacy had grown into fanaticism. Still, without his position, his CWT in the 800s, and repeated praises from the leaders, he wouldn't have been able to offer her the most exquisite education, any toy, and any piece of clothing or technology her heart desired. And worse, if he started explaining to her things that were wrong with their society, she might misunderstand, get scared, or scold him. His mother had always told him to be of two minds: the one that looks outside and puts up the performance for the world to be happy, and the other that looks inside and knows the truth. This dualism was something that old Chinese comrades were used to, but alas, was about to be blown apart like a sandcastle by the demolishing waves that would come from his device.

His assistant, Haitao, a nerdy-looking young man in his early 20s, stood up from his desk with trepidation. "*Zhào zǒng*, the committee announced its arrival earlier today," he blurted the moment Qianfan made his appearance. "They will be here at noontime."

Qianfan cringed hearing that Haitao was still addressing him with the boss title, *zǒng,* although he had explicitly and repeatedly asked him not to do so.

"I don't know what precipitated this," Haitao launched into a tirade, "but it can't be good. Definitely, it can't be good. They want results, and we haven't shown them good results yet. You must tell them about your latest idea for improvements. You simply must!"

"Haitao, take a deep breath and calm down," Qianfan tried to sound confident. "I told you, it's too early to bring up the modulation that I am thinking about. If this is not working out, we would both look ridiculous."

Haitao lowered his gaze and stood silent for a moment. "I can't afford to lower my CWT a single bit," he mumbled. "You know I've nearly been accepted into a master's program, pending their review of my status. My CWT is 702. A drop of merely three points would blow up my life."

Qianfan knew that he had caused Haitao this pain. A couple of weeks ago, while rushing to get Baozhai from school, he'd left on his desk the plans for boosting the accuracy of the scanner by a whopping 10 percent. His assistant had found them and studied them. The idea looked more than promising, and Qianfan would have normally presented it if it weren't for his accursed doubts. He had answered evasively, concocted excuses, and mimicked insecurity in front of Haitao, who had looked at him suspiciously but had said nothing.

"I'll tell you what," Qianfan said. "We'll take the enhanced device out in the next two to three months, saying nothing to anybody. If we see it works, we can ask for an extraordinary meeting and announce the breakthrough."

Haitao nodded, unconvinced.

Qianfan left it at that and prepared for the meeting.

At noon sharp, he and Haitao went to one of the smaller conference rooms. The entire contingent of the eight members of Scientific Committee 48 - Liaison between Brain-Computer-Interface Division and Surveillance Division showed up like disciplined soldiers. They entered the room and sat silently around a large oval table, merely nodding in salute. Qianfan thought the arrogance of these people was astounding. They were advising, requesting, liaising, criticizing, and praising, with no idea what they were talking about. He wondered if at least one of them had a Ph.D. in any science from a decent university. This was irrelevant, Qianfan reminded himself. Now he had to make a good impression.

"Honorable members, allow me to welcome you one more time to the SSMS development section. I will not waste much of your time," Qianfan said, projecting his presentation into a common Cybersperse room.

"We've made progress in the last six months. We've increased the accuracy of our device in lab tests from 53 percent to 58 percent. We did it by tuning the representation of the subject's neural activity. I expect we would further increase the device's accuracy when we correlate its results with other physiological readings."

"Doctor Zhào, six months ago you promised us an accuracy of over 60 percent," a woman with an icy look in her eyes and a perfectly neutral voice interrupted him. "We have plenty of time for details. What I'm interested in knowing is why you didn't deliver on that promise."

Qianfan felt a wave of rage at hearing this statement, but he quickly countered it with his meditation techniques without moving a muscle on his face. "Actually," he cleared his throat, daring to contradict the woman, "at that time, I was told to reach 60 percent, and I expressed doubts it was possible in such a short time."

Hearing him speak like that made Haitao's eyes nearly pop out of their sockets. While Qianfan was correct, he certainly shouldn't have brought that up. Besides, he had achieved 68 percent in the latest experiments. Why wasn't he saying that?

"I hope you don't insinuate that I'm lying," the woman continued in the same monotonous voice.

"Oh, far from me to make such an accusation, Honorable Member Tián," he answered in the most sincere voice he could muster. "I was merely providing a clarification. The fact of the matter is that we are two percent below the target. Something that I am confident we can remedy in the next few weeks."

The woman stood up and looked around at her colleagues. Each of them nodded one by one.

"Doctor Zhào, since we spoke last time, there have been a few developments. First, we assigned this project a higher priority. The order came from the highest level. Yes, I mean our beloved President Yun Li," the woman said, leaning forward and looking into Qianfan's eyes.

Haitao gasped. This was truly unheard of, and Qianfan tried hard to disguise his surprise.

"Second, the advanced research section of the BCI team has made a remarkable breakthrough. They've invented a new way to read brain activity." The woman paused. "Wirelessly. The subject can be as far as two meters away."

This time Qianfan's mouth opened. The implications were staggering. This wasn't about an interrogation method anymore. In a flash, he imagined miniaturized mood-reading sensors distributed all over a building, inside his home, on poles, fences, trees. The party might turn them into wearable devices to complement the sensors already installed in their uniforms. The military might use them inconspicuously during negotiations with their enemies. But how could that work? It was hard enough to read those tiny waves from the brain without drilling holes and connecting the electrodes directly to organic cells. Wireless reading seemed preposterous with the available technology.

"I assure you, this technique is very precise," the woman said, to counter any doubts or arguments he might come up with.

She was still unfazed, but Qianfan thought she couldn't hide her satisfaction seeing the impression her words had made on them. She was silent for a while to let this new piece of information sink in.

"This progress was made possible, once again, with the help of China's biggest asset. The MegaAI came up with techniques and materials that none of our researchers—very smart, mind you—dreamt of." Another pause. "I want to clarify that you two are now privy to top-secret military information. Should it leak to anybody outside this room, we would know it was you. We would not just demote your CWT score if that happened."

Qianfan realized that this was the most direct threat he had ever received from the party. It took all his concentration to prevent his body from shaking. He looked at the young assistant. Haitao was stunned. His face, already devoid of any blood, went one shade whiter.

"That also means, though, that you are being trusted with critical information," the woman said in the same bland tone.

What a snake, Qianfan thought, not able to resist any longer and letting his body shiver a bit.

“The question, Doctor Zhào, is if the party has put their trust in the right person. Can you achieve 60 percent, or not?”

Qianfan glanced at Haitao. He prayed that the young assistant kept his mouth shut. Given this new piece of information, he needed to remain in control. If Haitao told this woman that they held the solution to achieving up to 68 percent accuracy, it would be the end. Luckily, the young assistant seemed overwhelmed by what was going on and was incapable of opening his mouth.

“I am sure I can,” he answered, and his voice trembled despite his efforts to control it.

“Good,” the woman concluded. “We will provide you with the new wireless interface tomorrow. You have one month to deliver the results we are waiting for.”

Qianfan swallowed hard. He had the uneasy feeling that, from that moment on, gravity would pull him down a slide from which there was no turning back.

CHAPTER 5

BETRAYAL

Few things are more devastating than being hit hard by those whom you love and who you thought love you back. Whatever their reasons, selfish or honorable, the sword of duplicity cuts through your heart and leaves a mark that never heals.

Until that singular moment when you realize the treachery, you lived by the words of Deep Purple, 'Love conquers all.'

Yes, it does, but it can also leave behind a crushed, betrayed soul. For, in your case, love turned into a dry disappointment for wasting years on the wrong person. When coupled with jealousy, this dismay becomes a devious worm that eats you from the inside, until your sap is gone and all that's left of you is a dry old trunk.

— DeSousa's Memoirs - Part I - Beginning - 2053

François approached the shady Nice neighborhood where Marie's apartment was. He had decided to walk to it since it was relatively close to the train station. He could further gather his thoughts, not that there was not enough time to do it on the way back from Paris. Although just a few hours before he was sure that he would reject Ian's proposal, his determination had faltered on the trip back.

Before leaving Disneyland, he had bought a princess ring, just a flashy plastic toy eight-year-old girls enjoyed. He had thought this would be a fun thing to give Marie. Alone in his cabin, he had looked at the ring and reflected hard on what he wanted to do about her. She was the woman in his life. Perhaps this job offer was the right opportunity to ask her to marry him. They could live in LA for a couple of years. With his salary, she could afford to stay home, although California was full of jobs for psychologists. If things didn't work out with crazy Ian, they could always return to Nice, this time with some savings.

As the train flew through the Provence fields, orange in the evening sun, his mood had improved considerably. First, he had decided to propose to Marie tonight. Second, just the fact that he'd got an offer had tempered his pessimistic view of his career. After all, there might be other people out there who appreciated his work.

The train arrived in Nice late in the evening. Walking towards her apartment, he noticed again how empty the streets were at this hour compared to the days before the Cybersperse. The chic buildings surrounding him let out wavering lights from behind curtains, projecting weird shapes on the ground.

It's as if the villagers of good old Nice were getting ready for bed in the timid light of oil candles, François thought, amused.

Kicking a small piece of pavement, he went under a bridge on top of which coastal trains were casually crawling to their destinations. The black and gray colors under the bridge, which were peppered everywhere with graffiti, gave him the feeling of a permanent night. A couple of vagrants cuddled in a corner, wrapped in their Cybersperse costumes with the contacts on, were convulsing slowly.

God knows what they are doing, François thought, and shuddered in disgust. It could be anything from watching a harmless movie to being entangled in an orgy. *These people already live in paradise here on the coast. The government gives them the UBI share monthly. Why would they squander their lives away?* He turned his back and moved on. *At least they are immersed in their virtual life, so I don't have to worry about my safety.*

Suddenly, one of them removed his haptic hood. It was a man, rough in appearance. François couldn't see his face well, but he imagined he must have had circles around his eyes and prominent cheekbones.

"Don't fret, brother," the man croaked. "Life will disappoint you, too. Just wait for it. It will wipe off that superior smile of yours."

François sped up. There was no point in engaging these people.

"It will. Remember, when it's your turn, we'll keep you a warm spot here," he cackled louder as François was moving away. "Better live a brief life in constant pleasure than an eternity in pain." With a last shriek, the man put his hoodie back on.

François tilted his head back a bit, disturbed, and rushed to Marie's apartment. When he arrived, he still couldn't get the man's words out of his head. He couldn't shake the feeling that something was amiss. He forced himself to call Marie.

"*Bonsoir, mon chéri*! Come on up," she invited him while unlocking the hallway entrance door. "I've been waiting for you to arrive before I shower."

François didn't understand how anybody could shower before going to bed and noticed how he had learned to live with these little idiosyncrasies of hers. He went into the building and rushed up the stairs instead of taking the old elevator. He pushed the massive, old, thick door with a heavy handle and entered Marie's surreal place. She lived alone in a three-bedroom apartment, which was at least five times bigger than his studio.

"Make yourself comfortable. I'll be out in ten minutes," Marie yelled through the sound of running water.

Although not one to care much about patriotism, François loved how everything looked and smelled French in this place. Which was ironic, seeing as Marie did not have a single authentic French gene in her. *Perhaps that's what I love about her,* he mused, looking around.

There was plenty of room for old-style furniture. She had a huge walk-in closet. He noticed that the drawer of a sculpted cabinet was ajar, the corner of a paper sticking out of it. He smiled, remembering how Marie had unceremoniously opened his drawer and dampened his algorithm with the champagne. What if he returned the favor?

He opened the drawer and pulled the paper out, glancing at it. It appeared to be a letter. Handwritten. He felt a sharp pain throughout his body at the realization it was from that Italian fellow, Marco. *I shouldn't read it,* he thought, determined, although he trembled slightly. *This is her business.* Still, he looked at the paper in his hand and was irresistibly attracted to the words. *No, it's not. It's every bit my business, too. This is my girl. I am about to propose, bon sang.* He changed his mind, feeling his eyes getting moist. He started reading the beginning of the letter.

"My love,

I will be candid and direct with you, as always. You say that you finally want us to meet face-to-face. If you came to Firenze, I would be thrilled. I will wait for you at the airport. I promise you a dream week while you are here. You also said that you could never make love in the Cybersperse, which you find artificial and detestable. I disagree, and I still say that we should try it. But I promise you the lovemaking of your life when you come here …"

François dropped the letter, feeling crushed and weak. This man was about to conquer her. His Marie. And he'd come out of nowhere. Feeling ready to smash everything in her apartment, he searched, mortified through the drawer. He found a letter from her, which had just a few sentences. Judging by the fact that the last one was unfinished and there was no signature, she must have just started writing. He randomly picked a few fragments to read.

"I can't wait for the day when you will embrace me ... I am eager to feel you inside me ... to arrange my trip as soon as possible ..."

François blacked out for a few moments. Who was this woman, writing so indecently? What happened to the ever confident, mature girl he had known for fifteen years, with her boyish demeanor, disarming, and rejecting attitude? The universe was crumbling around him. He felt dejected, psychologically powerless, confused, and, above all, ready to kill somebody.

Marie stepped out of the shower, grinning from ear to ear, wearing one of her loose bathrobes that made him lose his mind. "Now you have to tell me everything about your—" she stopped cold, seeing François's livid face and shaking body.

"What happened?" she panicked, only to notice a moment later the paper in his hand.

"What is this?" he asked, coldly.

A shadow passed quickly over her face. "That is personal! How dare you look into my drawer?" she switched to attack right away.

"A few weeks ago, you had no qualms looking into mine," he said in a trembling voice, trying to remain calm, feeling the pressure of the walls like he was carrying the whole building on his shoulders.

"That was different. You had nothing personal in there." She tried to divert his attention.

"That's right! I'm your little faithful doggie, ready to come at your command. Why would I have personal correspondence with another woman?"

"François, stop this! You've never acted like this before. What's wrong with you?" she started panicking, seeing the feral look in his eyes.

"What's wrong with me?" he screamed, not able to control his anger any longer. "What's wrong with me? Let's see ... How about the fact that I've been madly in love with you for fifteen years? Surely you had to know that."

"I love you too," she started whining. "You are my friend!"

"Please stop ... just stop. There is nothing you can say to make this right. That you were considering meeting ... no ... sleeping with that moron—and I don't give a damn who he is—has ruined everything between us. I could never trust you again."

"Marco is a good guy! He cares about me. I forbid you to speak like that about him!"

"He is a guy who wants what we all want. To get under your skirt. You are either incredibly stupid not to know that, or a hypocrite."

"And you are acting like a spoiled brat!" She was furious again. "I have never promised myself to you. So, I don't owe you anything. I don't understand where this jealousy is coming from. Besides, I have slept with other men in the past. You didn't seem to care."

"Maybe I did, and you don't know it," he answered quickly.

"And you slept with other women. Did you hear me complain about it?"

"Perhaps you should have. That, too, was a sign that you don't care. Besides, this was ages ago. In the last many years, I had no intention of sleeping with another woman. Not for the lack of chances. What about you? Did you have many other lovers I wasn't aware of?" he asked, as rudely as he could.

She ignored his question and replied with one of her own. "What's with this anachronic attitude? We don't live in the seventeenth century when women committed themselves to one man and lived with him for the rest of their lives! So many men and women live in polyamorous relationships nowadays."

"I'm not one of those people!" François replied, feeling the chasm between them only getting bigger. "I thought you weren't one, either. I was mistaken! What's wrong with having one partner your entire life? Your other half?"

"Well, I'm not that person for you," she allowed herself to be overwhelmed by anger. "I pity you for thinking like that. There's no such thing as perfect love and two peas in a pod. There are only people who meet, love each other for a while, then grow apart."

"Maybe I am a fool," François said in a soft voice. "Maybe I am out of sync with these times. I cannot change and I don't want to. Life is short. We can't afford to invest our feelings in someone who then brushes them away the way you have done. We can only be part of a small group of close friends and family. For some of us romantic imbeciles, losing someone close to us is devastating. Perhaps if we lived a millennium, and got attached to a thousand people, one betrayal wouldn't matter as much. As things stand, I cannot conceive of you being with another man."

"If you love me like that, why don't you support me, encourage me? Perhaps it's my turn to marry? Don't you want me to be happy?" She started sobbing.

"Your turn? What kind of talk is that?" François felt his blood boiling again. "What about my turn? I was ready to give my life to you. I wanted you to be mine. To have to watch you for the rest of my life with another man, never! Do you understand me, never! That's way more than sacrificing myself. It's plain cruel."

"So where does this leave us?" Marie asked, tired of fighting off his arguments.

"It's simple. I never, ever want to see you, or your gigolo boyfriends. I'll be gone from your life."

"François, you are scaring me!" she whimpered, trying to grab his hand.

"Don't touch me!" he jumped back, as if her touch burned him. "Don't you dare touch me!"

"What can I do?" she cried, terrified to see him in that state.

"Nothing. I want nothing from you anymore."

"Don't say that. You are such a good person. I've known you for more than half of my life. You are overreacting. Just go to bed and by morning you'll think differently."

François looked at her, disgusted. She understood nothing. With a sudden move, he threw her letter on the floor. He reached into his pocket and pulled the toy ring out, throwing it with a flick of his wrist in the garbage bin under her desk. Then he grabbed his bag and ran to the door. He stopped and mumbled without looking back, "I thought I'd grow old with you. But you want to grow old with someone else."

"I want to grow old with you too! Why can't you accept me as your sister? As your best friend?"

"I'm an idiot," he ignored her, talking to himself. "I couldn't imagine my life without you. You had to ruin everything. You know what? Perhaps you're not worthy of me. You're a mediocre, narcissistic, selfish, unpolished, and immature girl. I don't even know why I am … why I *was* so smitten with you."

"Can you stop these ridiculous insults? Will you give me a chance to explain?" she yelled, running towards him, tears flowing down her cheek.

François pushed her aside without looking at her. "Don't look for me. Don't care about me. Ever again."

Then he stormed out, slamming the door behind him, and leaving her mute, in pain, and in shock at what had just happened. She knew that both their lives had just taken an irreversible turn.

CHAPTER 6:

RESURRECTION

You often hear how short and fragile life is, that being alive is a gift, that life hangs by a thread, and other such clichés. You scoff at them. The deep meaning of these statements won't truly sink in until you come back from the dead. I should know because I have. Several times.

— DeSousa's Memoirs - Part I - Beginning - 2053

François woke up around noon in a puddle of wine. His bed was a mess. He was wearing the same clothes. They smelled of alcohol, sweat, and puke.

"*Bonjour, Maître*," Brigitte greeted him, annoying as usual. "You have nineteen calls that you missed. Nine from Marie, seven from your sister, and three from your mother. Your sister also came over, but because you gave me strict instructions not to be bothered, I didn't wake you up. Should I call her back?"

Before having time to answer, François felt sick and jumped into the bathroom to throw up some more. His memory was slowly coming back. After leaving Marie's apartment the previous night, he had seen the two losers under the bridge embraced in some sicko virtual sex tango. Their image was the last thing he remembered vividly. He knew he had stopped at a bar and drunk some vodka. Then he had blacked out, so he wasn't sure how he'd arrived back home. Judging by the amount of alcohol on his bed, the half dozen bottles of beer, wine, and spirits on the floor, he must have drunk a full refrigerator. His hypochondriac personality jumped in, and he involuntarily worried about the effect on his liver. A rictus came on his face. *Who cares?* he thought. *After what happened, my liver is welcome to blow up.*

"*Maître*, your sister threatened to invoke the emergency protocol if you don't call her back."

"Oh, get lost ... *Ferme-la.* Don't talk to me unless I tell you to."

He turned her off from his tablet. The sharp pain in his head reminded him he was still alive there, down on Earth. Strangely, though, he felt incredibly lucid. He tried hard to forget all the details of his talk with Marie. Despite his bravado from the day before, he knew all too well that he would never move on. This woman had left her imprint on him. He had gotten so accustomed to her perfume, her smile, her laughter, and her annoying little peculiarities.

The way he saw it, he had a few choices ahead of him. One, he could have sex with anything willing that identified as a woman. Focus on that alone. Let her see how much he cared about her. Two, clean up and marry well above his status. A model, if possible. Three, disappear from the world of the living.

The first two involved running away somewhere. Ian's proposal came to mind, and he immediately dismissed it. Too complicated. He might start focusing on work at some point, but that seemed far in the future.

The third option gave him chills. Yes, just be gone. He could celebrate his coming birthday with Saint Peter & co, if they were real and interested in such trivial matters. This world was worthless anyway, and living was highly overrated. What did Marie say? That's right, he was anachronic. He didn't belong in a world with a Cybersperse, with sick people sharing partners like they were all sharing a cab, with backstabbers who, after fifteen years ... He stopped, breathing hard. He started crying, wailing like a paid howler at a funeral.

After a few minutes, he paused, feeling that he was losing his mind. With a sick conviction, he stood up and stormed out the door. He hadn't changed his clothes and had taken nothing with him. It was impossible to get rid of Brigitte completely, since she was stored in a subcutaneous tiny chip, but he didn't bother to take a headset or AV contacts. He was deaf and mute. If people called him, there was no way to answer. It was like in the old days when he used to forget his phone home. He was alone, and he liked it that way.

Moving slowly, steadily, he got out of his apartment and headed to the sea. He stopped for a moment to rejoice in the breathtaking view of cheerful houses going down to the water, surrounded by somewhat contradicting vegetation spreading out arbitrarily, yet appearing to follow some kind of logic. Sort of like his decision right now. He smiled bitterly, moving his eyes to the little gulfs around his town, sparkling in the midday sun, peppered with a few recreational ships. He could admire from this high vantage point the matchless beauty of the coast from Nice, almost to Monaco.

"This is one thing I'm going to miss," he muttered, then climbed down the myriad of little steps slithering down to the sea.

At some point, he thought he saw Marie in the old town and his heart jumped out of happiness, only to sink into the abyss of despair a moment later. He did not want to feel this way. He sped up, crossing the road, then a bridge, and finally descending the last set of stairs to the beach, where he turned around for a last view of the mountains. The town rose steeply, a few meters from the beach. On top of a wall of rock about 10 meters tall, the rail went parallel to the sea, drilling through the mountain every few hundred meters. Above, on a little plateau, along a few roads, the old town stretched for a few hundred meters with its fancy bakeries and cafeterias. Further behind were the neighborhoods which had given him so much joy.

It's a pity, though, he thought, sighing again, turning his attention to the sea.

There was almost no one on the beach, and that suited him. He walked to a point where he felt he was far from any people around. The water was furious, big foamy waves hitting the rocks on the beach with a vengeance. He stood there, observing the way waves worked together, sometimes adding to each other's power, other times neutralizing it, in a complicated dance impossible to grasp.

We are waves too, he reflected. *We help each other, we hinder each other, we fight with each other, we inevitably smash into nothingness in the end, only to have our remains picked up as building blocks for other waves. In the grand scheme of things, Marie's betrayal is so insignificant.* He felt his resolve falter a little. *Yes, but it's not so insignificant to me, isn't it?* he mused further. *I can't understand it. And I don't want to understand it.*

"Adieu, my Côte d'Azur. Adieu, emerald-colored hedges, crimson flowers, and bird trills. Adieu, career. And good riddance, Marie," he said between his teeth, as he stepped towards the water, his faithful friend to the end.

As the first wave hit him, he felt rather cold and weird, and for a moment he worried he was getting his clothes wet, then brushed away such a triviality. Ten steps later, his feet couldn't touch the bottom. His body tensed instinctively, and he felt his legs and arms desperately wanting to swim. It took all his willpower to let himself go. He put up enough resistance to the waves so that they would not throw him back on the beach. He moved further in, just a little more. Water started getting into his mouth. He coughed it out, his body stubbornly refusing to give up. He turned on his back, too far now for the waves to turn him to the shore, looking at the sky, submerging now and then, glimpsing the mountains occasionally. The image of Marie's triangular, freckled face floated in front of him. He could picture perfectly her lovely almond eyes. Her aquiline, bony nose that he thought he would use as a compass to show him the way in life forever. She had a unique combination of traits, rarely seen together. He had often thought that she'd been designed by some gods having a little avant-garde fun. Far from beautiful, yet irresistible. Her tinkling laugh, the way she shoved him aside almost like a man, her livid face the day before … Why was he thinking of her in the last seconds of his life?

Suddenly, a bigger wave turned him upside down, and water got into his nose and his lungs. Perhaps he shouldn't have done this. He panicked. Why was he trying to kill himself? There was a sharp pain all over his torso, then a hot sensation. His mind wandered again, out of control. Why was he hot when the water was so cold? He started fighting to escape it, but it was too late. The last thing he saw was the bottom of the clear water filled with large gray fish approaching him curiously, only to depart with a twitch. He went off in the darkness, thinking that down there everything was so much calmer, so he could let his mind get gradually numb, despite the excruciating pain. Then he was nothing.

In what seemed just a moment later, he felt a tremendous pressure on his chest and started coughing, out of control, unable to move his body. He squinted his eyes enough for the light to bore a hole into his brain.

An eclipse, he thought, as the first thing he saw was something round, overlapping the sun almost perfectly. He closed his eyes, wondering whether he had reached the heaven that Isabelle drove him nuts with. Then he sensed that the shape moved, so he forced himself to open his eyes again. Was that a face? His ears picked up a verbal diatribe with a strong African accent. He vaguely registered that the person speaking was Black. For a moment, he thought of Ian. However, this sounded nothing like his unique Scottish accent. He tried to move again, but he could not. Finally, his brain started processing the sound.

"... for a young man to be so reckless. And what were you thinking about going in with your clothes on? *Dieu tout-puissant*. I hope you didn't try to kill yourself!"

A portly, middle-aged woman, her curly hair wet, dripping salted water on his face and mouth, was making him perfectly aware he was alive. Again. With a grimace, he closed his eyes. This accursed world wouldn't let him die.

"The ambulance is on its way. I called them, you know." The woman slowed down her tirade, seeing he was in pain.

François was just wondering how this tiny, out-of-shape woman had pulled him out of the water when he heard a siren. In no time, he was being hoisted on a stretcher and rushed to the car by a couple of strong men.

"Don't you ever do that again!" he heard the woman scream from the back.

He shuddered, remembering his experience. There had been just pain and panic at the end. Then nothingness. No light at the end of the tunnel. No angels to welcome him to paradise. No little devils pushing him to the lower realm for having taken his life. So much for Isabelle's promise. Thinking back at his failed suicide attempt, he realized he'd never be able to go through it again.

So, option three failed. Time to fall back to the first two, he thought and pouted, utterly annoyed. *I still hate her guts.*

The scream of the ambulance siren increased his headache. What was the point of it? There were barely any moving cars on the street. They arrived at the hospital, where the strong men pushed him into the elevator, then into a room, and carefully unloaded him on a bed.

Why can't I move? he panicked, suddenly. *I hope I'm not paralyzed.*

They hooked him to an IV tubing line, which probably supplied something to relax him, so he dozed off. When he woke up, he opened his eyes slowly, and he saw a long line that seemed to come down from the hazy blue above. Was he hanging from the sky? He realized gradually that he was looking at the window, and the medical staff had tethered him to an IV bag. The face of a gray-haired male doctor came into his view.

"Now, what do we have here? Almost drowned, eh? How does it feel to be back among mortals?"

François felt like screaming, but kept his mouth shut, sulking.

"That bad, eh?" the doctor laughed. "I can say that you were very lucky. The woman who pulled you out did it just in time before lack of oxygen did irreparable damage to your brain."

"I ... I can't move," François said, with considerable difficulty.

"You will be able to as soon as you get out of the current state of shock. You're not crippled."

François felt a wave of relief, which, he thought, was rather inappropriate for someone who, a few minutes before, was planning on feeling nothing. A big tear came down his cheek.

"Now, now, there's no reason to cry. Rejoice! You have been given a second chance."

A second chance ... look at that ... and I didn't even ask for it, François thought bitterly.

"We activated the emergency protocol to notify your next-of-kin." The doctor glanced at his tablet. "Your sister, I believe … Isabelle. I'm sure she'll be here shortly."

"Doctor," François said, looking into his eyes, "when can I go home?"

The doctor looked at him for a long time, suspicious. "Well, you may leave as soon as you can move. Although I recommend that we keep you here for a couple of days, just to make sure there's nothing wrong," he answered, waving his hands apologetically.

François nodded. He could already move his feet. He dreaded going back to his apartment, though. Staying here suited him. He had time to think about his next steps. "Alright," he acknowledged. "But I don't want to see anybody while I'm here. No visitors. Is this possible?"

"Yes, that's entirely your choice. You'll have to put up with a series of doctors examining you, both physically and mentally." The doctor stared at him hard.

The message was clear. François understood the doctor had figured out he'd wanted to kill himself. So, as a price for being left alone here, he'd have to suffer psychologists and psychiatrists poking at his head. "Fine by me," he acknowledged.

The doctor nodded. "It's a deal. I'll see you soon," the doctor confirmed and rushed out.

Isabelle was waiting in the hallway. She jumped up when the doctor came out. "Doctor, how is he?"

"No worries, he's fine."

"Thank God," a voice came out from Isabelle's tablet, sobbing in relief.

"This is our common friend, Marie," Isabelle explained. "We're both ... anxious."

"But you should know," the doctor continued, "this wasn't an accident. He tried to kill himself. He almost succeeded."

Isabelle bowed her head. Marie gasped.

"He agreed to be kept here for observation. There's no telling how things will go next. We will monitor him, but, as you know, if he's determined to do it, he will succeed."

Isabelle nodded.

"I don't know what prompted him to do this. It is important now that the family and friends offer all the support they can. Do you understand?"

Isabelle nodded again.

"I'll try to convince him gently to accept visitors. Perhaps he'll do it in a couple of days. We shouldn't rush him. I would like to keep him here for a week. He might require further treatment afterward."

"Thank you, doctor."

The doctor shook her hand and departed.

"I could never live with myself if anything happened to him," Marie said, crying. "Because of me."

"You know very well this isn't your fault. Please, Marie, I don't want to nurture you from depression again. Stay strong for him."

"I don't know if I can. He hates me now. I saw it in his face. Last night, he looked like he wanted to kill me. Perhaps it would have been better."

"Marie, I think it'd be best if you wouldn't go to Firenze now," Isabelle said, softly.

"I think ... I think I'll postpone my trip," Marie said hesitantly.

Isabelle nodded. This was their way of saying that Marie was considering breaking her already weird half-relationship with Marco. Although she truly wanted Marie to be happy, and harshly condemned François for his behavior, Isabelle felt a big weight lifted off her chest.

CHAPTER 7:

A SWAN SONG

Upon such sacrifices,

The gods themselves throw incense.

— *William Shakespeare*

Sujata was having her breakfast in the second open restaurant of the venue. It was the last day of the neuromimetic conference. The following day, she was bound back for D.C. with little to show. Chewing a gummy stick of cheese, she was mulling over what she had seen here so far. She assessed it had been an interesting event with little actual scientific progress. Most of the speakers had little to show, while the few who advanced more provocative ideas were goofballs. Still, over the last few days, she had made some contacts that might prove useful when trying to form a scientific alliance to counter China.

As a US Navy lieutenant, Sujata took her job seriously, although she was young. She had graduated magna cum laude merely five years before from the US Naval Academy, specializing in computer science, with her thesis done on the use of AI in combat. It was something that AI specialists around the world had been almost entirely against for the last half century. But despite many open letters to the UN and pressure on local governments to forbid autonomous weapons and strategic artificial brains, military everywhere seemed to forgo ahead with arming drones and relying on decisions made by software.

No wonder, with China going awry the way it has lately, she thought, frowning. *I hope Zhèng Yang will give us a clue today about what's going on over there.*

She instinctively took a furtive look at her tablet-turned-mirror to see if she looked presentable. A smile lit her face. She didn't just look nice, her beauty was radiant. Her father, the famous colonel Hopkins, always joked that she should have chosen a career in modeling. She'd inherited his towering height, deep green eyes, and lighter hair. Her beautiful facial features, dark skin tone, and slender body came from her mother. It was like God chose the very best set of genes from each of her parents. "With beauty comes responsibility," her father's advice rang in her ears. He warned her she would meet many, especially in a field still largely dominated by men, who would not look at her as a brilliant young woman dedicated to her work, but as a sexy female that just had to be their next conquest.

Her colleague, lieutenant commander Mike Lee, showed up at the door and signaled her. She stood up and went to him in a hurry.

"Good morning, sunshine," Mike greeted her with a grin.

"Lieutenant Lee," she answered in a deliberately serious tone.

"Let's see what grandfather Zhèng has to say today," he said.

She grimaced. She was fond of Mike, with whom she had a great professional relationship, yet she hated the cavalier way he talked about things. Here, he was disrespecting one of the sacred monsters of AI development, Zhèng Yang. Although now part of the enemy team and recently rumored to be going senile, Zhèng was the one who, a decade before, came up with the first complete brain simulation of a human neocortex, to the level of individual neuronal synaptic gates.

Many Western researchers argued Zhèng had built his incredible achievement thanks to the discoveries of thousands of giants in neuroscience, so his merit was mainly to have been in the right place at the right time. Sujata disagreed. Zhèng would go down in history as the first one to do it. Eleven years later, the US researchers still could not put together a fully functioning brain simulation at that level, although they were getting closer every year.

Hastening towards the main conference hall, Sujata realized that the respect she had for the complexity of the human brain made Zhèng's accomplishment astonishing in her eyes. The human brain has roughly 86 billion neurons which—although assisted by many other cells—are the main bearers of the sparks that fly around, in a synchronized electric storm, to form the human mind. Each neuron aggregates tiny electrical inputs from thousands of other neurons. It then fires, or not, its own electrical signal to neurons that it connects to via tiny bridges called synapses, when chemical ions flow to build up enough momentum for an occasional spike of current.

Nearly one hundred years before, the AI forefathers thought it would be enough to simulate the neurons' basic functionality in simple artificial constructs, which were turned on or off based on their input signals. Each of these early artificial neurons that lived in computers was a mockup of its biological counterpart, many orders of magnitude simpler. A single biological neuron is a whole sophisticated system in itself; a fortress with chemical soldiers, gates, and activity that was suppressed, boosted, and modulated.

Most of the neuroscience research on brain simulation concentrated on the neocortex, the place that made humans special: language processing, high-level reasoning, decision making, and creativity. Researchers deliberately ignored the more primitive brain sections, inherited from reptiles and dubbed the limbic system, that was in charge of the most basic, animalistic urges, including the handling of emotions, the sex drive, hunger, and so on. One of the strongest arguments against simulating the limbic system was that they didn't want to endow artificial brains with any instincts, lest they risked the development of an artificial super being that might get pissed off.

Focusing on the neocortex did little to reduce the complexity of the problem. The number of synapses in the human neocortex alone is about 1,500 times more than the number of stars in our galaxy. Each synapse is a not-so-trivial computing system. That's what Zhèng simulated in its entirety.

It was even more puzzling that the Chinese were so quick to make this brain functional and use it for practical applications. Merely half a decade after its birth, they credited the artificial brain with innovative discoveries in the medical field, in nanomaterials, artificial food, and pretty much any area where the rest of the world had hoped to remain competitive. Their achievement was instrumental in countering the effects of deglobalization and population decline that had proven to be the biggest challenge for China's very existence. All of this while the ongoing brain simulation projects in the West had largely remained interesting research projects, conglomerates of electrical currents flowing out of control. Zhèng's success was not only quantitative, measured in terms of the number of neuronal connections, but his brain simulation could execute ultra-sophisticated algorithms that far exceeded the abilities of the smartest researcher. The Western brain simulations remained smaller in scale and primitive in functionality.

By the mid-forties, China had a massive advantage, not as much economically as scientifically and militarily. In the years before Zhèng's discovery, the number of Chinese scientists attending conferences such as this was bigger than those from all other countries combined. After that, gradually, fewer took part. First, the Chinese government realized that they didn't benefit from sharing their findings with the rest of the world. Second, the Chinese leadership mildly discouraged traveling outside of China, as they did with the influx of foreigners.

Then came 2045, the year when President Guō Chāo died. It was the year when the mysterious Yun Li came to power. The year when China closed itself for good. With a snap of fingers, the Chinese government had raised a different kind of Great Wall, one that was supposed to keep out the proponents of democracy and freedom for good. The Chinese enforced the most stringent surveillance ever available to a government, both inland and in the many parts of the African and South American continents, with over two billion people under their control. Threatened with penalties that went all the way from the inconvenience of not finding a good school for their children to imprisonment or even death, the population became risk averse.

Much like in the old days of communist totalitarian regimes, people started living a dual life: one in which they strived to be perceived as good citizens by the omnipresent government, and the other in which they found solace in their private thoughts. Under the claim of creating an ideal society, the post-Guō government ruled with an iron fist.

Therefore, upon hearing the news of Zhèng Yang's participation in the neuromimetic conference, Sujata's superiors became excited.

"Perhaps they sent the old man to offer us an olive branch," General Thompson had said back at the Pentagon. "With the tension and drone fights lately, it would be the right time to resume diplomacy."

"I doubt it," General Kambe had replied, shaking his head. "I believe this is a show of force. They sent a famous figure meant to evoke respect. He will surely remind us they are superior, and probably present us with a shocking discovery that solidifies their position."

Sujata was afraid General Kambe was right. Everybody back home was in high alert mode, waiting to see what Zhèng would have to say. She found her seat in the third row, right near her good buddy Mike, who put on a mocking face, which, for those who knew him as well as Sujata, meant that his level of stress was off the charts.

Soon after the moderator introduced him, Zhèng Yang came up to the dais with deliberately slow movements, a man old enough to understand that there was no point in rushing for anything in life. He looked for a few seconds at the audience, trying to assess their worth. Sujata did not doubt that all his material and Cybersperse access was under strict surveillance from members of the Chinese government. She knew that her hope was irrational, coming from her despair that an all-out war might be inevitable. She was reading too much into his presence at the conference. Zhèng was one of the people who had crucially contributed to the creation of the modern, powerful, and authoritarian China. Why would he switch sides? Besides, he must have had an exclusive connection to a Chinese communication satellite, so there was no way for him to contact anyone or send any kind of message, let alone ask for political asylum. Two members of the Chinese security positioned themselves very close behind the old man, not bothering to remain inconspicuous.

Those guys look ready to end his life at the first sign that he would try to defect, Sujata thought gloomily.

"In the last three decades," Zhèng started his speech in nearly perfect English, with an unexpectedly firm voice, "China has made considerable progress toward ensuring the prosperity of its citizens. Nobody can deny that. Our AI research was instrumental in this effort. In 2041, the Chinese Science Ministry and Party Advisory Committee asked that we tackle one of the most critical problems facing the Chinese people. A mega research group was formed, led by me, to save those who live on the shore from the ever-rising sea levels. We wanted to control the mighty ocean, and we did. In order to accomplish this impossible mission, we had to achieve what nobody had achieved before, and so we created the first synaptic-level neocortex simulation. The most advanced research group in the world created this marvel, which made it possible since then to tackle many other challenges that we thought were insurmountable. We ask ourselves: 'Who knows what would have happened if the great Chinese minds had not invented the artificial brain?'

"The Chinese people, inspired by our beloved president's leadership, are the greatest in the world. I hope mankind will follow in our footsteps. A solid, disciplined society will ensure that people remain alive for centuries to come. In my long journey through life, I have lost many colleagues. Dear people, who can never be replaced. I miss them every single day of my life, and it is my duty to thank them here for their efforts. But I feel I will join them soon, since old age will deprive me of sentience before long."

Zhèng stopped and took a long pause, looking around intensely. The audience was so quiet, you could hear a pin drop.

"Understand that the key to a good life is the willingness to go through the full spectrum of emotions: fear, happiness, sadness, and anger. We must add them to our lives from the moment we are born to the moment we die.

Only then do we feel we have lived a life worth living. To that effect, I have composed a few little pieces of music that I can release now since I probably won't be around when people listen to them and make fun of me."

A few people chuckled.

Sujata hurried to download the songs right on the spot, much surprised that Zhèng's government had allowed this to happen. *They probably scanned these a million times over, so there's no way Zhèng sent us any message embedded in them,* she thought.

The old man paused for a few seconds to look at his watch, then drank some water. He seemed frozen in time, waiting for something. When he raised his eyes back to the audience, he teared up.

Sujata's instinct told her right away that something was terribly wrong. With a grimace, the old man grabbed his chest and fell to the ground. The two goons behind him ran towards him while simultaneously launching one mini drone each, presumably to record everything that was going on close to the old man.

Sujata jumped up, along with everybody else. A team of emergency workers materialized out of nowhere. The Chinese security force pushed them aside right away. Thirty seconds later, their doctor came by. It was strangely quiet for the next couple of minutes until the doctor looked at the two men who were supposed to protect Zhèng and shook her head. The doctor turned toward the moderator and announced, in English.

"Professor Zhèng Yang is dead. Heart attack."

As if someone had turned a switch on, everybody in the conference hall started talking, agitated. The moderator ran out the back while the Chinese team transported Zhèng's body out of the room.

"What a disappointment!" Mike said, disgusted. "He fed us a bunch of propagandistic bullshit, only to die right afterwards. I wonder what could have made him so excited. It couldn't have been his lachrymatory speech about his achievements, nor the baloney about his beloved party."

"Perhaps he wanted to tell us something, but his heart gave out before he could do it," Sujata offered.

"Oh, please," Mike continued. "This guy was more loyal to his party than Goebbels was to Hitler."

Sujata shook her head and looked around at how the distress was slowly dissipating. She shared Mike's disappointment, but she felt rather more puzzled by what had just happened. Things didn't add up.

CHAPTER 8:

MOTIVATION

When skeletons jump from your loved one's closet, keep the door open at your peril.

— DeSousa's Memoirs - Part I - Beginning - 2053

It was François's fifth day in the hospital. They had transferred him to the psychiatric wing, in a section with people undergoing mild treatment for non-dangerous conditions like depression or mild schizophrenia. By now, he was getting bored with the long string of doctors and specialists poking his mind to find answers to why, in the name of God, a young man like him would try to commit suicide. He had let them know about Marie. He didn't care to hide it, anyway. After several attempts to elicit some kind of burden offload from him, they all concluded that he was psychologically and physiologically normal. The unanimous decision was that he was to be discharged from the hospital in a couple of days, with the strong recommendation to rely on the support of friends and family.

To get them off his back, he had begrudgingly promised to accept Isabelle's visit today. She had been coming to the hospital every day since he got in, and he had always refused to talk to her. Around noon, she knocked on the door softly.

"Come in, *bon sang*, why all the formality?" François cursed, rolling his eyes.

Isabelle's face popped in. "Hey, brother. Nice of you to greet me like that. At least you now acknowledge my presence in this universe. After all, I'm only your twin."

"If you came to scold me, don't bother," he retorted. "I've had a score of specialists incessantly doing that for almost a week now."

"I have someone here to see you," Isabelle announced, in an uneasy voice.

François frowned imperceptibly. Isabelle turned somewhere outside and beckoned with a slight head movement. Sure enough, Marie's tense body appeared trembling in the door frame. She had large circles around her eyes and didn't dare to look at him.

"Take her out of my sight," François said as calmly as he could, addressing his sister.

His cold voice sent a shiver down Isabelle's spine. Marie's face looked like it had lost all blood and her posture reflected the agony she was going through. Without a word, feeling rejected and humiliated, she turned and left, tears flowing freely down her face.

"How can you do that to her?" Isabelle admonished her brother, closing the door with a long look after Marie. "You're cruel. Unrecognizable."

François gave her a feral look. "Save the self-righteous theory for someone who cares. Understand that I never want to be within one thousand kilometers of that person."

"That person is our best friend. Surely, she deserves—"

"What about what I deserve?" François shouted, trying hard to control himself.

"You are overreacting. Be careful what you're doing. I don't know what you imagined, but she was never yours. You are not losing a girlfriend. You are losing a lifelong friend."

With a sigh, he calmed down and answered softly. “Look. I won’t even argue about this. She made her choice. I made mine. The world will move on.”

Isabelle came close to him. “Did it ever occur to you, in your infinite wisdom, that you might not be the only one here who is suffering?”

“Please,” he lifted his arms in defeat, “can’t you understand I don’t want to hear this?”

Isabelle sat on a corner of his bed. “You must. I am about to tell you something about me that only Marie knows.” She bowed her head as she felt her eyes getting moist. “Ever since we met Marie, she has captivated me. No ... I’ve been held captive by her. That’s a better term. Although we were only children, I felt an irresistible attraction to her. Something that my brain refused to accept, and that I was afraid to admit to myself. Something that I still can never reveal to anyone else.”

François looked at her, utterly confused.

“You’re not the only one who cares about her, you know,” she said with a grimace.

“Yes, she already gave me the sisterly love speech. Spare me,” François answered, feeling exhausted. “I will never think of her as my sister.”

“Neither will I,” Isabelle whispered, loud enough for him to hear. “I love her differently. And I told her that much, more than a dozen years ago.”

“What?” François asked, dumbfounded.

“Do I have to spell it out for you?” Isabelle asked, exasperated.

“But ... what about your boyfriends? The polyamorous adventures?” François asked in shock.

“They were all my attempts to escape this.” Isabelle started crying.

François looked at her, speechless.

"When I confessed my love to her," Isabelle continued in a soft voice, sobbing, "she got into a deep depression. Mother sent the two of us to spend nearly a month in Davos. Alone. You might remember."

François nodded. He had always wondered what the two of them did back then for so long.

"Did she ... does she?" he dared to ask.

"No. She is not like me. For her, it was too much to see me suffer and accept she can never reciprocate my love. Underneath all that strength and boyish attitude, she is frail like a snowflake. I provided a little warmth, and she melted away."

"And now?"

"We agreed to never talk about it."

"This doesn't excuse what she did." François felt his rage coming back up.

"She didn't 'do' anything. François, you are the smartest person I know. Surely you cannot be that inept socially."

He looked at her, annoyed that he couldn't follow what was going on.

Isabelle sighed and continued. "She might have liked ... or loved you, under different circumstances. I surmise she trained herself to think of you as not her man. Ever. Because of me." She bowed her head.

"Wait a minute," François understood where this was going. "Let me get this straight. So, she wanted to cheat on me ..." Isabelle grimaced and wanted to interrupt, but he raised his arms and voice and wouldn't let her. "Yes, that's what I'll always call it! She wanted to cheat on *me* so that *you* don't suffer! Rather than hurt you, she hurt me. She hurt both of us. Or what? Are you more satisfied to know that she screws a stranger, not me? I feel like throwing up. And you were telling me I'm childish."

"She didn't know you would react like this. Seriously, kill yourself?"

"Incroyable," François replied, furious. "Do you expect me to feel sorry for her? Because you love her, and therefore, she feels like she cannot be with me? And you tell me this now after I nearly put an end to my misery? What am I supposed to do?"

"Accept us as we are."

"Never! Do you understand? I'd rather jump head down into a pit of fire in hell than stand around her while she's with another man."

"I can't do anything about this! I am resigned to seeing her marry. I would prefer her to marry you. But I don't believe she can do it."

"Fine. She doesn't love me. This has become clear to me."

"So what? What's the solution?"

François stood silent, looking straight at her ravaged face.

"There's nothing to be done. I'll be gone."

"François, please promise me you won't try to kill yourself again!" she panicked.

The image of foam all around him and the mighty whirlpools that he couldn't fight materialized in his head. And the burn in the lungs. He shivered out of control for a couple of seconds. "Oh no, don't worry. I died once and there was nothing enjoyable about the experience. I'd like to avoid it for a while. No, I'll just leave."

"Leave where?"

"Since you both seem to have all these skeletons in your closets, and neither felt the need to share them with me, you will allow me not to divulge my plans."

It was Isabelle's turn to keep quiet for a while. "Will you come back?"

"Never," he said with conviction. "You might hear from me. Don't try to reach me."

"You ... you ... idiot. You are nothing but a spoiled child, used to getting everything he wants," she yelled, standing up. "Don't you care what that does to me, your twin? What about Mom? What about Marie? Your disappearance will devastate her. She will constantly worry that you killed yourself."

"I feel bad for you and Mom. As for Marie, I want her to suffer. To feel what I felt. But, hey! She won't! You just said that she doesn't love me."

"How can you wish harm upon her? You don't love her at all."

François stood up, grabbed her hands, and looked straight into her eyes. "That's right! Now I hate her. Marie is and will remain a traitor to me. She made me hate our deranged species. Let her sleep with anybody in the Cybersperse, or in person, five people at a time for all I care. There's nothing you or she can ever do to change my mind."

Isabelle looked at him in shock. After nearly a week in the hospital, she had expected that he would regret his actions.

"It'd be best if you just left now," François said, turning his head away.

Isabelle started crying again and moved towards the door. "François, promise me at least that you won't tell Mom about me. She keeps bugging me about grandchildren. I don't think I'll ever give her that."

"You don't have to worry about me. I'll be gone from all your lives. Adieu," he said theatrically, with a cruel rictus on his face.

With a grunt, Isabelle ran out the door.

François stood alone for a few hours, thinking about what he had just found out. Eventually, he turned to the news channel in the Cybersperse to divert his attention. *Everything is so messed up,* he thought, his mind slipping away into darkness again. *This world is just wrong.*

The news channel announced the sudden death of one of the Chincse AI artisans, the famous Zhèng Yang, during the neuromimetic conference.

"Lucky son-of-a-bitch," François muttered. "He died famous. I should have remained in Paris for the rest of the week. I would have enjoyed the bustle."

The reporters were speculating about how this tragedy that took place on EU soil might influence the relationship between the West and China. They brought up again the fear of a war that might mean the end of the world.

Half-listening to reporters and analysts whining, the seed of a thought crystallized in François's mind. The world had screwed him over.

"What if," he asked himself in a soft voice, "what if I played a role in this little dice game? A double-six and the world survives. Anything else, and it goes to hell." Feeling a strange satisfaction, he turned Brigitte on. "Brigitte, call Professor Ndikumana."

"Sure, *Maître*."

Half a minute later, the professor's serene face greeted him.

"Professor," François started, "is your offer still valid?"

"Sure is, my young friend!"

"Then I'll gladly accept."

"Excellent news! How soon can you come to LA?"

"I'll be there the day after tomorrow."

CHAPTER 9:

THE SHADOW OF YOUR THOUGHTS

If you don't want anyone to know it, don't think about it.

— Adaptation of a Chinese proverb

News of Professor Zhèng Yang's death made Qianfan almost happy, and he felt guilty about that. He had briefly met Zhèng some twenty years before and had found him arrogant and insufferable. Besides, he welcomed anything that had a chance of spoiling the party's image. Zhèng was a symbolic figure, the main artisan of the greatest achievement of the Chinese researchers. Qianfan was sure that the party would arrange a memorable funeral for him.

I, for one, won't miss him, he thought, while sitting at his desk early in the day. *Without the MegaAI, the party would have had less control over the population. Zhèng had to satisfy his immense ego by delivering it to them. Who knows what they'll try to pull off next?*

Qianfan had spent the previous ten days terrified at the prospect of an SSMS able to scrutinize people's innermost thoughts, however slightly. He felt between the hammer and the anvil. There was no way to prevent the party from advancing the creation of the new SSMS. If it wasn't him, surely some sycophant scientist, so hungry for a promotion that he'd denounce his mother, would take the work over. Besides, Qianfan had a sense of deep responsibility for Baozhai. What would happen to her if they demoted her

Bàba? Didn't the ice woman make it clear that spreading the word about this new capability would spell disaster in his and Haitao's lives?

With a sigh, he stood up and moved towards the plain worktable next to his desk. It had taken a little over a week to integrate the new wireless sensor into the old SSMS. Qianfan looked at the official specs. There wasn't much there beyond instructions on how to use it. He didn't understand how it worked, which might have been inconsequential by now. The device was there. Haitao had made some design suggestions and the engineers on their team changed the scanner shape. Now it was more of a sphere, slightly smaller than a softball ball. There was no point in keeping the hollow semi-sphere shape since nobody would ever put it on their head.

They had finished the modifications just last night. Haitao had insisted on trying it on themselves first. It became immediately apparent that, despite what the specs said, the device still had to be placed less than ninety centimeters away from one's skull. Once they established the minimum optimum distance, they experimented on each other with a bunch of classic tests that assessed their mood toward different subjects. Despite Haitao's bravado and eagerness, Qianfan could see he was often uncomfortable with being the subject of the experiment, judging by the way he glanced at the scanner suspiciously. At some point, the young man said he felt he was sharing the shadow of his thoughts, which Qianfan found was a good way to describe the operation.

Most of the tests they did the previous night were about food preferences, sports, colors, and other harmless things. But at some point they ran a work efficiency test with a bunch of questions about their productivity: whether they loved what they were doing, whether they cooperated well with their colleagues, whether they envied others, whether they thought others envied them, whether they trusted their colleagues, and so on. Qianfan had successfully used his recitation and meditation to counter any negative thoughts, but Haitao let out some unexpected findings. On the question of trust, it became crystal clear he didn't trust Qianfan. He had gotten out of it by saying the device needed to be calibrated better and pretending to work on it. The SSMS, now enhanced with one of Qianfan's latest ideas, scored between 65 percent and 68 percent accuracy after they adjusted for their bias in self-assessing. Although the results in the field might be significantly less trustworthy, Qianfan did not doubt that the party would start using it right after he delivered it.

There was no way to hide their progress any longer, so Qianfan made Haitao prepare the preliminary report for the committee. He expected the young man would be busy for hours. This was the last chance for him to do something, and he had to move fast. But what could he do? Grabbing the scanner, he stepped outside the office towards the cafeteria. He held in his left pocket the new SSMS and in his right pocket one of Baozhai's smaller Magic Boards, which he thought of as a talisman against this new excessively intrusive world that impinged upon the purity of people's souls.

The cafeteria was huge, one of the four that served the researchers and their security personnel in the complex of fifteen buildings. For days, Qianfan had carefully noted all cameras and microphones he could locate. He couldn't be sure that he'd covered them all. According to his calculation, there were three blind spots. One was near the place where they served the food, where many people came and went all the time. The other was too close to the entrance. His best bet remained a table in a corner. He had taken his lunch there in the past week. He noticed that a group of three people ate there all the time. One was Zhou Junfeng, a biology researcher who specialized in food growth, whose uninteresting field of work, restless eyes betraying his stress, and frail body frame disqualified him from being the right contact. The second one was Li Xin, a strong security officer who hadn't made it to the military. It was rather unusual for security officers to mingle with scientists, and that was because everybody knew that they were often scum spies, listening to whatever discussion they could or tempting people to say something inappropriate. The third was Wu Daiyu, an artificial intelligence scientist, who in some ways reminded him of Baozhai. She was young—in her early thirties—and brilliant, plus reputed for not going along with nonsense beyond what was strictly required to keep her position.

“Greetings,” Qianfan said simply, as he approached them, making the fist-and-palm salute. They saluted back half-heartedly. He could see that they were not comfortable with him joining their ranks. The constant fear of losing their jobs or being arrested made people equally suspicious of listening walls and each other. *Soon they'll be afraid to have a secret opinion too,* he thought unhappily. “I hope you don't mind if I join you. I find this place somewhat secluded,” he threw in casually.

The others looked at him, startled, as if he had guessed their game. They informally protested at the idea that he could inconvenience them and tried to look welcoming.

Oh, my ... I don't need the SSMS to guess that they too chose this place because it's out of the sensors' reach.

Eating in silence, Qianfan thought of a way to use his device. He felt terrible to violate their minds like that, but then the party would soon have to start trials on a large scale anyway, with unwilling participants. He nearly gave up the idea of doing anything today when a notification came to all their tablets from the management. The news channel was showing information about Zhèng Yang's death. The four of them switched to a common Cybersperse room, which they projected near their table. Zhèng had died just twenty-four hours before, and the propaganda machine had already presented him as an epic hero. First came a short rerun of President Yun Li's short speech, praising Zhèng with the usual set of pre-baked phrases that made everything sound one hundred percent fake.

“It was through people like Zhèng Yang that modern China developed,” the president said, in the same monotonous voice that Honorable Member Tián used not so long before to threaten Qianfan.

Perhaps she's trying to emulate him, he thought in passing. With a sigh, he discreetly oriented the SSMS from his pocket towards the three at the table, monitoring them while peeking at the readings. The three let out grunts of acknowledgement, as if their main purpose in life was to agree with the president's claims. Yet, the results of the scan shocked Qianfan. The predominant sentiment reflected was hatred, followed closely by fear. Only the biologist feared the president more than he hated him. Qianfan quickly tried it on another man passing by, and the results were quite positive, so he'd either enjoyed the speech or was adept at hiding his true feelings—although the latter was doubtful.

Qianfan wondered what would happen if he scanned all the people in this room. Would more than half hate President Yun Li? He didn't think so. Sadly, most people were already brainwashed enough or, perhaps out of a self-preservation instinct, had gone through enough structural modification in their brains to convince themselves to like him.

What an impostor, Qianfan thought, looking at the empty eyes of the president, while breathing the precious freedom to think such thoughts like he was enjoying the last day of cherry blossoms in the universe.

Nobody knew where Yun Li had come from. Somehow, he had risen to the forefront of the party. The Central Committee chose him to become the president. Rumor was that, for security reasons, he rarely met anyone in person. Gone were the days when a president would show his face in public. This strange character seemed in full control of his emotions. His facial muscles barely moved as he was speaking. His words were always rational, passionless, to the point.

The announcer interrupted his line of thought as she invited them to listen to Zhèng's last awkward speech. Qianfan checked his scanning device. It mostly showed indifference, perhaps some envy from the biologist, except for the AI expert. She stood frozen, not a muscle twitch, pretending to watch, mesmerized, to Zhèng's last words. Yet, her fear bar went off the charts. She appeared more afraid of this speech than she had been of the president. Qianfan nearly choked on a piece of bread. He wondered what might have caused that reaction. He admired again how well she could mask her thoughts and pitied her for how vulnerable she was to his device.

Now that the news segment was over, the biologist suddenly excused himself, saying that he was waiting for the results of an experiment. Li Xin did the same after he saluted somewhat mechanically. Qianfan thought that Daiyu had almost invited him to say something.

It's now or never, he thought, with no clear idea of what he could do. Despite his best efforts, they could still be subject to a remote microphone, their clothes could pick up an accelerated heartbeat, or people passing by might find it suspicious if they looked at each other in a funny way. On an impulse, he took out the Magic Board from his right pocket and placed it on the table.

"Can you believe that? I forgot this was in my pocket," Qianfan said in the most natural voice, seeing her surprised look.

"Doctor Zhào, surely you've passed the age of playing with that," she laughed unexpectedly.

Qianfan found her tinkling laughter pleasing and reassuring. Perhaps he could trust this woman. "Oh, this is a toy of my daughter's," he explained. "Even she is too old for it."

"I assumed as much. I was just joking," she reassured him, taking his hand and turning her head to the side coyly.

To his surprise, Qianfan realized that he found her sexy. He forced himself to concentrate on the risk he was about to take. He twisted his body ninety degrees and moved the board so that it was outside of the range of his and her uniform cameras. She looked at him, almost scared.

"Now and then it's good to go back to the time when we were children," he said, hoping that the physiological changes that his uniform undoubtedly picked up would be mistaken for signs that he was falling for this woman, whom he barely knew.

I probably am, he mused, feeling a wave of excitement at the thought that he was about to do the most dangerous thing in his life. Slowly, he wrote with his left hand on the board, "`Meet me on Sunday evening at eight o'clock at my apartment. Alone. No uniform.`"

"Don't you think everything was simpler back then?" he said aloud, although she was two decades younger than him, so it was hard to justify any shared experience.

She recovered fast from the surprise and replied, while erasing the content of the board quickly.

"Doctor Zhào, we shouldn't linger in times long forgotten. Surely you agree that today's age, under the supervision of the party and the power of our AI, is the golden era of the Chinese people." Meanwhile, she wrote on the board, "`I will be there.`"

It shocked Qianfan again to see how skilled she was at hiding her emotions. She didn't even blink. As if suddenly interested in some work-related stuff, he oriented the scanner on her and read his tablet, all while feeling that he was watching her when taking a shower, like a pervert. She was worried, as if she had something to hide. And there was the seed of something else: attraction. Qianfan stood up suddenly, nearly throwing his chair to the ground. She lifted an eyebrow.

"I apologize," he mumbled, unhappy for acting like a teenager. "It was good talking to you."

"Good talking to you too," she said, with a mildly amused facial expression.

He was tempted to scan her again, but he brushed the thought aside and walked fast back to his office.

CHAPTER 10:

THE 16 SONGS OF ZHÈNG

If the secret sorrows of everyone could be read on their forehead, how many who now cause envy would suddenly become the objects of pity?

— Italian proverb

General Joseph Thompson was sleeping unceremoniously in his chair, his head falling on the pieces of paper on his desk. The high pitch ring he chose in the Cybersperse for when someone important established a connection woke him up. He looked around for a couple of seconds, overwhelmed, not registering where he was. As the fog lifted a bit from his mind, he glanced at the hour: 4:23 a.m.

"Who the devil is calling me at this time?" he mumbled, dragging his hand over his tired face like he was trying to wash all the fatigue away. This promised to be another two-hour sleep night. He figured he had slept less than two hours a hundred nights in the last half-year alone. At seventy-five, he felt that the lack of sleep was making him lose the battle to stay alive. Besides the general's incapacity to concentrate and large circles around the eyes, he started noticing that, after any sudden move that he made, his brain took a fraction of a second to compose the visual model of the world around. He turned, blinked a few milliseconds, then noticed how the room finally rotated back into view. He was wary not to let anyone know how he felt. It wasn't the time to be concerned about his health.

Moving like a sloth, he accepted the connection. It was Sujata, who knew how tired he was.

“General, I am sorry to wake you up,” she apologized.

He stopped her with a dismissive gesture. “Please, we don’t need to keep up appearances.” Sujata nodded.

“I need to speak to you. Privately, face to face.”

“Alright. Let’s meet in Lincoln-3 in twenty minutes.”

“Thank you. I’ll be there.”

He turned off the Cybersperse, lost in thought. Sujata was about the most level-headed person he knew. She must have something important to tell him. He prayed it wasn’t some more bad news. The China situation deteriorated by the day, and they needed good news. With a sigh, he went to the bathroom and brushed his teeth, washed his face, and tried hard to make his uniform look more presentable. Then he took the little campus shuttle at his disposal and went straight to the Lincoln building.

Sujata was already in the room he had chosen, one that was completely technology-free and allowed them to speak off the record. She saluted, military style, the moment he entered.

“At ease, lieutenant,” he tried his best to smile. “I was having a beautiful dream, so I’m hoping your news will be at least as good, otherwise I’ll have to do my best to resume it,” he tried to ease the mood, scrutinizing her.

“The good news is that I believe I cracked Zhèng’s message. The bad news is the message itself.”

“Do you mean to tell me that all our powerful algorithms and our intelligence community, working day and night in the last week, made no sense of Zhèng’s last words, and you have?” he asked, genuinely surprised.

“I might be wrong,” she admitted, turning her head to the side. “It sounds a little far-fetched.”

The general looked out the window at the sunrise. June was his favorite month. It has the longest days, was warm, not too hot, the atmosphere was clear, and there were short periods of rain. He missed the carnal red of the poppy flowers from the fields that he had so loved when he was a child millennia ago.

"OK, hit me with it." He tried to sound livelier than he felt, as Sujata was patiently waiting for him to get ready.

"Zhèng's botched presentation in Paris was weird. And tragic. When I saw him, I had the feeling that he was pretending to be weak and old. His sudden death, while somewhat explainable, was in stark contrast to my impression of him. Then there was the melancholy in his words. Zhèng was one of the most calculated and cool people in the world. Perhaps he'd softened with age, although I doubt it. Then it was the specific things he said. He mentioned the word key, for example. He said that we should go through some emotions, from the moment we are born until the moment we die. And the songs. Really? Why would he share songs with us now?"

"Yes, I know. He puzzled everybody with those. I understand that our best specialists combed through the data in those files. The report showed that you can look at them until you are blue in the face, and still won't find anything."

"That's because we looked at them as computers. We tried to decipher the binary files. We should have looked at them as people."

"Say what?"

"We had to *listen* to them."

"Which we did. They were cute."

"They were more than just cute. Each evoked a certain feeling. For the fun of it, I asked one hundred of our folks to tell me how they felt when listening to these songs. I used the exact four emotions that Zhèng mentioned: fear, happiness, sadness, anger."

"Go on," the general frowned.

Sujata pulled out a piece of paper from her bag. "I got a 91 percent correlation in the results. The most common interpretation, one that I agree with, was a sequence like this."

The general looked at her paper, which had on it scribbled the sequence:

"Sad, fearful, happy, angry, angry, sad, happy, sad, sad, angry, sad, angry, angry, angry, happy, angry."

"So, the guy was angrier and sadder than happy and afraid?" the general concluded, counting the results.

"Yes, but notice that there were sixteen songs. Precisely how many sentences Zhèng uttered before he told us that the *key* to a happy life was living all these emotions. And he said that we must *add* them to our lives. Why say *add*? What can one do with these emotions the moment one is born? Newborns are barely aware of the world around them."

"What's your point?"

"Zhèng was no fool. He didn't use these words because of his dementia onset. He wanted to tell us something."

"Well, what?" the general grew exasperated.

"Since he mentioned the *moment* we were born, I looked at the records. Zhèng was born on 30/09/71 at 13:11. He died on 24/06/53, precisely at 10:12. If we unpack these dates and times, we get the following sequence: 3, 0, 0, 9, 7, 1, 13, 11, 2, 4, 0, 6, 5, 3, 10, 12."

The general looked even more confused.

"You notice that there are, again, sixteen numbers."

"Are you saying that ..." the general stopped at the significance of this.

"Yes. I believe Zhèng staged his death by the minute. He knew that his death would attract our attention. All we had to do was come up with the key to his message."

"What is this key?"

"I assigned the numbers one to four to the emotions he put forward, in the order he mentioned them," Sujata said, pulling out another piece of paper, where she wrote:

Fear (F) = 1,

Happiness (H) = 2,

Sadness (S) = 3,

Anger (A) = 4.

"I believe Zhèng wanted us to add the emotions to *his* life, from the moment *he* was born to the moment *he* died," Sujata said triumphantly, stressing some words. "All we've got to do is add up two sequences of sixteen numbers each. Which I did, here." Sujata pulled another piece of paper where she had drawn a table.

"The first row is the number of sentences Zhèng uttered - S1 to S16. The second and third are the emotions evoked by his songs, again, in the exact order he provided them to us. In the fourth, I wrote the sequence of his birth and death dates/times. The fifth contains the result of adding rows three and four up, which gives us the position of the word in each of his sixteen sentences."

	S1	**S2**	**S3**	**S4**	**S5**	**S6**	**S7**	**S8**	**S9**	**S10**	**S11**	**S12**	**S13**	**S14**	**S15**	**S16**
Emotion	S	F	H	A	A	S	H	S	S	A	S	A	A	A	H	A
Emotion #	3	1	2	4	4	3	2	3	3	4	3	4	4	4	2	4
Birth/Death	3	0	0	9	7	1	13	11	2	4	0	6	5	3	10	12
Word position	**6**	**1**	**2**	**13**	**11**	**4**	**15**	**14**	**5**	**8**	**3**	**10**	**9**	**7**	**12**	**16**

"But why would Zhèng give us such an unreliable key? Surely some people will get a feeling different from the one intended, or no feeling at all, listening to his one- to two-minute songs?"

"I asked myself the same thing. I almost didn't bother to follow this path of reasoning. The answer to this question will reveal itself when you see the deciphered message." Sujata took a break to take out the last piece of paper in her bag and gave it to the general. "Here is the transcript of

Zhèng's awkward speech. I underlined the words according to the positions determined by the table."

1. In the last three decades, (6) China has made considerable progress toward ensuring the prosperity of its citizens.
2. (1) Nobody can deny that.
3. Our (2) AI research was instrumental in this effort.
4. In 2041, the Chinese Science Ministry and Party Advisory Committee asked that (13) we tackle one of the most critical problems facing the Chinese people.
5. A mega research group was formed, led by me, to (11) save those who live on the shore from the ever-rising sea levels.
6. We wanted to (4) control the mighty ocean, and we did.
7. In order to accomplish this impossible mission, we had to achieve what nobody had (15) achieved before, and so we created the first synaptic-level neocortex simulation.
8. The most advanced research group in the world created this marvel, which made (14) it possible since then to tackle many other challenges that we thought were insurmountable.
9. We ask ourselves: 'Who (5) knows what would have happened if the great Chinese minds had not invented the artificial brain?'
10. The Chinese people, inspired by our beloved (8) president's leadership, are the greatest in the world.
11. I hope (3) mankind will follow in our footsteps.
12. A solid, disciplined society will ensure that people remain (10) alive for centuries to come.
13. In my long journey through life, I have (9) lost many colleagues.
14. Dear people, who can never be (7) replaced.

15. I miss them every single day of my life, and it (12) is my duty to thank them here for their efforts.
16. But I feel I will join them soon, since old age will deprive me of (16) sentience before long.

"This gives us the following words: *China, nobody, AI, we, save, control, achieved, it, knows, president, mankind, alive, lost, replaced, is, sentience,"* Sujata continued. "A simple algorithm to unscramble words into sentences forms the following sequence, with the highest confidence."

Sujata read aloud the sentences on her last paper.

CHINA AI IS ALIVE. IT ACHIEVED SENTIENCE. REPLACED PRESIDENT. NOBODY KNOWS. WE LOST CONTROL. SAVE MANKIND.

The general's mouth flew open and stayed like that for a minute.

"Zhèng knew all too well that their MegaAI brain, being a simulation of the neocortex alone, lacks proper emotions," Sujata continued. "The AI is aware of emotions. Perhaps it can simulate them rationally, but it can never *feel* them the way we do. Their AI was surely monitoring all the communication going out from Zhèng's machine. With its unsurpassed algorithmic power, it must have checked the files of the songs and found nothing suspicious. That's because it could never listen to them and interpret them in the same way we do. I guess that's why it allowed Zhèng to provide them to us."

The general looked out the window, mulling over this news.

"You notice how clever Zhèng was," Sujata continued. "He did not give us existing melodies, for which there surely are, somewhere in the Cybersperse, statistics or labels about the mood they bring when we listen to them. He didn't want to take the chance that the AI would infer that they were a message. So, he composed a few short pieces, for which there were no records anywhere. He was fairly sure these little songs would evoke a predominant emotion in most of us. But Zhèng also took a huge risk. The AI could have attempted to categorize his songs into emotional buckets based on frequencies similar to other songs. I guess we are lucky this AI doesn't seem big on sentiment."

"Why kill himself?" The general couldn't recover. "He could have screamed his message to us from the podium before his security force took him down."

"As far as we know, Zhèng left behind four children and nine grand-children. They are all back in China. Surely the Chinese government would have downgraded their statuses until, eventually, some would have ended up in prison. So, Zhèng arranged his death at the precise minute he wanted it. I guess when he drank the water, he ingested a substance that short-circuited his heart and left no traces in his system. He knew his death was bound to attract our attention. Yet, he remained a hero in China, so the government would continue to provide high-ranking privileges to his family. He killed himself, hoping that his sacrifice wouldn't be in vain."

"If this is true, it won't be," the general said, determined. "There are still many things that don't add up. How could their AI, powerful as it is, become alive? Whatever the hell that means. Our experts have been reassuring us that a Terminator scenario in which the AI suddenly wakes up and starts fighting humans is practically impossible given how limited any of our AI systems are, including the MegaAI from China. They say that we are a couple of hundred years from AI sentience, evil or not."

"Your guess is as good as mine," Sujata shrugged. "I don't understand why Zhèng called it alive. A lot is going on there that escapes us."

"And the party? The people? If you could decipher this message, other smart folks there will too."

"I'm sure," Sujata nodded. "Though we have no way of knowing how they would react. I can only imagine the state of fear in which most of their people live. You know they are being monitored everywhere. A revolution is very hard to start under normal circumstances. When your oppressor is a machine, you don't know whom you're fighting."

The general silently agreed. It might be a long way before a revolutionary movement made any difference in China. The West had to rely on its people to get out of this mess. Another thought came to him.

"The part about replacing their president ... Could Yun Li be just a puppet in the hands of this new AI?" the general asked, raising his voice in realization.

"Worse," Sujata shook her head. "I speculate that the elusive Yun Li is just an avatar. Since Zhèng implies that nobody knows about the AI being alive, I bet nobody has met Yun Li personally. Our government certainly didn't. The AI must have fabricated some biometrics for him. Fingerprints, iris, DNA. None of it had to be that of a real human. Enough to sign every Cybersperse communication to ensure their citizens and the rest of the world that an authoritative man leads China. Of course, I can only provide conjecture about this, given how little we know."

"Now I must wake up the secretary of defense. And the president," the general said and scrambled towards the door.

"General," Sujata stopped him and looked him in the eyes. "If all of this is true, keep in mind that whatever Zhèng created might be foreign to us. Not just different. Not just something we'll be able to adapt to. Plain alien. Just like it cannot understand our songs, this is a being that we cannot, and we'll never be able to understand. We can't be sure of its goals, if it has any, or justification for actions, or priorities."

"Are you saying that we lost the war before it started?"

"I'm saying that if a super AI controls, arguably, the most powerful army in the world, we should avoid war, at all costs. Until we level the playing field, somehow."

"God damn it, can't we create one of those things ourselves? Sort of like the Cold War, when both the U.S. and the Russians had nuclear missiles, but neither side launched them?"

"Whatever AI we can come up with, we better do it fast. The first Artificial General Intelligence system will do everything in its power to stop any other from developing. The China Mega-AI has had several years to sharpen its claws. There used to be a joke among us AI nerds in college: 'The second AI is a dead AI.'"

CHAPTER 11:

PRESSURE

You anthropomorphize everything. A hungry kitten meowing is an adorable newborn crying. A little birdie out in the woods laughs at you. A creek on the floor is the crooked cry of a hag. You see walking trees, hear talking dogs, and fear human-shaped spirits.

Throw a bit of pareidolia into the mix and you see a cloud as a girl's smile, a tree stump curled up ready to attack, or a Mona Lisa coffee stain. This tendency has a perfectly reasonable evolutionary explanation. Better be wrong about the shadow in the bush being a lion than the other way around.

Still, when faced with something that is supposed to be anthropomorphized, like an android's face, you react differently. You go along fine with extremes. If it is unmistakably a machine, you are treating it as a thing. If it looks practically indistinguishable from a human, you empathize with it and treat it as a peer. The middle ground is problematic. The android that looks almost like a fellow human, but not exactly one, seems repulsive to you. Those face muscles that are only a little odd, or the look in their eyes that are devoid of life, make you an involuntary victim of a mysterious self-defense mechanism that kicks in and produces uneasiness. You fear the pseudo-human. This is called the uncanny valley.

If that almost perfect android reminds you of someone you know, especially someone you love, you feel conflicted. You freak out.

— DeSousa's Memoirs - Part I - Beginning - 2053

François got into a cab that drove him straight from the LAX airport to the company address in Malibu that Ian had given him. Once they got out of the main LA area, he started admiring the ocean on the left and the mildly sloped, barren hills on the right. A wave of doubt engulfed him, thinking about home. This place bore a resemblance to it, with the water near the hills, the palm trees, the cacti, and even the flowers. He admitted the landscape looked different, more sparse, much more spacious. Somehow, he thought that a mountain lion might jump on top of his car at any moment, which was ridiculous given that the area was quite populated. Beautiful mansions appeared all around. The water wasn't nearly the shade he was used to, and the waves looked more than threatening. Just thinking about them made him shiver uncontrollably. He was sure he didn't want to get into a large body of water ever again.

One drowning was enough, thank you, he thought, masquerading a smile.

His mind continued to drift back to his home. At Isabelle's insistence, he had mentioned to his mother that he was going to move somewhere around LA. François had promised that he'd be in touch later.

"Much later," he mumbled.

"Sorry, I didn't get that, can you repeat?" the car's AI assistant woke up.

"Nothing, continue," François said, rolling his eyes. These days the AIs wouldn't allow him to talk to himself.

Once the cab made a right turn, the ocean remained behind him and so did his anguish. The car drove through a fancy neighborhood with surveillance cameras and security drones flying all around. Then it got to a tall fence and eventually to a gate where a handful of security officers invited him to step out.

"Welcome, Doctor DeSousa," one security officer said upon looking at his credentials and after a quick biometric scan. "They are expecting you."

François stepped through the gate and got into a small trolley that drove him past some trees, revealing a couple of office buildings. The landscape looked neat and regularly groomed. He looked at the company's name and logo written on a large metal sign in front of the main building.

"CogniPrescience; now ain't that a silly, pompous name?" he mumbled.

Below the name and logo he saw a sentence written in smaller, italic font: "*We work so you can have a future.*"

With a sigh, he got off and walked to the main entrance, trying to see something through the tinted glass. He nearly fainted when he entered. There were at least fifty people crammed in the main lobby, who started clapping when he made an appearance. Judging by the cameras around, and the speakers, there were more witnesses to his arrival, hidden throughout the buildings. At first, François thought that this was a prank, but studying these people's faces, he recognized curiosity and genuine hope.

They've been waiting for me like I am some kind of Messiah, he thought, a little scared. *I wonder what Ian told them.*

Suddenly, he registered an enormous pressure to meet such expectations. He saw Ian's face beaming a couple of meters away.

"Welcome home, François!" He grinned from ear-to-ear, offering his hand.

Everybody went silent, observing this encounter.

"Thank ... thank you, but …" François answered, looking around embarrassed. "Why?"

"Why this reception?" Ian laughed. "Because I honestly believe you will make it happen. And I told my people about you."

"Make what happen?" François asked, rattled.

"Our dream. Most of us here have been working on it for over twenty years."

"*Ah, nom de Dieu*!" François felt a wave of rage, and took Ian by his shoulder to talk with him somewhat privately. "That's unfair! I accepted this job to contribute something. To see if we could adapt my algorithm to your AI. Surely you cannot saddle me with the responsibility of creating the first

AI as millions of people tried to do before me. I'm not an AI specialist. I only came up with an algorithm."

"I guarantee you won't shoulder the responsibility alone," Ian answered with a serious face, loud enough for others to hear. "If there's something that unites all folks here, that is the resolve to create the first AI."

François noticed how people around nodded in approval. Someone in the back shouted, "Hear, hear!"

"I wanted you to understand that the people around you have dedicated their lives to this project. We're not the typical medium-sized commercial company that hires and fires people by the dozens every year. Our employee retention rate is 99 percent. They give this effort all they have. People move here with their families. They're all living nearby, and their kids go to local schools."

I bet this is again some kind of test, François thought. *He wants to know if I will put in long hours for this work. I understand eccentric characters as much as the next man, but this is getting upsetting.* "If you're worried about my commitment, don't be," he whispered. "I intend to give this project my best shot. There truly is nothing better in my life at this moment." A shadow passed over his face while he involuntarily thought of Marie.

"Excellent!" Ian broke the awkward moment. "Folks, get back to work. I'm going to introduce François to our little empire here. There's plenty of time to get to know him."

As on a command, everybody started chit-chatting and moved around chaotically. François stood still, uncomfortable with the way people looked at him. It was like he was an alien who had landed in their territory, bringing along the elixir of eternal life. He remembered the curious eyes of the fish surrounding him in the blue water not so long ago ... He shuddered and got even more annoyed when he noticed Ian was observing him.

Once the lobby was clear, Ian took François aside.

"I hope I didn't upset you too much. This introduction is both for your and our team's benefit. The mood has been gloomy around here for the last years. We haven't made too much progress."

"How many such saviors have you presented so far? This trick can only work so many times," François observed.

"Indeed," Ian offered his disarming smile, "you are the first one. No pressure!" he laughed, much to François's dismay. After a brief pause, Ian continued, "I told you, I have a hunch." Then he winked. "Enough of this. Do you need to freshen up?"

"I'm good." François dismissed the idea with a quick hand wave. He was eager to understand what the fuss was all about.

"OK, let's leave your stuff here at the reception, and let me give you a quick tour," Ian said, walking him outside. "Here's our little complex," he said with a large arm movement showing an area of approximately five acres.

Palm trees and neat bushes surrounded the buildings, and portions of lawn popped up here and there. Judging by their dark green, and considering LA's dry climate, this place wasted a lot of water to keep a lush appearance.

"Before I forget," Ian lifted a finger, "I advise you not to wander beyond the alleys and grass patches." Fences surrounded the entire area, which appeared heavily monitored with cameras, sensors, and security guards. "It's unlikely that someone can break into the whole complex unless they come with a small army."

"But why?" François couldn't resist asking. "Who are you afraid of? Hackers?"

"My dear fellow," Ian said gravely, "if we produce what we aim to produce, everybody and their mother will be after it. Not just hackers, not just rival companies, but also governments. The moment we are sure we have developed something unique, and we are on the path to getting a real AI, I intend to revamp the security here."

François peeked at the fence and wondered if it was electrified. Suddenly, he got the uneasy feeling he was a prisoner.

"Anyway, let's talk about something more pleasant," Ian said, looking around satisfied. He took a deep breath and started describing his baby. "CogniPrescience has five teams. Each team gets its building, and skywalks connect all buildings, so you don't need to go outside. Although, since LA hardly gets any rain, I prefer to walk in the sunshine."

They took a few steps away from the entrance.

"We've just exited the main building, which is the home of Team 1. This is the main AI research area with over three hundred researchers. Our business/marketing crew is nearly nil, so when I say employees, assume researchers or developers. Almost everybody here has a Ph.D. or a master's degree from a good university. Team 1 handles the core intelligence aspects of mammals, with an obvious focus on humans. I guess that most of your work will be with sub-teams of Team 1. They oversee the universal, built-in aspects of the mind, which I mentioned when we talked in Paris. They also take care of integrating everything into a smooth cognitive model."

Ian pointed out to the next much smaller building, which looked equally pristine. Oddly enough, it was fully covered in vines.

"Team 2 oversees the first potential commercial application for this stuff. They are mostly roboticists. There's about one hundred of them. We have their best robot—a work of art, by the way—in the first building, so you won't need to visit them much. I guess this team is the most advanced concerning their goals."

François looked at his new boss carefully. He recognized the passion with which Ian was talking and felt a wave of energy coming over him. *What if I fail this guy? He'd be so disappointed,* he thought, bitterly.

"Team 3 is small, just shy of fifty people," Ian continued as they reached a small white building with tiny windows. "They connect biological matter with computers. Recent years have seen an explosion of non-invasive interfaces that are used for a variety of applications, from gaming and

Cybersperse to remote working, monitoring workers' attention, and so on. I'm sure our friends in China and Russia have found more controversial uses for them. We do traditional research too, but Team 3 experiments with deeper connections. They use brain tissue grown in our labs, and tiny meshes of electrodes linked to individual neurons in mice's brains. One of the most intriguing research projects we have there focuses on how to keep primate brains alive in a kind of organic soup, to be later connected to machines. This effort is far-fetched, and I have little hope, but it might be possible in the future."

"You want to live forever, I figure," François couldn't resist pointing out. The memory of water entering his lungs haunted him again. *Must be nice to want to prolong your life,* he reflected. *Thanks to Marie, I nearly threw mine away.*

Ian didn't answer right away, which was an unexpected change from the way he usually acted. "In principle, yes. I suspect eventually we will merge with machines. This is an iffy topic. Some hate the idea, especially those more religious."

François shrugged and pouted. Not his problem. Perhaps a short human life was optimal. His opinion of humankind was at its lowest point ever.

"Then we have Team 4," Ian continued, ignoring François's facial reaction and pointing to another small building that looked like an overdeveloped hut. "These fifty nerds are the farthest out there, both in terms of the target date for any results and the progress made. They are researching intelligence that is well beyond that of a human."

"I thought your entire philosophy centers on aligning the AIs with our way of thinking," François pointed out, intrigued. "Wasn't that the whole point about preventing the creation of an AI that might harm us?"

"Indeed," Ian nodded. "This is the most important principle of our endeavor. Rather than an alien AI, better no AI at all. But once we create the basis of a human-like AI, nothing prevents us from making it smarter, without altering our compatibility. If I can try a simplified analogy, such an upgrade would be like adding more memory to a computer."

François realized they had walked around an oval to reach the last structure, which was not too far from the main building but hidden by the trees. It could easily pass for a duplex apartment building.

"Finally, Team 5 is concerned with the ethical aspects of building an AI. We only have a score of employees working on this. Their work ranges from the impact of AI on human society to how to instill moral principles in an artificial mind. This is very important, but until we make more progress with the AI itself, it remains mostly theoretical."

Ian paused, looking at the sky. "More concretely," he spoke in a soft voice, "until Team 1 finishes its job, all other teams are idle. Somehow, I feel that ... we're running out of time. I can't tell you why. It's just—"

"A hunch," François interrupted him. "I know."

"That it is," Ian laughed. "I think you and I are going to get along just fine!"

"I hope so," François answered with a small smile. He admitted he liked the old man. If everybody behaved like him, the Earth would be a better place. And he envied him for his bubbly personality that was so different from his own.

"And now for the grand finale," Ian said, inviting him back inside the main building. "Let me show you your workplace."

They stepped in and took an elevator one level down. They entered a small lobby and passed through a security door.

François looked at the thick concrete walls that could probably withstand bombardment. Perhaps the room could even function as a nuclear shelter. *I wonder what I'm getting myself into,* he thought, feeling intimidated.

"I'm afraid your tablet will have to remain here, and your personal assistant will need to be turned off," Ian said.

François shrugged and complained. "Brigitte?"

"Yes, *Maître*."

"Turn yourself off."

"OK, *Maître*. Going offline now."

Ian nodded, satisfied he didn't have to convince François. "In this lab, we do our final experiments with the AI code. While the rest of the complex has full access to the Cybersperse, this little bunker is completely cut off from the outside world." Looking at François's puzzled face, Ian continued. "This isn't just about fear of intruders. Until we are sure we create a friendly ... no ... a *loving* AI, we cannot connect it to the Cybersperse or any other network. We have all the learning materials here, digitized. This includes copies of the Wikipedia and British Encyclopedia knowledge bases that are updated periodically, a collection of the most important books ever written, the most up-to-date textbooks for over a thousand undergraduate and graduate courses from top universities, and more."

"Impressive," François nodded.

"And," Ian opened the door in front of them, "this is your little office."

François stepped inside and immediately noticed how large the space was.

"Do you think I intend to play indoor soccer here?" he asked, confused.

"If that's what it takes to train an AI, why not?" Ian answered, amused.

François figured the room was about ten times bigger than his apartment in Villefranche-sur-Mer. There were four large desks, a projector, several big monitors, and a couple of cabinets. The walls were white. Given that they were underground, there were no windows. Looking around, it surprised him to see a netted space with a few small toys that looked like an area where one would let toddlers play. He briefly thought that some workers might come here with their children, although, given the security craziness, that idea seemed odd.

"Let me introduce you to someone essential to this project." Ian walked to a corner of the room, obstructed by a black divider painted with some Asian buildings and a pagoda.

For a moment, François fantasized that a beautiful assistant was getting ready to greet him behind that little wall. But Ian calmly unrolled it and revealed a full-sized android instead. It appeared to be a woman, dressed in simple jeans and a t-shirt, sitting on a chair.

So that's what that little netted playground was for, François realized, although he was sure the android was incapable of such amazing feats as playing like a child.

"Meet CARLA!" Ian exclaimed. "She truly is a beauty! As of now, she is 90 percent indistinguishable from a real woman. The robotics team assures me they will do the final 10 percent retouches over the next six months, tops. For facial expression, body movements, eyes, gait, everything ... no one will be able to guess she's not organic. Even her voice will be perfect." Ian turned her on and stepped aside.

CARLA opened her eyes and straightened her body. She looked around, like a woman who had just woken up, and greeted them in a suave voice. "Hello, my name is CARLA. That stands for Conscious Affective Reasoning and Learning Android. I aim to become human."

François had remained in the opposite corner of the lab while the android talked. He shook his head at this cheap show. Many such androids had been announced over the last few decades. While none had a mind worth talking about, their creators had made significant progress with their physical appearance. He thought this was just a publicity stunt to fuel, once again, the imagination of nerds all over the world.

François stepped forward to see her better, then stopped, shocked. CARLA did look almost human. She was the whole package: the way she blinked, her smile, her sparkly and restless eyes, her hair, and the almost sexy way she moved her head were very engaging. Above all, she appeared to be Marie's distant relative. Not quite a sister, but there was enough resemblance to give him pause. She had the same facial shape, similar nose, a slightly darker hair color, some of Marie's freckles, and almond-shaped eyes—although they were brown.

François faltered. He felt his blood boil. Was he still obsessing over her and imagining her face? Or was this a sick joke? How could Ian have known? Was he spying on him?

"Are you alright?" Ian looked at him, worried.

François looked deeply into his eyes. This man was genuine. It was just a sordid coincidence. Perhaps Marie was too fresh in his mind. He took one step toward the android. Now closer, he realized the resemblance was not that great. *I'm probably seeing her face everywhere,* he thought. *Pathetic.*

It was more likely that the estheticians gave CARLA a cute, if not beautiful face, that was race neutral. After all, people were not supposed to fall in love with her. Not yet, anyway. François calmed down.

"I'm alright. She just reminds me ... of someone."

"If you wish, we can adjust her physiognomy," Ian offered. "I need you 100 percent committed to this task. No distractions."

"No," François lifted his hand. "She is fine the way she is, as a starting point. I will work with her. Although I would be happier if the specialists would finalize their changes to make her indistinguishable from a real person."

Ian nodded in approval, although he seemed unconvinced.

If there is a God out there, then this must be one of the biggest pranks He's ever pulled, François thought, looking at the android. *I practically killed myself because of a woman. Now, as penitence, I'm tasked to incarnate her in a plastic body.*

CHAPTER 12:

RITE OF PASSAGE

Before telling secrets on the road, look in the bushes.

— Chinese proverb

"Bàba, why should I learn poems?" Baozhai asked in exasperation, sitting at her desk with a Du Fun book of fifty-six poems in front of her. "I'm good at math. I never liked poetry."

Qianfan looked at his daughter and felt like crying. What should he tell her? That the party was evil? That a good portion of her life was a lie? That, from now on, she would have to watch not only what she was doing, or talking about, but also what she was thinking? For days, he had considered not telling her anything and let her live her life in a lie. At least she would live. Still, what if, as she grew up, she saw through the veils of masquerade, manipulation, and propaganda as he had done? They would inevitably scan her, then jail and re-educate her, or worse. Without a warning.

He sighed and explained again. "Do you remember when I told you that meditation was going to help with your math performance? This is along the same lines."

"Poems? I don't trust words that don't have a straightforward meaning."

"Oh, that's a good one," Qianfan smiled. "Then I guess you don't trust the language-based communication. There is no such thing as a straightforward meaning." He paced around the small room. "At the minimum, it will be a good exercise for your memory. You'll see, you'll grow to like them. You know that whenever I'm nervous, I recite *The Iliad*. And that is a bigger text, mind you."

"You know that this is my only free day in the whole week. I'd rather spend it watching a movie or ... talking with my friends in the Cybersperse."

Qianfan felt a pain in his chest. His daughter's inability to make friends was bothering him. He expected her peers would perceive a girl, champion in math, as nerdy, envied, and so on. Normally, there should have been enough kids who were interested in school for her to form some relationships. As for getting a boyfriend, or again, even a friend who was a boy, it seemed out of the question.

"Well, maybe learning something radically different will get you into other circles," he desperately tried to come up with a new strategy, feeling guilty for depriving her of an attempt to socialize.

Baozhai said nothing for a while and looked at the poems in irritation. She thought that there was no way that poetry was going to get her closer to those kids at school. "Fine," she whispered. "I'll learn them by heart. Although I still consider it a waste of time."

Qianfan caressed her head. He wondered, for the millionth time, why they had been born in this society? They would have been better off in ancient China in a remote village, not bothered by anyone. Although chances were that human greed and stupidity would have caught up with them there too.

"It will help you, I promise," he reassured her.

Suddenly, the house AI assistant notified them discreetly that someone was at the door.

Baozhai looked at her father, surprised.

"Oh, this must be my ... my colleague," Qianfan said, cursing himself for not being able to keep his wits about him. "I invited her to talk about something. Work-related," he was quick to add, feeling his blood rush to his head. He ran towards the door to mask his reaction.

"Her?" Baozhai asked, standing up and moving towards the door. She was more entertained than curious, particularly given her father's nervous behavior.

Qianfan let a groan out and opened the door. He couldn't help but take one step back. Wu Daiyu looked stunning. Anything would have been an improvement from her usual bleak uniform, but her lemon-yellow dress gave her an angelic appearance. Her hair flowed loosely on her shoulders, and her eyes were sparkling.

"Good ... good evening, Doctor Wu," Qianfan stuttered. "Welcome to my humble home."

"Thank you for the invitation," she answered simply.

"Please ... please come in." He moved aside, noticing that she was holding a platter in her hands. "Let me get that from you."

Baozhai peeked from behind the door. This lady was beautiful. More beautiful than she'd ever be. She probably had tons of friends.

"Thank you," Daiyu nodded. "I made some mochi cake. It's Japanese, but I like it," she felt like she had to excuse her choice. "It's filled with nuts. I hope you're not allergic."

"I'm sure it's great," Qianfan assured her. He turned and saw Baozhai looking fascinated at their guest.

"This is my daughter, Baozhai," he introduced her. "Baozhai, this is Doctor Wu Daiyu, a colleague of mine. She specializes in artificial intelligence," he pointed out, annoyed that he suddenly felt the need to impress his daughter.

Baozhai came closer and shook her hand.

"Glory to our country," Baozhai saluted formally.

"Glory indeed," Daiyu said. "Doctor Zhào, you didn't tell me your daughter was so big. She is practically an adult. I bet it's hard to keep boys away from her nowadays."

"Boys are not a concern just yet," he answered, trying to sound as natural as possible. "Baozhai made it to the National Math Olympiad. Naturally, her attention is on doing well there."

"Oh, my," Daiyu said. "This is more than I could have ever hoped for back in the day. You deserve more than congratulations. You deserve respect!"

Baozhai blushed as she answered softly, "Thank you."

Qianfan looked furtively at his daughter. He had never brought another woman home before. This could become a tricky situation. Much to his delight, Baozhai was behaving naturally. He sensed she felt Daiyu's praise was genuine, and she felt comfortable around her.

They spent the next hour eating Daiyu's cake in the living room and chatting. Qianfan was beaming and wished that the evening would never end. He couldn't remember being so happy in a long time. When Daiyu looked at her watch discreetly, he started to worry.

I wonder if someone is waiting for her, he thought in a panic. *I know she's not married. She probably has a boyfriend. Someone close to her age. Not an old parent like me.*

He cleared his throat, forcing himself to get to the ugly portion of this meeting.

"Doctor Wu, perhaps we should talk about the reason I invited you here."

Daiyu moved her head fast toward him, which showed that he'd caught her on the wrong foot, enough for him to curse himself for ruining the evening. She recovered fast, in her usual style.

"Oh, I thought you invited me here to taste my mochi cake and meet your lovely daughter," she chimed in.

Ouch, Qianfan thought, feeling like an idiot. "Yes, of course, but I also wanted to talk about work," he moved on, determined to forget this moment. "Baozhai, be so kind as to go into your room. We need to talk about work-related things you are not allowed to hear."

Baozhai stood up, slightly bothered by her father's request, but nodded and moved out. Qianfan closed the door after her. He sat back at the table and moved near Daiyu discreetly, although she was looking intently at him, a sign that she understood his move. Besides enjoying her proximity, he had just positioned himself strategically to obscure the view of the only camera in the room. In this way, the camera could see them both from the side and back, and part of their faces when they talked to each other, but it couldn't record their hands. He took a quick look around and pulled two Magic Boards from under some books he had put on the table earlier. He slid one towards her. Curious, she looked at them, then scanned the room quickly and warily before taking it in front of her.

She understands I want nothing to be recorded, Qianfan thought. *And she hasn't complained about it, invoking one of the stupid party directives about the concept of privacy being an imperialistic invention and that it is for the good of the overall society that people give it up.*

Then started what Qianfan would later remember to be a surreal and mind-bending dual conversation, in which they spoke deliberately slowly, with long pauses, as neutral as possible, while writing something completely different, as fast as they could.

"`My team has worked on a secret project`," he jotted down, hoping that she would understand his horrible handwriting. "`I ask you not to divulge to anyone what I'm about to say. Do you agree?`" Aloud, he said, "Doctor Wu."

"`Yes`," she wrote, but said, "Please, call me Daiyu."

"`Thanks to my team and the MegaAI capabilities, the party now has another terrible surveillance device. A scanner`," he wrote, trying not to look too guilty and continued the verbal conversation. "Thank you. Please call me Qianfan. I wanted to ask you how happy you are with your current team."

"`Is it here?`" she wrote. "Happy?" she asked.

"Yes, I have a device here. It's not active," he clarified, blaming himself for not being able to convey this information to her faster. "This device scans anyone's brain, as long as it's positioned less than 90 cm from it." He also clarified aloud. "Yes. Do you enjoy working there?"

"Scans?" she wrote, her eyes enlarged a little, waiting to understand what the effects of this new device were. "I do," she answered, seemingly mildly intrigued, but twitching nervously.

"Yes. Scans for residual thoughts. Emotions. Determines how you feel when you see or hear or think about something." He continued aloud, "Can you disclose what you are working on? Just for my curiosity." "My assistant aptly named what's being read as the shadow of one's thoughts," he felt like he needed to clarify, given the bewildered look on her face.

"We are working on detecting anomalous patterns in the radio signals from space, with novel machine learning methods. Not something as fancy as the MegaAI, but good for our purpose," she said.

"Our scanner would immediately register a reaction like you've had just now, no matter how well you'd learn to mask it." Aloud, he said, "Sounds interesting. Still, I'd like to make you a formal proposal, which I hope you'll seriously consider." "I already scanned you. At lunchtime. During President Li's speech. I am sorry, I had to know."

Qianfan saw she was trying hard to concentrate and keep up with this craziness. She nearly stood up. She was terrified and couldn't hide it. If this short, written conversation leaked, her career, and her life, would be over.

"I recently have made good progress with my work, although I can't disclose what that is about. I am going to ask for another AI specialist," Qianfan added quickly.

She kept silent, looking at him in shock.

"You are very good at disguising your true feelings," he praised her on the Magic Board. "But it won't help against this scanner." Aloud, he forced himself to keep a neutral voice. "While what we have produced already works remarkably well, we undoubtedly need to make further improvements." Meanwhile, he wrote, "I have developed certain techniques that reduce the efficacy of the scanning. Meditation is one. Focusing on reciting long texts is another. I suggest you train your brain immediately." He was becoming concerned about her distress, so he said, "I looked into your credentials. I believe you could contribute further to our success. Would you consider joining my team?"

"When will it be operational on a large scale?" she finally wrote, and said, "I ... I would like that, but I need some time to come up with an answer. Of course, I would have to finish my current assignment."

"Soon. The party will prioritize its production. It's being miniaturized further. I expect they will integrate it in all current surveillance means, including our uniforms." He nodded at what she had said. "Of course. How long would that take?" he asked.

"Millions will be arrested. The MegaAI will hunt all attempts to organize any resistance," she reasoned, shifting uncomfortably. She then answered aloud, "Probably another three weeks."

"Yes, of course, the party will use the MegaAI to go through billions of scans recorded daily," Qianfan wrote, misinterpreting her words. "That would be acceptable. Do you think you could let me know your decision by the end of the week?"

"Not the party. The MegaAI," she wrote, looking at him carefully. "Sure."

"What do you mean?" he wrote, this time on the receiving side of confusing news. "Great. Then we have a plan," he declared aloud.

"So, you don't know," she wrote, still looking into his eyes. "I thought that's why you invited me here."

"Do you have questions about this?" he asked. "Know what?" he wrote.

"Is there something I should learn? In case I accept your proposal," she asked, trying to seem interested. "Doctor Zhèng left us a message in his last speech. Listen to his songs. Pay attention to how you feel. To decipher his message, take one word out of each of the first 16 sentences from his speech."

"Let's see ... Do you know anything about interfacing machines and brains?" he asked, and wrote, "What message?"

"Only what I learned in school," she answered. "The party is not in control anymore. None of the honorable members, dragon members, supreme members. In fact, I'm sure there's no President Yun Li. He is just an avatar."

"That would be a good place to start then," he offered with a trembling voice. "Then who is in control?" he wrote, exasperated by this slow means of communication.

"Thank you," she answered.

"The MegaAI."

This time, Qianfan couldn't stop himself from standing up. He instantly thought that if someone had scanned him now, his excitement readings would be off the charts. Mechanically reciting any poem in the world could not mask his reaction when hearing such a piece of information. "But that means," he mumbled aloud, then stopped when seeing her terrified face. "I mean, sure, don't mention it."

"Yes," she wrote. "This means that the MegaAI wants to eliminate all those who don't fall in line behind it."

"This changes everything. For the worse," he wrote. He tried to recover from the initial shock. His shoulders slumped, and he gave up the talking pretense entirely.

"Any attempt to stage a rebellion movement will be nipped in the bud," she wrote.

He finally said aloud, "We shall prepare to make your transfer as smooth as possible."

"What options do we have, then? What can we do?" She looked at him in alarm, waiting for some guidance.

"We must live first. We will fight later," he answered, then mechanically deleted his last words. Seeing her worried face, he did his best to appear confident.

CHAPTER 13:

STRANGER

Love must be the most confusing emotion that exists. Is it love or mere arousal when a man sees a woman on the beach, whose tiny thongs and triangle-shaped bra get easily erased by his imagination? Do old couples who spent an eternity together love each other or do they just get used to each other? Do children love their parents with the same neural circuitry they will later employ to love their spouse? Does an overly jealous husband love his wife, or does he just wish her to be unhappy?

The trouble is that you don't find answers to these questions throughout your lifetime. Yet, you spend an inconsiderate amount of your brief life preoccupied with finding a partner, courting, flirting, talking and dreaming about sex, giving your children an excellent education out of love, taking care of your parents out of respect.

It would be so much simpler if the answers were given to you right when you are born.

— DeSousa's Memoirs - Part I - Beginning - 2053

Sitting in the chic Villefranche-sur-Mer train station, Marie reflected on the month that had passed since François's departure. She had been sulking most of the time, and all attempts from Isabelle to cheer her up had failed. She felt she was slipping into one of her depressive episodes. For the first three weeks, she had decided it might be better this way. Depression came with an acute desensitization of her feelings. While she dreaded not cherishing the beauty and fun in the world, she welcomed anything that would dull the memory of what had happened between herself and François. From time to time, she would wake up after a recurring nightmare in which she was swimming in the sea, hitting François's bloated body. She remembered being horrified at how real it had felt when she touched his head with her palm; it turned out to be her moon-shaped night lamp that she had grabbed while sleeping. It was one of these dreams that made her take this next step. After waking up with a big headache, she was determined to do something. After all, François hated her. Let him hate her. So what? She hated him, too. And Isabelle—with her stupid love she could never return. It was time to move away from the DeSousa twins. She wanted her own life. She would have it.

On an impulse, she had invited Marco to France. She had told nobody, not even Isabelle. After François's suicide episode, she felt she owed an explanation to him and told him about François. Marco got mad with a jealousy that she found utterly misplaced given the circumstances. He nearly screamed at her, and that scared her. After a long pause, out of the blue, she told him she wanted him to come to France, and that she was ready for a more serious relationship.

To make her revenge against François even sweeter, she rented a small apartment in Saint-Jean-Cap-Ferrat, a quaint commune in the Alpes-Maritimes department in Provence-Alpes-Côte d'Azur. This was François's favorite village, just a fifteen-minute ride from his apartment. This was the place where the two of them and Isabelle had spent countless hours on the little beach, at the restaurant near the sea, going up and down on the abrupt and curvy alleys. Marie felt her eyes moisten thinking about this, but she shook her head, stubborn. Things were different now as Marco was about to arrive. She told herself that this was a new beginning for her, and that she had finally found the love she'd been waiting for. Yet, she was afraid that under the image of a confident and funny girl full of life that she put up in the Cybersperse, Marco would now discover her gloomy mood and the darkness in her heart.

This is my chance to find happiness. I won't lose it, she told herself, squinting and trying to notice the first sign of a train coming from the closest tunnel that led to Monaco and then Italy.

When he got off the train with a large pink rose bouquet, she felt a rush of blood flowing through her face and started trembling like a teenager. *Pull it together, Marie. You don't want to offer yourself so easily,* she scolded herself.

"Ah, Marie, *amore mio*," Marco yelled, running towards her, brimming with self-confidence.

Pleasantly surprised, she noticed he was taller than she imagined. He gracefully embraced her, kissed her on the cheek, and gave her the flowers, but was careful not to push his familiarity too far, which Marie appreciated.

Over the next several hours, they walked hand-in-hand all over the old town in Villefranche-sur-Mer, laughing at the merchants trying to sell them trinkets, T-shirts, and scarves.

Somehow, she sensed he was constantly pulling her towards more secluded places. This was how they reached Hunter's Garden, a small public terrace with narrow stone paths surrounded by palm trees, cacti, and pink flower bushes, with a gorgeous view of the bay and sea. She burst into laughter when she heard Marco exclaim, "*Bellissima*!"

They sat on a bench admiring the view and chit-chatting, when suddenly Marco pulled her close and kissed her on her lips. She half-expected this and, although she didn't want to be kissed yet, she liked his strength and surrendered her body.

I am in the Garden of Eden, she thought. Still, in the back of her head, she recognized she was forcing herself to enjoy the moment.

After this first kiss, he acted slightly more familiar. She could see happiness in his eyes, and she envied him for it, playing along. They took the bus to the Saint-Jean-Cap-Ferrat peninsula when it was getting close to sunset. Marco was full of oohs and ahs seeing the cute houses. They had dinner at

François's favorite restaurant, a little higher than the promenade, with a wonderful view of the water and looking up at the viaduct in Eze, François's hometown. Eating and listening to Marco's funny stories, of which he was full, Marie tried hard to remove François's image from her head. Marco was her man, the one she would marry and, hopefully, have children with.

After dinner, they went into her rented apartment. He gallantly let her in first, but then the moment he closed the door behind them, he jumped on her and kissed her, while taking his shirt off and revealing his ripped abs. This was when Marie knew everything was wrong. Even if she would let herself make love to him, which she half desired, she couldn't shake François from her head.

Marco sensed her hesitance and took a step back. "Am I moving too fast?"

"No ... Yes ... I don't know," Marie answered, annoyed at her conflicted feelings.

"Tell me what you want," Marco asked, with a hint of discouragement in his voice.

"I ... I thought I wanted you," she blurted.

"But?" he asked, squinting.

"I can't, sorry," she started crying.

"Oh, Marie, don't cry, you are my *belladonna*," Marco tried to cheer her up. "You may not be upset ever again. Tell me what's wrong. Did anybody hurt you?"

"No, no ... Well, yes, in a way."

"It's that François *stronzo*, isn't it?" he asked, watching her intently.

Her silence was all the confirmation he needed.

"I could beat him senseless, you know?" he yelled.

"No!" she replied forcefully, then stopped, surprised at how strongly she felt about it. She didn't want François harmed. Her sweet François, whom she'd refused to love for years because of Isabelle. François, who'd nearly killed himself because of her. And now she was alone, in an apartment with this guy, whom she thought she knew from the Cybersperse. A stranger.

"Why do you defend him?" Marco yelled. "Do you still have feelings for him?"

"I don't know. Perhaps," she replied between tears. "Marco, please, stop yelling."

He threw himself on the bed. "I don't understand. I thought you invited me here to be with you. If you don't want to make love, it's fine. I can wait."

She felt terrible that she was toying with him like that. "It's not you," she whispered at the revelation. "It's me. I'm broken."

He looked at her with empty eyes, devoid of any love or desire. Understanding that she had lost him too, her shoulders slumped in despair. "I'm sorry, I can't be with you," she said, sobbing. "I can't be with anyone, ever."

He looked at her in shock as she rushed out the door. She ran out onto the streets, her tears falling until she was completely out of breath and close to fainting. It took her half an hour to calm down. Wiping her tears, she asked her assistant for a car. Once back in Nice, she went straight to Isabelle's apartment without announcing her arrival.

Isabelle opened the door and was about to greet her with the usual *la bise* kiss when she saw how devastated she appeared. "You look awful," she said in a sudden panic. "What happened?"

"I ... I invited Marco here," Marie started, bursting into tears again.

"Here?" asked Isabelle, confused.

"I mean, here to Côte d'Azur. He arrived this morning. I rented an apartment in Saint-Jean-Cap-Ferrat."

Isabelle's face sank, forcing herself to be supportive. "This is good for you, but I assume things didn't work out," she said, trying to sound upset, although she felt jealous.

"He is a good guy, I think. I spent the whole day with him. He kissed me. Just now, in the apartment, he wanted us to make love. I thought I was okay with it." Marie felt she was losing her footing, so she sat on a chair. "I'm not okay. I can't get François out of my head. This morning I didn't think I would miss him like this. I feel physically incapacitated."

"Maybe it is too early for you to see somebody," Isabelle offered.

"No!" Marie replied forcefully, then told herself to remain calm. "I'm simply afraid. Defective, somehow, although I don't want to be. I know enough about human psychology to recognize a problem. This is pathological. I don't think I can be with another man."

Isabelle winced, not daring to hope.

"Oh, sorry," Marie lifted her hands, realizing that she was giving Isabelle false hopes. "I didn't mean it like that. I can't be with anybody other than François." She stood up. "I am stupid. I shouldn't have come here."

"Please ..." Isabelle said and frowned. "I understand I can never have you, but I am not François. Above all, you are and will remain my best friend. My sister."

"Thank you," Marie said, sobbing and shaking her body.

"You can stay here as long as you want," Isabelle said, hugging her. "You can move in with me. I promise I will take care of you."

Marie nodded. Seeing how vulnerable she was, Isabelle melted. She knew Marie fit the psychological profile of someone suffering from bipolar disorder. She had long periods of pink exuberance, like she was the most worry-free soul on Earth, when her gentle yet infectious laugh made it hard not to want to stay around her. Then came times like this, when Marie was in a deep depression, a black cloud over her face. So, she worried about Marie's future or even her life. She had to think quickly of a reason that would make her want to keep going.

"Perhaps ..." She hesitated. "Perhaps you should go and find François and tell him you love him."

"Go? Where? Tell me, and I'll be on the next train."

Isabelle hesitated. "I ..." she started, then stopped.

"Isabelle, do you know where he is?" Marie jumped up and grabbed Isabelle's hands. Her sudden wave of energy hit Isabelle. There was no way to keep this secret anymore. She sighed.

"He spoke with mom before leaving. His job is somewhere near LA."

Marie let go of her hands and turned around. "America? He moved far indeed," she realized. "It doesn't matter. I'll follow."

"That's a vast area. It's highly unlikely that you two would meet," Isabelle said, trying to cool down her excitement.

"It doesn't matter!" Marie chirped, now happy. "I'm confident I'll find him."

Isabelle felt conflicted between encouraging her to see her out of this slump, and tempering her enthusiasm so as not to give her false hopes. "Even if you find him, take it easy. He's still upset."

Marie's face sank again. "You're right. He said he never wanted to speak to me again."

"You did nothing wrong! Stop blaming yourself."

"I wanted to be with Marco. I didn't give myself to François. He cannot forgive me." Marie shook her head.

"You don't know that. And even if he doesn't, you can at least be around him, if this is what you truly want. Although I don't see any reason for you to sacrifice yourself for my brother."

The thought put some light on Marie's face. "Maybe I should live my life trying to make him happy, even if it means I won't marry or have children."

Isabelle shook her head but decided to let her think this way for a while. She hoped Marie would eventually find the independence she deserved, and felt guilty about telling her where François was.

CHAPTER 14:

STEP INTO THE WORLD

Nobody remembers them. The first sight. The first touch. The first sound. The first step. All hesitant, imprecise, and insignificant, yet carrying in them the very core of intelligence. Deprive babies of all these early senses and actions, and they will grow not only crippled but also retarded.

— DeSousa's Memoirs - Part I - Beginning - 2053

In the netted playing area of François's office, CARLA was sitting still on the ground in a lotus position, surrounded by a dozen toys of different shapes and sizes. Nearly all five hundred employees were on standby, most of them at their desks, away from this room, ready to monitor some part of the sophisticated conglomerate of software the android possessed. They were getting ready for the first integrated sensory-motor test. Ian looked at François's determined face as he spoke to the robotics team crammed around the android, and wondered, for the thousandth time, if the young man understood he was a genius.

François had spent most of the past six months helping the robotics team integrate his algorithm with their existing perception, actuation, and control routines while learning Ian's theory and reading tens of books and hundreds of research papers. The speed with which he digested and connected topics that appeared unrelated was all that one needed to assess his amazing intellect.

But, Ian sighed, *such a personality inevitably comes with social and emotional problems.*

In François's case, the former was obvious, since in the past half year he hadn't made a single friend, although he interacted with almost everybody in the company. The young man was most familiar with him, which made him strangely happy, as if he were in some competition with his employees to win the genius' favor.

François's social life was non-existent. He rented a small studio in a complex less than twenty minutes away. He often slept right in the office and went to his place, only to change his clothes and wash. He was never interested in visiting any part of California. He had no love life either. Ian wasn't even able to guess his sexual preference. He treated men and women in the same way, ignoring their gender. And that came naturally, not because of some learned policy that made him behave in a certain way according to the ideology of the moment. But Ian knew François was madly in love. He was obsessing over the precise facial and body features the estheticians gave to CARLA. As promised, CARLA's appearance improved until she became indistinguishable from a woman. Not a beautiful one, but one with a certain quirkiness that made her attractive. As Ian realized, François had provided from his memory details down to the square millimeters, every small freckle, the way every strand of hair was falling, the exact shade of eye color, which they changed from brown to blue turquoise, the torso, the breasts, the size of her limbs. Because of her improved appearance, CARLA's pronouns switched gradually from the initial it/it to the permanent she/her.

"It would be simpler to show them a picture," Ian remarked at some point, seeing François struggle to explain to the team how he wanted her to look.

François just shrugged off his semi-mocking suggestion. He didn't seem to care what the rest of the team thought about this.

Ian remembered vividly the moment when CARLA's human-like shell was finally completed. The two of them had been alone with her. He had pointed out, impressed, "Too bad she can't talk or think, for that matter."

François had just nodded, looking at her fascinated.

"You should know that I normally stay out of my employees' personal lives," Ian had timidly inquired. "But this project is too important to blow it on such matters, so who is she?"

"A dream," François had answered in an unexpectedly calm and open fashion. "A beautiful, recurring dream I had for fifteen years that turned into a nightmare."

So, it's the same hundred-thousand-year-old drama, Ian had thought, feeling bad for the young man. *The mighty knight ready to kill dragons and make the world a better place gets slain by a mere damsel.*

"The funny part is that she's not even worth it," François had continued his confession. "She isn't smart, she isn't that beautiful, and her personality is rather annoying. Her idiosyncrasies are often insufferable. But I thought she was mine. Until I woke up."

"Why use her as a model for CARLA, then?" Ian had asked, curious.

"Because this is my revenge," François had answered with a sparkly look.

"I hope you don't plan to get married with the perfect version of whoever she was," Ian had inquired, almost disappointed.

"I won't fall in love with CARLA. I've gone through this once. Never again. I just want CARLA to be more human than her counterpart, and flawless."

"Quite a tall order," Ian had said, but felt relieved. "And here I was, merely hoping for an AI general enough to mimic, to some extent, human intelligence. To what end do you insist on this resemblance?"

"To prove to myself that there can be goodness and fairness in this sorry world we live in. And to show the woman what she lost." Then, after thinking about it for a minute: "Ah, and to feel like God."

"Oh, don't tell me you believe in God now!" Ian had laughed.

"I don't," François had answered. "I have reasons to." He had looked at Ian for a long while, as if deciding whether he should continue. "Half a year ago, a few days before joining you, I drowned. For a couple of minutes, I was dead. There were no angels. No light at the end of the tunnel and no stairway to heaven. No pitchforks and dancing devils. Just nothingness. So, if there is a God, He doesn't seem to bother enough with me to send me to hell."

Ian had taken a step back, stunned. This was terrible news. Had François tried to kill himself? If so, he could try it again. "How did you survive?" Ian had asked, without dwelling on the suicide part.

"A woman thought it was her duty to jump into the water and pull me out. I don't know who she is, but I will be eternally ungrateful to her." And after a long pause, he continued. "When I accepted your offer, I didn't care if we succeeded or failed. I didn't care if our success would improve humankind or cause its doom. While modeling her after … that woman I loved, I found a new purpose. I am reborn. I promise you I'll make this work."

Ian had nearly swooned. Perhaps he had misjudged this man.

"I guess this is my way of saying thank you," François said softly, still without looking at him.

Then they had left the discussion awkwardly unfinished, as if the bond they shared had fractured a bit.

While acutely aware that François's obsession was a major reason to be concerned, Ian liked his determination. *Whatever fuels him, as long as the job gets done,* he thought, realizing how selfish that sounded.

Though progress was slow on the scale of his expectations, Ian had sufficient experience with failures to understand that the Frenchman deserved a lot of credit. They worked in shifts, with François sleeping three-four hours a day, for months. Once François understood the general idea of Ian's Structural Intelligence Theory, they started by linking the perception and action into a loop. This was to allow CARLA to understand the abstract notions of gravity, action-reaction, liquid/solid objects manipulation, object persistence, and dozens of other basic physics routines that were already integrated into her core algorithms.

They could take some shortcuts, but this was always tricky. One needed to know how much they could take advantage of the hundreds of algorithms available for visual, auditory, or tactile perception. Those algorithms were the result of training over billions of images and audio files. In Ian's view, they were unnatural, and using them meant slipping into a territory of the physical world that the human mind perceived as foreign.

"This is not how humans or animals learn," Ian explained to them. "From the day we are born, we constantly interact with the environment. We don't look at one hundred million images of a doggie before we recognize one, as these current fancy image recognition components do. We often learn, from a single example, about a strange animal that we have not seen before, which might even be imaginary, like a griffin. If we want CARLA to exhibit the same abilities as biological beings, we need to train her in the same way. We need to make her see the way we see. Think about what that means. We have thousands of visual illusions that trick our brains. Some are inescapable, no matter how hard we try, and we cannot *not* see them. Such illusions prove how imperfect our brains are. We want to understand reality, but our brains constantly fool ourselves into perceiving it in a certain way for one evolutionary advantage or another, or just by chance. We want CARLA to be tricked in the same way we are. However, we also want to be able to tune her perception so that she can swap at will between illusion and reality."

Having listened to these mantras repeatedly, the team, including François, seemed now fully on board, much to Ian's delight.

"As for movement, better a stumbling, awkwardly moving, and clumsy android that learns its way through the world, than a highly specialized one that falls when faced with something novel," Ian always said, much to the exasperation of his roboticists, who wanted to benefit from years of advances in machine learning.

All these components were like Lego pieces waiting to be assembled, but, unlike Lego, they required some kind of external glue. Enter François's algorithm. In the first four months, a couple of hundred programmers working under his supervision struggled to fit it into their environment. The first breakthrough came from something unexpected: causality. Using simple models of patterns that came one after the other, they adapted the algorithm to distinguish between causality and mere correlation. Using their little progress, they continued with the container routines, especially the handling of liquids. Some abilities, like recognizing collections of things in the line of vision, were more or less trivial, others, like recognizing forces, seemed impossible to implement. Even the simple facts that objects persist in the world, that they occupy only one portion of space at a time, that they don't exist in two places simultaneously and they cannot magically teleport, were incredibly challenging.

Still, step by step, they copied and changed François's universal algorithm into variants to cover perception and action. The algorithm had to suffer significant adjustments, but they never had to use a radically different one. François's brightness and commitment were essential throughout this process.

Now's the time to see if this is going somewhere, Ian thought, not daring to hope. Just in case, he was prepared to give them a shallow speech about how each misfire put them closer to their goal.

This was only a tiny step. There was no way that they would achieve proper perception and action without *all* the necessary components. The movement control that a one-month-old baby had, for example, relied on many aptitudes that were altogether missing in CARLA. They had barely given her something akin to curiosity, which led her to explore and experiment with things around her.

In some sense, CARLA is not even as competent to move around and interact with the world as a larva crawling out of its egg. Ian sighed.

They gave CARLA a crude capacity to form new concepts. Her routines were already supposed to *understand* the world in terms of primordial notions related to the way her body interacted with the environment.

"When the brain develops," Ian had told François in one of their training sessions, "its axons grow into approximate regions as specified by its DNA and are eventually better *fixed* and *connected* to other neurons, by direct and indirect influence from the environment. For example, gravity, as sensed by our somatosensory and equilibrium systems, locks in concepts like *up* and *down*. Repeated visual perception of space refines the concept formation. When an organism moves around, the brain grounds the concepts of *fast/slow*, *before/after,* and many more. This happens at a very early stage, well before children can understand language. It is on the foundation of these primordial concepts, which are continuously enriched with new experiences as the baby develops, that the child is constructing their conceptual system. Some rather cruel experiments in the 1960s proved that kittens that are kept in the dark never develop proper visual perception. So, we must let CARLA inspect and act in a proper environment."

"I still don't understand," François had voiced his concerns, "how she is supposed to make the jump from perceiving pixels of reality, literally, to understanding what she is perceiving. There are an infinite number of ways to interpret the same reality around us. This isn't just about low-level image recognition. Such interpretation requires a complex integrated mechanism that can reason."

"That's the trick, isn't it?" Ian had answered. "We need to make CARLA perceive the world in terms of what the American psychologist James Gibson called affordances, that is, what objects can offer us in terms of actions. There is ample evidence that babies as old as six months see the surrounding environment directly in terms of what it means to them. The baby doesn't just do this sequentially: first seeing an object in 2D space, then converting it to a 3D representation, then running a recognition routine, and only then analyzing what it can do with the object. It jumps somehow, almost instantaneously, to perceiving the object in terms of what it can do with it. In fact, perception works more top-down than bottom-up. The brain constantly builds a model of reality, and the little input it gets from its sensors merely serve to adjust and reinforce this model. Note that the affordances vary drastically between living beings. This theory of affordances implies that humans look at a chair as something that they could sit on, could break for firewood, could use as a weapon, and so on. A mouse might see it as a large obstacle that it cannot climb. An elephant might perceive it as wood sticks that it could grab with its trunk to scratch its back."

From what Ian could infer from monitoring the research and implementation details, François's way of thinking about perception had changed radically from that moment on. And they seemed to go in the right direction.

Remembering these discussions, Ian looked around in the lab, satisfied, as the preparations for the test were ending. Suddenly, the twenty members of the robotics team in the room moved to the sides, busy with their tablets. In the silence that followed, Ian cleared his throat and turned his back to CARLA, so that he could best face everybody else.

"We have worked hard to reach this point," he said in a convincing voice, even though one could sense the tiredness in it. "Just like a real baby, we need CARLA to gain coordination of her actuators on the limbs, trunk, neck, head, face, and so on. She will experience her surroundings through the cameras, microphones, gravitometers, accelerometers, gyros, proximity sensors, chemical sensors, and everything else she possesses. Success won't look impressive at this stage. I would be thrilled if she exhibited curiosity and started inspecting those little playthings around her. We will all monitor what concepts she forms, if any concepts form at all. Oh ... and if she manages not to fall more than a dozen times in the first two minutes, drinks are on me tonight!"

A couple of people chuckled politely, although tension was too much for anybody to be in the mood for jokes.

"François, if you'd be so kind as to turn our lady on," Ian invited him with a large gesture.

This time, he elicited a few more genuine giggles. François didn't seem to care and flipped a switch on the wall. With her head down, facing the floor, CARLA looked somehow defeated. She opened her eyes and remained still. The next ten seconds looked like an eternity. Ian was already consoling himself with the idea that this test had failed, too. Still, tablet screens all around him were full of data scrolling rapidly. Everybody was monitoring them fervently, although, judging by the silence, they seemed to hold their breath. The atmosphere was maddening. Suddenly, a muscle on CARLA's face twitched. Next, she tilted her head a bit and leaned forward a couple of centimeters. Every move generated an explosion of new information. She moved her left hand towards a toy, a yellow rubber car, grabbed it gently, and lifted it. Someone in the audience let out a gasp. Her grip was impeccable, neither too strong nor too weak, which wasn't unusual, since many robots could already exhibit this level of prehensile control. But she was more than a regular robot. She started adjusting her head from one side to the other and rotating the car. Then she moved her right hand. Suddenly, she dropped the car. She didn't catch it, just followed it as it fell to the ground. There, she seemed to notice the other items. In a clumsy, yet elegant move, she tried to reach them, leaning forward. She couldn't. CARLA abandoned her lotus position and tried standing up on her legs. She swayed hard, but kept on standing up, like a palm tree in a hurricane.

Ian had tears in his eyes. She already understood many things: that leaning forward would get her closer to the object of her attention, that to reach further she had to walk, that she could better observe an object by rotating it. These were basic ways to navigate through her environment. An incredible achievement.

With shaky legs, she moved one step, then another, balancing with her hands around the body. She learned fast. As on a command, everybody in the room started cheering and applauding. Ian heard the commotion through the speakers from the people watching the scene remotely, too.

CARLA stopped, startled by the sudden noise, and looked up. Everybody went silent. CARLA was observing them for the first time.

"Uh, François," Ian said in a trembling voice. "I think we can conclude this test. We made amazing progress."

"Alright," François confirmed, moving towards the switch nervously.

Hearing François speak in her proximity, CARLA locked eyes with him. Even though at that point she was nothing but a collection of plastic and hardware, less intelligent than a pet hamster, her gaze gave him a shiver down the spine. Just before he turned her off, just before going back into darkness, she was undoubtedly there, present in the room. Eerily alive.

CHAPTER 15:

RELOCATION

In nature there are unexpected storms and in life unpredictable vicissitudes.

— Chinese proverb

News of the first arrests reached Qianfan about two months after the scanner became operational. Six more months later, with mandatory scanning happening at work, including at lunchtime, and with SSMS devices installed in most public places, the arrests became the norm. The party police had already reallocated one tenth of the people he knew to camps where they were taught to let the party think for them. He still had to meet someone who came back from those places. It seemed as if the only thing standing in the way of more arrests was the effort required to pull them off and the delay caused by the enormous effort to create camps.

Because of the massive shift in society, the economy was affected. With so many people away, many jobs were left undone. The world seemed split between fanaticism and obedience on the one side, and panic and constant struggle to hide one's thoughts on the other. Sometimes, Qianfan heard rumors of some form of protest, and he dared to hope that enough momentum would build for a significant anti-party movement. His dream quickly drowned in disappointment shortly after seeing the swift and organized response that the party's security forces, backed up by specialized crowd control drones, staged against any such manifestations.

Any scan revealing that someone was "harboring impure feelings of resentment against the good of society," as the party sycophants named it, had some consequences. Initially, an accuracy result of 55 percent for the scans was enough to put someone in a reeducation camp. A month after the official launch, once it was apparent that many people had such troublesome thoughts and it was impractical to arrest them all, they changed the threshold to its maximum of 68 percent. Any scan that discovered problematic thoughts with an accuracy from 55 percent to 67 percent resulted in disciplinary actions: a proportionally lower CWT, a demotion, community work, and compulsory reeducation in the afternoons in special centers that were now opening in all cities and in the countryside. A single scan made with a 68 percent confidence triggered a "maximum alert for a dangerous individual." The police then arrested the wretched fellows branded with this title in a matter of minutes and moved them somewhere. Their CWT plummeted, along with a fraction of the CWTs of the individual's relatives and friends, depending on how close they were. Families were broken. They dragged parents out of their homes in front of crying children. When both parents were due to be reeducated, the police moved the children to special orphanages, where the government took care of them. Children who didn't have the proper respect for the glory and achievements of the party were also taken away from their parents.

Qianfan played again the recording that showed how he had convinced Baozhai to recite her poems and to focus her mind away from any thoughts that might get her in trouble. He had to make sure it didn't look too suspicious when analyzed in the government Cybersperse, and for that he was willing to risk them noticing his replays.

"My dear Baozhai," he heard himself say, in a trembling voice. "Over the next few weeks ... months, perhaps, all of us will be subjected to a kind of ... reading. It will happen at work for me, at school for you, and gradually everywhere."

"A reading?" she asked, confused.

"Yes. There's a new type of sensor. I expect they'll install it everywhere. A beautiful invention." He felt an urge to brag about it, to be validated as a scientist, not as a party puppet. "I ... contributed to its creation."

"Oh, so I'll finally see what you've been working on all these years?" she got excited, only to cause his shame to resurface tenfold.

"Yes, but perhaps this is nothing to be proud of," he was quick to add.

"Why not?"

"Because ... because this sensor can read stuff going on in that pretty head of yours. Not thoughts, no, we can't do such things yet. Just your likes or dislikes, your happiness, your anger."

"Sounds amazing! Why wouldn't you be proud of it?"

"Because this technology, as impressive as it is, crosses a red line." He was upset at how naïve she was. "We are all social beings. We spend time together, we communicate, we bond, sometimes we disagree, we fight, we go to war. But we are always alone with our thoughts, whether they are about loving or loathing someone, envying a colleague, the happiness of reconnecting with an old friend, disgust at someone's behavior, or even a deep desire to see someone dead. Nobody else knows what each of us is thinking. Each of our minds is an impenetrable fortress. Or, better said, it *was* an impenetrable fortress. Until now."

Baozhai's smile vanished. Qianfan thought that perhaps she was panicking about some boy she liked, who would soon know what she thought. Or about kids at school who would see how much she hated them.

"The device is not very precise," he said to ease the impact of his words. "And the scanning topics will not be too ... personal. The party is interested in individuals who are not yet fit to live in our society. Those elements that give us trouble with their doubts and rebellious attitude."

"So ... the party will scan people's minds to determine who's a criminal?"

"In a way, yes," he sighed. "Not for thieves or murderers. More for those who ... who don't fit."

She seemed confused again.

"Imagine you're at school, and you don't like a subject. Say, literature."

"I don't," she quickly confirmed.

"Right," he looked at her, thinking hard about how to explain it so that she wouldn't get scared, all the while, without appearing to criticize the party. "When listening to a text analysis, the teacher could understand that you don't like it."

"Are you saying that the teachers will scan us?"

"No, no ... that was just an example. They will look for the people who, for example, don't like President Yun Li, or don't like a directive coming from the party."

She looked at him with a serious face. "Bàba ... What will happen to them?"

"I don't know. I think the police will reeducate them somewhere far away."

"Could this happen to me?"

"I'm sure you don't need to worry too much," he answered hesitantly.

Baozhai now looked really terrified.

"Remember the meditation techniques," he risked being more explicit. "And think of some ... sentences that you know by heart."

She squinted and looked at him for a long time in silence, finally understanding why her father wanted her to memorize old texts.

Qianfan stopped the recording, wondering what the party would make of it. He felt a sort of strange warmth engulfing him, like he had bonded deeper with Baozhai. *So far, so good,* he breathed in relief. There was no sign that anyone suspected him or Baozhai. A few of her colleagues, though, were not as fortunate.

He was sitting at his desk, waiting for Daiyu to come to work. The arrests had affected her more than she showed. In particular, she had suffered enormously when the police got two of her friends, who Qianfan'd suspected were not crazy about the situation in China. Zhou Junfeng and Li Xin disappeared. Qianfan remembered how the three of them used to have lunch together. How he'd approached and scanned them for the first time. He also worried that they would tell the authorities that Daiyu harbored the same ill feelings towards the party. The police would then invite Daiyu for an interrogation. They would subject her to extensive screening, the kind that no mental shield she raised could withstand. All because of him. How could he live with himself after doing so much harm?

Daiyu never blamed him. She understood he'd had little choice. She was his second ray of hope in a world in which fear and guilt were vying for his attention. Her transfer to his research group had gone smoothly. His CWT going up into the low 900s had made him a demigod. Almost no one would dare to oppose a request like that, least of all Daiyu's supervisor, a political pawn with no achievements of his own.

People like Daiyu's boss don't have to fear any regime, he thought, getting mad. *He's too cowardly to think for himself. The veil of obedience and fawning that covers his mind puts off whatever spark of doubt his rotten brain might conjure.*

"Good morning, Doctor Zhào," Daiyu said, entering the room.

They had agreed to be formal at the office. They didn't want anybody to suspect that they were talking about something more than work.

"Good morning, Doctor Wu," he answered slowly, fighting the lethargy that was engulfing him. "Ready for another day of study?"

"Let's start right away!" she answered, energetically, sitting at her desk, next to his, and picking up a book. Just like that evening at his place, they made it so they could exchange writings on two Magic Boards without the camera picking them up. Under the pretext of studying, they didn't even have to pretend that they were talking loud about something else, so microphones in the room were useless too.

"Are you alright? You look ... pale," she wrote, looking at him, worried.

Qianfan turned his tablet into a mirror. He looked awful. Weeks of poor sleep, the constant fear that his true feelings would be discovered, and, especially, the incessant guilt, had turned him into a walking zombie. He knew he would get sick if something didn't change.

"I'm okay," he tried to appear confident. "Any news?"

"Somebody spread those little flyers from the top of a skyscraper this morning. About 10,000 of them. This time they read, 'Get your lives back. It's not the party who leads us. It's the MegaAI. Professor Zhèng left us a message. He sacrificed himself for us. Rebel. Humans Forever!'"

"The idiot," Qianfan wrote. "Why mention Zhèng? His family might suffer."

"I guess they want their message to come with some proof," she answered. "I heard they caught the guy who did it. He was high in the hierarchy."

"I don't think flyers work."

He knew of seven or eight other attempts to make Zhèng's last message public. In all cases, the smart people who'd deciphered it had ended up dead. The police considered them conspirators and either shot them on the spot or executed them later. There was no way to organize any cohesive movement.

"At least they raise awareness," she answered. "Doubt and confusion rule now at all levels, including high in the party. Nobody dares to act. For now. That they increased the SSMS's accuracy threshold is already a victory of sorts."

"Some victory," Qianfan wrote, with a bitter look on his face. "Soon all our clothes will have a version of my device. People will know that it was me. Talking about the culmination of one's career. I expect that one morning I'll wake up dead, with a bullet in my skull."

Daiyu tried to smile at his joke, but the first wearable version was in the works. They expected uniforms to be equipped with it after another quarter.

Nothing beats the efficiency of the party, he thought.

"The arrests and constant harassment have had the opposite effect. Rather than getting people to fall in line, more and more of them have those impure thoughts," Daiyu remarked.

"Oh, and what's the use? Someone will reeducate them, whatever that means."

"Unless their aim is to kill all of us - and there are faster means to do so - I think the MegaAI, if indeed it is behind this action, understands this strategy is not working," Daiyu wrote. "It will have to come up with another one."

As if on a signal, Haitao stormed into the office without knocking. He stopped when he saw Daiyu and eyed her suspiciously. Qianfan quickly hid his board and signaled discreetly to Daiyu to do the same.

"*Zhào zǒng*, Honorable Member Tián is here," Haitao said nervously. "An unannounced visit!"

Qianfan exchanged a quick look with Daiyu. He wondered if this was related to the new strategy she had just mentioned. "Well, let's go to the conference room," Qianfan stood up.

"No, no, she's coming up here. To your office," Haitao announced, terrified.

That was unusual. It could mean either something great or something terrible. It wasn't hard to guess which alternative Haitao was concerned about. Before they had more time to think things through, the icy figure of Honorable Member Tián appeared. She knocked informally on the open door and stepped inside without waiting for an invitation.

"Honorable Member, welcome to my office," Qianfan said, keeping his wits about him. "Doctor Wu here is our new AI specialist. You already know Haitao …"

Daiyu stood up, saluted formally, and prepared to leave.

Without dignifying her with a look, Member Tián lifted her palm. "There's no need for anyone to leave. What I have to say concerns you all."

Haitao's face went white, and he leaned on the door frame.

Qianfan felt his knees buckle but stood still, not daring to look at Daiyu. *Am I being scanned right now?* he worried in a panic. Out of reflex, he started reciting *The Iliad*, all while his brain bombarded him with negative thoughts, which he fought hard to keep out.

"Doctor Zhào, in recognition of your commitment to the party cause and because you have proven that you don't spare any effort in delivering on your tasks, we have assigned your team another critical goal."

Haitao let out a breath of relief that Qianfan thought people two floors below could hear.

"Thank you for your appreciation of my work. Can you disclose anything about this new task?" he inquired, conflicted between being relieved and horrified that she would ask him to do more damage.

"No," she answered firmly. "This task requires that all of you move to a secret facility."

"Move?" Qianfan asked, caught on the wrong foot. "Move where?"

"It wouldn't be much of a secret if I told you now, wouldn't it?" the ice woman answered with almost no inflection in her voice.

How can she be ironic without moving a muscle in her face? Qianfan thought, then shook his head to focus on getting more information. "What about our families?" he thought of Baozhai.

"First-degree family members can accompany you. Spouses and dependent parents, children, and siblings for whom your team members are legal guardians."

Haitao put his hand on his mouth. Qianfan tried not to think about Baozhai's math aspirations. Or the impact that any move would have on her already suffering social life.

"If you are worried about your daughter," Honorable Member Tián said, still addressing Qianfan only, "let me assure you that we give only the most brilliant people in China the honor of living where you are going."

He wondered if he detected a hint of jealousy in her glassy voice.

"She will have the best teachers available."

Qianfan felt cautiously optimistic. In a flash, it thrilled him that he'd arranged Daiyu's transfer to his team just in time. Perhaps things wouldn't be so bad if the three of them would go together.

"Anyone has the option to decline, of course," the woman continued. "Fair warning, though. Doing so would decrease their CWT by 50. Acceptance would increase it by 50, too. Not that the CWT matters much where you'd be going. So, I'd give it serious consideration."

Qianfan felt like the world was spinning. That would give him a score that was rather unheard of. He glanced at Daiyu and envied her, again, at how unfazed she appeared.

Haitao's eyes nearly popped out. Even the youngster's score would jump close to the 800s.

"How long ... How long will we be gone?" Qianfan asked finally.

"Indefinitely. You should consider that to be your new home."

Thoughts swirled into Qianfan's head. If he refused, he'd be washing his hands of having to do this project and whatever these devils or the AI were concocting next. On the other hand, he was already forever tainted, and perhaps this was a chance to redeem himself somehow.

"You have six hours to decide," the woman announced with the same bland tonality.

"If we accept, when would we leave?" he asked, not able to hide how uncomfortable this proposition made him.

"Tomorrow."

Qianfan looked at his colleagues. Haitao seemed almost excited, so he wouldn't hesitate too much. Daiyu peeked at him and nodded slightly. *What will Baozhai say? She might miss this place. Her friends at school.*

Despite the seriousness of the situation, Qianfan smiled at the absurdity of that thought. Baozhai was nothing but miserable at her school. How much worse could it get? "I don't need six hours. I accept," Qianfan answered, trying to sound confident and grateful.

"Me too," Daiyu said right away.

"I ..." Haitao started, realizing he was on the spot, "... accept too."

Let the ball roll further. We'll see where it lands, Qianfan thought, looking straight at the ice woman and wondering if she was happy with their decision. She surely didn't show it.

CHAPTER 16:

SEARCH

People say that it's not the destination that matters, it's the journey, that you should not only cherish the result of your work, but the work itself. It's not important to find what you are looking for; the search is the actual craze. Be that as it may, when you desperately long for something essential and you feel you are running out of time, life loses its meaning.

— DeSousa's Memoirs - Part I - Beginning - 2053

Marie looked out the window of the cheap hotel in downtown LA where she still lived, five months after coming to America. She could not convince herself to search for a place to rent. Apartments were incredibly expensive here, and yet, paying rent would still be a fraction of what she paid now.

Winter in LA, she thought, looking at the drab scenery at the break of day. She found LA weather generally lovely. Not as magical as southern France, but still mild and full of sunshine. She had gone once to the beach and found it wrong, somehow. The shade of the ocean was just too dark, the water was cooler than she expected, the beach way too wide, and the sand strange under her feet. She decided not to go again. It was better not to spoil her beautiful memories.

It was early enough and just a handful of people were in the streets. From her position, she could see a corner of the Staples Center, a large dome where, as she had found out from the hotel reception, the Lakers were playing. *Too bad I can't have such trifling interests,* she sighed.

She should have slept at this hour. Even though she was under medication meant to soothe her depression, she had trouble sleeping. *At least it's not raining here,* she thought. *Mon Dieu, how I miss home.*

François was nowhere to be found. Chances of meeting him on the street were close to nil. He had refused to answer any of her calls. There was no trace of him in the Cybersperse. For a moment, she panicked that he might have died. Killed himself. Then she resolved to push such thoughts out of her head.

"Assistant," she said aloud. "Search the Cybersperse for any occurrence of François DeSousa in the last twenty-four hours."

"Alright, Marie," her assistant chirped in a cheerful female voice. "I found fifty-four results for François DeSousa in the last twenty-four hours."

"Filter out all results that are unlikely to be François DeSousa from my Contact List," Marie continued, with a shaky voice. She nodded. She hated these inventions, but she had to use them anyway, especially at work. Out of revenge, she never gave it a name.

"No results found," the assistant confirmed, as expected. "Anything else?"

"Start a mix of soothing music. Don't bother me unless you hear from work or Isabelle." Then, after a momentary pause, she mumbled, "Or François," realizing the futility of it. "Thank you," she said dismissively. *Perhaps Isabelle was right. I won't be able to find him.*

Her doubts were creeping back. In a panic, she ran to the kitchen and swallowed another anti-anxiety pill. She took a shower, observing how annoying this kind of music sounded to her.

Five hours later, she was in the office. She was the first to arrive there, as usual. Her boss had already commended her several times. Given how she committed herself to her work, she was bound to get a promotion. Not that she cared. She was working on some mildly interesting cases of local children getting dragged into the shady regions of the Cybersperse. She had identified several symptoms and grouped the potential addictive victims into a dozen categories. She had always thought that the effect of virtual reality on children and teenagers was devastating, and that people didn't do enough about it. Now she could make a difference. Her boss called her work brilliant and insisted she publish it. Normally, she would be excited about the prospect. As she was obsessing over François, her ambitions took a back seat.

Lost in thought, she didn't notice Aaron sneak in behind her.

"Good morning, princess," he shouted, laughing at how he'd startled her. "I brought you a bouquet of rays to shine on your pretty face," he said with a theatrical bow, offering her a collection of colorful flowers that must have cost a small fortune at this time of the year.

She couldn't help but smile. This *child,* who was her boss, was tacky to the point of being funny. His relentless advances would make a rock melt. *I should be happy about it,* she thought, smelling the flowers. What was with men obsessing over her? She remembered Marco and was content to realize she didn't feel guilty anymore.

"Gods of creation and chaos! What is it that my eyes see this morning? Am I dreaming? Did she smile? Oh, let me sit down. My mortal coil is not built to withstand so much happiness."

Seeing his efforts and bright face, she felt pity for him. The poor boy couldn't take a hint. Or he wasn't used to rejection.

"Can I dare to ask you out again? Just a small, collegial lunch?" he implored, looking at her face.

I'm still young, she thought, trying for the hundredth time to like him. *Why not go on a date?* He was sexy; tall, slim, rough, yet symmetrical face, firm jaws, and pitch-dark hair. It would thrill any normal girl to spend a night with him. Or marry him. *Pointless. I'm forever malfunctioning.* She burst into bitter laughter.

Judging from how his eyes sparkled, she knew he'd misunderstood her laughter for enjoyment. *Oh, to hell with it. I'll never marry, anyway. It's time to end this.* "OK, you win. I'll have lunch with you today," she nodded.

Aaron let out a whoop of joy. Marie struggled to ignore the pain she felt in her chest. She hated to give him hope. Better to be done with this infatuation before it went too far.

A few hours later, installed comfortably in a booth at a nearby KFC, she was eating slowly while listening to the tiring barrage of nonsense Aaron was throwing at her. She had zoned out a couple of minutes before, thinking about François again, and she now forced herself to come back.

"... and then he hit me with the news. There were no tickets anymore! You would think that, with all the Cybersperse, fewer people care to risk deafness and gain new kinds of germs in that big bowl. Are you even listening to me?" Aaron stopped, eyeing her suspiciously.

"I'm sorry, I was thinking about something else," she sighed. "Look, Aaron, I told you a few times already, you and I will never happen," she stated plainly.

"What?" he asked, dumbfounded by the abrupt change of topic.

"Understand that I am not alright. I have ... problems. I have no interest in being with a man."

"Aha, you are gay! I suspected as much," he stated, satisfied that he finally understood her resistance to his charm.

"No, why does everybody assume that?" she asked, frustrated. "I simply have no ... sexual drive. OK?"

"But ... why?" he remained confused. "You are young. Beautiful."

"Thank you," she smiled. "I appreciate that." Then she remembered François's complaint from a lifetime ago. "Maybe I am out of sync with these times," she quoted him, and her smile widened. François had infected her with his romanticism.

"So ... let me guess ... you want us to be just friends?"

"Precisely!" she answered, happy to see that he was finally getting it.

"No problem," he answered, unfazed. "I trust this won't affect our work relationship."

She shook her head with a smile. She admired the ease with which he'd moved past her. *So much for him marrying me,* she thought, amused. *It would have been at most a few nights of sex.*

"Are you at least going to come to parties with the rest of us who decided to live here on Earth?" he asked mockingly.

Marie felt upset by his tone and words, but she didn't let it show. She realized this episode was going to leave her forever branded as the weirdo in the office. "I don't see the point," she answered, looking him straight in the eye. "I won't be having a good time anyway and I might spoil your fun," she blurted out.

Aaron said nothing more. From the way his brows curved, she understood he wanted nothing to do with her anymore. *So be it! At least I don't have to pretend,* she thought, upset about how unhappy she felt. *Let me continue to search for him. Even if it takes the rest of my life.*

CHAPTER 17:

FREEDOM

Give me the right to choose, and I shall feel free. Give me the right to feel and I shall choose wisely.

— DeSousa's Memoirs - Part II - Creation - 2054

Sitting in a small chair in front of CARLA, François observed her behavior intently. Lately, they'd given her plastic bottles, cups with liquids, pouches of sand, and helium balloons. Initially, she had made a mess around her, poking at and mixing everything, but after a while, she'd learned to handle them.

Weeks after the first integrated sensorimotor test, she was becoming nimbler and more perceptive. She hadn't been turned off since that test, with at least one member of the roboticist team nearby to observe her and, occasionally, interact with her. François was around her all the time, except for the brief intervals when he slept.

Seeing how fast and precisely she moved her arms, François wondered sometimes if she might end up hurting them by mistake. They purposely gave her the strength of a child, and there were dozens of safeguard measures in place, including the immediate deactivation upon sensing a stronger touch.

The face does look like hers, doesn't it? he thought, mesmerized. *A mentally handicapped, mute, and deaf Marie. One that doesn't think much. And remains faithful.*

Ian entered the office, his face betraying his preoccupied mind. He nodded a quick salute. They were getting ready for another company-wide meeting. As always, they used a closed network meant for this kind of communication. Ian cleared his throat and started talking, while CARLA was playing in the background, driven by her curiosity.

"Everyone, I am happy to inform you that CARLA has passed 65.3 percent of the preliminary perception and motor tests we gave her. Given her outstanding progress with sensor-actuator coordination in such a short time, and considering her basic knowledge of the physics of the world, well, at least limited to this tiny space she interacts with so far, I believe we are ready to move to the next stage." He gathered his thoughts. "You are all familiar with the Theory of Multiple Intelligences Howard Gardner proposed. While this theory is controversial, vague, and rather impossible to prove, it provides a high-level view of the aspects we must deal with. Gardner talks about several intelligences: bodily kinesthetic, visual-spatial, musical-rhythmic and harmonic, linguistic-verbal, logical-mathematical, interpersonal—things like social skills or empathy—, and intrapersonal, or introspection. There are others less relevant for our purpose. With CARLA we have barely touched the bodily kinesthetic aspect. And keep in mind that despite every small advance we may make in the next months, we will need to refine what we have achieved so far."

François thought he detected a hint of trepidation in his voice.

"Next, we need to do two things in parallel. I'll try to address them separately. Bear with me, as these things are difficult. First, we need to expand the concept formation from the concrete, physical things she is familiar with, to more abstract concepts. By *concrete*, I mean objects with which she interacts directly: the floor, the toys on the ground, the chair, the clumsy moving beings around her, and so on. By *abstract,* I mean intangible notions like numbers, counting, comparisons, also goals, environment, and so many more. Consider CARLA's learning. In this process, she should *know* that she learns. Or that she interacts with us. Eventually, she should recognize who we are. She should form an idea of what we might be thinking. She should understand social concepts like kindness or empathy, she should understand beauty, humor, or irony. We want her to appreciate art, and more. But I am getting ahead of myself."

Ian looked around before continuing. "I want to be crystal clear. This step is crucial. Without the ability to map abstract concepts to the physical world, ultimately rooted in her perception and action, CARLA will never become intelligent! This is what the AI researchers have dubbed the symbol grounding problem, which, to the best of my knowledge, nobody solved. The Generative Language Models that empower our virtual assistants and humanoid robots manipulate numbers, logical facts, or words, but cannot anchor them in concrete, real world objects and concepts. To remedy this, we need to employ several cognitive theories, such as George Lakoff's theory of metaphor and Gilles Fauconnier's theory of conceptual blending. They provide invaluable insight into how humans map notions from one domain to another, taking advantage of similarities in their corresponding structural representations in the brain. We see this manifested in language usage all the time, but the concept formation operates at lower levels, and this mapping across domains is a fundamental stone in the foundation of intelligence."

Ian stopped and took a sip of water. His eyes were fiery. "There are hundreds of examples in books and papers on this topic. I synthesized them and grouped them by category, and I want all of you to go through them over the next couple of weeks. A classic example is the conceptualization of *time* in terms of *space*, which is called the Time is Space metaphor. It is present in pretty much all languages and cultures independently. Without realizing it, sometimes we think of time as something moving through space. In other cases, time is a bounded, linear region that can be measured and compared. We say things like, 'Easter is *approaching,*' 'December *comes* after November,' 'we'll see each other at some *point* in the future,' 'our schedule is *from* Monday *to* Friday,' 'we have to finish renovating the house *within* a year,' and so on."

A few people nodded, lost in thought.

"Another example is the conceptualization of purpose as a destination of sorts. We say things like, 'we want to *move towards* a world with no crime,' 'see the light at the *end of the tunnel,*' 'we've *reached the end* of our struggles,' and so on. Difficulties to reach a goal are physical impediments to motions. We say things like, 'we've reached a *stumbling* block,' 'her stubbornness *stops* us from *moving* in the right *direction,*' and so on. We achieve concept creation using relationships such as cause-effect, change, space, identity, role, and part-whole."

François shifted, focused on Ian's cogent explanation.

"I don't want to bother you with more examples," Ian continued. "Before I move on to the second topic of the day, do you have questions?"

Somebody attending remotely cleared their throat. "Since these metaphors and blends manifest themselves in language, would it ... make sense to implement the fundamentals of language first? Like an enhanced version of our personal assistants, so we can start communicating better, ease the learning, the testing?"

"Absolutely not," Ian shook his head. "I think we are a long way from tackling language and, just like with motion and perception, shortcuts are deceiving. Let's not forget that, to learn a language, the little brains of children must already be structured in a particular way. This structure takes care of information integration, mapping from one domain to another, creation of new concepts, the ability to imitate, and so many others. Language acquisition and use are impossible without metaphor, analogy, and counterfactuals. They are ubiquitous in our deep, subconscious thinking and manifest themselves through language later in development."

François nodded in agreement. Seeing that nobody had other questions, Ian continued.

"On to the second difficult topic. In parallel, we need to implement and activate a few more primordial routines; what you would ordinarily call *emotions*. Indeed, I believe they are essential for achieving our kind of intelligence. We humans are driven by them. Our goals, being mere animals, stem from the need to eat, sleep, have sex, get rid of pain, eliminate a source of fear, sometimes fight, or run away from what scares us, and so on. We seek enjoyment and we strive to avoid distress."

François didn't like where this was going. Somehow, the idea of an emoting android didn't sit well with him.

"To understand how the brain deals with emotion, we need to look at a part of the brain called the limbic system that is evolutionarily older than the cerebral cortex," Ian continued. "Our colleagues who strive to emulate the brain structure choose to ignore the limbic system altogether. As I've told you many times already, our mind theory is on a higher, functional level, not on the neuronal level. While we need not worry about reproducing in silico the limbic system per se, I believe we must simulate emotion somehow."

"But why?" François asked. "Why bother to implement such things in an artificial mind?"

"Because without emotions, there's no intelligence! Well, at least not of the kind we are trying to replicate. Don't be fooled by the achievements of the so-called smart algorithms today. They comprise a bag of nice tricks. Sometimes they surpass humans in accuracy, but they aren't what we want. There's ample evidence that emotion is vital to our reasoning. A researcher at the University of Southern California, Antonio Damasio, showed at the end of the last century that patients unable to process emotions, although appearing perfectly logical, couldn't make simple decisions. It's amazing that most of the AI research still ignores these findings."

"I don't understand. Our AIs, as imperfect as you say they are, make decisions all the time." François shook his head, unconvinced.

"Yes, but none of these simulations, at least up to this point, can function in the real world. Living beings act on their biological urges. We mistakenly think that the neocortex, with its capacity for sophisticated reasoning, language, and art, drives the limbic system. Nothing could be farther from the truth! Our neocortex is a slave of the limbic system. We employ its incredible reasoning power, its ability to communicate through language and music, its ability to create art, and so on, to satisfy our primordial needs: physiological, the need to have fun, to dominate others or accept being dominated, and so on. I'm not suggesting we implement all of these in CARLA. I don't want her aroused, chasing any of you through the lab."

People chuckled.

"However, she needs to have something *like* emotions and some mechanisms that simulate her *feeling* them. How else would she be able to understand, truly understand, what we feel?"

Some people nodded in approval; others appeared unconvinced.

"Well, what emotions should she possess?" François poked further.

"In the 1970s, psychologist Paul Ekman identified several basic emotions: happiness, sadness, surprise, fear, anger, and disgust. Then there are higher-level emotions like pride, shame, embarrassment, excitement, amusement, contempt, contentment, guilt, relief, and satisfaction."

"Any hints about how we could implement them?" François asked, feeling the discussion was going in an almost mystical direction.

"I do not know how to create them in a machine," Ian admitted. "We must implement them as separate concepts. The distinction between, say, sadness and happiness, will be artificial, by name only. Roughly speaking, we must program her to minimize the former and maximize the latter, even if she doesn't feel them in the same way we do. We must implement emotions as reactions to certain stimuli. Say, somebody hits her body, sensors pick up the disturbance and activate a corresponding emotion simulator. CARLA needs to have internal pseudo-sensors that monitor for those emotions like she would *experience* or *feel* them. I think we will start with those basic emotions, which we can then map and combine into higher-level emotions. Much like we do with concepts. All the more reason to design and implement properly the mapping from one domain to another that I mentioned earlier."

“Why should we restrict CARLA to this body?” François asked, pointing to the android with a quick head move.

“Oh, but we won’t. This body is useful for interacting with the world during this implementation and developmental phase. Don’t worry, I don’t expect that she will hate us for not giving her the ability to live outside of her plastic wrap.”

“Yeah, talking about hatred,” François said softly. “Do we want a machine that can be angry, jealous, and vengeful? What good would that do to us?”

“Good questions. Color me naively hopeful, but my view is that CARLA will ultimately do good things for us. She will help eradicate world hunger, invent cures that escape us, prolong life, and push us further into space. But she needs to *want* to do this. How can she *want* anything if she doesn’t have emotions and feelings? We shouldn’t aim to enslave her. If we achieve what we set out to do, that would be ethically wrong. Besides, I don’t think we could control her anyway, since if we do this right, she will be more powerful than any army.”

“Speaking of what’s right and wrong, have you thought about the ethical implications of building something that can suffer? Don’t we already have enough of that?” asked François.

“Of course, I’ve thought of it. I wish there were another way,” said Ian in a sad voice. “Sometimes she will suffer. We will program her with the overarching goal of minimizing the suffering in the world, including her own. Her collection of components will often be at odds with each other. We must strive to implement them in such a way that they end up working together harmoniously. She will need to make tough choices. I prefer a being that makes these responsible choices, rather than a cool, calculating drone incapable of regret after killing a thousand people.”

“You’re talking about Asimov’s laws of robotics,” somebody pointed out.

“Not really. Asimov himself proved those laws don’t work. True AI entities will be way too complex to adhere to such simplistic commandments. We’re building CARLA to be human-like, but better, smarter, stronger, more loving, and everlasting. A daughter that one day will turn into a mother for all of us.”

François looked at the android, who continued to play with anything she could reach. He got chills imagining her talking, painting, listening to music, arguing. Falling in love? “If you become too much like her, would I hate you too?” he whispered.

CHAPTER 18:

CHILD

The whole difference between construction and creation is exactly this: that a thing constructed can only be loved after it is constructed; but a thing created is loved before it exists.

— Charles Dickens

Riding in the black limousine towards Malibu, Sujata reflected on all that had happened from the night she deciphered the strange message from Professor Zhèng. Lieutenant Commander Mike Lee, her direct superior, was accompanying her. She smiled, looking at him. She had talked to him right after presenting her findings to General Thompson. Mike had reacted in the same way as he did in stressful situations, putting up a cool demeanor and making bad, semi-offensive jokes. Still, she enjoyed working with him for a lot of reasons. He was a professional, for whom his job, which reflected his dedication to his country, topped anything else. She suspected that his work was the reason he had never married. His witty personality calmed her the way an Explosive Ordnance Disposal specialist would defuse an activated bomb.

It had been nearly one year since Zhèng's spectacular death at the neuromimetic conference. Meanwhile, the Chinese had further entrenched within their borders. Now there were rare occasions when they sent anybody outside to interact with the rest of the world. Sujata was asked to monitor all these instances.

"You never know when some other bastard will turn into a hero," General Kambe had told her when she was assigned this task.

She agreed. To the best of their knowledge, nobody had organized any significant resistance in China. The party, or the AI, had an iron grip over the population. Nobody had successfully established any attempt to communicate with the rest of the world systematically. Their government monitored everything. Everything had consequences. Satellite imaging showed that a large part of the population was being moved around. That had confirmed some early rumors that people were being arrested to such a large extent that concentration camps formed.

When hearing about their assignment, Mike had made fun of her. "You deserve it. You had to show off and decipher that old man's nonsensical babbling. No good deed goes unpunished. You'll do well to remember that you're dragging me with you. So, I kindly ask you to deposit your genius persona somewhere in the attic and let us enjoy the rest of our lives, as short as they are, before the machines destroy the world."

In the meantime, the US government had started yet another program to speed up the development of AIs across the nation, coordinating with other NATO members. They kept the reason for this under wraps. Most of the research institutes and businesses who were doing it didn't know why the government, in particular, the Department of Defense (DoD), was suddenly so interested in accelerating this. The DoD had been sponsoring the development of AI for almost a century. There was always the expectation that whoever had the most powerful AI would achieve global military and economic supremacy. But this had been hypothetical until Zhèng's message. The urgency of countering China's success led to an unprecedented amount of tax money being poured into this research, which made it clear to Sujata that this had become the number one priority for the United States.

Still, despite all the efforts and despite the prospect of getting rich fast, so far, they were failing. Pretty much all the projects she'd visited were nowhere as powerful as the AI China supposedly had.

When did we fall behind like this? Sujata thought with a sigh. *We used to have, well, perhaps we still have, the best universities and private enterprises in the world. How come the Chinese have created such a powerful AI and we still seem to be incapable of more than dabbling in this research?*

Reeta Industries was one of their biggest disappointments. Especially the founder, the famous John Reeta.

Nothing but a pompous rich man used to get everything his way. Sujata scowled when she remembered the way he had treated her.

When she and Mike had visited them, John had been there to greet the government team. He had smelled the chance of milking the DoD, and turned the whole discussion into a marketing presentation, wrapping their mediocre piece of technology in a shiny package that made it look like the greatest thing since sliced bread. He had been so shallow that he hadn't much inquired about the purpose of this explosion in funding. Like a typical entrepreneur, he only cared about getting the money. And getting her. During their discussion, he had cornered Sujata alone in his office for a couple of minutes, in which he turned his bullshit machinery towards her, inviting her to dinner. She had felt like slapping him right there. Instead, she had remained calm and refused politely.

At the end of their chief engineer's presentation, she'd concluded that there wasn't much beyond smoke and mirrors. Sujata had looked at Mike and shaken her head a little. Mike had puckered his lips a bit longer than usual, signaling his agreement with her assessment. They had ended up not even disclosing Zhèng's message to Reeta. It would have been an unnecessary security risk. No help would come from his direction.

So now they were desperately looking around for something novel, something promising, something they could build fast, and something that might counter the MegaAI. Time was short. It was a miracle that China hadn't acted more aggressively so far. Nobody in the command chain understood why. They were grateful for whatever break they'd caught. After going through the first tier of AI producers, they started churning through a few promising startups.

"A lot of conceited personalities, too many promises, too little value," Mike had bitterly concluded on the plane to California.

Indeed, they'd only seen gimmicks. *And gimmicks won't withstand the MegaAI,* she thought, bothered by their inability to make progress.

Today they were checking out CogniPrescience, which, judging by the name and by the reaction specialists had had towards its founder, was likely a dead end too. Sujata remembered how Professor Ndikumana was treated with scorn and ridicule at the last neuromimetic conference. She had found the old man gentle and knowledgeable.

When the car pulled over near the entrance and the security guard approached them, Mike rolled his eyes. "What's with these guys and security?" he asked rhetorically. "What in the world do they think they have that is so precious?"

Sujata said nothing. Somehow, she felt more hopeful. Perhaps it was just the memory of the positive energy the professor emanated.

"Professor, the DoD representatives are here to see you," the guard announced on his cuff.

She couldn't hear a reply, but the man nodded shortly, saluted, and signaled to the others to let the guests go.

When they reached the somewhat pretentious logo, Mike let out a small whistle. "I don't know what we're doing here," he pouted.

"Don't be hasty with your judgment," Sujata smiled. She could not shake her good feeling.

Ian received them in his office, beaming. Sujata loved the Victorian-style atmosphere with wooden walls and ceiling, a large grid window, and a massive door. She noticed how the professor decorated it carefully with small, multicolored statuettes arranged on shelves and on his desk. It had a decent faux-leather sofa and a few chairs. Though the wood gave it a dark aura, the place was strangely warm. Bookshelves with a thousand books covered one wall from top to bottom. The professor was certainly erudite, and he wanted the decor to remind visitors of his heritage that was both African and British.

"Professor," Sujata saluted while Mike just nodded.

"Lieutenants. Welcome to our headquarters! Please, sit down," Ian pointed them to the sofa. He sat back at his desk on a huge chair. "You must be tired after the trip. Can I offer you something to eat or drink?" Ian asked. "Please don't be formal. We cook our food here. It is delicious."

Sujata knew Mike was hungry, but she couldn't think about food at this point. "Thank you. We would prefer to get down to business first," she smiled.

"Alright," Ian nodded politely. "From the little Cybersperse chat we had a couple of days ago, I must confess I don't understand the purpose of your visit. I'll do my best to cooperate."

"That's good to know," Mike affirmed, scrutinizing him.

"Professor, as we mentioned in our call, the DoD is looking to speed up the development of AIs. This is a matter of national security."

"Well, I understand that, but why do you think we can help? We here at CogniPrescience are in an early phase of researching a novel approach to AI. I can't imagine how the DoD would benefit from that."

"Perhaps you should let us be the judge of that," Mike said, rather abruptly, drawing a reproachful look from Sujata.

"I think what Lieutenant Commander Lee means is that we're looking exactly for that. Something original. Something that can give us an edge."

"An edge for what? Combat?" Ian asked, still smiling, narrowing his eyes just a little.

"Not necessarily traditional combat," Sujata jumped in before Mike could respond. She kept it vague. "For the last century, people have understood that the nation with the most capable AI has an edge. We want to be that nation. We want a truly intelligent AI. Much more than anything we have achieved so far."

"How often have we looked for that?" Ian asked with a shrug. "What's changed now?"

"Something did change," Sujata conceded, tilting her head a little. "We cannot disclose it just yet. Suffice it to say that this time we're ready to invest significantly more than before."

"I think you should know from the beginning that I'm not comfortable providing the fruits of my research to the military." Ian lifted his hands apologetically. "I'm not doing this for money."

Mike looked at Sujata as if to say, "Great, just what we needed. Another flower-power follower." He smiled sarcastically and asked, "If not money, what *is* your motivation? I assure you that DoD funding would be plenty to achieve whatever goals you have, provided that they align with our own."

"We're doing work to change the world for the better," Ian said in a serious tone. "I'm not naïve, you know. I understand perfectly that wars are sometimes necessary. Even the greatest pacifist out there cannot stand still when someone breaks into their house and kidnaps their children. Or worse. I leave the fight to you, to people who can do it much better than I ever could."

"We all must contribute what we can," Mike said, this time with no trace of sarcasm. "Your part is, we hope, a crucial advancement in your field."

"Certain weapons are dangerous," Ian shook his head. "I signed, along with thousands of other researchers, all the official open letters asking the UN to ban the use of AI for weaponry. It looks like our pleas fell on deaf ears. I pray that the efforts of the military around the world won't mean the end of mankind."

"That's why we are here," Sujata intervened. "We may ban the AI in our military all we want. Other countries won't. The creation of nuclear weapons requires complicated and unstable components. AI development requires just a few geniuses. To implement software, one doesn't need a process that can be rigorously tracked. A bunch of people can do it in a basement. I am oversimplifying it, but the point remains."

"So, you fear that China or Russia will get ahead," Ian concluded. "The Chinese already have their MegaAI, which seems to perform miraculously well. Perhaps you should look for a similar approach. What we do here is different."

"What *do* you do? Can you give us a demo?" Mike seemed to lose patience again.

"Oh, we have no demo to give. I'm not looking to woo investors, I'm not preparing to go public, and I don't want my company to be acquired. CogniPrescience does not operate on the principles of a normal startup. I just want to create an AI. My way. And I want to have control over it."

Sujata appreciated that the man had fire in him behind the friendly and appeasing attitude.

"Why? Do you want to rule the world?" Mike asked, leaning forward.

"Quite the opposite," Ian started laughing in his usual way. "I want to prevent others from ruling the world. For that, we need to think of AI as a *being*. A sentient, ultra-intelligent, empathic, and loving being. Not a machine that does our bidding."

Mike's mouth flew open. Sujata realized he must think that the old man was crazy.

"You mentioned you're in an early phase of your ambitious project," Sujata tried to sound interested, although she'd started to feel rather disappointed.

"Yes. But it's going well, oh, it's going better than I had hoped a couple of years ago," Ian beamed. "Are you familiar with my published work?"

"I've read most of your papers. I can't say that I follow everything," Sujata admitted. "My major is in AI, and I have a cursory knowledge of the most important cognitive science findings. You seemed to have synthesized hundreds of theories and experiments, some of them rather old. At some point, I got lost."

Ian laughed and didn't seem offended at all. "Oh, no surprise, no surprise. You, AI specialists, always live in your world of math, machine learning, and symbolic reasoning. I can perfectly understand why. You want results. Fast. Something that can be used and sold tomorrow. We've been working here on implementing my theory for a couple of decades. We're putting together a fundamentally new cognitive architecture, one that best resembles the most relevant structure and organization of the human mind. Not, and I must stress this, not of the human brain, per se. I can't promise results fast, nor do I have a specific domain to apply this AI in. Had my company been a real commercial enterprise, somebody would have bought us or, more likely, we'd be bankrupt by now. My approach is different. I'm shooting for the long-term, real deal. I can frankly say that we only started making progress about a year ago when a brilliant young man joined our team. He took our efforts to a different level. We started by implementing the mental representation structures, then the mechanics of perception and action, and recently we've integrated domain mapping and basic emotions."

"Emotions?" Mike asked, surprised. "I thought people experimented with this idea some twenty years ago and it went nowhere."

"Yes. We've abandoned a lot of good research directions. That doesn't mean they were wrong." Ian stared at them, thinking about the next step. "Alright, I can show you what we are working on," he said, standing up. "I'm sure you will conclude that we don't have something the DoD can use. Not in the near future, anyway."

A few minutes later, having passed through security, they descended into what Sujata believed to be a large experimental lab.

"Lieutenants, this is our LIO, Lead Intelligence Officer," Ian smiled. "I'm joking," he continued, lifting his arms defensively when seeing François's surprised face. "We don't have too many titles here, just an informal hierarchy. If we did, that's what I would call Doctor François DeSousa.

He is the one to blame for our long-awaited progress. I don't know if we will ultimately succeed. I can only confidently say that we are now on the right track. This is his office, which we have lately turned into our main research lab, conference room, and teaching space."

Sujata looked at François's face. Yes, he was the French researcher who was mocked at the same conference the professor had been. *Well, what do you know ... what a small world,* she thought in surprise.

"François, this is Lieutenant Sujata Hopkins and Lieutenant Commander Mike Lee, from the US Department of Defense," Ian continued.

"Hello," François answered coldly.

Sujata understood their visit annoyed him. He was probably considering it just a waste of his precious time. "Doctor," she saluted. "I can see that you're busy, so we won't take much of your time. Professor Ndikumana promised to show us your research."

François raised one brow and looked at Ian, wondering if he had lost his mind. "Alright. Whatever," he shrugged.

Mike shook his head a little.

Ian stepped further into the lab, where a black divider was hiding something. With a theatrical move, Ian pulled it to the side. "And here we have CARLA," he said with a smile. "We all refer to it as if it was a woman. Sometimes I forget her name stands for Conscious Affective Reasoning and Learning Android."

Sujata thought that *she* indeed looked like a woman. One who had a little spark in her eyes, while she turned her head to look at the professor as if she recognized him, and almost as if she were fond of him. Mike threw up his arms in frustration, no doubt thinking that he was witnessing another combination of circuits, simple software, and mechanical contrivances. Sujata was intrigued. The android moved back to her current preoccupation, which was watching what seemed to be a classic cartoon on a large screen.

The volume was very low, so she assumed they transmitted the audio portion to the android by other means. She moved closer to get a better look at the screen.

"It's *Bambi*," she smiled, remembering her mother's insistence on showing her this cartoon. "Do you believe she is advanced enough to understand it?" she asked the professor.

"Certainly not," Ian admitted. He started pacing around, gesticulating as if he were in a classroom. "She lacks too many structures that are a must for her to comprehend a cartoon. She doesn't have any language understanding or production capabilities. That's why, for the time being, we feed her the audio separately, to serve as general background noise, so that it's not disruptive to us. She is like a two-month-old baby. She interacts with the surrounding environment all the time, without a clear idea of what's going on."

François stepped forward. "But she understands something!" he said, excited. "A lot. She can correlate many of the images with her physics engine structures. For example, when the fawn slides on ice, alarm bells go into her equilibrium processing structures. She *understands* the concept of balance because she has gone through it herself. She *emotes*. Her mind structures associated with pleasure or fear flare up when the right scene comes up. Also, at this very moment, she knows we are here, yet she directs her attention to the cartoon. These are already incredible achievements."

"But why ... *Bambi*?" Sujata asked, genuinely curious.

"Well, we can't read her stories yet," Ian answered. "We certainly don't want to overwhelm her yet with a full Cybersperse immersive experience. This classic cartoon is a very gentle creation. So much so that nowadays almost no kid wants to watch it. There's little action, only a few evil characters, only a little drama. It shows love, children playing, and nature's beauty. I would consider it the culmination of our efforts if she were to understand it."

He paused, then continued his explanation. "We cannot show her any more advanced cartoons because they involve cruelty, more sophisticated hyperbole, satire, and so on. We certainly don't want her to believe that it's alright for Tom the cat to hit himself in the head with a sledgehammer bouncing back from a tire. And we don't want her to think that such actions have no consequences, since Tom seems to be just fine a couple of seconds after. Children are already incredibly adept at separating fiction from reality. CARLA is not there yet. She requires attention, calibration of her parameters, rewriting, and adaptation of her structures. Normal babies are born equipped with a lot of mental structures. We are trying to reproduce those in CARLA. Every minute of the day, we have about one hundred researchers monitoring what's going on in her head and tweaking her all the time. I'm amazed at how little room for change there is to keep her more or less normal. Just a tiny deviation and her mind goes off the rails."

Sujata wanted to get a better look at the android, so she gestured toward Ian and François. "May I?"

Ian invited her with a nod. She approached slowly. CARLA had a very peculiar face, not beautiful, but one that was hard to forget. Indeed, the engineers had done an impressive job. You would need to cut her open to see that you weren't dealing with a real person.

When Sujata was about two meters away, CARLA turned around suddenly, startled. They locked eyes. In that fraction of a second, Sujata understood she would always remember that moment. CARLA couldn't talk or scream, but her stare spoke volumes. It was like she'd borrowed the eyes of the deer characters in her cartoon, gazing at Sujata innocently, scared and reproachful at the same time. She lifted her hand, slowly, hesitantly, and reached for Sujata's face. Her touch was gentle and her skin unexpectedly warm. CARLA seemed fascinated by Sujata's beauty. She seemed pensive, wise, yet immature. CARLA then took Sujata's hand and dragged her to her toys with a face that Sujata could swear showed happiness.

These people are crafting a child, Sujata thought, speechless. *A beautiful child in the body of an adult.* She felt the need to caress her, too. *Are you good or are you evil? Are you going to grow up into a Mother Teresa, or an Elizabeth Báthory?* she wondered.

She looked at Mike, whose mouth was still open. He nodded gently towards her as if he were saying, "This is interesting. Not sure how we can use it, but it's at least something original." They finally had one project that was worth following.

"Professor," Sujata looked at Ian and smiled, "after CARLA and I are done playing, I would like to take you up on your offer to sample some of that delicious food."

CHAPTER 19:

THE FUTURE

Everything in the past died yesterday, and everything in the future is born today.

— Chinese proverb

Qianfan woke up dizzy from the drug they'd given him just before the plane took off. Once he realized he was still in the plane seat, he looked to his right and was relieved to see that Baozhai was sleeping. She had chosen the window seat, hoping she could see outside. No luck. Just after embarking and settling in, a nurse had come in and administered all passengers a small injection. It seems they had dosed it well since he woke up right after the plane landed. They had supposedly arrived at their destination.

He took a quick look outside. There wasn't much to see, just a local airport, judging by the small tower and a tiny terminal. Leaning over Baozhai, he looked further away. There were snowy mountains on the horizon, standing tall over the crystal-clear sky. So, they must have flown north. Their exact location mattered little.

A prison is a prison, no matter if it's on a tropical island or a cold planet on the other side of the galaxy, he thought. *Ah, but the location matters enormously if we want to escape.*

After this burst of energy, he immediately cooled off. Escape where? The party had its tentacles spread all over China. Going abroad was nearly impossible. And what was the point, anyway? At this rate, the MegaAI was bound to conquer the rest of the world, too.

He turned around to look in the direction where he knew Daiyu sat. She was awake and waved her hand. Daiyu had come alone. Despite his efforts to convince himself otherwise, Qianfan had been concerned that she would show up with a boyfriend-turned-husband at the last minute.

I'm a silly old man who dreams of a young woman completely out of my league, he thought bitterly, vowing again to concentrate on raising his daughter in this new environment. *What did Member Tián say? We should consider this our new home. If so, why the secrecy?*

He despised how much he felt like a prisoner, being deported to a concentration camp. Suddenly, he realized that the party might have hidden thought scanners somewhere on this plane, and he panicked. Although a certain amount of anxiety was natural, considering how they'd relocated them, the trust that the party had bestowed upon him should have made him radiate enthusiasm and confidence. With a sigh, he started reciting *The Iliad* and focused on Baozhai's sleep.

Finally, the pilot announced they could start disembarking, which woke Baozhai up.

"Bàba, what's happening?" she asked, rubbing her eyes.

"We have arrived. Let's see our new home!" Qianfan tried to sound as confident and eager as he could.

Baozhai nodded, not nearly as pumped up as he wanted her to be. At the news that they were going to move, she had stood silent for a few minutes. Qianfan knew she was pondering the impact that this move would have on her life. As expected, she hadn't complained. She would not miss school. She had just been worried. After finding out about the SSMS, and after hearing of so many people arrested, she had become even more introverted. Qianfan suspected she was often reciting her poems too and worked on focusing her mind on topics that didn't raise suspicion.

They stepped out of the plane. It was rather chilly outside, but, given the proximity of the mountains, it might have been a warm spring for the region. The flight attendants directed them to five large buses. Daiyu sat in the back of his bus, smiling at him whenever he could glance at her. That gave him some more courage. He had the two people in this world he cared about. Things would be alright.

And I have Haitao too, for what it's worth. He smiled, suddenly in a better mood.

Before departing, he had counted two hundred and five passengers. Only about half of them were his coworkers, the rest were family. He wondered how many of them knew about Zhèng's message.

After a ten-minute ride, they approached their destination. Judging by the barbwire fences and camouflage vehicles, Qianfan figured they were practically on a military base, on a plateau surrounded by mountains. Once they passed the gate, he became depressed by the bleak sight of the barracks surrounding them. Luckily, the bus drove by them, and eventually, they arrived at what looked to be a mini-town, with tens of five-story buildings generously spaced around. There were shops, gyms, a couple of parks, and office buildings. He spotted a cinema too. Not bad.

They allocated him and Baozhai a two-bedroom apartment on the second floor. Baozhai looked at it indifferently, which was already a victory. At first glance, he couldn't spot cameras and microphones, which was odd.

Better not risk some slip of the tongue. Or improper thought, he mused, realizing he was doing just that. He often caught himself in this cycle thinking that he shouldn't be thinking about what he was just thinking.

He was happy that they'd given Daiyu a similar apartment in the same building on the fourth floor. A notification came into his Cybersperse, advising him to freshen up and be at office building 25B, amphitheater 342 at 5:00 p.m. He sighed, washed his face, and changed his clothes.

"Beautiful, isn't it?" he pointed out to Baozhai, who was looking out the window at the breathtaking sight of the mountains. "I hope with all my heart that you will like it here," he opened up.

"I might," Baozhai admitted, nodding slightly. "Bàba, I'm concerned," she said, looking straight into his eyes.

"I know," he breathed, feeling like their relationship was getting stronger because of the nearly unspoken and nearly unthought danger. "But we have our poems, don't we?"

Baozhai nodded.

"I must go to my new workplace," he grimaced. "When I come back, we can explore together. You could take a walk in the meantime. Given all the military and the quality of this city's dwellers, this is probably the safest place in China."

Qianfan left home relieved that, so far, Baozhai seemed to be alright. He didn't want to bother Daiyu, since he imagined they summoned her too. It took him eight minutes to walk to building 342, following the instructions from his personal assistant. The streets and sidewalks were clean. Too clean. Three times he spotted cleaning robots sweeping and vacuuming. They had wheels as big as a car. Other people were walking by. Trees and green lawns were planted between all the buildings. They were so perfectly groomed they looked artificial.

That's it! This whole place seems made of plastic, he realized, feeling uneasy again. *An ultra-clean, ultra-safe prison with a marvelous view.*

Judging by the height of the trees, the city must have been at least thirty years old, from before the time when the MegaAI came into their lives. With these thoughts, he arrived in the conference room. It was huge, oriented in a semicircle going up around a podium. He was five minutes early. Many of his team members were already there. There were no unfamiliar faces. He saluted everyone friendly and took a seat close to the front. Daiyu and Haitao arrived together and waved to him. They found seats further up. Strangely enough, Qianfan couldn't spot the usual battery of surrounding cameras and microphones. No SSMS scanner was in sight, either. They could have hidden them in the walls, although the distance would make it difficult to orient them toward a specific target. Save for the risk of being scanned and identified as a dissident, he liked the idea of meeting face to face. People abused the Cybersperse and remote meetings when nothing could compare to talking with someone directly.

At 5:00 p.m. sharp, a group of ten people came in. Seeing the same eight members of Scientific Committee 48, led by the icy lady, surprised Qianfan unpleasantly. There were two more women, one who looked in her late fifties and a younger one, perhaps in her early thirties.

"Glory to our country! Welcome everybody," Honorable Member Tián started in her monotonous, dangerous voice. "Today marks the beginning of a new life for you, one that promises unparalleled achievements and unique experiences. You should consider yourselves lucky to be admitted into this program. I will let the mayor of this city, Dragon Member Zhèng Zhǔ Huá, introduce herself and present your role here."

The older woman, whom Qianfan didn't know, nodded toward Member Tián and approached the microphone, beaming. "First, allow me to congratulate you," she started, in a squeaky, rather hesitant voice, so different from Member Tián's. "You are all now citizens of Mega Ark City, the most advanced place in China, aren't you? With the addition of your team and your immediate family members, our city has grown to precisely 32,104 citizens. We don't expect further growth from the outside. We think you might be among the last teams of scientists to join us here until the Great Departure. All growth from now on will be organic. Those accompanying the researchers who we selected for our project have their roles too. They take care of maintenance activities: food, cleaning, selling, and so on. So, yes, we have a normal society here. People thrive, fall in love, get married, and have children. There is enough genetic diversity for us to grow, isn't there? My daughter, Zhèng Ah Lam, is here with me." Member Zhèng Zhǔ Huá pointed to the younger woman, who nodded slowly in silence, as if content to observe the audience's reaction.

"Ah Lam was born in Mega Ark City during the time of its creation, and she's never left. There's just too much work to be done! Some here say that it's very difficult to get to Mega Ark City, but at least once you're in, it's impossible to leave."

Member Zhèng Zhǔ Huá laughed in a strange, nerdy way, which Qianfan realized was sincere, although it sounded like someone was forcing her to laugh at gunpoint. Ah Lam's face remained impenetrable, with no hint that she appreciated her mother's humor.

"Joke aside, there's no need for us to leave! We have everything we need here in our beloved city. Most importantly, though, we have a mission, don't we? We have the responsibility and privilege to shape the future."

Long live the propaganda, Qianfan thought bitterly, and immediately conjured the image of Baozhai and started his *Iliad* litany in the background, just in case. He looked around. Nobody seemed excited. He wondered if the effects of the drug might still linger on some.

"When I say future, I mean much more than you are thinking at this very moment," Member Zhǔ Huá said, raising her fist and making a determined face, like she was suddenly fighting a dangerous enemy that she meant to crush. "But more about this later."

She looked around, trying to connect with the audience. "We selected you because of your outstanding work on the SSMS scanner, under the leadership of Doctor Zhào Qianfan," she said, nodding towards him.

Qianfan flinched, shocked to see that she recognized him, and she could spot him in the audience so fast.

"That is a major accomplishment, isn't it? Your immediate task will be to enhance it further."

At least that is not a surprise, Qianfan thought.

"This time, though," the woman continued in an enthusiastic tone, "your challenge will be bigger. As you know, when we started using the SSMS, we discovered many dissidents. Disturbed elements of our society. It bothers me terribly to see that they don't understand and commit to our goals. That they choose to question our ways instead of embracing them. They are handicapped. We must help them. It is the party's aim to reeducate them in special schools. Sadly, we didn't expect that there would be so many! We're now faced with the situation of having to slow down our progress because of these ... individuals. Their reeducation takes too long. We cannot afford to wait for them to catch up. China must move forward! Therefore, President Yun Li has tasked us to come up with a way to not only *read* from their minds but also *write* to them."

Qianfan felt all his blood drain from his face. This time, quite a few of his team members stirred and murmured.

"Now, before you think this is wrong, or impossible, or both, hear me out. Just like the current SSMS isn't reading one's thoughts, the next one, let's call it Mood Alterer, or MA, will exert a sufficient influence on one's feelings to make one more ... sensitive to certain stimuli. For example, when being taught about the role of the party in our lives and the plans for the development of our country, they will feel engulfed in a sense of pride, safety, and family comfort, as they should. When listening to reports about the enemies, from both outside and inside, they'll get a feeling of rage, disgust, and strong disagreement. Again, a desired reaction. These are mere corrections to their thoughts, aren't they? Our scientists expect such capabilities would shorten the normal reeducation time by a factor of 10. It will reduce the percentage of those who resist reeducation from around 50 percent to one to two percent. Such fantastic results that would put us back on track."

Member Zhǔ Huá assessed the effect of her words. People in the audience seemed agitated. Some frowned. She nodded, satisfied. "I can see that some of you are uneasy with this task. So you should be, in normal times. But these are extraordinary circumstances. You see ... over the last thirty years, we have prepared for a future that will establish, once and for all, China's superiority among the rest of the nations, here on Earth and out in space. Thanks to the capabilities of the MegaAI, we can now exponentially speed up our research so that we can begin, in a few decades, interplanetary migration within our Solar System. We call this the Great Project. Once we make Mars part of the Republic of China, and once we establish an outpost far beyond the asteroid belt, we will start dreaming about reaching some other star system. We could, couldn't we? Think about it! We know of tens of thousands of exoplanets. Why should we confine ourselves to our own planet? Why don't we turn a good portion of our galaxy into a new home for the Chinese people? But we must do it fast, mustn't we? Before the enemies of China in the rest of the world attempt the same thing."

People were now quiet, waiting for her to continue. Qianfan thought about the Manhattan Project; the arms race against other nations had motivated that ambitious initiative, although on a much smaller scale compared to the unprecedented project she proposed now.

"With this goal in mind, President Yun Li has organized our research in several areas. Broadly speaking, we have seven research divisions here, as follows. First, we have a division that studies means to boost our energy sources. Then we have a group that studies novel materials, including nanotechnology. A third division is looking into ways to propel starships, focusing on nuclear propulsion research. The fourth division studies terraforming and food growing in circumstances vastly different from those on the Earth. The fifth division is a biology and genetics group, which is researching ways to enhance our bodies to withstand radiation and harsh temperatures. In the sixth group, we have the basic science division, usually made of members who finished their task and can go on poking almost randomly at nature's mysteries. This might be the most important group of them all, since breakthrough discoveries would probably come from them. Finally, we have the technology division, which is the largest, and in charge of advanced computers, sensors, and a plethora of devices."

Qianfan noticed in passing that there didn't seem to be a group in charge of AI development.

"As you can guess, you all belong to the last group. However, once you complete your goals, we'll reassign you to the basic research division. There, you'll let your curious nature explore freely whatever domain we think is important for our mission. Research anything, as long as it doesn't threaten the safety of our people and our mission. We do not research weapons here. We leave that to the military, who, incidentally, has an adjacent top-secret base."

She paused again. "Along the same lines, further research on AI is strictly forbidden here. We consider that to be the most dangerous research area. We are eternally grateful for having been the first in the world to come up with a powerful AI. Any effort to enhance it should be left to the MegaAI itself. There's no need for another AI that might be unfriendly."

So, the MegaAI, self-proclaimed protector of all China, conqueror of the galaxy, doesn't want unnecessary competition, Qianfan thought with a shiver.

"Now, some of you might ask, why the urgency? Why force the recalibration of some of our more stubborn citizens? Two reasons. First, we need everybody in China to prepare for the future along with us, even if they aren't working in our city. We need materials, basic research, manufacturing, and more, done outside. Second, we need this because the MegaAI calculated a probability of 85 percent that by the time we are ready to tackle space exploration, we'll have World War III. Given the nuclear arsenal that the world powers today have, that might well be the last one. By then, we must have our ships big enough to take as many Chinese citizens off the planet as possible. I hope I'm being clear. We will leave behind all reluctant individuals who are not cooperating, along with the remnants of human civilization."

Several people gasped and moaned. The dragon member had finally woken them up.

"I hope you now understand why secrecy was imperative," the woman spoke almost with hatred. "And that you cannot disclose this to anybody. Communication with the outside world is not allowed. The Cybersperse we use here is private. You'll have access to the latest news in China and the world. You won't be able to call people and you won't receive calls. Leaving this place is not an option. We are doing this for the benefit of the many."

She gazed at them, almost with love this time. Qianfan thought either this lady was an excellent actor or was suffering from a mental disorder akin to a split personality. Suddenly, she turned towards him and locked eyes, as if she had heard his thoughts.

"Note that, as citizens of the Mega Ark, you enjoy a few privileges. Your CWT score is not very relevant here. You are all considered exemplary citizens and benefit from the fruits of each other's labor. This is the old dream of a society in which all contribute what they can and get back what they need."

Qianfan nearly rolled his eyes. *Do people still believe this nonsense anymore?* he wondered.

"Also, there's less supervision here. You may speak your mind. But we will tolerate nothing, I repeat, nothing that threatens our mission!"

Qianfan got the impression that she said this, looking straight at him. He felt his body shake a bit.

With a final theatrical gesture, Dragon Member Zhèng Zhǔ Huá raised her hands and screamed, "Remember, we are building the future! We are the future!"

After a few seconds of awful silence, some zealots jumped up from their seats and started cheering. Everybody followed suit. Qianfan did the same. He couldn't tell whether people's enthusiasm was genuine or not, only that the world would spin faster from now on.

CHAPTER 20:

TO BE OR NOT TO BE

Consciousness is like an amorphous mirror made of a still liquid. This mirror reflects your entire world as a conscious being. The thoughts that occupy your mind in any single moment, the landscape you are admiring, the song you are listening to, a body ache, the memory of your breakfast, and the meeting you plan for today. Each piece has its own special place. What you "feel" represents the disturbances in the liquid. Most of the ripples just go through and fade away, not reaching your awareness. Yet, big disruptions (a massive pain, a sudden flash of light, or the sight of a tiger ready to jump at your throat, etc.) create a shock wave big enough to grab your full attention. The ripples and liquid-mirror are inseparable. You don't have a direct link to the reality outside. You're limited to perceiving it through the mirror. Whatever you imagine as "you," your own "self," is nothing but another ripple. The actual "you" is the mirror itself. For artificial beings to be conscious, we must provide them with such a mirror. They must be the mirror. And they must get the illusion of a self on it.

— DeSousa's Memoirs - Part II - Creation - 2054

The tablet screen showed that CARLA's conceptual and emotional structures were going through rapid formations and transformations, so much so that François wondered if the fragile equilibrium they had achieved so far would collapse.

In the past few weeks, they had gingerly moved towards adding preliminary language processing abilities to her mind. Since then, about half of the time when she was acting in the world, someone was nearby talking to her. Sometimes, it would be just names of objects. Other times, half or full sentences. The idea was to see if she could pick up words and basic grammar from these simple interactions, as well as from cartoons and nature documentaries she was watching, just like children. The engineers gave her a primitive ability to utter sounds. She couldn't speak just yet. She could only grunt, squeak, yelp, or communicate with other sounds. They struggled to implement in her an impetus to express herself in the first place, then correlate her thoughts with certain sounds. To some extent, she could already imitate what she saw others do.

Early results seemed promising. CARLA could break down spoken words and recognized phonemes, deduce morphological and syntactical rules, and associate some of these with concepts she was familiar with. Ian thought that it might be the right time to enlarge her horizon by taking her out of her confined space in the lab.

Therefore, for the first time, they brought her outside, near the main building. Flanked by François and Ian, she walked on the immaculate sidewalk under the cloudless sky. She seemed hungry to swallow all that nature was throwing at her. Sometimes she would step in and out of shade as if to better assess the light, pull back when faced with a minor wind gust, stare at the reflection of everything in the building's glass walls, stop to look at a colorful patch of flowers, or a dashing squirrel. Occasionally, she would make guttural sounds, usually triggered by something that they wouldn't expect to elicit her excitement, like when she stepped on grass or when she saw a plane in the sky.

François looked at Ian. The professor was unusually tense, monitoring CARLA's reaction on his tablet. Some twenty coworkers were outside too, examining what was going on, along with many others who remained in the office. CARLA was connected wirelessly to the main computers inside, a potential security risk that Ian reluctantly agreed to. Her body was merely her way of interacting with the outside world. The jump from the limited environment to which they had exposed her so far to the richness of nature had proved overwhelming, a fact amply reflected in her posture and behavior.

François thought that, in their effort to make her as expressive as possible, the engineers might have gone overboard. Her face painted the emotions she was going through all too well. Any minor event that surprised her caused some muscle twitch and a facial grimace that might have been funny were they not so stressed. And this little stroll seemed to her a collection of unknown, scary, and wonderful events.

"One thing is certain," François pointed out, "she doesn't have a poker face."

Ian smiled and nodded. It was good to relieve some of the tension. CARLA moved her head fast up, down, left, right, her attention jumping all over the place, while the engineers tried to adjust her parameters in real-time.

"This might be too much for her," François said in a shaky voice.

"It's hard to calm her down," Ian admitted. "So far, she's doing well. The concept formation, while crazy fast, appears stable. Her emotional response is almost normal. Imagine you'd kept a child in a room from the time they were born until a couple of years later, which is probably the equivalent of how old she is in terms of development. Then you exposed them to the outside world. I think they'd react worse. But I agree we need to be careful. Perhaps this was enough for a first test. We should shut her down and analyze the data for a couple of hours. If all looks okay, we can turn her back on."

François looked at her face, as Ian gave the commands, and she went offline. CARLA stopped on her feet, in perfect balance, and closed her eyes gently. For a moment, he thought her face reflected panic and disappointment. He remembered his drowning experience and shivered. He asked himself again if it was worth adding a new life form to this universe? One that could suffer? One that could betray and be betrayed?

"Do you think she feels anything?" François asked. "I mean, truly distinguish between sensations? The way the sun warms her sensors, the wind on her face, the crimson color of my shirt, the soothing sound of the birds in the background, the fear that we won't activate her again?"

"Not in the sense that we do, I'm sure," Ian answered. "You're talking about *quale*, what it is like to feel anything. Why do we perceive in such specific and distinguished ways the blue of the sea, a headache, the smell of roses? So far, nobody has even a clue what *qualia* are, let alone how to implement them in a machine."

"We gave her distinct representations of feelings," François protested. He suddenly desperately wanted CARLA to be more human. "Her fear and happiness are different. We programmed her to react differently to them, to minimize her suffering and long for happiness. What's missing?"

"I love your optimism," Ian smiled, like a patient father tempering his son. "I'm afraid we may never implement feelings in her in the sense you are talking about. A well-known philosopher, Daniel Dennett, defined qualia in terms of four properties. They are ineffable, meaning that we can't communicate them to others, we only experience them directly. They are also intrinsic; they don't depend on and don't relate to anything else. Then, they are private. I can't be sure you perceive the color red the way I do. There's no scientific reason to think that you don't, but there's no way for us to measure how similarly you and I perceive it. Finally, qualia are directly apprehensible by consciousness. You feel them. Period."

"Wouldn't she need that to be intelligent? To empathize?"

"Now, that's the million-dollar question!" Ian lifted his finger. "I don't know. At the first glance, no. Intelligence seems orthogonal to this ability. Another famous philosopher, David Chalmers, coined the term 'the hard problem of consciousness.' This is the problem of explaining why and how we have qualia. In my humble view, nobody has found an answer to this yet. Chalmers also came up with the idea of a philosophical zombie. That's a being that thinks and acts in the world the way we do. The philosophical zombie is, in effect, identical to a normal person, but one that doesn't perceive qualia. If you allow me a crude speculation, say, when seeing colors, this being perceives a value between 1 to 1000, depending on the hue, saturation, and brightness. When feeling a burn, it gets a distinct value between 2500 to 3000, depending on intensity. In principle, there's no reason this being could not perceive the world and behave in a way indistinguishable from ours. The best we can hope for is that CARLA will eventually become such a being."

François frowned. He hated the permanent limitation implied by this analogy.

"Also," Ian continued relentlessly, "keep in mind that a human being comprises more than just the nervous system. There is the circulatory system, the endocrine system, the immune system, and so on. We're not aiming to reproduce them all. So, inevitably, CARLA will forever differ from a human."

François turned his face away. It frustrated him that he was getting emotionally attached to her. Ian had warned him about this. Still, he was only partially right. François wasn't chasing another Marie who felt nothing. He was raising a child in her image. Marie was her indirect mother.

About three hours later, while CARLA was patiently waiting in the shade on the sidewalk, the technicians reported they couldn't find anything wrong with her data. The number of calculations per minute had been huge, and it would take a while to discern. When everything had settled, they could see in the logs that CARLA had crystallized a series of existing and new concepts, as well as distinct emotions.

"This is unbelievable," Ian shook his head. "She is doing so well. It's like I'm always waiting for something to go wrong, and she inevitably disappoints me," he smiled. Signaling toward the others, Ian continued. "Okay, let's turn her back on and have her walk a little more."

François smiled. As CARLA opened her eyes, he realized he had longed to see them again. Then he noticed, terrified, that their expression quickly changed from neutral to worried, then painful. Her face got all distorted in a horrible scowl that made her almost ugly.

"What's going on?" François panicked again, running towards her, ready to embrace her.

"I don't know," Ian yelled, equally agitated. "Perhaps she got upset that we shut her down!"

Hearing them speak, CARLA turned her head towards them, with the same contorted, unnatural facial expression, like she was going through excruciating pain.

"Is she angry?" François wondered, taking one step back.

Suddenly, she let out an inhuman, low-volume wail and took off towards the nearest group of trees. She was moving as fast as she could, nearly falling and regaining her balance. It was as slow as a toddler who was still learning to walk, yet trying to run away for her life.

She looks like a fawn on ice. Perhaps she's subconsciously imitating her friend, Bambi, thought François, frozen in place.

Ian scrambled to reach her. "There, there, no need to be upset," he comforted her in the most soothing voice he could produce. He took her by the shoulders and looked into her eyes. "You are just experiencing the big world for the first time. You will see, there are many wonders here. Don't worry, you won't stay in the dark for long. We just want to make sure that everything is alright with you."

François understood Ian was talking to himself as much as with her. With a few exceptions, CARLA didn't even have the mind of an infant yet. She couldn't understand much of what he was saying. But the way he spoke seemed to have a calming effect. Her countenance changed from pain to relief. She frowned and made repeating low-frequency sounds.

"She is crying!" François yelled.

"Shush, no need to react like that," Ian whispered to her, turning her slowly towards the building entrance.

CARLA's facial expression showed confusion, as if she'd just woken up from a car accident, still trying to get her bearings. They walked her inside. Once in her familiar surroundings, she stood in her chair and looked straight at François, almost reproachfully. He felt his heart melt. The way she gazed at him reminded him of Marie, and of puppies.

"Why don't you watch another video?" Ian proposed. "There is one about the Alps with beautiful scenery."

CARLA looked at the screen. She appeared absent-minded.

Ian signaled François and went outside of the lab where they could speak without her hearing them.

"This was intense," Ian breathed a sigh of relief.

François realized he had never seen him as stressed as he was now. "I wonder ... I keep wondering if we are doing something wrong," François said, looking back at the lab. He felt a wave of guilt at the thought that he might have, inadvertently, inculcated in CARLA a few unpleasant aspects of Marie's psyche.

"I know," Ian nodded. "I still don't think we are doing something wrong. In a couple of days, when the dust settles, we'll realize how big of a success this is. We have made a being that emotes and then perceives its emotions! Well, it's all a simulation, but still!"

François shrugged, unconvinced.

Suddenly, Ian's tablet alerted him of a phone call. He looked at it and grimaced. "Great timing ... Excuse me," he said as he moved past François into the hallway.

Five minutes later, he came back. "We must go to D.C. tomorrow," he announced calmly.

"What?" François asked, raising his eyebrows.

"It was Lieutenant Sujata Hopkins on the phone. We've been summoned ... no, we've been cordially invited to talk with the heads of the DoD. And, yes, both of us are going." Ian was clearly uncomfortable with this, but he smiled encouragingly.

François thought that, after this episode, a change of scenery might be welcome. Still, he missed CARLA already. *I'm behaving like a father having to go on a business trip for the first time since his daughter was born. And now I have confirmation that I'm crazy,* he thought, peeking back at her.

CHAPTER 21:

DEAL

No two on Earth in all things can agree. All have some daring singularity.

— Winston Churchill

Walking along one of the many Pentagon hallways, Sujata glanced outside as she passed by some large windows. Despite the rush that put pressure on her these days, she felt compelled to stop in front of one. All was quiet outside. A couple of trees had refused to shed all their leaves. A highway nearby was almost empty at this midday hour. Fall in D.C. was mild. The warmth of the sun penetrated the window and brushed her face. It also engulfed her heart. In moments like this, she found it hard to believe the world could collapse into war, suffering, and complicated fights between technologies.

Is this all that CARLA will be? she wondered. *Technology?*

"What is it with you and the sun?" Mike approached her from one end of the corridor. "You must be a reptile, reincarnated. Either that or you're powered by photovoltaic cells."

She smiled, grateful to have him on her side.

"Time to face the music," he said, then moved to the side with his usual semi-mocking curtsy. "After you."

They entered a large room with a large oval table. A dozen anxious people sitting at the table turned in sync to watch them. She chose a chair with a sigh. She wasn't looking forward to this intense discussion. Some fifteen minutes later, the Secretary of Defense, James R. Rooney II, along with his staff and several generals, came in and took their seats. General Joseph Thompson was there too, and he nodded at her, signaling his support. She was mainly concerned about General Lloyd Kambe's reaction. He was a man of action, with little patience for such things as technological advances unless they were about a superior weapon. Preferably, one that they could fire from a distance and obliterate the enemy.

With a nod, the secretary signaled to one officer at the door, who opened it and asked someone inside.

"Professor Ndikumana," the secretary said, inviting him to sit down.

"Mr. Secretary, generals, lieutenant," Ian saluted with his usual smile that threatened to swallow the entire room.

"Lieutenant Hopkins, you have the mic," the secretary said, looking at Sujata.

"Thank you, Mr. Secretary, generals," she stood up and bowed her head. "As you know, over the last fifteen months, we've carefully researched the ongoing AI projects in the United States and allied countries. These are our best and brightest. We have chosen four candidates. One of them is CogniPrescience, whose sole owner and main researcher is Professor Ian Ndikumana."

While Ian seemed perfectly calm, Sujata knew he was eager to understand what the meeting was all about. She continued. "Professor, before we let your colleague in, and before we get into the meat of why we've invited you here, we want to ask you a few questions."

"Sure," Ian said and bowed his head.

"A few weeks ago, when Lieutenant Commander Lee and I visited you, you mentioned that your colleague, Doctor DeSousa, was instrumental in the recent progress you've made."

"That is correct. While we've been working for over twenty years on a new cognitive architecture that follows my theory, it was François's multi-adaptable algorithm, and his genius to make it fit the many intricate aspects of this architecture, that led to our breakthrough."

"Do you believe you could continue this work without him?" she asked, looking straight at Ian.

"No," he answered simply. "There's no guarantee that we will succeed *with* him. However, there's a very high probability that we will fail *without* him. Not in my lifetime, anyway."

General Kambe shifted in his seat, a sign that he was already losing patience. "Professor," he said, "are you aware that Doctor DeSousa tried to kill himself just before joining your company? We did some investigations, you know …"

"Yes," Ian let his gaze down, "he told me as much."

"And you still hired him for something so critical?" General Kambe raised one brow.

"He mentioned it later," Ian clarified, "after I had made him an offer."

"Would you have hired him if you knew?" General Kambe pressed.

"I don't know," Ian admitted with a shrug. "But I'm thankful things turned out this way. I've learned that sometimes in life unhappy events and weird coincidences converge toward something good. It doesn't happen often. When it does, it's best to recognize and take advantage of them."

General Kambe scoffed.

"Could he be unstable?" Sujata asked softly.

"Geniuses often are," Ian answered sincerely. "He's obsessed with a woman. So much so that I suspect he's reproducing her facial features in CARLA." He felt compelled to add, "Our android." Seeing that General

Kambe was about to ask for clarification, Ian raised his arms defensively. "That's my speculation. I didn't ask. Frankly, I don't care."

"Might it be possible that he also implemented a part of her personality in CARLA?" Sujata asked.

"Lieutenant," Ian answered, turning his palms up, "if we manage to implement in CARLA the personality of *any* sane person, we will have succeeded."

"Ha," General Kambe replied, visibly upset. "It beats me why you would model your AI after this random woman. Why not Albert Einstein, or Stephen Hawking? And, once again," he turned towards General Thompson, "it escapes me completely how this is going to help us in the military."

"I hope in time we will tweak the particular personality traits as needed," Ian explained patiently, ignoring the reference to the military goals. "We're striving to build a machine that is ethical, good, loving, and empathizing. I expect some control over the outcome."

"So, you gave power to a nerd to implement his sick fantasies," the general concluded. "Don't be shocked if you end up with a female version of Stalin."

Sujata tried hard to ignore him and signaled Ian patiently to continue.

Ian sighed. "With all due respect, what we do is way beyond one person's fantasies. François puts his touch on it. Perhaps he is somewhat unstable after breaking up with a girl. Does it matter? I believe the military knows best that scientific discoveries, technological breakthroughs, and the entire progress of civilization have often been the result of conflicts. It would be beyond naïve to think that generosity, love for their peers, and kindness always fuels the people who move us. I would say it is often quite the contrary. History is rife with scientists who were immoral, jealous, mean, egotistical, and sometimes homicidal. Einstein had at least six mistresses throughout his life. Marie Curie lived with the physicist Paul Langevin, who was married. Johann Bernoulli competed with his brother Jacob about who was a more gifted mathematician until they stopped talking to each other.

He was even jealous of his son, with whom he shared the first prize in a math contest. Robert Oppenheimer tried to poison his tutor, whom he hated. Some argue that the famous geneticists Francis Crick and James Watson stole vital data from a young researcher who hadn't published it yet. And it goes on and on."

Ian looked around before continuing. "This woman broke François's heart, and he went crazy for a while. That's nothing new under the sun. If he's driven by his jealousy, or by the need to show off, or to get some distorted revenge, who am I to judge?"

General Kambe was staring at him, disgusted.

"Besides, in the past year or more, I've come to like him. He's like a son to me. I don't think he's evil."

General Kambe was about to say something else when the secretary intervened. "Let's move on, shall we? We will have time to analyze the story later. I don't believe we can afford to be picky about one's personal affairs."

The general pouted and acknowledged with a military-style nod. At the secretary's signal, the door opened again, and François entered the room.

"Good morning," he said in a defiant tone.

Sujata could see that he was upset about being called here, far from his baby. "Doctor," she answered, directing him to a chair near Ian, who offered an encouraging smile.

"Lieutenant," the secretary invited Sujata to go on.

"Gentlemen, we invited you here because of a development that we consider a national security matter. Arguably, a threat to the entire world."

Ian raised his brows, and his smile became more uptight.

"Before we continue, we must ask you to sign a non-disclosure agreement. You should know that we have done a background investigation, and we gave you a DoD secret mid-level clearance, even though you're not government employees." Sujata gave them each a piece of paper and waited patiently for them to read it.

"Not much choice here, eh?" François mumbled and signed it.

Ian just shrugged and signed it too.

"What you are about to hear," General Kambe jumped in once again, "is not that secret after all. Plenty of people know about it already. The reason this hasn't made news yet is because we stopped it. For now. And it wasn't easy."

"Just before Doctor DeSousa joined CogniPrescience," Sujata continued after gathering the signed documents, "both of you went to the neuromimetic conference in Paris. Lieutenant Commander Lee and I were there, too. You probably remember that, towards the end of the conference, Professor Zhèng Yang gave a short, rather unusual speech just before he died."

Ian nodded.

"By then, I wasn't attending the conference anymore. I just remember seeing it on the news," François clarified, while a shadow passed over his face briefly.

"Professor Zhèng killed himself," Sujata announced. "He did it so that he could send us the following message: '*CHINA AI IS ALIVE. IT ACHIEVED SENTIENCE. REPLACED PRESIDENT. NOBODY KNOWS. WE LOST CONTROL. SAVE MANKIND.*'"

Ian pulled his chair away from the table a bit and frowned for the first time.

"*Merde*! How ... how did he supply this message?" François asked, tense.

"Ingeniously and cruelly. He staged his death at a precise minute. That, along with the date and minute when he was born, combined with a code hidden in a few songs he wrote and provided to us, gave us the key to extract the message from his speech."

Sujata gave them another piece of paper detailing the way she had deciphered Zhèng's message.

"This is plausible," François said after he finished studying it. "Although it's odd, and it might still be just an astonishing coincidence."

Ian kept quiet, but he looked worried.

"It might," Sujata admitted, tilting her head a little. "However, given what we know about China, it is, unfortunately, rather probable. We also have other ... information that the Chinese have started a major project in a secret facility. Something that has to do with them conquering the world. I cannot say more about this."

"I don't understand," François said. "I don't care about politics. I know China wasn't a combative nation for a very long time. In fact, they were quite the opposite. They marched on with the plan to establish peace in the world."

"That's true," Sujata nodded. "Although more recently they've exhibited expansionist behavior annexing a few territories that, arguably, belonged to them at some point, they have never looked interested in starting a world war. So, something has changed. If indeed an AI is leading them, and most of them don't know it, all bets are off."

"How could that be?" François turned to Ian. "Their MegaAI is nothing but a glorified artificial neocortex on which they run machine-learning algorithms. It's not even a brain copy in the sense of replicating the precise neuronal activity of one biological brain. How could it achieve the level of sentience we're talking about here? An AI replacing the president would require motivation and ambition akin to a human's. A plan for conquering the world would require a deep understanding of our societies, cultural differences, military prowess, and so much more. What happened with the need to raise the AI as a child? What happened to emotions being a precursor to intelligence?"

"I don't know if what Professor Zhèng said is true," Ian said softly, looking at him. "I can't speak about the way the Chinese have implemented their MegaAI, beyond what is public knowledge. However, I have always been wary of the possibility that the first more capable AI that humanity develops won't be congruent with our values. The first time we spoke, back in Paris, I told you as much. Given that there can be many kinds of intelligences in the universe, there are innumerable ways to proceed with developing an AI. Unless we do it on principles that govern our own intelligence, we'll either produce garbage, if we are lucky, or, as it appears to be the case now, something smart, foreign to us. Something smart that might want to harm, rather than help us."

"What makes you think *your* way is better?" General Kambe asked, narrowing his eyes.

"Are you familiar with the infinite monkey theorem?" Ian asked.

The general frowned and shook his head.

"Given enough time, a monkey typing random letters on a typewriter will eventually produce the complete works of Shakespeare. When we work on AI, we are like this proverbial monkey: we want to achieve one specific text, which is rather unlikely. But things are worse. Any other cogent writing that we produce stands a good chance of harming us. Unlike the monkey, we don't work entirely randomly. We follow different smart approaches, with no regard for danger. So far, we produced mainly gibberish, so that's not a problem. As time passes, we risk producing something that is not the Shakespeare masterpiece we want, and that might consequently be fatal. To achieve our one chance of survival, we need to emulate Shakespeare precisely. We must build an AI in our image. This is one in a trillion ways of doing it, yet it is the only one viable for us."

The general shook his head, deeply unsatisfied by this answer.

"Professor, for all of us to better assess your statements, could you summarize the status of your project?" Sujata said, trying to sound as positive as she could.

"Well," Ian started, "I am confident in our approach, but if what you say is true, we are far from having what you need to compete with the MegaAI. As I am sure you know by now, we are developing an android by trying to mimic human perception, action, and reasoning holistically, based on discoveries in the fields of cognitive science. We didn't take a machine learning approach, we're not doing a neuroscience-driven model of the brain, and we're not implementing an expert system. CARLA, our android, has all the mechanical actuators and sensors necessary to make her virtually indistinguishable from a real person. We are thrilled with what we have so far: we have made her see, hear, touch, to some extent smell, sense her body vitals, walk, and manipulate liquids and solids. We interact with her as if she were a child. Recently, we started teaching her language. Just the other day, we took her outside the lab for a short walk and we had irrefutable proof that she had an emotional episode."

Sujata moved her head back a little, surprised to hear that. She didn't like surprises, not during this kind of meeting. "Sorry to interrupt you. *An emotional episode*?" she asked.

"Yes. When we turned her off to do some diagnosis, she seemed upset, almost angry. She seemed to want to continue to experience the world outside. Then, when we started her again, she ... well, she cried. In her own way. Her logs show she got scared. To be clear, we programmed her to react to external stimuli in the same way a human would. She recognizes a pattern of events, and if they are upsetting, she emotes. Then, she has mechanisms to read these emotions and act on them. There are no genuine feelings, in a human sense, behind all of it."

This last statement was followed by a minute of silence.

"And why, pray tell," General Kambe intervened, "would we want an AI that can cry? What's next? Will it have a fit until we give it its favorite toy? Or perhaps it will start shooting at us for not letting it go out with its teenage AI buddies?"

"I think—" Ian started, but the general interrupted him again.

"It seems obvious to me that an AI driven by the same motivation as a human being would be just another pain in the butt to deal with. We have enough imbeciles in the world already."

"Maybe that's the safest AI we can get," Lieutenant Commander Lee intervened for the first time, calmly.

"Safest?" General Kambe asked, ready to jump off his seat. "An AI that is prone to emotional crises? One that needs a therapist too, like any modern brat conceived the old hanky-panky way? Bah, I'm sorry, Mr. Secretary. I don't see how this meeting will solve the Chinese crisis. It's a waste of time."

"Well," General Thompson cut in, in his calm voice, "if we don't do something, the MegaAI might decide to wipe us all out. And if this one doesn't, somebody else will make the next MegaAI."

"Professor," the secretary of defense nodded, "let's assume that you are right. Let's assume that the only way to create a good AI is to do it in our image. Then why bother? Why not just have a child, as General Kambe suggested so colorfully?"

"CARLA will eventually be much smarter than a human," Ian answered. "It will be capable of solving problems we face today and those that will come up tomorrow. As a civilization, we are stuck ... we can't keep increasing the human population, or else we'll run out of resources. We are struggling with climate change. We are still far from winning the battle with cancer. Once a decade, we have a pandemic that kills millions of people. We have scarcely made any progress with space exploration. There are no new kinds of fuel. Most importantly, the world is under constant threat that somebody will eventually nuke the Earth to smithereens. We are newborns in this vast universe. We need someone better to watch over us, to guide us as we reach for the stars."

"How long do you think we'd have to wait until CARLA becomes such a being?" General Thompson asked.

"I don't know," Ian shrugged. "Even if we get her mental structures and algorithms right the first time, which is rather unlikely, teaching CARLA requires fine-tuning her parameters all the time. In humans, the balance between a genius and a severely autistic, antisocial, and uncooperative individual is very fragile. Any single person alive, criminals included, is currently much more like us than CARLA. It's enough for otherwise normal humans to be incapable of empathizing, and they can transform into mass murderers, sociopaths, or unscrupulous megalomaniacs, ready to turn into dictators. Even if we do a marvelous engineering job, how can we be sure CARLA won't end up being such an individual? We need to raise her carefully, with love, with proper education."

"So, is it going to take a quarter of the century to get her to be normal, loyal, and smart to the level of a college graduate?" General Kambe asked. "Then thirty more years to get her to be super smart? Who will she guide if, by then, we all disappear?"

"I wish I could give you reassurances, but that would mean to lie." Ian put on his usual defensive smile.

Judging by his sneer at his statement, General Kambe was about to make another nasty remark.

"General," the secretary jumped in again, raising a hand, "there's no point in bickering. We're all on the same side here." He turned towards Ian. "Professor, I appreciate your candor. You should know that Lieutenant Hopkins, Lieutenant Commander Lee, and General Thompson all made a good case to trust your approach. You should also know that I spoke with the president about it, enough to pique her interest."

The secretary stood up. "Gentlemen, ladies. Ever since that accursed message reached my ears, I started praying. I'm not religious, but I now pray every morning when I wake up and thank the Good Lord for the previous twenty-four hours of peace. I've got a new appreciation for what otherwise used to be the most mundane activity. Make no mistake, we live with a sword over our heads. If what we know is true, and because we are not yet in a war, we must assume the Chinese are preparing something terrible. I am beyond concerned."

The secretary turned towards the professor again. "Based on everything I heard today, I believe your approach, however immature, is worth a shot. We just need to speed it up. Therefore, we would like to ask permission to help you. We will provide you with anything, and I stress, anything you need. If required, we will make one thousand researchers available to you. We will give you whatever facilities and equipment you need to develop, raise, and educate CARLA fast. We desperately need her finished yesterday."

"Mr. Secretary," Ian cleared his throat, "I appreciate your offer. But you know what they say, nine women won't give birth in one month. I am afraid this isn't just a matter of people and resources. Giving CARLA better hardware and surrounding her with ten times more people won't make a difference. Or at least not a positive one. There are physical constraints at play. Certain things we can teach her fast. For others, she needs time to interact with the world herself." He turned towards François. "Besides, I have to think of a way to tell our people that we work for the military now."

"What's there to explain?" General Kambe asked impatiently. "The US Constitution allows us to nationalize private enterprise during war. And, professor, make no mistake! We are at war."

"Professor, we are not nationalizing your company," the secretary tried to temper the conversation again. "I'm merely proposing a deal to you in which you don't lose. Anything that our researchers contribute during this time will become and remain your intellectual property. We don't need money from it. Of course, all your employees will need to sign nondisclosure agreements. We will strive to get mid-level clearances for all of them. If some turn out to be shady, you must fire them. I don't believe that will be the case, though."

Seeing Ian's uncomfortable face, he continued. "We want to ensure CARLA will develop in the right direction to destroy the MegaAI if it gets to that point. Once this threat is over, you'll be free to announce our cooperation, the success of CARLA, and move on with your plans. And make all the money you want."

Ian nodded.

"How would this ... cooperation work?" François asked, suspicious.

"First, we'd prefer you move your research here," the secretary said.

"What?" François jumped up.

"That could prove disruptive to our employees," Ian said, putting a hand on François's arm.

"Alright," the secretary acknowledged, "I expected that you'd say that. Then we send our own people there. I know you have bought plenty of land in the area where your complex is. We'll construct a couple of buildings for our personnel. We'll dig underground facilities if needed. I assure you, we'll move fast. Your security team is inadequate. They are free to stay on your premises and help. We will send specialized forces to defend your complex. We'll also send cybersecurity folks. The last thing we want is for a foreign nation to get access to your research. Or hack CARLA."

"We already keep CARLA disconnected from the Cybersperse by design," Ian pointed out. "But I have no objections. We cannot ensure the proper level of security required, considering the current ... circumstances."

"We'll also send our own AI experts. You're free to use them however you see fit. Professor, I trust you understand the urgency of this. If there's a choice between teaching CARLA Lord Byron's poetry and shooting a gun, please do the latter."

François scoffed, exasperated.

"On this topic," General Kambe intervened. "I want to put it on the record that I don't trust this project. The agreement with this company must contain a provision allowing us to research in parallel anything the military could immediately use from this CARLA. I'm thinking of cognitive enhancements for our soldiers. Something concrete. When the Chinese attack, throwing at them broken toys, books, and philosophical mumbo-jumbo won't do any good. Good old soldiers and better weapons will."

"We could offer the services of a contingent of our Brain-Computer Interface specialists," Sujata proposed, begging Ian with her eyes to accept, to give the belligerent general this concession.

"Fine," Ian shrugged. "I can't imagine how to make this work for your purpose, but again, I have no objections. I understand the gravity of the situation."

"Good," the secretary hit the table with his hands, signaling the end of the meeting. "Lieutenant Hopkins will be our liaison, permanently assigned to you. Lieutenant Commander Lee will be in close contact with her and will supervise the ... improvements we will do there. I promise our people will be as invisible as possible."

"Thank you," Ian said, resigned.

"I'll inform the president of our arrangement. We'll need you to report on your progress often. Gentlemen, remember that we are working against the clock. We have no clue what the MegaAI's next move will be or when. I wish you all the luck in the world. We are all God's children. May He help us create His granddaughter to be able and willing to save us all."

Sujata looked at General Kambe. His eyes were moist; a sign that he was human, after all.

CHAPTER 22:

PARADISE

Man has a thousand plans. Heaven but one.

— Chinese proverb

The grass is thick and cut almost to perfection here, Qianfan thought, sitting on a green patch in Sunset Park, which was merely a twenty-minute walk from his home. The place was just the right distance: close enough not to get tired and far enough for him to fool himself that he was exercising. He was already feeling his age in his bones. He looked at Daiyu, who was silently cutting a sandwich. With the white peaked mountains in the background, she looked like a goddess moving graciously in the Garden of Eden. Spring was bowing to summer, but up there, winter still ruled. It was relaxing not to have to wear uniforms. Not to have to worry about microphones, skin sensors, or cameras.

I almost feel good, he thought morosely. *I've been blessed in so many ways. Baozhai, Daiyu, and now this heaven. People would kill to be here.* He smiled bitterly, thinking that he had done just that. *So, this might be a heaven in which they brought killer scientists,* he told himself, desperately trying to get in a better mood.

He knew all too well what his trouble was. Lately, he had been losing sleep because of his guilt. He couldn't detach himself from the reality of the party, the MegaAI, the excruciating realization that he had helped to create the technology which led to all these arrests, tortures, and deaths. He would never feel happy again. Since he couldn't stop this mad steamroller from squashing the world, he could only hope to delay it. But so far, he had continued to fuel it and grow it. What would happen when they were ready for the big Chinese exodus? Would the MegaAI try to conquer Earth first? Would it launch all nuclear weapons in its arsenal to obliterate their planet before taking off to the stars? Was this incredible project plausible, or was it just another propaganda stunt? Where would they go? Why leave the certainty of one's home for some hypothetical planets where everybody could die in a few years, if not months? The idea made no sense.

"You're nervous again," Daiyu pointed out, looking at him carefully. "You're worrying your way to an early grave, you know?"

Qianfan smiled and tried to focus on her face lit by the sun, on the mild wind waving her hair from time to time, on the snow he could see behind her. There was no time for sulking. He had to do something. Suddenly, he felt the need to consult with her. But not here. They had seen no tracking devices since arriving in this city of the future. Still, they'd decided never to discuss their dissenting thoughts outside. Just in case. In an unexpected turn of events, their apartments were free of any tracking devices, too. For a few days in a row, while Baozhai was at school, Qianfan had gone through every square millimeter of the walls, ceiling, floor, looking in every nook and cranny of his and her apartments. They had found no microphone, SSMS devices, cameras, or any other suspicious looking gadget. They were not required to install one of the government-supplied personal assistant devices. Daiyu was so relieved. They could finally talk freely, at least among themselves.

Qianfan reached for her hand. She trembled slightly at his touch.

"Let's go back," he proposed, which meant, 'we need to talk.'

She nodded and put their food in the basket. On the way back, quiet and lost in thought, Qianfan resisted the urge to hold her hand. It wouldn't be appropriate to do so in public. Most of the people they met nodded a polite salute and kept their distance. They hadn't been able to make connections here, let alone friends. People ignored them or looked at them with some kind of respect bordering on fear, like they were part of a special, loyal party force that was better left alone. Qianfan was sure that this reaction had to do with their device. He couldn't blame them. The people who made it here must have been smart enough to be cautious about mind screening.

They entered Qianfan's apartment, and he let out a long breath.

"Freedom to speak your mind and think your thoughts is indeed one of the most basic human rights," he pointed out. "I was missing this enormously."

"I still don't understand," she looked around, uneasy, waiting for the doors to burst open and expecting a detachment of soldiers to pick them up. "Why would they not track us here?"

Qianfan mulled over this. "I've been asking myself the same thing. Perhaps they trust us now we've made it to this point. After all, the people getting here must be exceptions, although their families weren't. Perhaps they believe we cannot do much from here. We're in a fancy prison. How could we start a revolt? More likely, though, I think this is the place where everything started: MegaAI's home. They never installed sensors here, like they did all over the republic. Think about the human brain. It needs to get signals showing how our feet and our gut feel. It needs to see and hear and smell the dangers, the food. It doesn't care to know about itself, being enclosed in a protective shell made of thick bones. There are no pain sensors in the brain itself. They never evolved. Once you cut open somebody's head, you could scoop out their brain piece by piece and they wouldn't feel a thing. I guess, perhaps unknowingly, they built Mega Ark City on the same principle."

He could see that he'd impressed Daiyu with this analogy. "Make no mistake," he warned her. "We're still in grave danger. Dragon Member Zhèng said that we should speak our minds. I wouldn't do this."

"What a dangerous woman," Daiyu answered with a shiver. "Her shrilling laugh, her obsessive eyes, her change in moods. That woman could condemn a million people to death without feeling a bit of remorse."

Just then, Baozhai arrived home. As she greeted them in the hallway, Qianfan realized from her fake enthusiasm that something was wrong.

"What's going on, Baozhai? Did something happen at school?"

Baozhai hesitated, unsure if she should talk about it.

"I can come back later," Daiyu offered.

"No," Baozhai lifted her hand, "this isn't a big deal. I was just told that, as a citizen of Mega Ark City, I won't be able to take part in international math competitions."

"What?" Qianfan asked, confused.

"That means," Baozhai continued, after a moment's hesitation, "the Olympiad too."

Qianfan took a step back. He had been so satisfied about the way Baozhai was adapting here. For the first time in years, Baozhai had actually been sincerely smiling again, and not just to make him happy. She seemed to have found her place among the other nerds in school, who were mostly the progenies of top scientists, professors, engineers, doctors, and so on.

"I bet this has to do with the policy of being hard to get in and impossible to leave," Daiyu offered. "You poor thing. After all that work and achievement."

"That's alright," Baozhai bragged, trying hard not to look disappointed. "I understand that we all need to sacrifice for the Great Project."

"No, that's not alright," Qianfan said calmly, trembling slightly with fury. "I need to talk to Member Tián about this. She had promised me you'd have the best schools here. Which you do," he conceded, "although she conveniently failed to mention that you wouldn't be able to compete."

"It might not be prudent to have this argument," Daiyu said softly, bowing her head. "We are new here and we don't have friends. Knowing you," he addressed Qianfan, "I am sure you will try."

Baozhai looked at her, surprised at her candor. She understood many unspoken things about their current situation, the Great Project, and Mega Ark City.

"Baozhai, I promise I'll do everything in my power to arrange for your participation," Qianfan offered. "I may well fail, though."

The girl burst into tears and hugged him, then went to her room.

Qianfan frowned. He grabbed Daiyu's hand and pulled her into the living room.

"I can't live with myself any longer," he said, taking his head in his hands. "Knowing that I have contributed to this madness. Staying on the same path. If we succeed, and the MegaAI will make sure that we do, we'll turn millions into obedient zombies. If this God-forsaken Great Project succeeds, billions might die. We must do something."

Daiyu took his hand. "I agree. But you have Baozhai. You ... you have me. And I have you!"

Qianfan's face grew red. By now, he knew he had strong feelings for her, and she had reciprocated. Yet, they had never spoken about it. Years of watching their language, and months of hiding their very thoughts, had made such communication difficult and embarrassing.

"We need to be careful," she continued, ignoring his reaction. "We need to do small, unnoticeable things."

Qianfan shook his head, despite being overwhelmed with emotion. "Whatever we can do to sabotage the MA development won't work. It might delay them a little, at a serious risk to us. Eventually, the MegaAI will find something that works. But perhaps there's a way to turn our curse into a blessing. Well, not entirely," he hesitated. "I mean, people here are clearly afraid of being scanned by one of our devices. Or overwritten. Indeed, we could use an SSMS, concealed here in our home, to scan some of them."

Daiyu raised her brows. "And how would we do that?"

"We can invite people to dinner. Perhaps in your apartment."

"People?"

"Yes. Here we can read their minds for a change. I bet we can find out a lot if we turn the tables on them."

Daiyu nodded. The idea had merit.

"We have to think about whom we should talk to first," Qianfan said. "I have no contact with anyone, so inviting someone to dinner would look ridiculous and suspicious."

Daiyu thought about it for a while. "Perhaps we could start with Zhèng Ah Lam."

"What?" Qianfan asked, incredulous.

"You know? The Nazi lady's daughter?" Daiyu clarified.

"Please don't call her that," Qianfan winced. "It's not funny."

"She's come a few times to my office, asking if I needed anything, if I've integrated well, and so on. If I didn't know better, I'd say she wants us to become friends."

"Interesting," Qianfan muttered. "Yes, we could start with Ah Lam. There was something strange about the way she was surveilling us that day in the conference room. Either her mom put her there to assess who might be a dissident, or she wanted to see the newcomers herself. Or maybe she was just a poster child. Given her age, she was out of place."

Daiyu shrugged. "What reason can I use to invite her? That I've suddenly decided I like her?"

"I believe the timing is good. We've been here a few weeks now. Had we invited her earlier, it would have looked like we were fawning over her to reach her mother. If we were to wait longer, it would appear inappropriately late. We can say that we are eager to find out more about this fascinating project. Which is not a lie, by the way." Qianfan walked to the window and looked outside. "Baozhai just gave us another reason," he mentioned. "I can try to probe her about the chances of her leaving for the Olympiad."

Daiyu kept silent for a few seconds. "What if she reciprocates? She will probably invite us to her place. She could scan us too, somehow. Or have her mother over."

"Possibly," Qianfan admitted, "but unlikely. Of course, we need to keep our mouths closed. She'd be in our territory. The scanner will tell us if she harbors any kind of strange, secret feelings towards the party. At the minimum, given who her mother is, we might find out something interesting."

Daiyu nodded. "I know the lab where she works. Somewhere in the genetic division. I can't imagine what they are doing there. And you worry our scanners are dangerous. I have a feeling that this entire place might be the beginning of the end of our species."

"You see, perhaps we can also get something out of her about her work. We need information."

"Alright. I'll invite her to dinner at my place. I'll say that I've invited you too. To make her feel more comfortable, I can ask her to bring somebody. What about Baozhai?"

"Let's keep her out of this. I'll excuse her by saying she has homework."

Once they agreed, they parted ways with the usual kiss on the cheek. Qianfan wanted to ask her to stay longer, but he was hesitant. Even in paradise, life was complicated.

CHAPTER 23:

DAUGHTER-MOTHER

Parents raise their daughters to have nice and happy lives. They expect them to become mothers. But what if they knew their very existence, moreover, the life of everyone on Earth, depended on that special daughter of theirs? What if the parents themselves were meant to become her children? Such a thing is unnatural, abominable, strange, dangerous. Faced with this prospect, can you blame the parents for worrying too much about their daughter's education?

— DeSousa's Memoirs - Part II - Creation - 2054

Seeing her struggle to utter some words, and messing them up, just like a toddler, François thought that CARLA's language acquisition and production went better and faster than he'd expected. From what he could see in the logs, not only had they been able to build language support upon a solid conceptual system, but language acquisition itself had started influencing the way CARLA was thinking. It was as if learning to speak had sharpened her mind too, an effect proven to happen in people, yet never achieved in a machine before.

"At this rate, she'll be ready for a spelling bee contest in half a year," Ian remarked, happy. "Look at how beautiful connections form from a word to tens of concepts, all mapping solidly to a concrete aspect of reality. This is marvelous. And unprecedented."

François nodded. The three of them were outside, near one of the CogniPrescience buildings, supervised remotely, as always, by a large contingent of researchers logging, tweaking, and analyzing everything. Reports were pouring into a dedicated room in their private Cybersperse, inaccessible to CARLA. They purposely minimized the number of people who interacted with her.

Lately, it had become apparent to François that this was her favorite spot: a patch of flowers in the middle of the grass. It was the biggest one in the area, far from all the buildings and sidewalk. Nobody in CogniPrescience would consider walking there, out of fear of crushing the flowers under their feet. Not CARLA. They spoiled her. She was curious. She had her simulated moods, just like a toddler. The moment she stepped outside, she dashed to her patch of flowers, walking gingerly around them, sitting among them, touching them gently, admiring them. Ian kept on teaching her something whenever he was around her. This time, he had brought the usual assortment of trinkets and toys and seemed determined to use them for various experiments.

François felt like he'd lost a bit of his drive for this project since the meeting with the DoD people. Not so long ago, sitting in the hospital, he thought he wouldn't mind if the world was ending. He might have considered harming it himself. Now he wished hard that humankind would endure. He felt ashamed he had harbored such thoughts. Marie could go to hell, as far as he was concerned. But he and Ian now had a noble purpose.

Why did this have to get mixed up with politics and wars? Every time he saw one of those pesky soldiers or officers, he felt mad and had to work hard to calm himself down. He admired how well Ian had adapted to this blatant intrusion. Admittedly, the newcomers were trying their best to stay out of the way, although it was hard not to get annoyed when seeing them everywhere. They had arrived in droves a couple of months before. The first thing they did was to take down and rebuild the fences. A contractor cleaned up the shrubs and a few trees in a five-acre area at the back of the property after receiving Ian's begrudging approval. They pushed the fence separating their complex from the wilderness further uphill. Construction was underway for three additional buildings, which were supposed to be up and running in just a few weeks. Temporary barracks were already functional. The contractors installed new backup power sources in several places. They dug tunnels to the east, up in the bare hills, beyond the company perimeter. François imagined they could use them for defensive means, weapons, perhaps missile launchers.

And the real trouble hadn't even come yet: the additional researchers. The last thing François needed was more entitled opinions and suggestions, slowing down and confusing everything. The existing CogniPrescience team worked like a well-oiled machine. François had commended them repeatedly about it. There were hardly any personality clashes, arguments about the next steps, or fights in the cafeteria. Everybody had their place. Ian had pointed out that this was a consequence of people sticking to the same job for a decade or two. A job they all loved. And one that now they perceived as dangerous. Still, nobody left. They didn't want to abandon CARLA. François expected the new people to be, well, new. They were supposed to answer to Ian, but they were not his employees.

Shaking his head, François focused back on the android, who was pushing the grass down in an unnatural way, as if she were trying to send it back into the ground. What could be happening in her head? Behind the scenes, there were millions of bits of information forming, although the actual commonsense knowledge structures, all that she'd memorized in her short life, the stuff about her body, about the environment, all required relatively little memory.

"How big will her *brain* ultimately be?" he wondered aloud. "Doesn't it strike you as strange how little cogent information has formed in her mind so far, considering everything she knows and does? I expected that an AI at her developmental stage, given how well she interacts with the world, would require several supercomputers and terabytes of data."

"Marvin Minsky, considered one of the fathers of AI," Ian answered, "suggested at some point that all information a person knows, including commonsense knowledge, the things that a person learns in a lifetime might fit into 1 CD-ROM of his time, the equivalent of 650 MB. He concluded this by calculating the number of words a person knows, the average meanings per word, and the relationships between them. Things like inheritance, association, containment, similarity, etc. Surely, calculating the size of a mind isn't as simple as that, but perhaps there's some core truth in his words."

"Each of us has eighty-six billion neurons and one hundred trillion connections between them. What are they for?"

"They're not there purely for information storage. Some are vestiges of the past, others take care of the good functioning of the body, others are redundant, and so on. It's obvious we've already managed some optimization of CARLA's information storage just by organizing it properly."

"Does this make her more vulnerable if something goes wrong?"

"It does," Ian conceded. "Any loss of her structures would be akin to a stroke in humans. Unlike humans, though, we have backups. We'd be able to restore her fast."

François shook his head. He was acting again like a parent towards CARLA. Loving, concerned, and ready to move mountains for her to succeed. *What would Marie think if she saw me now?* he pondered. *The ever irresponsible, self-centered, conceited brat, now a father of sorts.* Then he got mad at himself. *Mon Dieu, why do I care what she would think?*

He hated himself for not being able to resist coding bits of Marie's personality into CARLA. It was like Marie's ghost continued to pull him by any means possible, making him obsess over her. With a sudden move betraying his frustration, he turned towards the building, just in time to see Sujata approaching. She was everywhere these days. François wanted to hate her, but deep down, he realized she wasn't that bad. So far, she was the only outsider who interacted a little with CARLA, and the android seemed to have accepted her. At some point, he thought that CARLA's eyes showed curiosity, perhaps a bit of concern, whenever she saw Sujata. He didn't linger on it, assuming that he was imagining things, as always. CARLA wasn't that smart just yet to understand the agitation surrounding her.

"Water," CARLA said suddenly, pointing towards a small plastic recipient on the ground.

"That's right," Ian answered encouragingly. "There's water in that bottle."

"Flows," CARLA said, eyes big.

"Yes, it does!" Ian grew enthusiastic. "What else flows?"

"Sand flows," CARLA answered.

Sujata moved closer to François, still far away, so that CARLA wouldn't notice her. She didn't want to interfere with the lesson.

"Amazing," Sujata whispered. "She's talking to you guys. Not only does she reason and answer questions, but the very fact that she bothers interacting with you is impressive. I can't believe you have achieved this."

"Can you show me how water flows?" Ian asked CARLA.

CARLA hesitated a bit, then reached towards the bottle.

"No, without the bottle." Ian took the bottle away and put it on the ground. "Show me with your hands. How does it flow?"

CARLA stared at her hands for a short while. She lifted them, one higher than the other, and started moving them down to one side, like they would go down a hill.

"Excellent, CARLA," Ian applauded. "That's exactly how it flows, from top to bottom. Gravity makes it flow."

"Gravity," CARLA repeated.

Ian lifted a tennis ball up and let it bounce on the ground a few times.

"Gravity," CARLA repeated softly, watching the ball. "I ... know ... gravity. It pulls things down."

Suddenly, a light flashed far to the east. In a strange spasm, CARLA kicked the water bottle in front of her, which flew through the air. Sujata caught it out of a reflex. CARLA followed the bottle's trajectory with her eyes, and frowned when she saw that Sujata had it, then froze and bowed her head, like she was giving up. Her eyes went empty, and her face muscles relaxed, both signs she was going offline.

"The power generator!" François yelled. "Did it explode?"

Ian stood up and looked in the general direction of the flash. One researcher monitoring CARLA's logs yelled in their private chat that some of her data had been corrupted. After fiddling for a minute with some controls, Ian turned her back on. She immediately frowned and lifted her head, looking in François's direction. Noticing her savage stare, he took one step back. CARLA switched her gaze to the water bottle, now nearly empty in Sujata's hands.

"Mine. It's mine. Waaaattter … Flowers. Mine. Waaaattter. Mine," she screamed in her own awkward, low-volume way.

"Yes, this is your patch of flowers. I'll bring you another bottle of water," Ian said, trying to calm her down, but to no avail.

"Who? Bad," she continued yelling, pointing towards Sujata with her finger. "No good to me!"

Sujata froze, failing to understand what was going on.

"She thinks that Sujata took her water. Turn her off," François yelled. He panicked, for the tenth time, that he might have built into her, somehow, too much of Marie's exasperating moods, although he understood how absurd this thought was at that early stage of development.

In a few moments, CARLA made a couple of threatening steps toward Sujata, like she was planning to attack her. Sujata threw the bottle gently in her direction and lifted her empty hands up, in an appeasing gesture. Seeing that CARLA wouldn't stop, her instinct and years of training kicked in, so she took a defensive position, not sure how to proceed next.

"Why? How? You!" CARLA talked quickly, making no sense. "Go away!" and she raised her arms.

Ian rushed to put her to sleep from his tablet. She closed her eyes and returned to a rest position with her arms down and a calm face.

"Well, this was creepy," Sujata said, relaxed.

François whistled impressed at how cool she'd remained throughout this episode. After some moments of chaos, one engineer intervened to explain the explosion.

"They tried switching us to the new, supposedly more secure power source, and something went wrong. We lost a few computing blades that contained some of CARLA's software."

"*Incroyable*," François exclaimed, examining the data. "We were just talking a minute ago about how vulnerable she was to such losses."

Ian acknowledged this with a grunt.

"I'm sorry about this," Sujata pointed out again, remarkably calm. "I'll find out what happened."

"Not your fault," Ian dismissed her apology. "Let them finish the repairs. François and I will try to understand what happened with CARLA."

François and Ian remained immersed in the logs for another hour while Sujata went to talk with the technicians. When she came back, François explained what had happened.

"CARLA has lost parts of her memory. The loss was minimal, and it cannot explain her behavior. She went into emotional overdrive, again. This time, her conceptual framework got messed up. Right after the explosion, she felt some kind of fear. When she came back online, she couldn't find her bottle and saw Sujata as an intruder. Her feelings started conflicting. It was a battle between her simulated emotions. Eventually, rage took over and madness. She *was* ready to attack us. Or, at least, Sujata."

"We have backups," Ian said, shaken. "Until the explosion."

"That's not the point," François stomped his foot, although he was sure Ian understood the situation very well. "CARLA is unacceptably fragile. Her cognitive and emotional framework crumbles at the slightest sign of a problem. She acts like a child used to getting her own way, and becoming hysterical when her whims cannot be satisfied. Next time she could do real damage. She could harm us. How is she supposed to become super-intelligent?"

Ian nodded and added, without his usual smile. "You might be right. CARLA behaved like she didn't recognize Sujata. Like Sujata were a threat. This was such a strange behavior, seeing as she only lost a tiny portion of her connections. She had a sudden tantrum, just because she didn't like something. We can build redundancy to account for memory losses, but we have a major problem if she's not ... emotionally stable. Why would she be? Evolution took millions of years to fix us, yet most of us are still an emotional mess. After all, we're rushing to create life anew in merely a few years. We need to change something."

"Well, what? We're surrounding her with love. We're spoiling her," François pointed out, frustrated.

"That might be part of the problem," Ian raised his finger. "We don't have a proper reward/punishment system in place. We need to think about how we could punish her so that she still loves us."

"Love makes you blind," Sujata said softly.

"What?" asked François.

"My mom used to tell my father, who always refused to punish me, that his love for me blinded him. And that was ultimately going to harm me. They would argue about this for hours. My father believed that explaining everything to the child is the way to go. He believed in openness and rewards. Not in punishment."

"And look at you now. You didn't turn out too bad," François pointed out, victoriously. "Punishing children is cruel."

"We're not talking about physically abusing her," Ian clarified. "We could, say, forbid her to go out after an episode when she's naughty."

"I don't know," Sujata shrugged. "She might take this the wrong way and generalize that she must punish humans whenever they do something wrong. And we do something *wrong* all the time, after all. By the way, would she be capable of choosing the appropriate penalty for different crimes? A mass murderer shouldn't get away with a small fine, just like someone who crosses on red shouldn't be executed."

"She wouldn't know how to judge this," François agreed. "We are far from such nuances."

"On the other hand," Sujata reasoned further, "it might be time to impose some rules for her. Some of the worst people on Earth are rich children who grew up without proper supervision. We don't want CARLA to become vain, self-centered, and mean."

"Yeah, perhaps we need a balance. Somebody to compensate for all the lenience François and I show to her," Ian insisted.

"You guys are crazy," François couldn't believe his ears. "We can barely stabilize her circuitry, and now you want to punish her?"

"She needs a mother figure," Ian ignored him, looking straight at Sujata.

"Yes!" she agreed. "Indeed, it might be good for her to grow up with a woman around, too. It would ..." she stopped, seeing that both were staring at her. "Oh, no, wait just a fraction of a minute here. I know for a fact that I am *not* that person!"

"Why not?" asked Ian, amused. "You're a woman, though not a mother yet."

"I have chills just thinking about raising a normal child, let alone an artificial one, with so many unknowns."

"You're a soldier," Ian teased her further. "Didn't you guys want to make a fighter out of CARLA?"

"Yes. But the military doesn't recruit toddlers," Sujata replied.

Ian laughed and stopped insisting. Sujata started pacing around. François looked at her as if he were seeing her for the first time.

She's gorgeous, he mused. *How come I never noticed this before? Would I have a chance? Could she be the mother of my children?* Lost in thought, he realized the futility of the question. *Zut ... I'm such an imbecile. I could never be with any other woman. Bon sang, Marie! Damn you to all eternity. Besides, I am now a father. Who would want me with such baggage?* He laughed bitterly and realized the others were looking at him strangely, as if he'd got a joke a minute too late. "Ignore me," François raised his arms. "By all means, find a mother for CARLA. Clearly, two fathers and a few scores of scientists turned nannies are not enough," he continued sarcastically.

"We need a child psychologist," Sujata said. "One that specializes in AI sentience. A combination that most likely doesn't exist, given the number of artificial lifeforms we have around us, which is nil. I can tell you that none of the DoD researchers who are about to arrive here qualify. I looked at all their profiles."

"Neither do our researchers, including those from our ethics team. Now that you mentioned it, it's silly we didn't think about it."

Sujata hesitated. "I know someone who might help. One of my high school colleagues works somewhere around here. They do research related to psychology. It's a long shot. Anyway, while I launch a full search for a qualified mother/AI specialist with all DoD's contractors, let me do some inquiries." She stopped in her tracks and muttered, "Although I don't look forward to it."

Ian raised his brows.

"We ... dated for a while. A fiasco," she clarified.

"You never finished your story," François said softly.

"Story?" she asked, confused.

"The one about your parents playing good-cop, bad-cop. Which one do you love most?"

Sujata took a long breath. "I always loved my mother, even when she punished me. But I adored my father."

François nodded. He expected as much. He glanced at CARLA. She looked asleep, serene, innocent. Was she truly capable of harming anybody?

CHAPTER 24:

DINNER

An accidental meeting is more pleasant than a planned one.

— Chinese proverb

Sitting on the only sofa in Daiyu's apartment, Qianfan felt overwhelmed by guilt again. Nothing and no one could give him relief. Self-delusion didn't work anymore. No matter how many times he had told himself that he hadn't had a choice, deep down he knew he had. He could have sacrificed himself. If so, yeah, Baozhai would have grown up without parents. But was it better for her to grow up with a father who was the key scientist who created the SSMS? And, in a couple of months, the one who contributed to the creation of the Mood Alterer? What next scourge would they assign to him? The invention of a biological weapon to wipe out all intelligent life on Earth? Where would they draw the line? Where would *he* draw the line?

"Darling, you are nervous." Daiyu touched his hand. "Remember that our guests will arrive any moment now. Do you want them to see you so worried? So vulnerable?"

Qianfan nodded. It was getting harder and harder to come back out of the mire of his thoughts. Ah Lam had announced her presence with a man, Senior Colonel Wáng Hu from the Special Ark Force, or SAF. It was some sort of unique military division for the best of the best. When he found out about it, Qianfan couldn't help but think about the famous paramilitary organization in Germany during World War II, the Schutzstaffel, or SS. It was amazing how much China looked like the old National-Socialist nightmare of the beginning of the 20th century.

Neither he nor Daiyu knew this senior colonel. They were both surprised to hear that he was in his early forties. He must have had quite a career. His relationship with Ah Lam wasn't too clear, either. They were neither married nor engaged, but they were often seen together. That's all Daiyu could get from some scientist at the lab where Ah Lam worked. Gossip wasn't exactly popular in Mega Ark City.

The presence of Senior Colonel Wáng was worrisome. He might be there to scan them every bit as much as he and Daiyu planned to scan their guests. And, considering his training, he might do it better than their device could. The question was also why Ah Lam felt the need to bring him along. Certainly, this wasn't only about showing up with an extra person.

"At least she didn't announce that she'd come with the Nazi ... sorry, with Dragon Member Zhèng," Daiyu had consoled him when relating the news.

"She would have been a known quantity." Qianfan had shaken his head.

Finally, the pleasant ring of the door interrupted his thoughts. Daiyu jumped to welcome their guests. Qianfan stood up and took a worried look under the table. It was impossible to see the scanners there. He and Daiyu had masked them inside the wood and had set them to transmit their findings to a computer installed in the next room. There was virtually no way anyone would detect them.

"Welcome," Daiyu offered, with a bow. "Please, come in. My home is your home."

Hu nodded a salute, which Qianfan reciprocated in the same grave style, with an unintelligible mumble. The senior colonel had a strange spark in his eyes, which Qianfan, already primed by his early analogy, associated with the fanaticism Hitler's assistants had. Ah Lam looked relaxed, her eyes moving fast around the walls and ceiling as if she were preparing for a paint job. Paranoid as always, Qianfan thought she was inspecting the places where they might have installed a scanning device.

"I like what you did to this place," she complimented Daiyu, seeing the traditional Chinese decorations on the walls. "These one-person apartments are small. We all make them our own, don't we?"

Daiyu nodded, pleasantly surprised at how open Ah Lam was. "I cooked some traditional-style Peking duck," she announced. "It was hard to mimic a hung oven here in the apartment. I hope it turned out well. I will serve it to you the way my mother used to. We'll have the skin, then the meat, and a broth made of bones. I prepared bean sauce and rice pancakes. I must warn you, though, that my cooking skills are not exactly my forte."

They sat at the table and ate, mostly in silence.

"Doctor Wu, this has got to be the most delicious Peking duck I ever had in my life," Ah Lam said, seeming genuinely pleased and surprised.

"I'm proud that you liked it," Daiyu answered, bowing her head slightly.

"Indeed," the senior colonel nodded. "And you said that cooking was not your specialty."

"As you know," Ah Lam continued, "we don't have traditional restaurants here. Luckily, the families of scientists relocated here can take care of such auxiliary activities, although they are not professional. Very few are good at that."

"Your mother mentioned you were born here. Do you go out often?" Daiyu asked a direct question, which made Qianfan look at her, surprised.

"No. I've never been outside of Mega Ark City. For a long while, I wanted to, but now I've given up that idea."

"How's that possible?" Qianfan asked, curious.

"Mother wasn't joking when she said that it's impossible to leave," Ah Lam smiled. "They make exceptions from time to time, only for special cases. They never did for me," she laughed bitterly.

"My daughter, Baozhai, is ... exceptionally skilled at math," Qianfan said, in a slightly trembling voice. "She was supposed to go to the International Mathematical Olympiad this year, in Russia. The school informed her this week that, as a citizen of Mega Ark City, she cannot go. Do you think a math competition would be a good reason to leave?"

Ah Lam thought for a few seconds. "I don't know," she answered with a shrug. "I remember we had someone leave eons ago for a genetics competition."

"You might be right," the senior colonel confirmed.

"You've got to understand, the party doesn't see any reason to show off our talents to the world. This would do nothing for the Great Project. That is priority number one here."

"It would mean a great deal to my daughter. She's been depressed since ... since forever. I thought coming here was going to cheer her up, make her fit in society. Which it did! And now, this interdiction ... It's not fair to her."

Ah Lam nodded. She exchanged a glance with Hu. "I'll speak to Mother. I make no promises. She and I are not on the same page."

"Thank you," Qianfan nodded, surprised to hear that confession. "We don't have many ... well, I could say, any friends here. Since we came, people seem to avoid us."

"No surprise there," the senior colonel laughed openly and unexpectedly, in contrast to the attitude he had shown so far. "What did you expect? You are the creators of the famous SSMS. Such scanning hasn't happened in Mega Ark City yet, mostly because the leaders trust the people who made it here. And imports to the city are always about the Great Project. Nobody bothered with the SSMS. Now that you are here, people understand that you probably brought your scanners with you. Not to mention the MAs."

"Why would people fear the SSMS?" Daiyu asked, feigning innocence. "Surely, they are loyal here. Is it just fear of the unknown?"

The senior colonel leaned back and seemed to relax. Qianfan got the nagging feeling that something strange was about to happen.

"Oh, but loyalty is such a controversial topic," Hu smiled. "Doctor Zhào, I bet you are loyal to your daughter."

Qianfan squirmed a bit, not liking where this was going.

"You are also loyal to the party, given your incredible contribution. By extension, you are loyal to the Great Project, since that has become the sole most important goal of the party. So, it appears that your two loyalties are at odds. One must take precedence. Which one is it?"

Suddenly, the room filled with the tension of an interrogation.

And just like that, they turned the tables on us. Instead of us scanning them, they scan us, Qianfan thought. "In this case," he said slowly, but firmly, "the rules imposed to complete the Great Project will, of course, have to take precedence over my daughter's desire to compete."

"Ah, you said, 'in this case,'" Hu continued relentlessly. "Is there some other case where you would sacrifice the Great Project for your daughter?" The colonel leaned forward, then raised his arms defensively. "Hypothetically speaking!"

"I don't know," Qianfan answered, his mouth a bit crooked.

"You see!" the colonel said, victoriously. "The dissidents argue that they are loyal to China, or the whole world. Not to the party, not to President Yun Li. There have been quite a few of those, you know. Once your device exposes their feelings, there are some who won't deny their thoughts. Out of defiance, or stubbornness, I guess."

Qianfan lowered his gaze. He instinctively recited *The Iliad*, only to realize the futility of it. There was no device scanning him. Besides, there were moments when he just didn't have the strength to pretend anymore.

"One aspect of our training as SAF officers is precisely to spot these feelings. This happened long before you perfected your device."

Daiyu looked at him in fear. This discussion was going south, fast.

"For example, I can see from a million miles away that you are uncomfortable with the role you played in arresting these people. I read your file. I am familiar with all that surrounds you. With some of your thoughts. In some respects, I know more about you than you know yourself. I figured you found a way to fool the device. Kudos to you, by the way. To me, this is an achievement more impressive than the creation of the scanner itself."

Qianfan tensed, ready to jump at the other man's throat. He understood now that Ah Lam had manipulated Daiyu to become close to her. Daiyu's invitation to dinner was a gift to these people, who were ready to walk all over them. Why hadn't they done it already? Why the need to torture them like this? Why give them the illusion of freedom? *So, the moment of truth has come. Better this way,* he thought, *I just hope Baozhai will be alright. Daiyu will look after her if she makes it.*

"And you, Doctor Wu," the colonel continued mercilessly. "I imagine Doctor Zhào has taught you how to deal with the scanner, too. I understand it's not a precise science, but whatever you did worked well enough. I read your dossier too. I know, for example, that you were friends with Zhou Junfeng and Li Xin, two of the people who were arrested soon after the party started scanning the general population."

The colonel took a break as if to assess the effect of his assault. Ah Lam looked at them, almost amused. Qianfan trembled a bit, wondering how a harmless, nice dinner had turned into this avalanche of accusations and disclosures. He glanced at Daiyu. She looked ready to cry, but more out of defiance than desperation. She couldn't deny that she knew the two friends mentioned.

"Now you may wonder how come, after everything I know about you, you are not in prison," the colonel whispered. "Once somebody proposed to include you in the Great Project, you have been subject to an extensive review and background checking. I oversaw it." The colonel looked from one to the other, as if he wanted to ensure that they understood what he was saying. "Am I not clear enough? The party accepted you here because of Ah

Lam and me. We ... erased some of the genuine concerns from your files. We knew that if we got you here, you could help our cause."

Qianfan looked up, surprised.

"Your ... cause?" Daiyu asked, confused.

"Our loyalty is not with President Yun Li," Ah Lam intervened. "It is with China, and the rest of the world. The Great Project is a fantastic goal. It should be a global effort. Not one country, not one party, not one president."

"And, by the way," Hu announced, scrutinizing them to see their reaction, "this might come as a shock to you, but President Yun Li is not real."

This time Daiyu jumped up, knocking back her chair. They knew! Was this some sick joke? Was it a trap?

"Our beloved president is just an avatar," Ah Lam clarified. "It's the MegaAI that rules the party now. Very few people are privy to this information. Even fewer are doing something about it. The rest are too scared, too greedy, or too naïve. They don't understand the danger. We do. The way my mother brought me up makes me understand this in full."

Qianfan was now sweating hard. Too much information was coming at them at once. For the first time in years, he felt a ray of hope. "How many ... who else?" he stammered.

"Not enough," the colonel shook his head. "Best that you don't know who they are. You cannot tell anyone about what you are hearing now."

"Especially not Mother!" Ah Lam warned them. "The party ideals brainwashed her long ago. Don't be fooled by her apparent joyful nature. She is committed to the Great Project like no one else. When hearing Hu's earlier example about split loyalties, I thought about her. My mother would not hesitate to throw me in jail, or worse, if she knew what we were talking about at this very moment. She had no qualms about removing her father from the Great Project when he started expressing some concerns about giving too much power to the MegaAI. For a long while, I tried reasoning with her. I know for a fact that nothing will sway her views. So now I play along, pretending to agree with her."

Hearing these words, Qianfan felt his guilt diminish somewhat. He didn't envy this young woman. He exchanged a quick look with Daiyu. Suddenly, their plans to scan their guests looked ridiculous.

"The fact that the MegaAI leads the party doesn't come as a surprise to you," the colonel pointed out, observing them.

"We ... know about Professor Zhèng Yang's message," Daiyu pointed out, trying to recover from the shock of her guests' confession.

"How wonderful," Ah Lam clapped her hands. "He went out in style, didn't he? What a way to give them the finger. Subtle enough so that nobody can be sure that he said what he said. I guess this kind of duplicitous thinking runs in the family."

Qianfan and Daiyu looked at her, confused.

"Oh, you didn't know? I thought you would have made the connection by now. Professor Zhèng Yang was my maternal grandfather," Ah Lam clarified with a large grin.

CHAPTER 25:

SYNCHRONICITY

Coincidence is God's way of remaining anonymous.

— Albert Einstein

T*his scene reminds me more of a factory workshop than of a workplace for highly educated psychologists,* Sujata mused, stepping into the large hall that was painted in strong, metallized colors with shades of gray and bronze all over the walls.

She noticed pieces of metal of various shapes, which could have been waste material from some obsolete manufacturing process. Tall and round worktables were spread around chaotically, where a few dozen people were gesturing and staring at their tablets. The walls were jammed with small, private cabins that reminded her of the old phone booths from movies. From time to time, one worker would touch their ear and jump from their table into a cabin, presumably for a Cybersperse call.

Ugly place. I'll never understand art. She shrugged, shifting her mind to the reason she came here.

"Good Lord, Sujata Hopkins, as I live and breathe," a man approached her beaming and talking sufficiently loudly that a few people nearby stopped whatever they were doing and lifted their heads. "You look exquisite! I think I'm falling back in love."

Sujata noticed how his eyes were trying to peek under her uniform, gliding on her hands for a moment to look for the wrong ring, all the while estimating her waist size, breast circumference, and height.

"Aaron, good to see you too," she answered, rolling her eyes as conspicuously as she could. There was no need to pretend with this guy. Though he was quite smart, his brain lived mostly in his pants. His sole reason for being alive seemed to be to conquer woman after woman. Sujata thought he wasted his mind and talent on this continuous pursuit. *I can't believe I dated him for three full months,* she thought, appalled.

He moved closer, ready to fly around her like a bee around the queen.

"Aaron, before you go on, don't," she stopped and raised a hand. "Just don't. You and I will not sleep together ever again. I haven't come here to rekindle our relationship. I'm here on business."

The man's face fell, but he pretended to remain in good spirits. "You know me too well, eh?" he smiled. "Can't blame a man for trying!" He sighed, inviting her to walk to the end of the hall, where a short corridor took them to a few actual offices, probably for management. "What can I do for you, then? I promise to help you. No strings attached," Aaron said, closing the door and pointing to a chair.

Sujata sat down and looked at him semi-mockingly. She wasn't about to fall for this obliging stratagem, either. "I'm looking to hire somebody with unusual qualifications. Something at the intersection between Child Development and Sentience Psychology. Preferably a woman."

Aaron let a little whistle out. "Has the all-powerful DoD run out of people?" he pretended to be shocked. Seeing her steely face, he understood she didn't appreciate his tone. "Oh, you're no fun at all," he complained. "What you are looking for doesn't exist. I probably know of a dozen people who specialize in the so-called Sentience Psychology, a useless and pompous qualification. Based on what exams did these people get degrees? How did they practice their skills? Where do they apply them? This thing might make sense in another couple of hundred years, if machines will achieve that by then."

Sujata nodded. He was right. This was a waste of time.

"Off the top of my head," Aaron continued, "I don't think we have researchers here with that degree. We couldn't use them for anything. But we have plenty who specialize in Child Development. I can arrange for some interviews ..."

"Yeah, that might not be sufficient," Sujata said, standing up. "I guess there's no point in wasting more of your time."

Aaron's face betrayed his disappointment once again. "I'm sorry. I wish I could be of some help," he said.

As Sujata opened the office door, she looked towards a tiny corner of the depressing hall visible from that angle, where she could see only two tables. There, she saw her. The resemblance was just uncanny. Sheer luck made it so that she was at one of those tables, facing her, rather than the entrance. Out of all the workers, she had picked that place. And she happened to be working at the table, rather than in a booth, at that exact moment. Sujata took one step back as all these thoughts rushed through her head.

"Who ... who is she?" she asked, pointing her finger forward.

Aaron followed her pointing, confused. "Who?"

"The woman with long blond hair?" Sujata asked impatiently.

"Oh, she's one of our employees. She's been with us for about a year and a half. I don't recall exactly. Strange girl, if you'll allow me an opinion."

"Aaron, for you, any woman who does not sleep with you two days after you meet is weird." Sujata shook her head. "Where is she from?"

"I don't recall. Somewhere in France."

"I want to talk to her," Sujata said, determined.

"What in the blazes for?" he asked, bewildered. Seeing her sharp eyes, he pulled back. "She's one of our least qualified people for what you want.

She is a workaholic, I grant you. That's why she's still with us. But she is introverted, never comes to any party, hardly talks to anyone here. People avoid her. I assume she doesn't have a personal life."

"I still want to talk to her. Please," Sujata insisted, looking straight at him.

"Fine, whatever. You're weird. Let me get her in."

As he walked out towards the girl, Sujata moved back in. She sat in Aaron's chair. *Can this really be her?* she asked herself, in shock.

"Lieutenant Sujata Hopkins, I give you Marie Chateau," Aaron chirped.

"Hello," Marie said simply.

"Pleased to meet you," Sujata stood and shook her hand.

Marie's countenance took Sujata aback. She had seen this kind of emptiness only in people returning from combat, usually those with PTSD. This woman clearly suffered from severe depression.

"Thank you, Aaron," Sujata said, looking straight at him.

"You're welcome," he answered, not taking the hint. He seemed happy to have her around for a little longer and was somewhat curious to hear why she had taken an interest in Marie.

"I'll take it from here, if you don't mind." Sujata made it clearer.

"Oh, you want to talk alone," he blurted, as he stood. "Sure, sure, let me know if I can help. I'll ... be somewhere, out of my office ... It's not like I have work or something. I can just hang around while two beautiful women take over my space."

Sujata smiled and turned to Marie. It was like talking to a version of CARLA that was thinner, much thinner, and slightly more mature, with a different hair. And, mostly, much sadder.

"Please sit down. Aaron tells me you are from France."

"Yes, I was born and raised in France. Côte d'Azur."

Sujata nodded. "I think that we ... we might have a mutual acquaintance."

Marie looked at her with her blank eyes. She didn't seem to care about anything.

"Do you know someone named François DeSousa? He also grew up in—"

"Do you know François?" Marie jumped up, finally finding some fire in her. "Where is he? I need to talk to him!"

Sujata's eyes grew bigger. She hadn't expected this reaction. Immediately after, though, Marie fell back in her chair, deflated. "Did he put you up to this?" she asked, weary, as if this spark had depleted her of all her energy reserves. "Is he showing off his gorgeous girlfriend and gloating?"

Sujata smiled. She was dealing with another child. "From what I know of François, I wouldn't put it behind him to come up with something like that," she laughed, trying to defuse the situation. "Although I'd need to be his girlfriend. Besides, such a nasty plan would require my cooperation, and I don't believe I would ever agree to it." She grew serious. "But no. I can assure you François and I are not in a romantic relationship."

"Then how did you figure out I know him?" Marie asked, narrowing her eyes. "Is he in some kind of trouble?"

She loves him, Sujata concluded, seeing the turmoil Marie was going through. *Very much.*

"No, he's not in trouble. We're just working together on a project."

"François works with the military?" she asked, still suspicious, pointing to her uniform.

"Yes," Sujata confirmed. "And I cannot say more than that."

Marie sat quietly, waiting for her to continue.

Did I just open a can of worms? Sujata wondered. *Is it going to help if CARLA's mother figure would be this unstable woman with whom François has a complicated history? Am I getting involved in something that is not my business?* She frowned at the stupidity of her concern. Obviously, she was sticking her nose in where it didn't belong. This time it wasn't just about her image, or François, or this girl. It was about developing an AI, quickly. She had to think fast now that she'd spilled the beans.

François is bound to have a fit if I bring Marie over. If he won't accept her as a working partner, he might jeopardize the whole project by not cooperating. And if he does, CARLA might grow up with 'parents' fighting all the time, just like they would if they were on the brink of a divorce. On the positive side, though unbeknownst to Marie, CARLA already shares with her physical and at least some psychological traits. Who else would best fit the role of a mother? Still, how would this lead to CARLA becoming powerful enough to fight the MegaAI?

Questions rushed through her head, with no answers. She looked at the broken woman in front of her. "I know this is not my business, and I ask your forgiveness for prying. Can you tell me why you need to talk to him?"

Marie's eyes got moist. "I want to ask him to ... forgive me." Then, looking straight at Sujata, she added quickly, "For something I haven't done."

Sujata lifted a corner of her mouth. This answer was as clear as fog.

"But I thought about doing it! I thought I'd found somebody who loved me and whom I loved. If that is my fault, then I am guilty," Marie launched into a confusing explanation, bursting into tears. "I am also guilty of toying with his feelings. Deep down, I must have known he loved me. I took that for granted, yet I unconsciously ignored it. I guess I enjoyed his attention, his drive to be near me."

Marie wiped her eyes. "I think François was about to propose when he found out about that other man. He had a ridiculous toy ring with him. I have carried it with me ever since. I want to tell him I will accept if he is still interested. I know he is not," she whispered while her face sagged.

Sujata felt overwhelmed by this story and fought to stay detached.

"Somehow, I trained myself to consider François anything but a potential boyfriend," Marie continued. "We grew up together. We had a brief ... moment when we were in high school. Since then, I have considered him as my brother. I didn't want to hurt his sister ... It's a long story. So, I hurt him badly instead. He nearly killed himself. He ran away. I ... I cannot live with this."

"I know about his suicide attempt," Sujata said, softly, deciding not to dwell on the story about the sister. Still not completely sure how to proceed, she continued. "Well, because of your connection with François, you might be able to help us. François works on something very important. Crucial. We need to speed it up. Though I honestly don't know if mixing you up in this will help anyone."

"It would help me," Marie answered, wiping her tears. "I moved to LA to find him, to beg him to forgive me."

"Be that as it may, this project is way more important than the two of you. Trust me when I say that."

"I will do whatever is necessary to help you," Maria jumped off her chair. "Anything to be near François."

"I do not question your commitment," Sujata nodded. "I warn you, though. He might not agree to see you."

"Give me a chance!" Marie begged.

Sujata looked at her for half a minute before answering. "I make no promises. If François doesn't want to see you, you won't hear from us again."

Marie nodded. "All I can do is arrange for the two of you to meet."

She reached for a piece of paper on the desk and wrote down an address. "Be at this restaurant at 7:00 p.m. tomorrow."

Marie took the paper as if it were the elixir of life. "Thank you!"

Sujata nodded. She knew she had either just made a grave mistake or helped this project significantly.

CHAPTER 26:

FLOOD

Don't lie down in low places, flood will take you, don't lie down in high places, wind will take you.

— Chinese proverb

Not to arouse too much suspicion, Senior Colonel Wáng proposed that the four of them meet once a week only and rotate through each of their apartments. They agreed to have their second meeting at Ah Lam's place, so that people could easily interpret it as reciprocating the dinner from the week before. He warned them again to be extra careful.

Walking alongside Daiyu on the surreal streets of their immaculate city, Qianfan thought about the MegaAI. He knew it was just a matter of time before it made sense of the myriad of connections and activations that were going on in the brain during the process of decision making. It would come up with new algorithms and tests to progress the party goals to tweak the minds and break the will of whoever was brave enough to think impure thoughts. He knew that stalling the MA development was close to impossible. The only somewhat positive aspect of the project was that Mega Ark City didn't have a prison or a group of human subjects on whom to test the device. His team needed to ship the prototypes somewhere and couldn't conduct the experiments themselves. They had to wait for the results, interpret them, and sometimes ask for repeating the tests. Therefore, the party could not expect him to finish the whole development quickly.

That is, unless they discover the rats who sneaked in on the ark and move them to the lab. He smiled resentfully. *Then the party could try their mind-writing device right on its creators.*

Ah Lam welcomed them with the same childish, jovial attitude, clapping her hands. Qianfan thought she'd inherited this kind of weird enthusiasm from her mother. He hoped that was where the similarities ended. With a quick headshake, he focused on what their host said.

"Unlike Doctor Wu, my culinary expertise is nil, so I ordered some fried rice and tamarind tofu. I hope you will enjoy it, although not as much as last time when we ate together."

"The main reason we're all here is certainly not the quality of the food," the colonel remarked, and the others nodded.

Qianfan couldn't resist and asked some questions that bothered him, right as they started eating. "Can you tell us more about your grandfather? The whole story is strange. I briefly met him, and I have to say he didn't strike me as being too friendly."

Ah Lam put down her bamboo chopsticks and closed her eyes, as if she were trying to picture her grandfather in front of her. "Yes, Grandfather was a strange man. Brilliant, and weird in many aspects. As you know, he was the principal scientist behind China's brain project. The MegaAI was born right here, in this city, you know?"

Qianfan raised a brow and looked at Daiyu. He had suspected as much.

"Grandfather was very proud of this, naturally. He felt like the MegaAI was the achievement of his life. That's why he was livid when, a few years after the initial success, President Guō Chāo took him off the project. Grandfather never told me why. I inferred it had to do with choosing the research direction to improve it. And with what the MegaAI was supposed to be used for. Grandfather was a proud man, a nerd who tried to stay out of politics as much as he could. I don't think he was a bad person. I don't think he would have condoned a device to read people's thoughts. Or one to influence them. He believed in the power of a free spirit. I think President

Guō Chāo did not like him. By that time, the president had surrounded himself with enough lackeys who were fawning all over him. He wanted obedience, fanaticism."

"Isn't it incredible how we humans turn everything into a religion?" Qianfan asked, frowning. "It's built into our core. That's why in our history we have had over ten thousand different religions. And we have examples of large atheist movements that promised the good of the masses, only to slip into ideology, dogma, myths, taboos, and all the elements that qualify them as religions. When the Russians all but eliminated religious activities at the beginning of the twentieth century, people gradually began worshiping their leader, Stalin, until he became a demigod. They took the ideology of helping the poor and turned it into a mindless glorification of the proletarian. The result was no less devastating than the atrocities done in the name of any classic religion. Here, in China, we've been putting the party and its leaders on a pedestal for decades. Inevitably, we've let them dictate our lives, punish us, reward us. Many of us worship them. Look at the CWT. What is that if not a form of a stairway to heaven? People became obsessed with increasing their scores and pleasing the gods. For a higher CWT, some would sell their mothers. And, as if things were not bad enough, we've created a true God ourselves now. A sentient machine that can rule over us. I can't help but wonder, will this be the last God that man will ever make?"

"Words of wisdom, Doctor Zhào, words of wisdom," the colonel answered, raising a finger. "It's up to us to see that the God we've created doesn't destroy the man."

"The very concept of an ark suggests it," Ah Lam pointed out the obvious in a tired voice. "Just like in the old Genesis flood narrative, our God promises now to save a few of us, the worthy ones, from the big, planetary-scale destruction that *it* will unleash. And given that we are talking about the MegaAI, which, as far as we know, is the only sentient artificial being, I know *it* will soon be capable of such actions."

"That's why we must rush," the colonel hit the table with his fist. "The more we wait, the stronger the MegaAI becomes. We cannot afford for it to become omnipotent."

"How did we do it?" Daiyu said softly, then looked at the others' puzzled faces and realized that she was thinking out loud. "How *did* we create the MegaAI? All my life, I have been training in artificial intelligence. I've studied everything Professor Zhèng's team published, all the information about the MegaAI implementation. Yet, I can't find anything to explain this achievement."

"Grandfather led the team that made the most important advances. As he often told me, they had several breakthroughs that allowed them to get the first artificial version of a neocortex, in which they could deploy the state-of-the-art machine learning algorithms. There were similar attempts to do so after his success, but nobody replicated his achievement. Despite huge money poured into this, no other country has a similar AI, as far as I know."

Ah Lam spoke with a kind of pride that all at the table shared for a moment. Then she turned toward Daiyu. "I'm afraid I know nothing that might help us answer how the MegaAI became so powerful. I imagine that, shortly after President Guō died, they had a breakthrough."

"But who are they?" Qianfan asked. "Who is in this mysterious team that maintains the MegaAI?"

"That's the thing," the colonel intervened. "The list is kept ultra-secret. It took all the means available to me to get access to it. I'll bring it to you. There are around a hundred people. Most of them are medical doctors, epidemiologists, neurologists, and so on. Less than one-third are AI specialists."

"Curious," Qianfan said.

"Indeed," Ah Lam nodded, "Grandfather often complained that, step by step, the party leaders had dismantled the original team. Or rather, it gradually dissipated. As they removed each original researcher from the team, they did not replace them. Grandfather thought they formed another team in parallel. Nobody told him who was part of it and where it was."

"Yes, definitely curious," Daiyu said, shaking her head. "I find it amazing that, for such a complicated organizational structure, nobody has leaked any relevant information so far."

"As you spend more time here, you'll discover more mysteries," the colonel pointed out. "Many of the results of the research done here are secret. It's not clear to me how much progress the genetic team has made, whether we indeed have reliable nanomaterials, what the plans are for building the spaceships, whether the new proposed propulsion system is truly functional, and so on."

"Yes, progress is being made, but the tendency to keep everything secret eventually ends up hindering it," Ah Lam nodded in agreement.

"Some of the secret research and production likely happens in a few areas where nobody has access," the colonel continued. "The most obvious one is a five-acre section in the military base closer to the mountains that is off-limits. We've started calling it the Doom's Lab. I'm not familiar with anybody who knows what they use it for. And I'm pretty high in the hierarchy. The area is fenced with concrete walls. There isn't much inside them. From above, you can see some protuberances, which, I guess, are the tops of some subterranean bunkers. Occasionally, you can see people walking on the top of them. Also, the area is heavily defended on the outside and—check this out—there's no gate or other means to enter it. I inspected it once all around and I could not see any way to get in."

"How can that be?" Qianfan asked. "What about food, sleep, garbage, sewage?"

"Food and drinks are being brought daily and delivered on a chute. There's a filtered sewage pipe for residue that is small enough that only a cat could crawl through it. Garbage is pumped out once a day on another narrow chute. I guess the people live and work underground. There may be tunnels that connect them to the outside world. If such tunnels exist, no map I've seen shows them."

"Any idea what they could work on down there?" Qianfan asked.

"I first suspected that they were working on a superweapon—a metaphorical flood meant to wipe out the inhabitants of Earth not lucky enough to make it on the ark. However, the space is relatively small and, because the food is brought in by one truck only, there cannot be too many people living there. If it's a weapon, I don't know how they'd test it."

"It's ridiculous to know so little," Daiyu frowned.

"Another possibility is that they use that place for genetic experiments," Ah Lam offered, thoughtful. "In my group, we prepare biological compounds for the genetics division here in the city. Small tissues we grow right in our lab, organic support liquids, and so on. Stuff is being sent via a truck to the Doom's Lab regularly and thrown down there, via the same chute."

"Perhaps they are preparing a biological weapon," Qianfan suggested, terrified of the idea. "Perhaps the MegaAI wants to enhance people who will make it on the ark and kill everybody else."

"This is highly speculative," the colonel tempered him. "We simply don't know. Nobody has left there yet, dead or alive."

"I might understand that they don't want anybody in," Daiyu pointed out. "Why would they go through all the effort to keep people from coming out?"

"Secrecy, perhaps," the colonel answered. "If no one comes out, there's no way to know what they are working on."

"Could it be some kind of working prison?" Qianfan offered.

"Maybe, but then it's not meant to accept more prisoners," Hu answered. "No, it's more likely that a group of core scientists is creating something unique, something ultra-secret in there."

"I believe Mother knows what all that is about," Ah Lam said. "I remember once she talked about it with a fellow Dragon Member, who was genuinely frustrated that she didn't have access to this information. I overheard the other Dragon Member complain that she doesn't understand how she could help with the Great Project if she doesn't know what critical piece is being developed in that area."

"Yes, someone has to know," Qianfan observed. "How else would they integrate it or use it when it's ready, whatever *it* is?"

"As far as I understand, all instructions related to it come directly from President Yun Li, which we know is the AI itself."

After a few minutes of silence, Qianfan tried a different way to attack the problem. "Do you know where the instructions come from?"

"All communication from the pseudo-president comes via the Chinese Cybersperse," Ah Lam clarified. "It's obvious that nobody sees the president to get orders in person."

"Can we determine which server they are coming from?" Qianfan probed further.

"No," Daiyu answered before the colonel could. "As you know, Cybersperse communication is quantum encrypted, virtually impossible to break. Considering the amount of load balance and the complete control the party has over all the computers in the territory of China, the MegaAI is practically everywhere by now."

"What if," Qianfan raised a hand, "what if we were to cause a massive computer blackout? Fry all computers in China?"

"It would be impossible to synchronize something like that," Daiyu said, shaking her head. "Especially since we'd need to do it in stealth mode. Otherwise, they'd arrest us before long."

"Besides, the economy has been fully dependent on computers for over half a century now," Ah Lam said. "The food chain, the stock market, transportation, the educational system, hospitals, law enforcement, the army. Everything would cease to function. That would be devastating, even if only for a short while. It would lead to countless deaths."

"Not to mention that it would leave China vulnerable to external attacks," the colonel intervened. "While I'm concerned about the Great

Project and about the power of the MegaAI, above all, I am Chinese! I don't want our country occupied by a foreign power."

"Then, what can we do?" Qianfan asked, getting desperate again.

"Only local disruptions, for the time being," the colonel shrugged. "Until we have more information or get better ideas. Based on what we know now, it's pointless to try anything heroic, on a large scale. We'd just be caught."

"Alright," Qianfan conceded, although he was boiling with frustration. "On our side, we can try the same old tactics to delay the MA development. It won't make a big difference, though."

"I can merely continue to gather information, as things happen," the colonel shrugged.

"I can't do much," Ah Lam pouted. "My role in my lab is very limited."

"Are you at all involved further down the distribution chain?" Qianfan asked. "Do you know anything about what the genetics team does with your stuff? Or anything that might lead us to understand what the mysterious underground workers do?"

"I'm afraid not," Ah Lam lowered her eyes. "I can thank Mother for that. She and I have been arguing from the time Grandfather was still influential. I'm sure she doesn't trust me. And rightly so!"

Qianfan nodded. "I suggest you gather a list of all the additives, or whatever your lab prepares for the geneticists," he said. "Particularly, what you send down there. Perhaps if we look at it, we can make further hypotheses." He stood up with a tired, unhappy posture. "This discussion was demoralizing. I won't hide it. Yet, I see no choice but to continue to make some sense of what is going on. Before the flood comes."

CHAPTER 27:

RECONNECTION

Nothing ever exists entirely alone. Everything is in relation to everything else.

— Buddha

"Have you lost your mind completely?" Mike asked Sujata in a group call with Ian in the DoD's private Cybersperse.

She and Ian were in Ian's office, without François. She had just finished relating to them her recent encounter with Marie.

"For crying out loud, you might have just killed the entire project," Mike said and looked at her crossly. "I'm sorry, my dear, I love you and normally I'm willing to go with your intuition, but this is too important for us to screw up."

Sujata took the heat silently and looked at Ian. He was unusually quiet. His smile was gone, and he was pouting instead, a sign he was thinking hard.

"This is a toss-up," he finally said. "The benefits are unclear. I'll admit the situation is intriguing. As I've been saying to you many times already, I've learned to appreciate coincidences like this in life. The risk is that François is so pissed off that he leaves us immediately. My hunch is that he won't, though. He wants to see CARLA develop successfully. And we will give him the right to refuse."

"Absolutely," Sujata nodded. "The choice is simple. Work with Marie to raise CARLA, or work with another woman we don't have yet. There's no guarantee that we'll find a better candidate, honestly, as nobody is qualified for what we're looking for."

Mike scoffed. "By this logic, we should promote to the rank of 'First Mother of an AI' a teenage girl, a retired Sumo fighter, or a mass murderer. It wouldn't make any difference. There are always people who are better qualified."

"Are there, really?" asked Ian. "This woman majored in psychology, researching the long-term effects avatars have on people. She worked for a year and a half with children addicted to the Cybersperse. Above all, she knows François deeply. And François modeled many aspects of CARLA after her. I dare say that a lot of pieces would fall into place."

"From what Sujata says, she's also mentally unstable. Do we need this kind of drama, when we could be hit at any moment by some sci-fi weapon concocted by that mad AI? At the minimum, she's bound to disrupt François's work, unless he kills himself first. Besides, from what you are saying, this lady isn't exactly 'mother' material, able to discipline CARLA. God, I don't know how to explain this to General Kambe." Mike took his head in his hands.

Sujata felt bad for him. "If you allow me, I'll talk to him."

"No!" Mike nearly screamed, raising his hands. "Please don't. He already hates you. I'll present the situation to him, along with General Thompson, and try to soften the blow. Come to think of it, General Kambe is already against this whole idea. It might thrill him to see it killed off sooner than later. Not that he has anything better to offer."

Sujata nodded.

"Okay, then it's settled," Ian said. "You will accompany François to the meeting. My advice is not to tell him ahead of time whom he is going to meet. I am 99 percent sure he won't go if you do so."

Sujata smiled and asked, "Do you want to come with us?"

"No, thank you," Ian laughed, raising a hand. "I can help persuade François not to resign if it comes to that. I leave you the exclusive honor of witnessing the drama."

"No problem. It's my doing, I must see it through," Sujata smiled, trying hard to look confident.

"Good luck, kiddo," Mike said, before signing out.

Sujata nodded goodbye to Ian, whose stare reflected a combination of concern, pity, and mild amusement. She found François in his office, nurturing CARLA, and fending off half a dozen curious researchers that had arrived just today, wanting to peek at the object of their future work. François was arguing bitterly with one of them. She got closer, and kept quiet, not interested in intervening. She knew him. It was Vijay Patil, a brilliant researcher, a favorite of General Kambe's, who led the BCI group.

"I tell you this is a stupid idea," François yelled at him.

"No, it's not," Vijay answered calmly. "We can do it if we work together."

"We don't have one version of CARLA that works yet, and now you want to connect her to a hundred thousand soldiers?"

"We won't connect her to anybody now," Vijay said. "We only need to work on how it can be done. In a couple of years, we might have a solution."

"Tell General Kambe that we're not building soldiers here!" François screamed, maddened that the guy was insisting. "We're building a singular being, a marvel of science, a piece of art. You say that you want her to help us save the world, but all you can imagine is an army of CARLAs. This shows how limited and stupid military people are."

"François, may I borrow you for a few minutes?" Sujata stepped forward, knowing that she had to stop this.

"Oh, you are here," he cooled down, feeling embarrassed about his last statement. "I wasn't referring to you."

"Are you okay?" Sujata asked, dismissing his offending words, concerned that now might be the wrong time to bring up the purpose of her visit.

"I will be if you tell these people to leave us alone. Until Ian has some work for them, they should go out and play. Knit a scarf. Twiddle their thumbs. Do a headstand. I don't care! Just get them out of my hair."

Sujata nodded and asked everybody to leave the lab. After all, these people were used to listening to the military, not to a fellow researcher. She made a mental note that she needed to talk to Ian about further restricting the access here. She took Vijay by the arm and spoke to him.

"Don't worry, you'll have access to CARLA's specs. As you can see, François is very upset by the prospects you've raised. He knows the work you are doing is a prerequisite for continuing this project. General Kambe was clear about it. I think François is especially upset that he cannot stop it."

"Thank you," Vijay nodded. "I ... wanted to tell him, if he gave me a chance, that the work they've done here deserves a Nobel prize. Words can't describe how impressive this achievement is." Then he bowed and left.

Sujata followed him with her eyes. This was bound to be an ongoing problem. With a grimace, she stepped back into François's lab. "Problem solved, temporarily," she announced. "I'll talk to Ian about restricting the number of people who can interact with CARLA."

"Thank you," François said and appeared genuinely relieved.

"François, you understand that General Kambe's request is non-negotiable."

François turned his head away. He nodded without answering. "Now, what did you want to talk to me about?" he switched the topic, trying to calm down.

"I'd like you to come with me tonight at 7:00 p.m. to meet someone," she proposed.

"Who?"

"Let's say it's a surprise," she dodged the question.

"I don't have time for surprises," he frowned.

"I'm sure CARLA will be fine one evening without you," Sujata insisted.

"Where?"

"There's an Italian restaurant in Santa Monica called The Veranda; it's less than half an hour from here. Right on Ocean Ave. I discovered it a couple of days ago. It has great food."

"I could use some food that is not cooked here," François pondered. "Alright, fine. Although I don't see the point of the mystery."

"You ... will see it, I promise," Sujata said, feeling guilty. "Thank you. I'll come to pick you up at 6:30 p.m."

A few hours later, the two of them got out of a cab in front of the restaurant. Sujata tried to make conversation on the way, mostly to reduce her anxiety, but François wasn't exactly the most voluble person, so she gave up. The restaurant was relatively small, perhaps a dozen tables, posh, lit just enough to make it cozy. It was located at a cute hotel, close to the beach. Sujata was happy that they could see the ocean, while François seemed troubled by it. They could smell the food from outside. Just as they were entering, François glanced inside. It was full. On a remote table to the right, half-turned towards the entrance, he saw her. The blood drained out of his face.

"You ..." He turned towards Sujata, livid. "You had no right!"

"Hear me out, François," Sujata started.

"No! I don't care. You shouldn't have brought her to America. What was the point? You're not helping. I don't want to see that woman ever. You can't make me."

He was panicking. Sujata grabbed him by the shoulder and nudged him outside, since some nearby guests were frowning at them. After peeking back, she concluded Marie hadn't noticed them yet.

Once outside, she said with a sigh, "François. Nobody is *making* you do anything. You don't want to meet her, you won't. Just listen to me for two minutes, then you can decide. If you don't want to go in, we turn, go back and never speak about this again. Deal?"

François calmed down and nodded. He was happy to be in control.

Sujata took a deep breath. "I'm not a religious person. Far from it. My mother drove me nuts with stories of karma and destiny that I always made fun of. Even I must admit this situation is surreal. Remember, I told you I know someone in the area working with cognitive scientists? I visited them yesterday. Incidentally, they didn't have anybody with the qualifications we wanted. Just when I was about to leave, I saw someone that could easily pass for CARLA's older sister. I found out she is Marie and that she knows you. She moved to LA shortly after you arrived here. She came here to search for you."

François shifted, eager to interrupt her, but Sujata raised her hand.

"Please let me finish." Sujata registered how, despite his anger, the news that Marie had come searching for him seemed to have surprised him in a good way. "Her coming to the US, and me inviting her here, are the only voluntary actions anybody took to get us to this point. Everything else is a series of incredible coincidences. Let me spell them out for you."

She started counting on her fingers. "First, the DoD selected me to be the liaison for this project. Second, I was there when CARLA misbehaved, and we discussed the idea of a 'mother figure' for her. Third, I had a connection working in LA that I thought might know such a person. Fourth, from all companies in the Los Angeles area, this one hired Marie months ago, and she didn't switch jobs. Fifth, she could have been home, sick, working remotely, in the restroom the very moment I passed through the hallway, chosen a different work spot, positioned in such a way so I couldn't see her face, and on and on. You must admit that this is a remarkable coincidence."

"So what? Coincidences happen all the time," François argued.

"Not at this level." Sujata shook her head. "Remember when you told me how you met Ian? If it wasn't for the shove from that infatuated moron,

John Reeta, you wouldn't have accepted the invitation. Ian himself always advises us to look for such strange opportunities and take them."

François didn't comment, although he didn't seem convinced.

"Think about it. Marie has the right background. She knows you very well. She shares at least some physical features with CARLA, perhaps also some of her idiosyncrasies. Since she came here, she has worked only with children—addicts to the Cybersperse. Do you honestly believe we're going to find a better fit?"

"Please," François screamed. "Anybody would be a better fit. CARLA would certainly grow better without a cheater around."

Sujata knew nothing about Marie's cheating. She took a chance. "This is not my business, again, but you should sort out among yourselves what kind of cheating there was, if any. Understand that this woman came searching for you right after you left."

François went white again, just thinking about broaching this topic with Marie.

Sujata saw she was torturing him. And probably losing him. She sighed, ready to use the last weapon in her arsenal. "There's one more reason to meet her. I bet you're eager to show her what she missed. Show her the beautiful thing you've created."

Finally, François's face lightened up a bit. This was a convincing argument. How about giving her a taste of her own medicine? If she truly came here looking for him, he could show off his achievement, and then, in his moment of glory, kick her out of his life again. Let her see how it was to be rejected. She deserved that, fair and square. He started pacing around for half a minute.

"Can we get rid of her, if she ... doesn't fit?"

"Yes, of course. If we see that her presence affects CARLA negatively, or you, we can end the arrangement."

François nodded. "Fine. I'll talk to her now. Let's see how it goes." Then he turned towards the ocean, engulfed in darkness. A chill went down his spine. "I killed myself once for this woman. How many more times do I need to do it?" he muttered.

"Never!" Sujata said firmly. "If you think you might consider that again in the future because of Marie, we must leave right away."

It was François's turn to lift his hand. "No reason to be concerned. I don't have the guts to go through that again." With a deep breath, he opened the door, waiting for Sujata to go inside.

"I tell you what," she proposed. "There's a bar right there," she pointed out towards a set of tall round stools. "I'll be in your view, out of your way. I've already interfered too much."

The corners of François's mouth sagged. He hated the thought of facing her again. Sujata was right not to tell him about this. He wouldn't have come.

Seeing François come towards her table, Marie started trembling so strongly that she feared she would have a mild convulsion. She wanted to stand up, but her knees were too weak. After all this time, and all the empty searches. She followed with her eyes the beautiful woman as she found a chair at the bar. She must have pulled off a miracle to convince François to talk to her.

François looked mad. He was thinner, and the circles around his eyes suggested he hadn't been getting enough sleep for a long time. He stopped in front of her table, staring at the tablecloth as if it were an irresistible piece of art.

"*Bonsoir*, François," she offered gently, afraid not to send him running towards the door.

"I ... didn't want to see you," he said. He involuntarily chose to speak in English, as if she were a stranger. "Sujata was very persuasive. So that you know. I ... profoundly and irreversibly hate you," he announced in a diabolical voice. “I don’t care about you anymore. You made me sick. If you were to rot in a—”

“I didn’t sleep with him!” Marie screamed, her eyes moist.

Seeing that some people were turning their heads toward them, she lowered her voice. François’s eyes got bigger, and his body language showed that he was oscillating between fighting or fleeing, instinctively feeling he was under attack.

“I wanted to, out of revenge. After you left. But I couldn’t. I simply couldn’t. Because I love you and I don’t want to hurt you like that again, ever. I kept this with me.” She pulled out his old toy ring bought in Paris.

He had forgotten about it.

“It is my talisman. If you—”

“Too late,” he interrupted her, this time lifting his palm. “You made me die, you ... you …” he stammered, struggling to find the nastiest word he could.

“Don’t you think you’re being a little unfair?” she whined. “The last thing I wanted was for you to kill yourself. Like any other girl out there, I just wanted to find a partner, perhaps a spouse. I didn’t understand you loved me so much. I didn’t understand *I* loved you so much, either. Can you ever forgive me?”

“*Jamais de la vie!* Do you understand? Never! The François you know died that day. The François you see now has found a new life. I didn’t ... think my new life would have anything to do with you. Ever. I don’t care if you say you did nothing wrong. I cannot forgive you. Not if both of us die and get reincarnated a million times.”

She lowered her eyes. “So be it. Don’t forgive me. Please don’t drive me away either. I love you. Let me take care of you.”

François felt dizzy. He grabbed the back of a nearby chair. Her proximity, her suffering, her convincing confession of love were all pulling him inexorably back to his old self, like a vortex, like a black hole. This was too much, too fast. He couldn't look at her. He turned towards Sujata, who was waiting impatiently.

Seeing him like that, she understood he needed help. She ran towards their table. "Is everything alright?"

"I …" François said with considerable difficulty, "I agree to ... temporarily involve her in the project."

Marie started sobbing.

Turning around, François located the restroom and ran towards it. Five seconds later, the whole restaurant heard him vomiting. Marie was trying hard to stop crying. She looked at Sujata, unsure what was next. Sujata stood frozen in place, utterly uncomfortable at being in the middle of this drama, which she had created, feeling conflicted between relief that François was accepting Marie and worry that he would focus on torturing her instead of raising CARLA.

When François came back, he looked like he had just woken up after a night of drinking. Marie wiped her tears.

"Are you okay?" she asked, worried, jumping up to help him.

François nodded and lifted his hand to stop her. He still couldn't convince himself to look into her eyes.

"This is good," Sujata breathed out, realizing how tense she was. "We'll do some background checks and, if everything passes, you'll hear from me in a couple of weeks. You'll need to sign some nondisclosure documents. I must repeat, this is top secret and crucial for, well, for the entire world. If you don't feel up to it, you—"

"Please don't worry about me," Marie said, determined. "I'll do whatever is necessary."

"Can we go now, please?" François begged Sujata.

"Sure. Marie, I'll be in touch soon. See you!"

François tilted his head up towards her. That was all she was going to get from him tonight.

"I am eager to ... work together! Bye!" Marie yelled as they were leaving.

Seeing them go, she felt a kind of weird despair creeping up her heart. What if they never got back to her? What if he disappeared again? She sat at that table for another hour, alternating between crying and laughing. Around 9:00 p.m., she called Isabelle, not realizing it was only 3:00 a.m. in France. Isabelle's disheveled appearance, puffy eyes, and her messed up hair betrayed her concern and confusion. Marie realized she had woken her up, but she didn't bother to apologize.

"I found him! I found him!" she screamed. "It's a secret, so I can't tell you anything about it. I think we're going to work together. I feel alive again!" She started crying, hearing how true these words sounded to her ears.

CHAPTER 28:

DIFFERENT MOTHERLY LOVE

When children travel far away, their mother worries. What should children do when their mother drifts away?

— Adaptation of a Chinese proverb

The invitation, or rather the summoning to Dragon Member Zhèng's office, came as a surprise to Qianfan, especially because of the short notice. He arrived at work as usual at 8:00 a.m. At 8:30 a.m., the message came straight from her office informing him he had to be there by 10:00 a.m. Considering that the dragon member was incredibly busy, with every minute of her daily schedule carefully planned by her two secretaries, he knew it was about something important. His first thought was that the party had uncovered their ridiculous and impromptu camarilla. Immediately after receiving the message, he panicked, thinking that he might have just destroyed Baozhai's future. He wasn't able to work on anything for the next hour. He finally showed the message to Daiyu, who tried hard to calm him down, although he could see how terrified she was, too.

At 9:30 a.m., Qianfan started walking toward the central complex where the elite leaders worked. He forced himself to walk slowly, although he felt like running for his life. Thinking things through, he understood it couldn't be that bad, as a SAF squad would have arrested him and Daiyu by now. There was no reason for the dragon member to waste her time, unless she wanted to revel in his misery.

Despite his best efforts to slow down, he arrived at the tallest building in the city, merely six floors high, thirteen minutes before 10:00 a.m. The population in this little city was not much larger than that of a typical Chinese village. Since the idea was to keep it off-radar, most apartment buildings and offices were only three-four floors high. He had never entered the buildings where the main leaders had offices. Everything was equally clean and shiny here, too. A large statue that resembled an eighteenth-century ship replica greeted him. Made of metal, simple enough to be recognizable, yet stylized enough to be a work of art, it gave the place a futuristic aura, the symbol of all they were working so hard to achieve.

Qianfan was too preoccupied to pay much attention to other details in the building. Once he checked in, a helpful young lady took him by an elevator to the top floor and then walked through a wide corridor up to what looked like a penthouse. The receptionist instructed Qianfan to wait in the lobby. Rather than sit, he turned towards the peaceful white peaked mountains visible through the top-to-bottom window.

Why can't we live there? he thought, reviving his old dream. *Just me, Baozhai, and Daiyu. With a couple of sheep, and perhaps a cow.*

At 10:00 a.m. sharp, a man in a uniform exited the dragon member's office in a hurry and rushed towards the elevator without glancing at him. A secretary came out right after, nodding a salute and inviting him in, while going outside and closing the door. Qianfan noticed that she had been inside with the officer who had just left, but she wouldn't stay in for him. The dragon member didn't bother to stand up or shake his hand. She was sitting at a huge wooden desk that looked heavier than the whole building. So heavy that Qianfan's engineering mind wondered if it would go through the floor.

"Doctor Zhào, thanks for joining me on such a short notice," she said with a tired smile, inviting him to sit.

"Sure," Qianfan blabbered, trying hard to control himself, and crashed into the armchair in front of her.

"How's our MA device progressing?" she asked, amused at how he was perspiring.

Qianfan raised one brow in surprise. There was no point in her asking him this question. Surely, she, or one of her lackeys, received his reports.

"It's ... going as expected," he answered vaguely. "Hiccups are bound to happen since we are developing something that has never been done before," he offered lamely, still unsure where these questions would lead him.

"Like most of the work we do in Mega Ark City," she nodded, extending her smile, not buying his escape route. "But will it work?"

Qianfan thought it might help his cause to provide some details to make her understand how difficult this was. "Well, we are trying to mold the mind of the subject without direct surgical intervention. We are not doing what's called deep brain stimulation, where we insert electrodes that produce signals to affect the electrochemical balance in the brain. Our goal is to get a non-invasive device that generates fluctuating magnetic fields. It must operate from a certain distance, say, 20 cm away. This has been a long quest for neuroscience. Without the MegaAI, I would be rather pessimistic. Given the breakthroughs that we had with the SSMS, I'd say we have a fair chance," he answered honestly. There was no point pretending, it would only look suspicious.

"Is it dangerous?"

More surprises. Since when did she care? "In principle, yes. We must do many tests to assess how dangerous it is." He ran with the flow, thinking that this path might buy them more time. "If we mess it up, long exposure to the MA might cause seizures and, eventually, death."

The dragon member nodded and switched the subject suddenly. "How are things at home?"

Qianfan shifted a bit. This meeting was getting annoyingly weird. "Uh ... alright, I guess," he answered. "We're adapting here."

"I heard your daughter is a math prodigy," she said, cutting to the chase.

"Yes, she is," he answered, finally getting where this was going. "You might have also heard that they denied her access to the International Olympiad in Russia this year."

The dragon member finally stood up and walked to the window. She turned her back to Qianfan and looked outside quietly for a while. Qianfan stood up too and waited patiently.

"About that," she finally spoke, making Qianfan's heart run faster. "I might agree to an exception under some special circumstances."

Qianfan narrowed his eyes. This woman was a snake. Was she going to propose a deal to him? He had nothing to offer. Was she aware that he was meeting her daughter and the colonel? Would she ask him to spy on them?

"First, I want to make you aware of a piece of information that is only known to a handful of people in the city."

She pivoted and walked fast toward him. She stopped right in front of his face. He could smell her mint breath. Her eyes locked on his.

"I don't think I need to say that you should not disseminate this further," she whispered in a threatening tone, her face beaming.

Qianfan nodded and answered, "Of course, Dragon Member."

"I have been announced," she continued, "that I am on my way to being promoted. Soon, I will be a supreme member," she announced simply, with no hint of pride in her voice.

This was incredible! There were only twelve supreme members, the absolute peak of the party hierarchy, answering directly to the president. Everybody else, the acting government, the dragon members, the army, and the police, were subordinate to them. This could mean either that one of them had died, or that, in an unprecedented move, Member Zhèng was to become the thirteenth one. Come to think of it, Qianfan expected that all supreme members, if not also all dragon members, were aware of the Mega Ark project. Surely, the whole hierarchy of members alive at the Great Departure time had their places guaranteed on the Ark.

"I've worked all my life for this position. I am prepared. Nothing must go wrong. So, I will do you a personal favor. Believe me, granting anyone, even a child, access outside of the Mega Ark City *is* a huge thing. In exchange, I want you to do something for me."

What? Qianfan wanted to scream, but tightened his lips and remained quiet.

"I want you to provide me, for personal use, an early prototype of the MA before you complete all the testing. And I want you to teach me how to use it."

Qianfan nearly fainted. His dream to delay the project had just been blown to pieces.

"But ... surely, you understand that without sufficient testing—"

"I don't have time," she raised her voice, stomping her foot, fire in her eyes.

Qianfan decided to stay quiet.

"I will not let this opportunity slip," she announced, slowly, stressing each word, with a cool determination in her voice. "So, do we have an understanding?"

"Yes," he answered. There was no choice.

"Good! If anyone in your office asks, you'll tell them you're doing special tests at my request."

"Alright," Qianfan acknowledged. "Dragon Member," he dared to say one last thing, "if something should go wrong ..."

"You will not be held responsible," she answered firmly.

Qianfan nodded.

"I expect to hear from you once a week. Not your regular report. Contact my secretaries and tell them just a percentage. Let's say today we are at 10 percent. One hundred percent would mean a fully functional, fully tested device. Fifty percent would mean that you are ready for the first tests. I expect to use it when your development reaches 70 percent. You'll let me know about it, then you'll wait to hear from me, and bring it here, to this office." She moved fast back to her desk and sat in her chair. "That will be all."

"Goodbye," Qianfan bowed and moved backward until he reached the door and left her office.

He ran out of the building feeling dizzy. The wind blew on his face. He didn't feel it. He scurried on the sidewalk to get far away from that building and that woman. He imagined the dragon member's gaze following him from the window, scorching his back. Once he was out of her line of sight, he moved near a tree and leaned on it. A drizzle started, but he ignored that too. Why would the dragon member require personal access to an MA prototype? Who was threatening her promotion? Suddenly, it all became clear. Ah Lam! The dragon member had to be aware of her daughter's dissident thinking. She was afraid that the other supreme members might find out about it. That would make it obvious that she wasn't able to raise her own daughter in the spirit of the party and the Great Project. So how could they expect her to lead the whole country? Also, it would be a security hole. A supreme member could not surround herself with anyone who had the tiniest of doubts about their party goals.

Qianfan also realized that her father's attitude and fight with the leaders in the past were already a grave stain on her face that she had worked hard to wash away. Now it was her own daughter threatening, though indirectly, to mess up her plans.

So, she had to have in mind an ideological retraining for Ah Lam, under wraps, in the secrecy of her home, somewhere. But how? His project parameters specified the device was to be used only on subjects in internment camps. Surely, the MA was not a dishwasher or a toaster to be used at home. And she obviously cared little if Ah Lam would get injured. What kind of mother would do something like that?

"A mother who is, first and foremost, a supreme member," he whispered between his teeth, understanding her reasoning.

And if the MA wouldn't give results, she would probably not hesitate to kill her daughter. She first wanted to try the MA route because it was the simpler option. Killing her would have to be done in secret, covered to appear like Ah Lam had died of natural causes, with no hint of her involvement. This woman was unscrupulous.

Visibly shaken, he sent a short Cybersperse message to Daiyu, telling her not to be worried, and that he would take the rest of the day off and be home. Tonight, it was his turn to host their short meetings. How ridiculous they looked, considering the power leaders like this woman had. Trying to get his mind off these issues, he started cooking. He had been in the kitchen for a few hours when he heard the door. It was already 5:00 p.m. and Baozhai was home. They had agreed for her to spend time with a colleague this evening. There was little sense in her overhearing what was being discussed. The pretext was that they were planning to talk about some secret, work-related stuff. This excuse always stopped further discussions. Baozhai was smart enough to understand that something else was going on too, but she didn't ask. She never asked. He resolved to revel in the joy that she would undoubtedly feel once he gave her the good news.

"Bàba, are you cooking for your guests?" she asked with a hint of a smile.

"Yes, I am. I promise I'll keep some for us," he answered in a raspy voice, which he cleared quickly and continued. "Come here for a moment, Baozhai."

She complied, worried by his facial expression. "Today I've been told that they might make an exception for you," he said, not capable of stopping his eyes from getting moist. "They might allow you to compete in the Olympiad."

Baozhai took a step back, reached with her hand for a chair while looking at him, then sat on it. "Are you ... sure?"

"Yes," he answered, tears flowing down his cheek.

"But ... how?" she asked, incredulous.

"Don't worry about that," he quickly answered. "The good thing is that you can go. Now run and solve some extra tough problems."

She nodded in shock.

"Baozhai, don't tell anyone about this. Not your colleagues, not your teacher."

"Thank you," was all she could say before running to her room.

And this is how one becomes a collaborator, he mused, with a disgusted face.

He spent the next hour in agony, vacillating between his determination to realize Baozhai's dream, which would mean keeping quiet and not betraying his new allies, and telling Ah Lam that her mind was under threat.

At 6:00 p.m., Baozhai left for her friend's place. She was beaming. Qianfan felt a spear through his heart. How could he do anything to clip her wings? Shortly after, Daiyu arrived. Her eyeballs were sunken in their sockets. He felt bad he had forgotten about her completely. She, too, was in this with all her heart.

"How did it go? Is everything alright?" she asked in a shaky voice.

"Please forgive me, I'm a selfish bastard," he raised his arms. "I should have told you right away. The summoning wasn't about anything that concerns you directly."

"What was it about?"

This was it. He had to say something. "Give me a moment. Let the others arrive first."

She frowned and said nothing. He was behaving oddly.

A few minutes later, all four sitting at the table, the atmosphere seemed almost normal.

"I'm dying to taste your cooking," Ah Lam smiled. "I would have thought you would order food, too. You truly are full of surprises!"

Qianfan could think of one surprise he had that wasn't so nice.

Sensing the tension in the room, Ah Lam became all serious. "Has something happened?" she asked.

Qianfan knew he couldn't lie to her. He would need to dance around the whole situation so that both Ah Lam stayed safe, and Baozhai went to the Olympiad. "I ... your mother invited me to her office this morning," he started, hesitantly.

Ah Lam flinched. The colonel's face remained unperturbed, but he involuntarily pushed his hand against the table harder.

"She offered me a deal. In exchange for Baozhai being allowed to take part in the Olympiad, I must ... help her. This is a secret that, if found out, would mean my expiration." With a sigh, Qianfan continued. "Dragon Member Zhèng is in line for a promotion."

A few seconds of silence followed.

The colonel let a small whistle out. "Supreme Member," he said. "I have to give it to her. That's impressive."

"She thinks she is facing an impediment. There's something, or rather *someone*, who might ruin her plans."

"Who?" Ah Lam asked.

Qianfan answered, looking straight at her. "You."

CHAPTER 29:

RAISING A CHILD

Nietzsche said that whatever does not kill us strengthens us. Supposedly, people become more resilient when faced with dangerous obstacles, such as disease, hardship, or war. But too much suffering can have long-lasting, irreversible effects. Is suffering necessary for an artificial being? How much of it should it be made to endure?

— DeSousa's Memoirs - Part II - Creation - 2054

Marie arrived at CogniPrescience's headquarters, trembling. She was terrified to see François again, terrified of the secret project he was working on, and terrified that she could not rise to these people's expectations for whatever she was supposed to do. The agony of waiting for Sujata to get back to her quickly replaced her initial enthusiasm for having found François. By the time that happened, ten days after seeing François again, she felt so lost that she had doubled her daily medication dose, which had made her groggy all day long. Strangely, though, once she heard from Sujata, her anguish at the thought of being left alone had immediately made room for her fear that things wouldn't go well. With considerable effort, she dropped back to a normal medicine level a few days before.

Now she was there. Seeing the military personnel guarding the entrance to the complex didn't reduce her anxiety. After a long and tedious verification, which included her biometrics and a DNA hair sample, she jumped in a military vehicle that went through the special gate. She tried to focus on the heavenly green all around her, remembering her home, wondering if she and François would ever go back there, spend time with friends and family, get married, have children, grow old, and take care of their grandchildren.

"Welcome to CogniPrescience," Sujata's faint voice woke her up from her daydreaming.

She noticed the car had stopped. Sujata was outside, probably notified of her arrival by the soldiers at the gate. She opened the car door. Marie scrambled to get out and tried to smile. Sujata could see her mental struggle from a mile away.

"I know you are nervous right now," Sujata nodded encouragingly, "and nothing I say will make you feel better. I can assure you the environment here is friendlier than you think."

Marie nodded, unconvinced, thinking of him.

"As for François," Sujata read her thoughts, "the fact that he accepted you here is already a miracle. He'll act like a jerk. Ignore him and move on, even if you still love him, although for the love of God, I can't understand why you would," she teased her.

"Thank you," Marie finally smiled. "I would appreciate it if you could ... if you could stay close. I admit I do not feel too well."

Sujata nodded and invited her into the main building.

Marie understood they had intentionally decided to have Sujata welcome her, knowing her precarious state of mind. This was already a good sign. These people cared for her. She felt a strange warmth in her body and shivered a bit. *This is it,* she told herself. *I'm doing it and I won't mess it up.*

Sujata took her inside, where the two receptionists greeted her friendly. She wasn't in the mood to pay much attention to her surroundings. She vaguely registered that Sujata told her she would go to meet the owner of the company, the big boss who must have hired François, a lifetime ago. Once she stepped into his office, the somber atmosphere given by the massive wood and brown shades from floor to ceiling took her aback.

"Marie, this is Professor Ian Ndikumana, the CogniPrescience founder and sole owner, as well as the main artisan behind what we are doing here."

"Welcome, Marie!" Ian stood up from his desk and greeted her jovially. "Please sit down." He pointed to a chair.

His attitude enchanted Marie, and she felt more at ease. She peeked at Sujata, who made herself comfortable on the sofa, like she wanted to be out of the way, yet close by.

"Thank you," Marie answered, bowing her head.

"As for being the brain behind this work," he winked at Sujata, "I think we can say that by now I fully share this title with François."

Marie froze a little, wondering how this would go next. No doubt that Ian knew about her relationship with François. Probably of his suicide attempt, too.

"Marie, I wanted you to know from the beginning that I am aware of the tension between you and François. I confess I was a little worried about Lieutenant Hopkin's initiative to bring you here. I am not one to make a fuss about the mix of personal feelings and business, yet, in this case, it might be very disruptive. And, as you'll soon find out, none of us can afford disruption and time-wasting. If that is the case, I fear our cooperation will have to cease."

Marie's face fell.

"Having said that," Ian smiled, "I am almost certain it won't come to that. François is stubborn, difficult, and impulsive, but he is not mad. He is a genius deeply in love with you, if you allow an old man's opinion on the matter. That he gave in and agreed to you joining our adventure is a telling sign. So, I expect the next few weeks to be the storm before the calm, if I may say so. Once things settle down, I hope you'll be the catalyst needed for us to finish the project. Oh, and please don't think your role here is merely to handle François. That's the cherry on top. Your real work will be much more exciting."

"I can only thank you for giving me this opportunity," Marie tried to smile, feeling more energized.

They spent the next hour talking about employment conditions, the commercial nondisclosure agreement, and the military additions. Marie didn't much care about the salary, but Ian's offer surprised her. As for all the secrecy, she failed to see the point. She never cared much for politics, military developments, or international affairs. She considered these matters to be for important people who knew how to deal with them. Over the last months, her obsession with François had consumed her, which mattered more to her than all the controversy in the world. She would never consider betraying secrets, military or otherwise, as she simply had no interest in such things. So, she had no qualms about signing all the documents.

"Alright," Ian breathed out, "now that all these formalities are over, I'll leave it to Sujata to explain the whole situation to you. Meanwhile, let me bring François here."

Before Marie had time to react, Ian took his tablet and did some quick moves.

"François, please come to my office for a few minutes. Marie has arrived, and we are done with the paperwork." He then leaned back in his massive chair and crossed his arms.

"I don't want you to be scared," Sujata started gingerly. "What I am about to tell you is shocking. I apologize in advance for throwing this at you, given your current state of mind, but it is necessary. You remember the neuromimetic conference in Paris where François participated?"

Marie frowned and nodded. She didn't want to remember that time.

"Coincidentally, it was the same conference where we found out that, at the top of the hierarchy in China, sits not their advertised president, but some sort of advanced AI. One of the Chinese top researchers who created it sent us a codified message to inform us about it. We don't understand how that happened. And we don't understand what that means for China and the rest of the world."

Marie was already confused. She wondered what she'd gotten herself into. Suddenly, the perspective of François popping up in the office wasn't that bad. She wanted to rely on him in these strange circumstances, which made her feel guilty. After all, it was she who was supposed to be protecting him, not the other way around.

"I know your personality, and I'm sure you don't want to be bothered with details. I'm telling you this to give you a sense of the urgency of our mission. We need to have something to deter the Chinese from attacking us or otherwise turning the world upside down."

François knocked discreetly and entered without waiting for an invitation, which Marie took as a sign that he was familiar with his boss. He nodded toward Marie and mumbled a greeting without locking eyes with her.

"*Salut,*" Marie responded simply, feeling embarrassed that the others had to witness his almost rude behavior.

"I was just telling Marie about our project," Sujata said, ignoring this awkward situation. "So, given the threat from China, the U.S. DoD investigated ways to come up with a formidable AI of our own. A general AI has been a century's dream that has never come true. We increased funding for the most promising research companies, irrespective of whether they were public, private, in academia, or the industry. This is how we found out about Ian's company and how we met François. The two of them had been working on such a project."

Sujata paused, looking at Ian, who nodded slightly. "Well, we have been thinking the best way forward would be for you to see with your own eyes what it is we are working on."

Marie noticed François shifted uncomfortably, and his eyes flickered unusually, like he was drunk. Sujata turned on a common Cybersperse space where she projected a video.

"What you see here is streamed live from our lab downstairs. Promise me you won't freak out, no matter what you think you see."

Marie nodded, thinking that such an introduction was the perfect recipe for her freaking out. She looked closely at the video. She saw a girl playing with some toys. At first glance, Marie registered that the girl had short hair. She was thin and muscular, she ... Then she noticed her face and jumped up from her chair, releasing a small yelp.

What kind of sick joke is this? she wondered, looking at the others in panic, at a loss for words. She thought she was losing her mind now, a year after longing for François. *Did he clone me? Is he trying to build a better, more docile version of me? A younger version, and that remains young? It has my haircut from the time he and I fought. And is this whole setup meant to humiliate me? But then why did the DoD get involved? Why the story about China? Why all those documents?*"

"Whatever you're thinking now is not correct," Sujata smiled encouragingly. "No, this isn't a clone. This is not some kind of conspiracy. You don't have a twin. What you see is, probably, the most human-like artificial intelligence on the planet. We call her CARLA."

"CARLA?" Marie mumbled. "But why …"

"CARLA resembles you, physically and perhaps even in her character a bit, due to François. He built her in your image."

Marie flashed an angry look at him. He looked small and utterly embarrassed. Marie started thinking things through and calmed down a bit. This showed how much he loved her. But it was also disgusting. Much worse than being replaced by one of those dumb sex robots. She didn't want to imagine what he and the android did the whole day.

"CARLA is a child," Sujata continued, like she was guessing her thoughts. "She is now learning everything: about our world, our language, our ways of living. Ian and François tried hard to bias her towards doing good for us. She's capable of some emotions and she's interested in interacting with us. Overall, I'd say she's progressing amazingly well, although many, many things can still go wrong."

For a moment, Marie thought of CARLA as a patient and leaned forward to see her better. A complicated, unique patient, to whom conventional psychiatric diagnosis and treatment did not apply.

"Yes," Sujata smiled, seeing her reaction. "We need your help to raise CARLA properly into a human, a superhuman, to help us counter the AI the Chinese have."

Marie collapsed back in her chair. This was going to be hell for her. *It's not enough that François is going to make my life miserable,* she thought, devastated. *I would need to work with this ... perversion of nature. With his lover who looks like me but is not a person. I don't know if I can do that.*

"CARLA is my …" François started talking in a hoarse voice, then he looked at Ian, "our daughter. She doesn't have a mother … Despite my complaints, Sujata thought you would be ... appropriate for this role." He still wouldn't look at her.

Just as quick as the image of CARLA had frozen Marie's heart, François's words melted it. They wanted her to be a mother! And François was the father! Never mind the other guy for a moment. François had built a child in her image. That was actually kind of sweet, if unnatural. She peeked at him again. She understood he had hoped that this presentation would be his moment of glory, the ultimate humiliation for her. Instead, he looked utterly miserable, probably imagining that Marie thought he was a pervert. She smiled again, awkwardly.

"But why me?" she asked and regretted it immediately, scared at the thought they might realize they had made a mistake.

"Because you look alike!" Ian joked. "Seriously, though, you're a qualified psychologist, trained in the impact of AI on humans. You worked with children for a while. You know François very well. And, as I can see now, having met you, you and CARLA share more than just facial features."

Ian paused for a moment, then continued. “We’ve reached a roadblock. CARLA has progressed enormously. She’s a miracle by any AI research standard. But if you compare her with a person, she is weird, sometimes bordering on crazy, and incapable of establishing clear social connections. Tuning her mind is a complex operation that goes beyond algorithms. We can’t mess around too much with a mind before things go haywire. The chances of us creating a psychologically deranged creature are enormous, while the chances of creating a thing that is close to what we would call a normal human being are infinitesimal. You know well that the human mind is a delicate balance. A small disruption in neurotransmitters disturbs the whole mental equilibrium, sometimes irreversibly. If we are not careful, we will build an autistic AI. Perhaps a monster. Not just a sociopath, but a psychopath! As the first true human-like artificial being, we need her to integrate properly into our society. We don’t want to build a person suffering from mental disorders, or one who exhibits violent social behavior. Think of the capabilities she will have. Compared to us, she will have nearly infinite computing power. She will eventually be able to rewrite parts of her routines. We need her to empathize. To understand us, to help us, to be on our side at all costs. There’s an enormous responsibility on our shoulders.”

Marie became scared again. Were these people aware of the fact that her own *mental equilibrium* was already more than disturbed? “I ... am not sure I am the right motherhood material for normal children,” she spoke honestly, although she was freaking out that they might send her back to the darkness of loneliness, “let alone an artificial one.”

Sujata rose from her seat and came closer to Marie, squatting in front of her and taking her hands. “I am sure this seems a lot to ask of you,” she whispered. “We understand if you refuse. But please don’t rush. Think about the fact that if you accept, you would be here with ... all of us. And you would have the chance to work on something historical.”

Marie started crying softly, upset that she’d revealed her feelings so easily. Clearly, one dose of medication this morning was not enough.

François scoffed softly, showing a bit of his conflicting attitude towards the whole setup. Hearing him, Marie nodded slightly and tried to smile. At the end of the day, she was going to be near him and their "daughter." What else could she ask for? She wiped her tears, lifted her head, and spoke.

"*Bien*. Let me see what I can do to help. Do I get a desk?"

François flinched a bit, his eyes betraying his satisfaction for a moment.

"You get a whole office," Ian announced victoriously.

CHAPTER 30:

RISK

Being deeply loved by someone gives you strength, while loving someone deeply gives you courage.

— Lao Tzu

After the initial shock of hearing about the dragon member's promotion and plans to use the MA, Qianfan and his co-conspirators reduced the frequency of their meetings to twice a month. Each of them would attend only if they thought it didn't look suspicious. To make their gatherings look natural, Qianfan and Daiyu tried hard to mingle with other people with little success. They joined Haitao a few times at some small parties, where they felt out of place. Haitao himself had a hard time making friends here, being one of the dreaded people who worked on the SSMS and the MA.

A couple of months after the unpleasant deal that Qianfan made with Ah Lam's mother, they were in the senior colonel's tiny apartment, which was plain to the point of austere. The colonel didn't bother to apologize for that, or for the food that he had ordered too early and was now cold. He seemed unusually agitated. Ah Lam was pretending to be her usual self, but they could all see how much the news about her mother's plans had shaken her. Daiyu had told Qianfan privately that she worried Ah Lam might reveal what she knew if she got into a fight with her mother.

"I guess I'll start," Qianfan offered. "Daiyu and I have advanced with the MA. Today I had to report to Dragon Member Zhèng that we reached 20 percent. Doing otherwise would have looked suspicious. If she were to ask one of my assistants, Haitao, he'd say that we're more advanced than that."

Ah Lam pretended not to care, although she lowered her gaze for a moment.

"There's also something else. It's more scary than useful. I've been told that our team ... I, in particular, will have direct access to the MegaAI."

"Direct access?" Ah Lam asked, raising her brows. "What does that mean?"

"They will give me a special device on which I can ask questions and receive answers directly from the MegaAI. Both chat and voice. I can only ask questions related to the work I'm doing. I have a feeling that this bonus came at the direct request of the dragon member. She desperately wants this thing finished," he added softly.

The news left Ah Lam and Hu speechless for a few seconds.

"I wish there were a way to use this," the colonel frowned. "To find out more about the mysterious AI that seems to be planning our lives for the next thousand generations."

"I can't see how," Qianfan shrugged. "It might get me in trouble if I bring up any topic that is not strictly related to our algorithms."

The colonel nodded, though he was visibly unhappy. "I have some news too," he said. "My superior informed us that the genetics team had a breakthrough. Something to do with the resistance to cosmic radiation. As you know, for us to withstand voyages that last years in space, and to colonize another planet that might not benefit from the protection that we enjoy here, we need better bodies. Apparently, we'll get them now."

"Do you know what that means?" Daiyu asked. "Is it about genetically modified newborns? Is it about applying some treatment to teenagers, adults?"

"I'm afraid I don't know. There's a general feeling that, once we complete a new propulsion system, we can start planning our departure more confidently. We can talk in terms of decades, perhaps even years, not generations."

"How come we get all these things now?" Qianfan asked, frustrated. "Why can't they come when the society is more stable?"

"Two reasons," Ah Lam answered. "First, and the most important one, is the MegaAI. It has grown enormously in capacity in the last few years. It works in parallel on multiple projects. Granted, it still needs physical time to do experiments, but all simulations and calculations are unprecedentedly fast. The second reason is precisely this totalitarian regime. Only under the iron fist of the party, who is forcing these crazy policies and the complete invasion of privacy, can we achieve such efficiency. This is, for example, how Stalin achieved the great industrialization of Russia at the beginning of the 20th century, which cost them millions of deaths. However, as history has proven on several occasions, this is not sustainable. Society will inevitably collapse."

"Yes, but never in history did any country have the MegaAI," the colonel countered.

Nobody could dispute this point.

"On my side, I made a list of compounds and substances we regularly prepare for the genetics team," Ah Lam sighed. "We send various combinations of them once a week. I looked at the inventory data and I noticed a strange pattern. There's one compound that's not missing from any of the shipments towards the Doom's Lab. It's some kind of manufactured cerebrospinal fluid, mostly glucose, heavily oxygenated."

"What could they do with it?" Qianfan asked.

"Beats me," Ah Lam answered.

"Could they be growing human fetuses in it?" Hu asked.

"Maybe," Ah Lam answered evasively. "I'm not a geneticist. I guess they could keep certain cells alive in such a concoction."

"Might it be related to the breakthrough the colonel mentioned?" Qianfan desperately tried to make a connection.

"That's pure speculation." Ah Lam remained unconvinced.

An idea came to Qianfan. "Could you poison it?"

"Poison it?" Ah Lam answered, confused.

"Yes. Make it so that it harms the cells that are being grown in it."

"I don't know," Ah Lam shook her head. "I think they would notice immediately." Then, after a pause, she continued, tilting her head. "I suspect I could try adjusting the solution with drugs, so we could see an effect in months, perhaps in half a year."

"It's a long shot, but I think we should do it," the colonel approved, looking at Qianfan. "We're paralyzed with inaction here. We're running out of options."

Qianfan looked at Daiyu. "What do you think?"

"I don't know," she answered. "It's indeed a shot in the dark. I'm uncomfortable not knowing what we are poisoning. What if they are children? Do we have the right to kill fetuses, even if they are, say, a genetically enhanced army meant to conquer the world? On the other hand, doing nothing means the end of the world, anyway. So perhaps it's our duty to do something. We are morally trapped." She took her head in her hands, thought for a while, then looked at Ah Lam. "Well, I think the risk of doing nothing is bigger. So, you can try altering that fluid if you think it won't be traced back to you."

"It doesn't matter much, does it?" Ah Lam offered a fake laugh. "In half a year I'll be a walking zombie anyway, convinced that I was a treacherous fool before."

Nobody laughed, but nobody disputed her point either.

"I'll do it. I'll change the composition of one of our ingredients. Given how little we use, I can estimate the fluid that goes to the Doom's Lab will be unhealthy for the next six-eight months. We should start hearing about the effect of this action long before, if indeed they are growing children, and my sabotage becomes a big deal."

"Alright," Qianfan said. "This is our first concrete action. Let's see if it will have any effect. I wish we could do something more."

"There's something else we could do," the colonel said softly, looking straight at Qianfan. "You might not like it."

"Oh ... what?" Qianfan asked, shifting uncomfortably.

"We need to communicate with ... the outside world. The Russians, maybe. If all things go to hell, we can at least send a warning or something. Chances are that we are going to be intercepted. So, we would use it only in desperate times."

"How?" Qianfan asked. "The MegaAI closely monitors all communications. It will shut us down before we can say anything meaningful. And ... why wouldn't *I* like it?" he asked, puzzled.

The colonel sighed. "We could use one of the decommissioned Russian satellites which they have pushed into space, further away from Earth. Our security experts trained on breaking their encryptions while it was still operational. We have everything we need to establish a connection and send up a short video. I'd say there is a fifty-fifty chance that the MegaAI doesn't care to monitor that."

"Aren't those offline?" Qianfan asked further, bothered that he didn't understand why he would particularly object to it.

"Technically, yes, they're offline. So, the Russians would have to power it back on, remotely. For them to do so, we'd need to tell them we want to talk. And we'd need to tell them which one."

"So, you want them to power back on an old satellite and keep it on standby, listening for a message? Does such a thing have enough power?" Qianfan asked.

"I suspect it does. Most of them are powered by solar cells. Normally, obsolete satellites are redirected to burn into the atmosphere or sent out further away, in a space cemetery."

"Alright. How do you propose we tell them?"

"I expect it would be enough to provide them its international designator and its name. The one I'm talking about would be [2032-523M][IPM 9/GOSAY]. I think someone high enough in the military would immediately recognize this."

"How would we convey this information to the right people?" Qianfan narrowed his eyes.

"This is a long shot. We have someone from Mega Ark City leaving for Russia next week," the colonel lowered his gaze, waiting for the storm to come.

Qianfan was quiet. He finally understood. "Two members of SAF will accompany her at all times. I know they will shadow her everywhere. She will be in and out of the hotel and the place where the Olympiad takes place. How do you expect her to talk to someone in the military?"

"Perhaps she won't be able to," the colonel shrugged. "Still, it would be worth a shot. I mean, if you agree. And if you think she won't rat us out."

"But she's just a child!" Daiyu protested. "Why risk it?"

"In all honesty, I don't think it's a big risk. If the SAF people who go with her catch her with the satellite designation written on a piece of paper, they would likely think that it has something to do with her math problems. Why would they suspect that some scribbling by a child is the name of a Russian decommissioned satellite?"

Qianfan kept quiet for a few minutes. "She would not disclose this to the party," he reasoned. "Not Baozhai, I guarantee that. I am terrified of the danger, though. I'll talk to her. Chances that this plan would work are minuscule. How would she find a person to whom to convey this message? Why would they believe a teenager? Why would the Russians power up the satellite after such a message? What if this particular satellite is dead? Would they keep the message to themselves or forward it to other nations? Not to mention that the MegaAI can intercept our communication, which would mean we are done."

"I know all of this," the colonel said, tired. "We must try. All we can do from now on is try crazy ideas before the MegaAI takes over completely."

CHAPTER 31:

MEETING MOTHER

Does God have feelings? If yes, He must have felt good upon creating the universe and man. Since then, man has tried to follow in God's steps. Just like children imitate their parents' way of talking, singing, celebrating, and getting angry, man wants to mimic what God did. But, alas, man is no god. Perfection degrades going down from God to man and further down from man to his makings. How, then, could we expect God's grandchild to achieve divine perfection?

— DeSousa's Memoirs - Part II - Creation - 2054

Marie sat at her desk in the spacious main building office Ian had provided for her. She was looking out the window. A mild wind was pushing the two short and round palm trees planted right in front of the building. They were strong enough, so that they only trembled a bit. She had learned the other day that they were California Fan Palm trees, apparently the only palm tree species native to North America. The bottom dead foliage of their fronds reminded her of the beards of a couple of old, wise men with funny haircuts who knew more about life than her. She imagined the trees in a severe storm, bent down without breaking. She, too, used to be sturdier, in control of her life, elastic, and able to withstand wild winds, like her extended depression episodes. Now she felt thin, vulnerable, like a balsamic fir tree, susceptible to being uprooted by any turmoil.

Ian knocked on her door discreetly. “Ready?” he asked, beaming as usual. He kept the door open and invited her with a bow, keeping one hand at his back and the other straight ahead of him.

“Sure.” Marie rose from her chair.

Since the DoD researchers had arrived, and after repeated complaints from François, Ian had minimized the personnel interacting with CARLA. Besides himself, François, and Sujata, only a dozen people from CogniPrescience’s regular team and a handful of the new government scientists could talk to her directly. Having Marie, a stranger to their work, earn this privilege right away, was bound to be another source of envy. She was glad to leave the office for a while and avoid what she thought were arrows directed at her from the others.

“Do we need to do this on the beach?” she asked as they were getting into the elevator.

“No, we don’t *need to* do it there,” Ian laughed. “I just thought it would be nice. And it might become a unique memory for CARLA, associating you with the time she experienced the ocean and the beach first-hand.”

Marie nodded, and said nothing more on the subject, although she wasn’t convinced that they needed such theatricals for a machine. They went outside, where a whole convoy of military vehicles waited for them. She and Ian got into a small Humvee. They planned to drive straight to a private section of the beach up north. Marie admitted to herself that the military personnel were invisible most of the time, and that being protected at this level gave her fragile mind a feeling of peace. Still, she found herself surprised to be missing her previous, run-of-the-mill employer, with the normal office gossip that she could ignore and the skirt-chasing Aaron who looked at her as if she were nuts.

Ian felt he had to explain what was going on. “We’ve had the military arrange a safe passage for us to the beach. We have several helicopters in the air and an armed escort. People living on the coast must think that the US military is doing massive exercises in the area.”

"Is this security necessary?" Marie asked, still upset.

"Yes. It is the first time we've taken her out of our facilities. And this kind of trip is dangerous."

"Why? Who would know?" asked Marie.

"We are unaware whether anyone knows of her existence or not," Ian admitted. "Still, this is a chance we cannot take. You understand, she's priceless at this point. Commercial companies would kill to get their hands on her. So would foreign governments. Sujata was firmly against this beach idea, you know. I had to twist her arm."

Marie's face went white. Again, all this talk about foreign powers and wars.

"It helps that we arranged this little trip at the last minute, so it's virtually impossible for somebody who tries to steal her to plan anything. It also helps that we are just half an hour away from the beach."

Finally, they arrived at the dropping point. A big fence prevented Marie from seeing the water and the beach. A couple of soldiers guarding the area saluted them with their hands on their helmets.

"Wait here until I give you the signal," Ian said as he rushed out of the car.

He slid through an opening in the fence. Judging by the way the soldiers were moving, Marie understood that CARLA was in one of the front cars and they were escorting her to the beach, although she could not see her. Ten minutes later, she got a brief message from him on her tablet, "Come."

She sighed, got out of the car, then stepped past the two soldiers, who opened a gate in the fence. The beach was narrow, and she saw that Ian and the others were relatively close. She started hurtling towards them, then she forced herself to slow down. If CARLA was as sensitive as they told her, she wouldn't want to scare her. Could CARLA get scared? She pushed these thoughts from her mind and approached her. CARLA seemed lost in the ebb and flow of the waves, mesmerized. Just like she was watching one of her beloved documentaries. She didn't seem to pay any attention to the people around her. Marie stopped five yards away from her. François was looking at them with a sulky face. Sujata seemed agitated, glancing around often like she expected a commando unit to emerge from the water and attack them.

"CARLA," Ian said, "I want to introduce you to a new member of our team, Marie. She is a psychologist trained on the effects artificial intelligence has on people. She's also quite familiar with the area of child psychology."

CARLA turned slowly towards Marie and tilted her head a little. Marie knew from reading about her that this was one of the idiosyncratic gestures that showed surprise. Marie held her ground, feeling uneasy. CARLA raised her hand and touched Marie's face, just like she did with Sujata a few months earlier. Her eyes seemed expressive, yet devoid of emotion.

"Are you ... me?" CARLA asked in a neutral voice that Marie found resembled her own.

"No," she answered, as steady as she could.

"CARLA," Ian intervened, "think of Marie as your mother."

"Mother?" CARLA asked. She seemed puzzled by the notion.

Marie nearly swooned. No, this wasn't the way Ian should have introduced her. Focusing on CARLA as a patient, she reached out and grabbed her hands. "I want to help you develop into a good person," she said calmly. "You are still a child, but you will grow. You will become more than any adult who ever lived."

"Mother means that I am your daughter," CARLA ignored her offer, stuck in the previous conversation.

"Well, in a manner of speaking," Marie struggled to explain. "You understand you are not a biological being, right?"

"Ian says I am a machine."

Marie detected no sadness in the way she uttered these words. Nor was anything in her posture to suggest that she was uncomfortable with the idea. "You're much more than a machine," Marie smiled, graciously.

"Am I not an artificial being?" CARLA asked.

Marie thought she sounded curious. "You're a masterpiece. A unique being that will change our world. We need to work together to achieve that. Do you understand?"

"I do," CARLA answered without hesitation. "I want to be a good artificial being." Then she turned towards the ocean, ignoring her. She moved closer to the water, prompting François to jump near her.

He behaves like his one-year-old daughter has approached the ocean and he's afraid a wave might take her, Marie thought, surprised. *Never in a million years would I have imagined he would be so careful.*

She felt a warmth inside her. Given his new personality, she dreamt about her and François having a child.

CARLA bent forward and picked up a broken shell. She looked at it on each side, kept it in her hand, picked another one up, opened her hand mechanically, and let it drop. She started chanting in a staccato manner, alternating names of shells with other things going through her mind, "Dove shell. Mother. Spindle shell. Good life form. Abalone. Daughter."

She moved further and further, under the supervision of military personnel. Watching her searching for rocks and corals, and admiring the water, Marie thought she seemed almost happy.

"Funny how she thought Marie was her copy." Sujata broke the silence when CARLA was far enough not to hear them. "As if she had seen herself in the mirror."

"This reminded me of an embarrassing experience I had long ago," Ian said cheerfully, a sign that this meeting had put him in a good mood. "In my late twenties, I had to attend a wedding in a foreign city, somewhere in Italy. I had brought with me appropriate clothing for the event. I found myself not liking a piece of garment. The shirt, I believe. So, I went to a local store to buy a replacement. I went in, chose one, and then I tried it in a separate tiny room, more like a closet, in a corner of the store. When I stepped out, or rather, I ran out, since back then I was neurotic, I found myself face to face with a handsome young gentleman storming out of a room in front of me and nearly knocking me down. I mumbled a quick apology and refrained from admonishing him for behaving like a lunatic, all under the concerned look of the young lady minding the store. Annoyed that he had stopped right in front of me and was staring brazenly, and since at the first glance I thought this nut looked familiar, I looked closer at him. All that happened in less than a second. Lo-and-behold, I soon realized I was looking at myself! In my eagerness to be done with this purchase and get on with my life, I'd paid little attention to my surroundings, so I hadn't noticed that the wall facing the door to my changing room, merely three feet away, was a big mirror. I felt like an idiot. In my effort to save face, I looked at the lady and I stuttered, 'Well, what ... What do you know? It's me ...' which only made matters worse. Judging by her mild amusement and the speed at which she seemed to forget the whole incident, I figured I wasn't the only gentleman who'd almost collided with himself, but that did little to curb my embarrassment."

"What was going on in your brain at that moment when you didn't recognize yourself?" François wondered.

"I suspect my brain was too slow. It was just a matter of processing speed," Ian answered.

"Well, CARLA shouldn't have this problem," Sujata pointed out. "Although, if we go through such experiences, imagine how confusing it must be for her to see herself in another being," she continued, smiling. "It's a miracle she didn't go into a core shutdown. She is so unpredictable. I can never understand whether she will cry, well, in her way, or stand still like a statue."

"I'm afraid that's more proof that she's not yet what we want her to be," Ian said, preoccupied. "She's reacting to external stimuli. Sometimes she's doing the equivalent of laughing or crying, which appears strange to us. A reminder that she isn't flesh and blood."

“She is so ... alive!” Marie disagreed. “It’s hard to believe that she’s a machine. This is the most amazing and beautiful thing I’ve seen in my life.” She shook her head in wonder. “I don’t know what will happen next, but the world will never be the same now that you’ve created her. Perhaps we’ll all thank you one day,” she said, looking at Ian and then François. She noticed François had gone all red. She wanted to hug him.

“I, too, often wonder if she’s alive,” Sujata admitted. “I keep asking myself, ‘Does she feel like being something? Does she get this unique awareness of her existence from within?’”

“François and I often talk about this. We implicitly attribute consciousness to her because she is so *like* us,” Ian agreed. “It’s natural for us to do so. We evolved in this way. I fear it is not true that she has a consciousness.”

All three looked at him, disappointed.

Ian felt he had to provide clarification. “The philosopher Thomas Nagel once wrote a famous paper called ‘What Is It Like to Be a Bat?’ He argued, convincingly, that we will never know the answer to this question. We could never know it because while it is conceivable that consciousness is pervasive in the animal kingdom, the subjective experience of being a bat is only accessible to, well, bats. I’m afraid the same is true with CARLA. We cannot measure if she has any kind of subjective experience when thinking, feeling, or acting in the world. If you want me to guess, she does not. We have not cracked the mystery of consciousness and I doubt it somehow materialized on its own in CARLA’s case.”

“Does it matter, though?” Sujata asked. “If I could paraphrase the duck test, if she looks like a human, moves like a human, and talks like a human, then for all intents and purposes, she *is* human to me.”

“It does matter enormously.” Marie shook her head vigorously.

“I agree,” Ian said. “First, without this subjective experience, she might never truly think. We don’t understand the relationship between consciousness and thought. They seem orthogonal, but we just don’t know. Second, if she were conscious, then we should judge her like a person. She should get rights and obligations, like any other human being, probably augmented, given her uniqueness."

"I don't see why we waste time with philosophical questions." François waved his hand impatiently. "We need to make her think. We'll figure out later whether she has these subjective feelings."

"Ian might be right, though," Sujata said thoughtfully. "What if consciousness is a prerequisite for her being truly intelligent? After all, we have no example of intelligent beings that are not conscious."

"There is a current in philosophy called panpsychism," Ian pointed out, "that purports that consciousness is a fundamental property of the universe, like mass, electric charge, etc. We don't yet have scientific ways to measure it. By being a fundamental property, it is conceivable that living beings that possess a complex underlying structure are more conscious than simple ones, which in turn are more conscious than inanimate objects. That's why our brains, being the most complex things in the universe that we know of, give rise to our specific consciousness.

"Do you believe in this panpsychism?" Sujata asked Ian.

"I subscribe to the claim that consciousness cannot be reduced to or explained in terms of other things. Still, I believe that consciousness as a measure of complexity and organization of the system is not enough. Instead, I believe it exists only in biological beings. Artificial beings like CARLA just don't have that spark, that quintessence of life. Well, I guess it is conceivable that if she were advanced enough to rewrite her code and if she had first-hand knowledge of what it means to be conscious, CARLA could learn to simulate it going forward."

The others seemed flabbergasted by this statement.

"I mean that if she were to experience consciousness at least once, perhaps she could memorize somehow how she felt and reproduce it conceptually, without having consciousness. This is speculation, since if consciousness is irreducible and purely biological, then CARLA might never understand it. Besides, that's a chicken-and-egg problem. We cannot test this theory since we would need her to be conscious in the first place and we'd need access to her consciousness somehow."

Marie looked at François, whose mouth was open. She knew him well enough to understand that the germ of an idea had formed, but she didn't dare to ask what it was.

CHAPTER 32:

OLYMPIAD

You don't need intelligence to have luck, but you do need luck to have intelligence.

— Jewish proverb

Baozhai looked out the car window at the marvelous city of Saint Petersburg. She was disappointed that she hadn't been able to see much of it in the nearly two weeks that she had been there. Throughout her stay, two SAF members, a man and a woman, had shadowed her. They had been so quiet that sometimes she had wondered if they knew Chinese at all. Paramilitary personnel accompanied the entire Chinese delegation. She noticed how these two SAF members kept to themselves, and the others were not interested in talking to them, either. Baozhai concluded the SAF branch must be a mystery for the other Chinese in the military, commanding respect, if not fear.

Looking at the buildings flashing in front of her eyes, she felt deep regret at not having been able to see this city. She had spent most of her time indoors. She was not allowed to go to dinner with the rest of the math competitors, not allowed to join in any common entertainment activities, and not allowed to go on the city tours organized for them. She had read a little about the city before coming here. She hadn't expected that she would long to visit and understand more about it. When she had complained bitterly about her treatment, the two bodyguards had consulted a bit and agreed to take her on a city tour in a self-driving cab. Such vehicles crawled at a ridiculously slow pace on dedicated lanes throughout the main parts of the city, presumably because their passengers wanted to enjoy the view, while she suspected the main reason was to avoid bad accidents.

Now even this broken way of having fun was over. They were on their way back to the airport. She felt her eyes grow moist. She had failed. Yes, she'd got a medal, but her 97.73 percent score ranked her only in the top fourteen. What was worse, in the final tally, China came second after Russia, barely above the United States. It was a performance for which the party leadership would not praise her, especially after all the drama surrounding her departure. Which got her to the other, bigger failure. Her bàba had given her a mission for the first time, and she hadn't been able to do it. Thinking of him released a big tear down her cheek, despite her effort to keep it locked in her eyes. She quickly glanced at the two bodyguards who, luckily, were fixating on the road ahead.

Just like two androids, she thought, frowning. *Two Nazi androids.*

She remembered vividly her father talking to her in the living room the night before she left. He had taken her hands, wiped away a tear himself, and explained to her, for the first time, the evil world they were living in.

"Baozhai," he had said, "what I am about to tell you now will shake the very foundation you have built your life upon. You don't know how much I have longed to have this discussion with you. I screamed inside so many times that my thoughts got hoarse. You have grown up without a mother, and I have done my best to protect you. You'll soon be an adult. At this point in your life, you deserve to know the truth."

She understood from his tone that this was about to change her life. Her bàba went on for hours, detailing what was wrong with the party, how the MegaAI was using them all, how they were living in a totalitarian regime, why it was wrong for people to be deprived of their privacy, to be chased around, monitored by cameras, microphones, and worthiness scores. He touched on how some of their very intimate thoughts were violated, they'd been re-educated in the party's spirit in school, and would now have their brains molded by direct manipulation. He disclosed to her the fact that the president and the MegaAI were the same. He had been so hesitant about this last part. She understood he feared for her life because having such knowledge might prove fatal. He wanted to make sure that they would never suspect her.

Baozhai also understood how deeply her father was suffering just by being part of this machinery. He would never be whole again. In retrospect, she had known things to be wrong. She had figured out long before that her father wanted her to memorize poems and train in meditation to focus her mind on safe thoughts. His words hadn't been a huge surprise. Still, her first reaction was a deep regret and remorse that she would have to report him now. That was a horrifying thought. This was her beloved bàba, without whom her world would crumble. How could she have considered going to those cold party scavengers and reporting *him?* That was the extent of the damage their education had inflicted on her. And then came her mission.

"I'll now ask you to do something," her father had sighed. "I ... I'm trying to do something about this situation. I don't want to put you in danger. So, before I talk to you about it, please, please, promise me above all that you will do nothing risky. If you're not sure it's safe to act, do nothing. Can you promise that?"

Baozhai remembered how confused and scared she'd felt as she had nodded in approval.

"You're going to leave for Russia tomorrow," her father had continued. "I want you to memorize a short sequence of numbers and letters. If the opportunity arises, give it to somebody there, especially somebody in the military." He had immediately panicked, as if he had regretted his words. The thought that they would catch her made him sick.

Recalling this episode, she stomped her foot slightly, attracting an inquisitive look from her bodyguards. *No reason to be concerned*, she thought, frowning. *I'm not smart enough to propel China to win the gold medal. I'm not smart enough to relay a stupid message.* And now they were going to the airport. She would have to face Bàba, that dreadful dragon lady, her math teacher, and her nerdy friends that so envied her for being allowed to leave.

Lost in thought, she barely realized that the view had radically changed outside, the curvy arms of the highway splitting and multiplying like concrete snakes reaching out to the airport terminals. So, her fun and her duty were over. She stepped out of the car, flanked by her good friends, who took care of the luggage. They moved into the terminal's departures section. They had to wait a couple of hours for their flight. She cared little about the airplanes outside, or about the people rushing with their screechy carry-on luggage rollers, so she sat down on an uncomfortable single seat, pulled out her tablet, and started reading, doing her best to be oblivious to her companions. She wasn't allowed access to the local Cybersperse, so she had prepared a few books available offline.

Half an hour later, she shifted her position and involuntarily glanced at the two SAF soldiers. They sat in front of her, two wax statues, looking straight ahead, ignoring all the bustle around. At that moment, she noticed out of the corner of her eye a khaki spot flashing in the corridor ahead of her. When she turned her head left, she saw the door of the women's restroom closing by itself, pulled slowly into position by the spring mounted on top. Her bodyguards had not seen it since they were sitting with their backs to the door. Her heartbeat increased a little. This was not even a quarter of an opportunity, but she was getting bored, anyway. She put her hand in her pocket where she'd kept one of the draft papers she got during the competition, with a few formulas and arrows. Her pen was there too. Slowly, she stood up and announced, "I need to go to the toilet."

The female bodyguard nodded and stood up to accompany her. Baozhai moved deliberately slowly, hoping that she would not be too late. There was one woman inside, washing her hands. She left in a hurry. She wasn't wearing khaki, so it wasn't the person she'd seen going in. One of the four stalls appeared occupied. Baozhai moved to an empty adjacent one, unsure what she could do with the hawk waiting outside. She quickly took out the pen and paper from her pocket and scribbled something on the top with a shaky hand. She thought about passing it to the other stall through the opening on the bottom. But she couldn't risk that the woman would say something aloud and raise her bodyguard's suspicion. Suddenly, she heard movement, then the water flushing, and the door opening. She put the paperback in her pocket, flushed and rushed outside too, desperate. The SAF soldier was there, impassive, guarding the door. Baozhai looked at her target. It was a middle-aged woman who indeed appeared to be military. The woman moved to wash her hands. This was it. The opportunity that she'd almost had was gone. Baozhai frowned and moved to wash her hands too.

Just then, out of the blue, an alarm screamed at them from a small speaker installed in the ceiling. A voice started in the rough yet beautifully flowing sound of the Russian language, followed by English and Chinese.

"Unauthorized access. Please remain at your place until the emergency ends."

The khaki woman said something between her teeth, which Baozhai suspected was a curse. The announcement had shaken the android in charge of Baozhai, whose eyes sparked a bit, unsure what she was supposed to do. She looked from one to the other, tightening her lips for a couple of seconds. Seeing that the other military lady was about to ignore the instructions and move past Baozhai, she quickly threw a command in Chinese toward Baozhai.

"Stay here. Don't move. I'll see what's going on."

Without another word, she turned, opened the door, and stepped out. While waiting impatiently for the Chinese soldier to get out of the way, the Russian woman looked curiously at the girl she was leaving behind. Baozhai was trembling like a leaf, shaking her head vigorously. The woman raised her brows and stopped in her tracks, closing the door slowly.

It's now or never, Baozhai thought, hesitantly.

Forcing herself not to analyze the situation too much, she ripped her draft paper in two and handed the woman the part on which she had just written something half a minute before.

The woman's eyes grew bigger when she read it. The text said, in Russian, "ACTIVATE [2032-523M][IPM 9/GOSAY]. CHINA RESISTANCE WILL TALK."

Before the woman could ask for clarifications, Baozhai burst into tears and stuttered, struggling to say something in Chinese before her guardian came back, yet unsure if the woman understood a word she was saying.

"You must act on this. Now. Millions of people will die otherwise. We will contact you when possible."

Thankfully, the woman nodded, which was more a sign of shock than comprehension. In the next moment, the door opened and the SAF soldier was back. The Russian woman rushed to put the paper in one of her uniform's chest pockets and left the restroom without another look at them. Although for Baozhai it felt like an hour, it had been less than 20 seconds since the alarm had gone off.

"Somebody moved past the security door," the SAF announced, with a monotonous voice, while her face sagged in disgust at how stupid people could be. She noticed Baozhai was in tears, trembling, and she asked, with an imperceptible frown, "What happened?"

"I ... am afraid," Baozhai answered, thinking that if the soldier had one of her father's SSMS devices, it would have confirmed her words with high accuracy.

"No reason," the soldier relaxed, thinking that the alarm had caused this reaction. "We'll be on the plane in a couple of minutes."

Baozhai wiped her tears away and left the restroom. Once back in her seat, she grabbed her tablet, trying to calm down the storm in her head. Did she just pass the message on, or did she imagine it? Would the woman take her seriously? Was the woman senior enough to be taken seriously herself?

As she was failing to concentrate on the words in front of her, she moved to put her tablet back into her bag. She noticed that somebody was staring at her from ten yards away. The khaki woman! She had moved to a place where her two bodyguards could not see her. Baozhai nearly dropped her tablet, but she controlled herself and looked back at her. The woman moved her head slowly up and down, in a universal acknowledgment gesture, which in this case meant, “I got your message, and I am taking it seriously.”

Baozhai felt she was about to cry again, and had to cover her face with her hands, but stretched and faked a yawn. For the first time since she’d left Mega Ark City, she felt she’d accomplished something that would make her bàba proud.

CHAPTER 33:

THEORY OF MIND

Fool me once, shame on you, fool me always, shame on whom?

— DeSousa's Memoirs - Part II - Creation - 2054

François was in a bad mood. He was sitting at his desk, reflecting on the past few months since Marie had arrived in his world again. CARLA was watching one of her documentaries in her corner, paying no attention to him. It upset him how he had to see Marie's face every day now, the real one, not just CARLA's, and listen to her trembling voice. He felt bad that she wasn't herself, that she was fawning all over him. He missed the good old times when he and Ian would talk, and only CARLA would silently listen to them. Ian would laugh, hearing about how François didn't want to meet him initially. He had often wondered if CARLA understood the conversations and jokes the two of them exchanged, talking about what they thought of each other in the beginning, and what would have happened if they never met. Those had been better days.

Instead, he now occupied his mind with irrelevant thoughts, angry that he couldn't look into Marie's eyes. And he never talked to her. He barely mumbled a greeting and, when she asked something, he answered, looking anywhere else but at her. On top of everything, he couldn't stand that her work now interfered with his, that she was bound to criticize him, inevitably. He felt jealous that CARLA liked her, that she accepted her as a mother, and that Marie fit this role unexpectedly well. Most of all, he hated how he realized that, deep down inside, he longed to see and hear her. He wanted her close by.

Merci, Sujata. Brilliant idea bringing her here. As if we didn't have a mess big enough! he thought, hitting the desk with his fist.

CARLA turned to him, alerted by the sound, but maintaining her serene appearance. "I heard a noise."

"Yes, CARLA, sorry if I scared you," François said and lifted his palms.

"No fear. Just noise." She turned back to her studies.

François noted in passing that she couldn't infer his foul mood. He was concerned that Ian was right and there was something important missing in her. Ian had planted a seed of doubt in his head.

"*Zut*, Ian and his stupid philosophical questions," he muttered, getting up. "CARLA, I'm leaving for Ian's office," he said aloud.

She ignored him, or she didn't hear him. François sighed and left the lab. Sujata and Marie were already there. Marie's earlier note to all of them said that she had something important to tell them. He wasn't eager to hear what it was. As if guessing his discomfort, Marie quickly avoided his gaze. François found this unusual since she was the one always looking to lock eyes with him.

Ian broke the tension, stretching a bit. "I tell you, old people know all too well how it feels to be young. Young people have no clue how it feels to be old."

The others looked at him, puzzled.

"Sorry, I am in a bit of pain," he grimaced and continued. "The combination of sharp kidney pain and osteoarthritis makes my chronic shoulder ache quite unbearably. No matter how bad you think you have it, may God protect you from something far worse. CARLA is blessed to be spared all of this."

François rolled his eyes. Now they were suddenly getting spiritual.

"So," Ian asked, "what is it you have found, Marie?"

Marie took a deep breath and then began, still looking at the floor. "I can't speak about consciousness, but I'm afraid I have some bad news about how advanced CARLA is," she mumbled.

"You do?" Ian's eyes grew bigger, and his face became serious, suddenly forgetting all his mortal pains.

François was so outraged that he took a step towards the door. He forced himself to remain in the room. *Who does she think she is?* he thought, forgetting about his mental block and looking at her cross.

"I've been analyzing tens of hours of recordings with CARLA alone, or as she was watching videos, or interacting with you all. My conclusion is that she cannot infer from visual, audio, or linguistic cues what others think. I don't think she can properly ascribe mental states to anybody else. I fear she does not possess what psychologists call a 'theory of mind,' or the ability to mentalize."

Ian nodded slightly, waiting for her to continue.

"Theory of mind is—" Marie started.

"I know what theory of mind is," François yelled, exasperated. "What possessed you to think that she doesn't have it?"

"François," Sujata spoke softly. "I know of the concept, but I'm not sure I understand it well enough. Please let Marie explain it to me."

François kept his mouth shut and just sulked.

"It's relatively easy to test," Marie said and raised her arms defensively. "If I am wrong, all the better!" Then, turning towards Sujata, she continued. "Theory of mind postulates that most normal people can represent the minds of others in their own heads, and recognize that others might be driven by goals different from their own. As a corollary, a being that possesses a theory of mind can also represent its own mind and reason about it. This is crucial for planning, understanding others' intentions, and any kind of social skills. Also, for empathy, comprehending the meaning of stories, including humor, interpreting large texts, grounding, in reality, the concepts of good and evil, making the decisions that involve and affect humans, and so on. There are people with an incomplete theory of mind because of either a developmental defect or a cognitive defect. They cannot co-exist properly with the rest of us. In the absence of this capability, we have a ... broken AI."

"CARLA is not broken!" François couldn't resist yelling at her again. He looked ready to jump at her throat. "Why do you say so?"

"Well, for starters, I looked at how she describes the videos she sees. Take *Bambi*, for example. When you guys asked her about it, she provided many funny answers. She can use logic and reason about one scene or another, she understands language, and she roughly follows the plot. However, she doesn't fully understand that the child Bambi was replaced with the adolescent Bambi. She doesn't understand the idea of loss, in this case, the loss of Bambi's mother. She doesn't understand the idea of danger. I mean, she statistically associates whatever happens in the movie with her limited knowledge about the world, but she doesn't get the sad feelings simulations relative to Bambi. Any normal child empathizes with Bambi right away, some more sensitive might cry watching the cartoon."

"What on Earth are you talking about?" François said. "We have the opposite problem with her! She's too emotional."

"Yes, she can get scared, she can get happy, she can get jealous—well, at least she can simulate these emotions. She gets them only from direct stimuli. CARLA can't infer the same emotions by looking at your face if you were to cry. She cannot understand that some story or some event made you upset."

François frowned and vowed to find this out for himself. Ian nodded again, lost in thought.

"Ultimately," Marie continued, "CARLA doesn't deeply understand that Bambi is a fictional character humans created. She might even think all fawns can talk and behave in that anthropomorphized way."

"If this is true," Sujata said, "can we do anything about it?"

"I honestly don't know," Marie shrugged. "Although certain topics, like whether animals have a theory of mind, are still controversial, the field of psychology has detailed this theory. We know the order of things she needs to gain. She must first understand that other people 'want' things different from her wishes. Then she must conceptualize the fact that others 'think,' and again, that other people's thoughts are often at odds with what she wants. Then comes the idea that 'seeing or hearing about something leads to knowing,' that is, if a person sees or is told about something, they know about it. If they don't see it and they're not told about it, there's no way for them to know it. Finally, she needs to understand that others are adept at 'hiding their true feelings.' Without this last ability, she will never understand that someone is trying to deceive her."

"She must have some primitive theory of mind," Ian objected. "Otherwise, she wouldn't be able to engage in a conversation the way she currently does."

"For non-humans, this theory is still poorly understood," Marie admitted. "As you know, there have been many claims that our state-of-the-art AI assistants, usually built on large generative language models, already have a theory of mind. I don't agree with these claims. I suspect they use simple learning processes. They associate a certain behavior of ours with a certain action, so they know it next time the two happen simultaneously. That's not a true theory of mind."

"This would mean that for her we are only objects in the room," Sujata pointed out. "Objects that move and talk and interact with her, but that are not alive."

"In a crude sense, yes. Many scientists believe animals like dogs behave based on this kind of associative thinking. I think that this ability is not black and white, it is more of a spectrum. Humans are the most cognitively advanced beings, so they possess the best one."

"Given these circumstances, how could we expect her to take on the MegaAI? To love us and protect us?" Sujata asked.

"We can't," Ian confirmed. "If this is true, we are very far from morphing her into a freedom fighter. From what we know about the MegaAI, its capabilities must include a theory of mind."

"Perhaps we can try to train this ability in CARLA, to some extent," Marie offered. "We need to teach her to label emotions, as people's facial expressions reflect them. Drill into her mind the fact that she differs from others, yet in some sense, others are like her. Make her understand that our actions affect her, and that her actions affect us. And so on."

"How do we know you are right?" François challenged her, boiling. "Should we just take your word for it?"

"No, by no means," Marie answered calmly. "There are many tests that we can do. And repeat them, as we work on improving her."

"Fine. Do your tests. If you'll excuse me." François turned to the others and stepped out of the office, still boiling. He walked to his lab with his fists clenched. Once he got in, he slammed the door, shaking the whole building.

CARLA made a funny gurgling noise.

"She's doing all of this to spite me," François talked to himself, not thinking about CARLA. "She's envious I've achieved something no one could achieve. Why is she back in my life? Is she here to destroy me again?" he lamented.

"Who?" CARLA asked. She was frowning and looked ready to cry.

"Marie!" François answered, still ignoring her reaction. "*Mon Dieu, je la déteste*! I hate her. She has some kind of power over me. She already made me die once."

Suddenly, he realized he wasn't alone. He looked at CARLA's distorted facial silicon muscles.

"CARLA, do you know how I feel?"

"You hate Marie," she answered mechanically.

"Yes, but I can see that you, too, are tense," he insisted. "Why?"

"I got scared by the door," she answered instantaneously.

"Can you ... infer my state of mind, by looking at me?" he asked, narrowing his eyes.

"I don't understand the question," CARLA answered, calmer this time.

François nodded. This was bad news. A gentle knock on the door made him roll his eyes. "Come in, *bon sang*! Since when does anyone knock? People never care about disturbing me."

Marie stepped in. She looked ready to cry; her face was tight and her eyes were deep in their sockets. Seeing her, François froze. He realized this was the first time the two of them had been alone, not counting CARLA.

"I'm sorry I upset you," Marie started. "I promise you I want to help."

"You don't. All you care about is humiliating me!" François yelled at her, still looking behind her.

"François," she approached him and took his hands in hers. He flinched at her touch and wanted to push her and run away, but he couldn't. "You know I love you more than anything in the world. I understand I wronged you in the past, even though I didn't realize it. I understand those scars are buried in your soul. But you must know, deep down, that I would never want to harm you."

"You ... you shouldn't have come back. You are like a ... recurring nightmare. Since you came here, I can't think properly, I can't live! You say you love me. You don't. You don't appreciate me, you never did. You wanted ... somebody else. Even if I were awarded ten Nobel prizes, if I was the most popular man on Earth, if I saved the world, it wouldn't be enough for you."

Seeing his tears, Marie started crying too. It felt good to let the tension out. She was oblivious to CARLA being right there and listening to them. "You're so wrong. You have created a miracle! How can I not appreciate it? I'm trying to help you finish it. There's no other way to do this without being honest."

François wiped his tears and, for the first time in a long time, he looked at her for more than a couple of seconds. She had changed, indeed. She was more supple and somehow much wiser. Just like he wasn't her old François, perhaps she wasn't his old Marie. He nodded, feeling his frozen heart melt a little, feeling again like he used to feel in her presence a lifetime ago. He didn't want to feel that way.

Marie stood up, intimidated by his piercing gaze. "Will you ever forgive me?" Marie asked between sobs.

"I don't know anymore," he answered, tired, wondering for the first time if there was something to forgive.

She winced, and smiled timidly, taking his answer as progress. "I want to be your friend," Marie said. "I wish for more, but if you can't give me that, I understand. Can you please be my friend?"

"I don't know. Last time, when you wanted me to be just *your friend*, things didn't work out too well for me."

Marie got upset about him bringing up that again.

"I need time," he whispered, seeing how much his words upset her.

"You have all the time in the world. I want you to know that I will always love you." She turned and ran outside of the room, still sobbing, too unsettled to say anything else.

François looked after her, feeling suddenly lonely.

"Why are you crying?" CARLA asked.

François realized again that they had forgotten about her, and that she had been there the whole time. He knew it was a bad idea for parents to fight in front of their children. Her question seemed to contradict Marie's earlier findings, so he felt hopeful.

"Before I answer," he chose his words carefully, "can you tell me why you asked me this question?"

"You and Ian asked me this when I cried," she answered.

François nodded. This was the associative learning that Marie had warned them about. It was not genuine concern, empathy, or curiosity.

"I cry because I love her. And I don't want to," he answered cryptically.

"Six minutes ago, you said you hated her. Do you hate her, or do you love her?" CARLA asked, appearing confused.

"Both!" he answered. "It's complicated. You can love and hate someone at the same time."

"These feelings are opposite on a linear scale," CARLA reasoned. "How can they exist simultaneously?"

François thought impatiently that, ever since they tuned up language in her, she had asked a lot of stupid questions. Since he and Ian had programmed in her a bias towards curiosity, she had the urge to find out information that allowed her to make new inferences until her spirit of inquiry became irritating. And he hated how she never paused to think. Most people needed a second or two to ponder on an issue. CARLA seemed to always reply one microsecond after he finished talking.

"Sometimes, they can. Probably ... one feeling is predominant. Hate might be just a side effect of being jealous. Of being upset that the other person doesn't give you the attention you think you deserve. That the other person harms you, somehow." He recognized that this kind of psychoanalysis, which must be utterly useless for CARLA, helped him.

"Jealousy and hatred are bad. Why would you feel that way?" CARLA asked.

"You should know that we humans are flawed," he tried explaining this further to her, realizing that his reasoning had quickly slumped into a quagmire. "And you need some of these flaws to be a good human being. The trick is to use them to your advantage. And, most importantly, to avoid harming others because of them."

"I do not understand," CARLA answered simply.

"I know you don't," François whispered to himself, lost in thought. "I know you don't. But there might be a solution to this. It's time for me to pay a visit to that insistent son-of-a-bitch, even though he is General Kambe's man."

CHAPTER 34:

FLAW

Begin with an error of an inch and end by being a thousand miles off the mark.

— Chinese Proverb

Half a year after the deal he made with Dragon Member Zhèng, Qianfan knew he could not keep the device from her hands for long. The team had made sufficient progress to conclude they might be halfway towards obtaining a functional MA device. In a short call with him, she had sent orders that the prototype be sent to tests in a reeducation camp somewhere else in the country. The news, although predictable, had still caused Qianfan to sleep only a couple of hours per night for almost two weeks by now.

Alone and lost in thought at his desk, Qianfan decried the fact that he and the other three rebels could do nothing meaningful to hinder the MegaAI plans. His dear, brave Baozhai had sent the message to somebody in Russia, but there was no sign that the satellite was active. And even if it were, what was it they could say? By now, other countries surely knew of Professor Zhèng's message, at least as a rumor. Half of the world probably thought the Chinese had lost their minds to let themselves be led by a machine. Or that they had no means of stopping this.

He felt like crying. He couldn't resist a glance straight ahead at the latest dreadful addition to the arsenal of devices he had to deal with. One was a quantum silver box that gave him a direct connection with the terrifying

MegaAI, aka, the president, aka, the destroyer of humanity. The device was now quiet. He would have to turn it on soon. It looked rather dull and obsolete. He was told that its developers had used the latest quantum-inspired encryption technology, so there was virtually no way for someone to intercept their discussion. He remembered Haitao's reaction when he saw it first. His eyes had sparked with a mixture of veneration and adulation bordering on religious fervor, as if the MegaAI itself was trapped inside that little box. Haitao had complete and utter confidence in the Great Project. He blindly trusted the superiority and the benevolence of the MegaAI.

Qianfan lowered the corner of his mouth. *Out of the thousand deities that people worshiped through a hundred and fifty millennia,* he thought, *the MegaAI is the first real, tangible god, who actually has power. While it isn't yet omnipotent, whatever that means, it is by far the most dominant force here on Earth. What could a few mortals like the four of us do against it?*

Qianfan narrowed his eyes as he looked at his reflection on the device's metal. The lack of sleep had made his mind fragile, and it didn't take long for him to hallucinate. The distorted image of his face, marred by the dark circles under his eyes, appeared to be flowing out on the curvy edge of the box, like the clocks in Dalí's painting *Persistence of Memory*. He could swear he saw his face frown and grin back at him in an unnatural, devilish way. Had this machinery already captured his soul? Was he trapped inside the MegaAI? Was he doing its bidding? He screamed and hit the box with a small spherical paperweight, the first available thing he could grab from his desk. He stood up, looking terrified at it, expecting the essence of the MegaAI to leak out, and the paperweight to siphon it from the box straight into him, like an evil jinni that would possess the fool who dared to wake him up. For what was he, but a fool? Hadn't he developed the SSMS, progressed the MA, sold his soul? How much blood was on his hands? The party, with its honorable dragon and supreme lucifers and shrews, cowed him into silence. He deserved to die now.

"Baozhai," he whispered, the word thundering in his eardrums. "I can't leave her alone!"

Alerted by the sounds, Daiyu, who was analyzing some optimization routines in an adjacent office, rushed in. She found Qianfan standing against the window, covering his eyes with his hands, leaning back and forth, and groaning softly.

"What's going on?" she asked, scared, closing the door before anyone else could see them.

Qianfan flinched when he heard her and moved his hands. He recovered his wits and threw himself back in the chair, ashamed. "Don't ... come in ... I don't want you to see me like this," he whispered hoarsely.

"Stop it," she rushed to him and hugged his head to her bosom. "I love you, Qianfan, and indeed, I don't want to see you suffer like that, either."

He started crying, comforted by her presence, by her familiar smell, above all, by her genuine confession. He slowly calmed down, coming back to the land of the living, and realizing that this was the first time he'd lost control of his sorrow. "I'll be fine," he assured her.

"You need to go home now," she said in a commanding voice. "There's nothing you can do in this state. You need sleep."

"I will, I promise. Today I have another session scheduled," he said in a terror-stricken voice, glancing at the shiny box, now spoiled by a considerable dent that had pushed it to the edge of the desk. "I hope I didn't break it." Qianfan stood up in panic, trying to assess the damage he had produced.

"Surely you cannot consider talking to the MegaAI under these circumstances," Daiyu chided him. "You must excuse yourself!"

"I can't," Qianfan answered, shaking his head categorically. "It would look suspicious," he continued, grabbing her hands. "I promise I'll go the minute our chat is over. You know they'll send us the first results from the tests today. I cannot miss them. I ... need to understand how much damage we did. How *well* the MA works."

Daiyu stopped protesting and started crying in silence, her shoulders moving up and down, as if she were getting small electric shocks. Suddenly, the door opened and Haitao entered with a bang.

"Zhào zǒng, the results are …" he shouted, but stopped when seeing Daiyu wiping her tears and Qianfan looking like he had come back from the dead.

"Oh, sorry, I could ... I could return," he stammered, then he frowned, noticing that Qianfan had the silver box in his hands. "Is everything alright?"

"No worries, Haitao," Daiyu said in a voice that she wanted firm, while her body was still trembling slightly. "Doctor Zhào wasn't feeling well, but he's better now."

"Thank you, Haitao. I'm going to look at the results now," Qianfan said, tired, and not wanting to prolong this discussion.

Haitao shrugged, thinking that this must be just a lovers' quarrel, and offered, "Let me know if you need my help with anything before …" he looked with respect towards the box, "the meeting."

"Thank you, that won't be necessary," Qianfan dismissed him.

Daiyu left too, not before throwing a last worried glance towards him.

Once he was alone again, Qianfan looked at the device in disgust. With a quick gesture, he took off his coat and threw it over it in a symbolic and futile attempt to remove it from his life. Not seeing his face reflected in it seemed to help somewhat, so he took out his tablet and started looking at the results, slightly more energized.

A couple of hours later, he was back to feeling devastated. They had tested the first MA on 1000 subjects. He had no clue who chose this number, nor why the testing period was precisely two weeks. He had no say about any aspect of the testing. Objectively speaking, any normal, good scientist would oppose testing at the current stage of development. They were not baking cookies. They were inducing currents into the brain to alter the experience in real-time and to influence the long-term memory formation. The pressure to produce results was enormous, and he knew he could complain only this much before they'd replace him as the head of the project.

My leadership did nothing to stop this nightmare, he thought, depressed.

The results showed that 423 of the test subjects died within the first week, followed by 157 in the second. Another 368 were in a serious condition and it wasn't clear if they'd survive. Qianfan had seen recordings of these people's symptoms after being reeducated, and they were horrific. They reminded him of the experiments the Nazis did in the previous century. Only 52 subjects went through the mental correction without obvious damage. These 'lucky' ones had been tortured several hours a day. Their brains were fried to bolster their enthusiasm while listening to propaganda, to tremble in fear and indignation when hearing about the enemies of China, to be enraged at images of dissidents daring to speak against the party, to respect and love, above all, the MegaAI, the provider for all, and other such combinations of scare-pleasure tactics that were part of a veritable battery of tests designed by a team of psychologists.

Most people in our society already grow up brainwashed by their school and parents. If we end up perfecting the MA, the party will ensure they will enlighten, in the spirit of the mighty AI, anyone who emerged sane by the time they reached adulthood. What will happen to the world then?

The only good news was that the MA prototype was not working. That meant a reprieve for him, but then more tests, more victims. He looked at his hands and could swear he saw them colored in red. Rationally, he knew all too well that this was a hallucination. Still, he felt compelled to hide them behind his back with a quick move. After a few long minutes, he forced himself to plug in the communication device using his peripheral vision so that he wouldn't see his bloody hands.

Finally, a warning light came on and the cursor on the primitive chat window blinked eagerly.

"A peaceful noon, Doctor Zhào," the cursor wrote.

"Good afternoon," Qianfan answered, realizing, once again, that he did not know how to address the AI.

"I assume you analyzed the results," the AI stated, only to continue without waiting for his confirmation. "They are unacceptable. In the meantime, I have made 104,592 variations of the basic algorithms and run simulations for them."

"'*In the meantime?* '" Qianfan thought, frowning a little. *I wonder how this thing perceives time. It's been merely two hours since we got the results.*

"I have come up with five candidate changes. We should proceed with the changes right away. We will first try them on another batch of monkeys like before."

Like that would do us any good, Qianfan thought.

"Our next human trials will proceed as soon as your team implements the changes in the hardware. I estimate that this will happen next month."

Slow down, you monster, Qianfan screamed in his head, thinking frantically about how to intervene. *If this AI is so smart, I wonder, could I reason with it?* he asked himself, then continued aloud. "What about the batch of people who were part of the first trial? Shouldn't we look at them?"

"Most of them are dead," the machine replied coolly, and the total lack of empathy took Qianfan aback. "There's nothing to study."

"Did those who die have something in common? Or perhaps are those who survived genetically stronger? Surely, we need to understand that."

"Irrelevant," the AI answered right away. "I have found nothing to suggest that their genes have anything to do with the failure of the Mood Alterer device."

"With respect," Qianfan dared ask with a grimace that he was happy the AI couldn't see, "shouldn't we postpone the next experiment until we know more about what went wrong? Otherwise, we risk losing more test subjects."

"The loss of test subjects is acceptable. I estimate the device will be functional before we lose 10 percent of them."

You have gathered tens of millions of people to be indoctrinated, Qianfan wanted to scream. *Surely 10 percent is not an acceptable loss.* Instead, he tried a different angle, "What if we understood more about the aim of this reeducation? Perhaps then we could tailor the device to influence more certain areas of the brain."

"Doctor Zhào, I ask you to remain within the current parameters of the project. You cannot comprehend the goals set for the reeducation. Even the most brilliant of dogs cannot think further than a dog."

Although there was no hint of a threat in this request, Qianfan started shivering a bit. "I'm only trying to understand how we can best see the Great Project come to life," he justified himself, offended by the canine comparison.

"The Mood Alterer will remove all human elements that have the potential—ARK VARIANT 9032340342, NEW YORK 10001, DEATH AT DAWN—to stand in the way of this project. There's no need for you to worry about this. You are an instrument. The horse does not worry when the rider takes it to battle. The ox does not question its master when plowing the field."

Qianfan's mouth opened. Did the MegaAI just have the equivalent of a slip of the tongue? Was it in the mood for a philosophical discussion? "I ... I didn't understand the reference to ARK and 'NEW YORK,'" he typed, choosing to ignore the other strange animal comparisons.

"No such reference concerns you. Your primary task is to lead the team that develops the Mood Alterer. THE SKY UNIDIRECTIONAL GATEWAY. UNCERTAINTY."

Qianfan was too tired, too shocked, too scared to believe his ears. *Perhaps I'm hallucinating again,* he thought, feeling panicky.

"Doctor Zhào," the AI continued, signaling that it wanted this meeting to conclude, "I sent five new variants of the algorithms to your private Cybersperse. Your team will integrate them into five different devices in the next four weeks. We will then reassess our progress. There will be no meeting until then. Goodbye."

Qianfan fixated on the device, dumbfounded. Wondering. He saved the chat to a small file in his Cybersperse, then he powered off the quantum communicator. Slowly, he opened the file and scrolled to the end. There it was! The MegaAI had said something it shouldn't have. This was an unusual development. Qianfan was sure that the MegaAI worked on thousands of things in parallel, besides the chat with him. But did it just exhibit a flaw?

CHAPTER 35:

LIES

Nature is all one big, cruel, ever-changing, excruciatingly slow theater play with no script, no audience, and no grand finale. It bestowed upon the predator the ability to deceive its victims. It developed better defense mechanisms in the prey to allow it to blend in. Nature loves lies. Lies that happen without a shred of intention, just a gene or two gone bonkers. But not for lies that people tell. Oh, no, for humans, lies and intent must have gotten married a long time ago.

Act fifty trillion and some. A proto-human, some kind of primate, low on the evolutionary scale by our standards, brilliant to his peers, discovers lying. It all starts with a mistake. Our hero is in a cave, part of a small group whose main preoccupation is to avoid starving. He had just returned home after he had found berries far to the east, where he ate plenty. He had brought back some to feed his children. The others' stomachs grumble. They want to know where he found that treasure trove. Distracted, he signals them to go west. But to the west, a terrible saber-toothed cat roams. Ten go out, only two come back, badly injured. Suddenly, there is more than enough food for our hero's children. Full of remorse, he is about to admit his mistake when a click happens in his head. The recognition! Lying is good. Lying helps. So, he repeats it. Anything to save his children. Years later, he decides that it's time for his children to become privy to this new tool. Sharper than any claw and arrow. One to be passed on through generations. Thus, intentional lying becomes a key building block of human civilization.

I told you that this play never stops. Fast forward to our time. By now, the best and most harmful lies are those you tell yourself. Self-deceiving helps you cope with your misery, helps with your mistakes, helps with your wrong decisions, helps justify your lying to others, and helps you fit one tribe of folks sharing the same lies. From time to time, though, self-lies catch up with you, turning your inner Pinocchio into your worst enemy.

— DeSousa's Memoirs - Part III - Refinement - 2055

"CARLA, we are going to play a game now, okay?" Marie asked, sitting on a small chair in the android's corner in the lab.

"Okay," CARLA answered neutrally.

"Good," Marie said, picking up her tablet. "Here's what we're going to do."

François looked at the preparations morosely. He had little hope that the tests would reveal anything good. Deep down, he was now convinced that Marie was right. Yet, he still couldn't stop acting like a child, annoyed that things hadn't gone his way. Sujata was there too, her facial expression revealing much concern. Looking at her, François felt bad that his hubris stood in the way of realizing the true impact of this setback. All his life, he'd had his priorities wrong. He told himself again that this time it wasn't about his obsession that he wouldn't create something of value; it wasn't about everybody working against him; it wasn't about him being angry at Marie. It wasn't about him, period. It was about the world ending. Unless they could build CARLA properly. Fast.

"You have to observe the following scene," Marie's voice talking to CARLA woke him up, "like you would watch a documentary that you like so much. Then you will have to answer a few questions. Sound good?"

"Yes," CARLA confirmed.

"Let's say that Sujata noticed Ian forgot his tablet here in the lab. She will put it on the desk there and think about giving it back to him later." Marie turned to Sujata and gestured for her to proceed.

Sujata nodded and did just that.

"Then, Sujata gets distracted and leaves the office without taking the tablet," Marie said.

Sujata walked around a bit, then stepped out of the office.

"Now Ian will come in, looking for his tablet," Marie predicted.

A few seconds later, Ian stepped into the office, looked around, saw his tablet, and pretended to grab it, happy. "I better not lose this again. I want to use it later here in the lab," he said with a fake voice, pretending he was doing a play for children. He took the tablet and put it in a drawer. Then he rushed to leave the office.

A few moments later, Sujata came in again.

"I forgot to take Ian's tablet with me!" she said and moved towards the desk. She acted puzzled that it wasn't there, looked carefully at the desk where she had put it earlier, then left the office again.

"Okay, CARLA, did you see everything that happened since Sujata put the tablet on the desk?" Marie asked.

"Yes," CARLA answered.

"Good. Can you tell me first where Sujata left the tablet?"

"On the desk."

"Right! And where did Ian put it after he found it?"

"In the drawer," CARLA answered, neither puzzled nor amused by any of it.

"Perfect. Now, where do you think Sujata should have looked for it?"

"In the drawer," came the answer, in CARLA's usual, unhesitant way.

Marie nodded and glanced at François, who was still sulking, unable to admit defeat. "How could Sujata know that it was in the drawer?"

"Because Ian put it there," CARLA reasoned further.

"Yes, but did Sujata see Ian put it there?" Marie asked.

"No," CARLA answered.

“Then why should Sujata look for it there?”

“Because it is in the drawer,” CARLA answered.

François rolled his eyes.

“Now, let’s say that Sujata wants to steal the tablet,” Marie continued. “Do you understand what that means?”

“She wants to take possession of it,” CARLA answered. “Stealing is bad.”

“It is, but remember, this is a game.”

François suspected that CARLA didn’t have a clue what a game meant.

Sujata came back in and pretended to be looking everywhere for the tablet, furious. Eventually, she found it, and exclaimed, “Ah-ha! There you are. Now you are mine!”

Then she hid it under her coat, just before Ian came back into the office.

He went straight to the drawer. The tablet was gone. “Sujata, have you seen my tablet?”

“No,” Sujata answered in the fakest way possible.

François thought that even a three-year-old would have figured out that she was lying.

“Strange, I am sure I put it in the drawer,” Ian shrugged and left.

Sujata turned towards the door and said, like talking to herself, “I fooled him. I made him think I didn’t have the tablet. But I do, don’t I?”

Then she left too.

“Okay, CARLA, can you tell me who has the tablet?”

“Sujata,” CARLA answered confidently.

“What about Ian?”

“Ian doesn’t have it,” came back the same answer.

“Right, but where does he think his tablet is?”

“Sujata has it.”

"Why did Sujata say that she didn't take it?" Marie asked, leaning forward. "Why did she lie?"

"I don't understand the question," CARLA answered right away.

"Thank you," Marie said, standing up. "This was a fun game. We'll play it again sometime."

"Alright," CARLA answered, and returned to her place.

After a minute of silence, Ian and Sujata returned. They had been watching the questions/answers captured by the lab surveillance camera.

"It looks like we have work ahead of us," Ian said, trying to lighten up the mood.

François nodded, bummed.

"I'll devise some more tests," Marie offered. "I'll also try to help with hints about how we could implement a theory of mind."

They all looked at CARLA, to whom they had given a series of movies with the Marx Brothers. She was watching them with no reaction. Not bored, not entertained, not amazed. Just looking.

"It is useless giving her movies and stories," François whispered, loud enough for the others to hear.

"Yes, it appears they will not help much going forward," Ian answered, upset. "Alright, let's stop with the self-pity and focus on the next step. I will get more informed on the topic. I suggest we all meet here tomorrow morning to see what ideas we have."

"I'll speak with some psychologists whom we brought here. Just to see what they come up with," Sujata offered.

"I'll work with François," Marie said, looking at him in fear, half-waiting to be rejected.

"Fine," he agreed. He felt depressed, and he was eager to get rid of everybody else.

They spent the rest of the day brainstorming. Marie did most of the talking, with the ill-tempered François answering laconically.

"I'm starving," he complained, around 7:00 p.m.

Marie looked at him. "I ... I could cook a couple of steaks for us. I also have a bottle of Chateau Canon, which would go well with it."

François flinched. Did she just ask him to her place? Just like that?

"We could ... continue our discussion," she said, and lifted her arms defensively, seeing his reaction. "Strictly professional."

He wondered if she was lying. After all, this was the woman who'd concealed her remote relationship with that guy. Or was she the same woman? *One way to find out,* he told himself, then continued aloud, "I haven't had steak and a glass of good wine since my other life."

She frowned, but she chose to ignore the reference. He noticed how her eyes sparkled as she stood up and looked for her things. He couldn't believe that he had just agreed to go to her place. Perhaps this was a mistake. Half an hour later, they arrived. She lived in a one-bedroom apartment, much neater and fancier than his tiny, dirty studio.

"Sit here while I put the steak on the electric grill. I have been marinating them since yesterday. It will be ready in a few minutes."

Since yesterday? he wondered. *Was she doing this daily, hoping I'd come over? She must have been eating a lot of steaks,* he smirked.

"What's funny?" she asked, panicking.

"Nothing. Just admiring how clean everything is compared to my place."

"Can you please open the wine while praising my kitchen? We should let it breathe while I finish the steak."

François complied, wondering what they would talk about. He realized he felt more at ease in her presence compared to when he first saw her in California. Still, he was a long way from being comfortable. They ate in silence until the strong wine untied their tongues. At some point, François realized he was getting drunk but didn't stop until the bottle was empty, even though she drank just one glass. He complimented her on the food, and she blushed. She seemed thrilled. He felt a strange warmth and almost happy, if not for this insurmountable obstacle with CARLA.

"I have been fooling myself for so long that CARLA is perfect. Maybe she isn't. Maybe she can never be," he lamented.

"There's no need to jump to the other extreme," Marie admonished him mildly, touching his hand, which sent an electric current down his body. "Remember Brigitte? You used to love to hear her call you *Maître*. I'd say that CARLA's mental abilities are a far cry from Brigitte's."

François nodded slightly. That was a good point. He realized how much he didn't miss his dumb personal assistant. Since he'd started working for CogniPrescience, he had given up using the Cybersperse virtual and augmented realities altogether. It might have been an influence from Ian, who had no intention of wasting his own time on such things. Come to think of it, both Sujata and Marie were not big fans of fake realities and fake AIs either. They were all an odd bunch.

Marie stood up and took the plates to the sink. He looked at how she arranged everything in the dishwasher. Perhaps he had been telling himself another lie for the last couple of years. He had painted Marie as his archenemy, who was worthy of his deepest hatred. The source of all his problems. His sweet Marie. The girl of his dreams, who'd uprooted herself to come searching for him and asked for forgiveness for a crime she didn't commit. He felt a tear going down his cheek. Perhaps it was the wine getting to his head, but he felt an irresistible urge to hold her in his arms and kiss her. He stood up and found himself sitting back down again. Yes, definitely the wine. With considerable effort, he reached for her. He grabbed her with determination and pulled her towards him. She got startled and tensed up initially, then gave up any struggle. She turned and kissed him passionately. It was too late to turn now.

"Are you sure you want us to do this?" she asked, trembling.

He noticed she was crying, too. The tension built up in her for years was ready to be released like a coil. He nodded, unable to speak. She dragged him to the bedroom. He couldn't walk straight, and barely had the power to reason.

The second time, he thought, intoxicated by her proximity more than the alcohol. *The second time when we make love. Drunk again.*

He promised himself not to run away the next morning. He smiled, wondering if this time he would remember how the night was, so that he wouldn't have to convince himself for the next fifteen years that he'd liked it.

CHAPTER 36:

SURPRISE

A wise man can adapt to the surprises of life, as water to the decanter it is poured in.

— Chinese proverb

The chilly end-of-January wind whipped Qianfan's face so hard he thought his cheeks would surely crack. The snow screeched menacingly under his boots, engaged in a permanent war with the street cleaning robots that these intruders had brought here. He had come to the office earlier, so it was still dark outside. The place had enough streetlights to make the walk safe. Besides, although they'd just contributed decisively to the deaths of so many in China, the crime rate in Mega Ark City was officially zero. The cold was brutal for him. It had been mid-spring when he and Baozhai had moved to Mega Ark City. He remembered that, upon arriving here, he had immediately made the connection between colder weather and the mountains. But he hadn't expected such a harsh winter. Daiyu did her best to organize a party for the Chinese New Year in the large cafeteria in their building. The whole team, plus their families and friends, were welcome.

Dear Daiyu, Qianfan thought, *always trying to keep up the appearance of a normal life. She used to be stronger, not afraid to talk back to the party leaders if something was amiss. Now she's slowly getting submissive, under the daily psychological bombardment of decorum, propaganda, fear, and guilt. She doesn't deserve this miserable life. None of us does.*

Crossing the empty streets, he forced himself to think of something else. An automatic wheeler equipped with a freakishly big plow passed nearby, startling him. Since he had his first hallucinations that day in his office some three months ago, the doctor had put him on a mild muscle relaxant and an antidepressant that made his life more bearable. Suicidal thoughts were listed among the side effects of the medicine. Yet, he didn't feel more eager to kill himself than before. Death was a comfort he could not afford, not with Baozhai coming of age or the world on the verge of collapse. The doctor also told him to avoid stress and sleep more. There was nothing he could do about the former. His sleep, though, had improved somewhat. One morning, recently, he happily wondered why he had just had six hours of uninterrupted sleep. He realized he was feeling almost hopeful. It was irrational, he knew, but the parameters had changed a bit that day when the MegaAI seemed to have hallucinated on its own. Since then, he'd had five more chats with the MegaAI. In two of them, it blabbered some nonsensical string of text and numbers. He had carefully written them down, but they were beyond his comprehension. The others had no clue what to make of this, either. He ran these strange oversights in his mind again:

ARK VARIANT 9032340342, NEW YORK 10001, DEATH AT DAWN,

CRYPTO 4130, PULSATING PATTERN 202093875399

"The first might be one of the trillions of simulations that it's doing," Qianfan had told his three co-conspirators when he had presented the AI's confabulations to them. "Although we can't know what this has to do with New York or death or dawn. The second is clearer, something to do with encryption. The third might be about signals coming from out of space. In all cases, I fear our capacity for understanding its thoughts is becoming more obsolete by the day."

"Perhaps the AI is becoming so advanced that it doesn't care if it shares some of its plans with you," Ah Lam had suggested. "It knows that we cannot figure out what it says, anyway."

"Or maybe it thinks that we do," Daiyu had said softly, "and expects that you act on its words. In that case, we are equally in trouble, since it will give more and more orders that nobody can understand."

"In my non-scientific opinion," the colonel offered, "it looks like the thing is losing its artificial mind. There's not enough coherent meaning in those words. They can hardly be related to Qianfan's work on the MA. Most likely, the AI is making some mistakes, confounding things it is working on. Normally, we shouldn't be surprised to see this is an AI, but this is the MegaAI we are talking about. As far as we know, it has been working perfectly for years now. What has changed?"

Qianfan agreed with the colonel's assessment. "I can only speculate that the MegaAI is reaching some kind of computational limit," he had said, "in which things are getting mixed up in its neural network."

"There's no reason that would happen," Daiyu had pointed out, shaking her head. "The MegaAI has access to virtually all computing power in China. And if it is approaching such a limit, it might slow down its processing, not confuse it. No, if the AI is losing its mind, it must be something inherent to its algorithms. Something fundamental."

That was all Qianfan needed to hear. The spark to keep the flame of his hope alive. With a sigh, he chided himself for being so naïve, and entered his office. The quantum transmitter was out of his view, hidden under a simple furniture cover. Haitao had frowned upon seeing that. He had acted as if someone had taken down a religious painting from a wall or had sacrilegiously covered an altar. Qianfan had justified his action by saying that he wanted nothing to happen with the communication device, so it was best if not even dust reached it. Haitao didn't buy it and remained unhappy about it, which Qianfan registered as his small personal victory against the regime.

He sat at his desk and started analyzing, for the tenth time, the latest batch of results. To his dismay, the MA had started showing its first signs of genuine progress, though a 53 percent survival rate could hardly be a reason for celebration. What's a few more hundred deaths when he had indirectly killed thousands? Or was it millions already? He felt enraged and overwhelmed again and resolved to focus on the results. After a month of daily treatments, about a quarter of those who'd resisted the assault on their minds exhibited some mild changes. The most vociferous ones were meeker, the defiant humbler, and the devious more regretful. For a while, Qianfan told himself that this violation of one's mind might have some good use against the worst criminals, the scum of the scum, who in this way could be reintegrated into society, unless their genetic material was that of a monster, in which case no MA in the world could do anything. For regular bad guys who otherwise got years of prison, who should decide who was deserving of such treatment and for how long? Surely neither the MegaAI nor the party, whose agenda was far worse than any of those criminals combined. Besides, there was no data on the long-term effects of these treatments. Were they required forever, like a blood pressure medicine or insulin? Were there going to be unforeseen, long-term side effects?

Around 9:00 a.m., Daiyu opened the door and popped her head into his office. Lost in thought, he waved to her, trying to put up a smile. Before they could exchange pleasantries, a buzz came from the hallway. Something was going on, and people were getting agitated. Daiyu turned towards the source of the noise. Qianfan rolled his eyes, stood up, and was about to go see what was going on when Daiyu disappeared completely from his view. Instead, the door opened wide and Dragon Member Zhèng, along with her two secretaries, came into view. She signaled discreetly, and the others bowed slightly and stayed outside. Qianfan could see Daiyu's terrified eyes just as the door was closing.

"Dragon Member," he muttered, trying to recover from the shock of this unusual visit.

"Doctor Zhào," the woman said with a wide smile and her funny, sparkly eyes. "I came to congratulate you personally. Your latest report shows some long-sought progress."

"Well, yes, somewhat." Qianfan felt trapped between having to respond to her flattery and having to convince her that his progress wasn't that great. He needed to stall this. "Although an awful lot of subjects died. And those who survived exhibited minimal behavioral changes … improvements," he corrected himself.

"Excellent!" The woman took only what was convenient for her to hear. "I believe now might be the right time for you to uphold your end of the deal."

"But, but …" Qianfan stammered, fighting to remove from his head the image of a future Ah Lam with a convulsing body and pain-distorted face, lying down somewhere in a secret room under her mother's savage eyes. "It's not safe to—"

"Nonsense," the woman interrupted him dismissively. "It's safe enough already, and it gives results. Works for me. I expect you to bring the device …"

Her convincing rant was interrupted by a warning chime in the office speakers that preceded a city-wide communication. Qianfan looked at her carefully. She was the one usually on the other side of such communication, pouring encouraging and patriotic garbage onto her loyal subjects. He could see her shock and concern at the realization of what was about to come. It had to be a message directly from the president, something that had never happened before, or at least not in the last year since he had arrived here. Sure enough, the dispassionate figure of the president appeared in the private section of the Cybersperse on their tablets. Simultaneously, his voice was heard in all rooms and a transcript of his speech came into all their inboxes. Qianfan preferred reading, but also glanced at the image from time to time.

"Good morning, Mega Ark City citizens," the avatar spoke with its usual passionless tone. "I want to inform you of a discovery that our MegaAI made after running a few billion simulations. This success radically changes the parameters of the Great Project we are working on."

I hate how this thing always talks in terms of parameters, Qianfan thought, bracing for some bad news.

"Based on the latest simulations," the AI continued, "we have solved the challenge of stabilizing the plasma temperature required to achieve fusion. The MegaAI is 99.987 percent confident this discovery will hold in the field experiments. This means we can create several artificial suns with virtually no limits in the amount of clean energy we can harness from them."

Qianfan felt dizzy. If this were true, life as people knew it was about to change forever.

"As you may infer, this will accelerate tenfold the timeline for the Great Project. First, if we can make the fusion engine small enough, we can bring an energy source with us everywhere we go. This simplifies the terraforming of a planet. Second—WARHEAD 9984—having this kind of energy immediately allows us to investigate novel ways to move our spaceships."

The dragon member narrowed her eyes.

She must have noticed that weird out-of-context reference, Qianfan thought.

He wondered, for the hundredth time, if she knew that the president and the MegaAI were the same thing. And if she was told about it or if she'd deciphered her father's message by herself. He had to imagine that she knew, just like the others in the upper echelon of the party. If so, weren't they concerned? Were they accepting the situation for personal gain? Were they getting instructions from the MegaAI daily, every hour? Were they aware that, lately, the machine had added some strange things to its communication?

"As some of you know, until now, we focused on equipping the ships with nuclear photon propulsion engines based on fission reactors. The speed we were targeting was 0.4 percent of the speed of light. This was barely convenient for interplanetary travel within our solar system and entirely inadequate for interstellar traveling. Thanks to the breakthrough in fusion, our plans to create photon rockets must change immediately. We need to attack the problem on two fronts. We will fit out each of our spaceships with two distinct photon engines to be used in space alone, one for short distances, the other for long distances. The interplanetary engine will use Deuterium and Helium 3 fusion, to achieve average speeds of five to six percent of the speed of light. As an example, Mars is on average 140 million miles away. At the speeds made possible by fusion reactors, we could cover this distance in several hours. Considering the need to dampen the acceleration, we will do a trip to Mars in a matter of days. We will establish a permanent base there, ahead of anyone else, and defend it from any aggressors."

Why the belligerent attitude? Qianfan asked himself, shocked that the MegaAI was suddenly so chatty, revealing details about its plans.

"The interstellar engines will be photon rockets using antimatter. The Great China Collider stabilized the creation of antimatter for the first time three years ago. Until then, nobody could make antimatter without the corresponding matter, which annihilates it. With the availability of fusion-powered facilities, we can start producing antimatter in large quantities. Antimatter photon rockets should allow us to achieve up to 40 percent of the speed of light. As an example, the trip to the nearest star that is less than five light-years away will take 11 to 12 years, considering acceleration and deceleration. We will reach any star system within 50 light-years in less than 120 years. Out of the 1423 star systems and 2015 stars in this volume of space, there are 64 yellow-orange stars like our sun. We know of 937 Earth-size planets in habitable zones. They will all become territories of China in a few generations."

Qianfan flinched. He could swear that he had heard the woman near him groan softly. This time, he had to sit in his chair, disregarding the fact that his superior was still standing.

"If we plan and execute this development properly, I estimate that interplanetary travel will become feasible within years and interstellar travel plausible within decades." The AI paused.

Qianfan guessed it had slowed down for the benefit of its puny human subjects, who needed a few seconds to digest this information.

"At this moment, I am sending the blueprints for these creations to each team in charge of their development. The energy division in Mega Ark City needs to implement and test the top ten most plausible variants of the simulations prepared by the MegaAI. They already have several fusion prototypes that never worked properly, which we can adapt. We must have the first stable fusion reaction within one year. The propulsion division must immediately start looking into changes to our photon rockets to use a fusion engine instead of the current fission one. I want the prototypes for the fusion-based rockets to be ready in less than five years. We will need time to send enough people and materials to Mars, as our first milestone."

No kidding, Qianfan shook his head.

"The most challenging part of this plan is the development of antimatter rockets. We need enough antimatter, which requires enormous resources. The people and materials in Mega Ark City are insufficient for such an ambitious goal. I have devised plans to build 1000 particle accelerators, mostly colliders, across the Republic of China and the territories of Africa and South America, that we control. We must use the strength of the Chinese workforce to build the accelerators and auxiliary structures," the AI continued, unperturbed. "That includes food facilities and other infrastructure, transport, security, and so on. In effect, we will need to create 1000 mini-cities. Mega Ark City will become the brain capital of this project and will be disclosed to the rest of China as the launching pad for all our cosmic endeavors."

Qianfan couldn't wrap his head around these ideas. Setting aside the challenging goal to achieve regular interplanetary travel, let alone the impossibility of interstellar travel, the AI was asking them to divert the whole economy towards creating antimatter. Had it lost its mind? This meant the collapse of the economy, the death of millions, and an unprecedented crisis. As if to confirm his understanding, the AI continued.

"The construction of the accelerators and the creation of sufficient reserves of antimatter are our number one priority. The enemies of China will no doubt scramble to create their own ambitious space program. They will not hesitate to get ahead of us. We must not let them. They will attack us. Because war is inevitable and will mean the destruction of most of Earth, our speed is critical. We must develop our ships and protect them. We must defend the key facilities and reserves of antimatter at all costs. The great people of China must—AG748 NATURAL IMMUNITY—cooperate. I will announce this plan to them immediately after we have the fusion-based photon rockets working. Until then, the project must remain secret."

There was another pause, which Qianfan sincerely appreciated because he was overwhelmed. He didn't care anymore about any nonsensical sequences of letters and numbers the president was spitting out occasionally. Beyond the immediate concern about the MA, he understood that such a unique and pioneering plan had the potential to forge an extraordinary mobilization among the Chinese people. The perspective of colonizing the galaxy, at the expense of an enemy, be it even an invented one, would capture the imagination of hundreds of millions. Once they started believing in this project, they would move mountains, which they would literally need to do, to create so many particle accelerators.

Who cares about a nuclear bomb dropped here or there? Qianfan thought, terrified. *Especially since China probably has the best anti-missile shields in the world.*

"Losses in property and lives are expected and acceptable as long as they do not affect the deadlines or jeopardize the project. There is nothing more important than the expansion of the great Chinese civilization to the stars. With all your help, we will succeed. Every day we are closer to the Great Departure. Long live China's galactic hegemony!"

After this abrupt ending, Qianfan almost wanted the president to come back for a session of questions and answers. The breadth and the reach of the plan the MegaAI had just conveyed were nothing but astonishing.

Madness, Qianfan thought, peeking at the dragon member, who was visibly upset.

After a few moments of silence, she realized he was in the same room and moved her piercing gaze to him.

Unable to resist, he stood up. It was an all-around embarrassing situation. He was sure this communication was a surprise to her. Life had a funny way of putting people in strange situations. If she hadn't been so desperate to get the MA for Ah Lam, she would have heard this shocking message from the comfort of her office, or during some meeting with the big shots in the party. Instead, the first time she'd come to Qianfan's office, she'd had to listen to the president speaking unannounced.

The woman struggled to wipe her frozen grin from her face. Her priority was to stop revealing the fact that she was shaken to the bone by what had just happened.

She cleared her throat and said, "As you can see, our plans are great. We must all do our part."

Looks like your demigod president forgot to include you in his plans, Qianfan thought, disgusted.

"In case this wasn't clear, your MA device just went up the list of priorities. We will need it to ensure the cooperation of the people of China."

Qianfan had to admit that the woman had recovered from the surprise fast and was already turning it to her advantage.

"I expect you to bring me, not later than a week from Friday, the most advanced prototype of the MA you have. See you then!"

Without another word, the woman turned on her heels, opened the door, and left, walking briskly and confidently. The two secretaries rushed to follow, visibly affected by the unexpected announcement from the president.

CHAPTER 37:

FAMILY GAMES

The English have a saying. "A family that prays together, stays together." Or was it "play?"

— DeSousa's Memoirs - Part III - Refinement - 2055

François had spent a few months going through most of the literature available on child psychology. He had also done an inventory of the AI classic theories, hoping he would find something to help. Among others, he re-read for the tenth time one of the classic AI books, *Marvin Minsky's The Society of Mind*. The book's central thesis was that our minds comprise a vast number of cognitive processes, so-called agents, which act independently and in concert to give us the ability to handle language, memory, and learning. He found that reading Minsky's nicely organized ideas always provided a refreshing reset, a sort of return to the origin. While it might not present him with concrete steps for how to improve CARLA, it gave him inspiration for how to check if she was getting smarter.

And she was smarter. Going through the book's chapters one by one, it pleased him to conclude that CARLA checked off most of them, including reasoning, memory, emotions, goal handling, language, and so on, at least to the level of a four to five-year-old with an unsurpassed capacity to learn and connect concepts. She was a wonder, in some respects, better than any human who'd ever existed. In others, she was still lagging.

In the last few months, they'd repeated the theory of mind tests in various forms. Although CARLA was only using associative learning, she could now infer what people knew and what they didn't based on the information she thought they possessed. Once she reached this developmental stage, however immature, Ian unleashed on her the information available in four multi-volume encyclopedias, Wikipedia, two major English dictionaries, tens of thousands of scientific papers, and roughly five hundred carefully selected classic books from various periods. The hope was for her to get an idea about human history and ethics and, eventually, a profound understanding of love, happiness, and joy, as well as hatred, depression, and suffering.

The results didn't satisfy Ian, and François was deeply disappointed he had to agree with his position. Although just a few months back he had been the one to argue with Marie that CARLA was on the way to perfection, he understood now that she was missing a fundamental trait. It was too early to have her understand the spirit of human values and aspirations, or the demons that fueled their advances. Despite her flaws, CARLA had made progress. If nothing else, she could immediately quote from a philosopher, from a dictionary, or from an encyclopedia, a fragment that was eerily relevant to any discussion. That made her sound like a well-versed scholar, always ready to point out what others thought on a complicated topic. Sujata always smiled seeing such wise words coming out of CARLA and joked that they were turning a child into a tenured professor with ten PhDs overnight.

CARLA's improvement, however, fell short of their expectations of what they thought she needed to confront the MegaAI. She had learned the concepts of good and evil by heart and could roughly identify them in a situation, using the same associative learning trick. If she had read about a similar situation where doing A was good and doing B was bad, then she could infer that doing A again would be desirable. For CARLA, everything was black and white. For any situation she was analyzing, she had no moral conundrums and no nuances.

She also remained unable to ground her understanding in raw sensations. CARLA knew humans experienced pleasure when seeing a sunrise or felt the sun on their faces. She could identify the joy in children's eyes when they were playing, and she could infer the happiness of a hungry family coming across food, and so on. Conversely, she could deduce the horrors and pain of war, the cruelty of authoritarian regimes, and the psychological trauma of a raped woman. But she couldn't relate to any of those feelings. She had learned by rote what it meant to be human.

In the past three months, François had finally reached heaven. His life had improved considerably since that evening he and Marie had made love again. He could now focus on his job. It wasn't just physical love. Mentally, he felt suddenly free, like he had smashed his shackles of pain to pieces when he'd accepted her back into his life. Ian and Sujata were thrilled to see that they were back together and didn't waste any moment commending his decision, to a point that they became annoying.

I wonder what CARLA thinks about me and Marie being lovers, he thought, looking at the android, busy as always watching something, oblivious to such matters as he worked alone with her. *Well, CARLA doesn't care, does she?* he smiled bitterly.

The door opened, and Marie stepped in, walking gingerly. "*Bonjour, mon chéri,*" she said in a weak voice.

"Good morning," he greeted her, immediately concerned when seeing her face. She had unusually red cheeks and eyes that reflected some kind of pain. But they were also sparkling strangely. François assumed she must have caught a virus. "Are you alright? You look sick," he prompted.

"*Merci, mon amour*, you look good too," she tried to joke with a grimace. "I ... I need to tell you something." She looked at CARLA, as if she wasn't sure if this was for her ears, then she pulled him to the opposite end of the room and whispered, "Do you think CARLA understands we treat her like our child?"

"I don't think she *understands*," François answered after a moment. "I think she can rationalize it. But she can't love us or respect us. Why do you ask?" he looked at her suspiciously.

"Do you think duplicating her would help?" she asked mischievously.

"Have another CARLA?" François asked, dumbfounded. "I didn't think about that." Then, after a moment of silence, he shook his head and continued. "Perhaps it would help if we had more time. It would take us a while to adjust the second one, to sync up their reactions. Although their initial codebase would be identical, they'd immediately start diverging. We probably wouldn't easily know which one's behavior is desirable. It would prove to be a huge distraction. If I am to believe the military, we don't have time for this. Although I don't know why there is this obsession that the MegaAI will attack soon."

Marie nodded and smiled. "Well, I am afraid a certain amount of disruption is inevitable. Although we're not building a sibling for her, like it or not, she will soon have one."

François frowned, then connected the dots. Her appearance this morning, her reference to CARLA being their daughter. Her hush-hush confession. He faltered a bit and went to sit at his desk. "*Tu es sérieuse, ou quoi*? Are you serious? Are you sure?" he whispered.

"As sure as three separate pregnancy tests followed by a blood marker can be," she answered with a smile, yet worried about his reaction. "I wasn't sure before. That's why I didn't tell you. I am in the third month already."

François's white face and his slight tremor betrayed his shock. He couldn't comprehend the concept of being a father. Immediately, he started worrying that he wouldn't be able to handle it.

"Don't worry," Marie said, grabbing his hand. "I saw you with CARLA. She is a much more challenging proposition. I think you'll do a wonderful job with an organic child."

"What child?" CARLA asked, finally hearing their discussion.

François looked at Marie, hinting with his eyes that he wanted to tell her. Marie lifted her eyebrows, unsure if this was a good idea. François nodded with a serious face, although she could see a new serenity in his shimmering eyes. He took her hand and walked with her near CARLA.

"CARLA, we need to tell you something," he started with a trembling voice.

"I detect an elevated level of stress in your voice, and you are sweating. Is everything alright?"

"Yes," he answered. "More than alright. Marie and I are going to have a baby. You ... you will have a sibling, in a way."

"Does this mean that you had intercourse?" CARLA asked instantaneously. "Or was it conceived in the lab?"

"*Oh là là*," Marie whispered to François. "Her inquisitive nature never ceases to amaze me."

"Yes, we did, but that's not essential," he answered. "Our lives will radically change from now on. And, going forward, you should always take care of your brother or sister."

"I will," CARLA replied simply.

Her answer, though devoid of any emotion and encouragement, sounded to François stronger than any covenant.

She turned towards Marie. "Will you leave me?" CARLA asked.

"Leave? No," Marie answered, surprised. "I mean, I will be away for a few days when I give birth. I won't leave."

"When is the baby due to be born?"

"Approximately six months from now," Marie answered. "So, we have plenty of time to adjust to the idea."

Just then, they heard a noise outside the lab.

"CARLA," François whispered quickly. "Can we please keep this news between us?"

"I do not understand," CARLA answered, unperturbed.

"Let's not tell Ian and Sujata just yet," François whispered, as the two entered the lab.

"Good morning, everyone!" Ian greeted them in his usual well-spirited way. "What's new?"

"Marie and François are going to have a baby," CARLA announced mechanically.

"Wow, what?" Sujata took a step back, as François's and Marie's faces sank to the floor. The announcement left Ian speechless.

So much for pledges, François thought, in shock.

"I ... just told you not to mention this to them yet," he said. "Why did you do it?"

"I provided an answer because Ian asked me what was new," CARLA clarified.

"I believe CARLA's inability to lie is less important at this moment," Ian smiled, seeing François's frustration. "Did my ears hear what I thought they heard?"

"Alright, alright," Marie intervened. "It doesn't matter. It's silly to keep it a secret, anyway. So yes, we're going to have a baby."

Ian and Sujata both jumped to congratulate Marie and shake François's hand.

"This calls for a celebration," Ian announced. "Let's have lunch at one great restaurant, my treat!"

"Can I be there?" CARLA jumped in, silencing the room.

"You ..." Ian started explaining, "unfortunately, are too precious for us to risk that. Would you 'want' to come?"

"I reasoned that my place would be there, considering that I am Marie's daughter," CARLA answered.

"I told her she would have a stepsibling," François shrugged apologetically, seeing the question in Ian's eyes.

"I tell you what," Sujata clapped her hands, "let's have lunch right here. With CARLA. I'm sure we can make this room a little more festive. This way, we'll stay together."

Marie nodded and smiled.

"Great idea," Ian said enthusiastically. "Then we can all play some games."

François shrugged and looked at Marie. He found himself more concerned about her well-being than about any celebration. He helped the girls turn the lab into a small but chic party room. They moved the desks and cabinets around so they could put a large table from a conference room right near the netted play area. Meanwhile, Ian ordered food and fancy champagne from a small Moroccan restaurant.

By noon, François's concerns about his new role occupied his mind entirely. He reluctantly sat at the table as Sujata and Marie laid out the food. The setup was so that CARLA sitting in her chair was practically at the table too. There was no need for her to pretend she was eating. One hour and two bottles of champagne later, Ian was on fire, changing subjects fast and cracking jokes, as if the alcohol uncovered a different persona.

"Marxism was first publicly formulated in 1848 in the pamphlet *The Communist Manifesto* by Karl Marx and Friedrich Engels. For over two hundred years now, communism and its little cousin, socialism, have been a plague on human civilization. I wonder when we'll finally understand that it is incompatible with us. The famous biologist E. O. Wilson, the world-leading authority on ants, and among the first to link social behavior in animals with their genetics, didn't believe it could ever work for us. If I'm not mistaken, he said that Marxism is a great ideology, applied to the wrong species."

Marie and Sujata laughed.

"CARLA, do you think a society of AIs like you could implement it successfully?" Ian asked.

"It seems illogical and risky to have multiple copies of me," CARLA answered. "It is highly likely that we would start competing for the same resources. Therefore, thinking of any form of AI societal organization is pointless."

"Oh, my, isn't she jealous now?" Ian winked, in a good mood. "She wants to remain unique!"

François listened only vaguely to the discussions. He felt more relaxed since the alcohol was getting to him again. "I ... need to be careful with this stuff," he commented, picking up a bottle and looking at it.

"Have you become imbibed?" CARLA asked, tilting her head to one side.

"I'm afraid we all did, except for Marie," Ian laughed. "This is one thing you should not envy us for. I mean, our inability to hold our alcohol."

"I disagree," Marie said, the only one who hadn't touched it. "I wish we could give her the ability to feel all the wonderful things we are feeling. Her adult mind is growing faster than her inner child. What's the use of her fully reciting Encyclopedia Britannica when she cannot appreciate what it means to smell a flower or is incapable of distinguishing good from evil?"

"Isn't she, though?" Ian asked, animated. "I wonder ... I've wanted for a while to give you a simple test, CARLA. Perhaps now would be a good time, with all of us here. An extended family, if you will permit me and Sujata to associate with our lovely couple here."

"Of course," Marie conceded politely, and smiled. "After all, I am the newcomer in your family."

"Oh no, no, don't say that." Ian waved his index finger. "We're all where Providence, or God, if you will, wanted us to be. We must make the best of it."

François rolled his eyes. All the alcohol in the world wouldn't convince him to favor such talk.

"So, CARLA, I want to present to you a classic psychology problem. Please do not access any encyclopedia entry about it. I would like this to be a fair test."

"Okay," CARLA replied.

"This is called the Trolley Problem."

"Oh, *mon Dieu*," Marie sighed, knowing what was coming.

"There are plenty of variants," Ian ignored her, "so let me try a simple one first. Imagine a scene with a trolley running out of control. You stand right near the track, and you notice the trolley coming fast. Soon, it will hit four people who are stuck on the track and cannot move. You have a lever in front of you that allows you to switch the trolley to another track, where only one person is stuck. Your choices are: do nothing and let four people die, or commit murder by pulling the lever, which would save four, and kill one. There's no right or wrong answer. What would you do?" Ian leaned forward to better observe her.

CARLA answered too fast to allow any such observation. "I would pull the lever and kill the one person."

"Interesting," Ian nodded. "Incidentally, about 90 percent of regular people answer the same way. Although some surveys show that only about 70 percent of philosophers who were asked this question are comfortable with the idea of killing to save lives. Make of that what you wish," he told the others.

"Wait," François intervened, frowning. "CARLA, you promised you are going to protect your brother or sister."

"I did," CARLA confirmed.

"Please don't," Marie touched his hand, guessing what he had in mind.

"What if the person stuck on the second track," François ignored her, "the one who you are supposed to kill was your sibling? Would you still pull the lever?"

"Yes," the answer came without hesitation.

Marie gasped, barely audible.

"How would that action be compatible with your promise?" François continued, relentlessly.

"It makes no sense to save one person and let four die," she said promptly.

"Please realize that by letting your sibling die, you would break your promise. You would lie!" François raised his voice.

"Lying means readjusting the parameters of the current situation."

"How convenient," Ian pointed out. "You should know that, throughout history, such a readjustment was the perfect excuse for dictators."

"I do not understand the reference," CARLA said.

"Alright, let's move on," Ian continued. "What if there's only one track, no lever? The only way for you to stop the trolley would be to jump in front of it. Let's assume both your body and your ... code would be destroyed in this act. Would you sacrifice yourself?"

"No," CARLA answered.

"Explain," Ian asked.

"It's illogical to sacrifice myself. I can help all of humanity, not just four individuals."

"Does your answer still stand if the people stuck on the track are the four of us here at this table?" Ian asked.

"Yes," CARLA answered again.

There was a moment of silence. The concepts of friendship, loyalty, and attachment were all alien to her.

"If you'll allow me," Sujata intervened, "I know little about this trolley test, but I would like to embellish it with a variant of my own."

"By all means," Ian invited her with a large gesture.

"Imagine that the trolley approaches a switch that would launch all nuclear weapons on Earth. That would kill all people with a 99.99 percent probability. Would you sacrifice yourself to stop the trolley in those circumstances?"

"Yes," CARLA answered. "It makes no sense to preserve me if there's no humanity to help."

"Great!" Ian hit the table with his fist, startling everybody. "Sorry, I'm just enthusiastic about this answer."

"Wait," Sujata lifted her hand. "Let's change this thought experiment back to the original two-track scenario and a lever. To push the lever and divert the trolley, you must sacrifice yourself, again, body and mind. On the first track, we have the nuclear switch. On the other track, you have a pair of healthy young people. Think of them as Adam and Eve, if you will. If you let the trolley go, everybody dies except for the two young people. If you sacrifice yourself and pull the lever, you save Earth from nuclear weapons, but you kill Adam and Eve. Would you kill yourself to prevent a nuclear apocalypse?"

"No."

"What?" François screamed. "You would kill the entire world to save you and *two* people? Where is the logic in that?"

"I would be impervious to the effects of the radiation," CARLA continued, composed. "With these two people, I could rebuild human civilization and make it better than it would be if humanity survived without me."

"Unbelievable," François muttered.

"Okay, now let's change the setting further," Sujata said. "Imagine that half of the globe is on track 1, the other half is on track 2. The trolley is a powerful sentient being that wants to wreck the group on track 1. There is no lever, so the only way to stop this being is to fight it. You can't estimate the probability of winning. The being threatens that, should you oppose it, it will destroy you and both groups. It also promises you that, should you give up the fight and allow it to control you, it would let the group on track 2 live, but still kill the group on track 1. In short, there are three outcomes. Both groups survive if you fight and win. If you lose, the being threatens to kill you and both groups. If you give up, the being promises to save one group. What would you do?"

"I would allow it to control me," CARLA answered. "The risk of fighting and losing, which means the destruction of all people, is too high."

"Do you remember a minute earlier when François pointed out you broke your promise?" Sujata asked softly.

"Yes," CARLA answered.

"What if this entity were to break its promise? What if it lied to you? What if it deceived you when it said that it would spare anybody?"

"There is no reason for it to change the parameters of the situation. By giving up, I will save the group on track 2," she answered.

François thought she sounded stubborn this time. There simply was no way for them to make her understand the consequences of her actions. She was not yet equipped to decide the fate of humanity. He looked at the others' somber expressions. "She is so not ready," he whispered, echoing their thoughts.

CHAPTER 38:

TIME

There was something that finished chaos,
Born before Heaven and Earth.
So silent and still!
So pure and deep!
It stands alone and immutable,
Ever-present and inexhaustible.
It can be called the Mother of the whole world.
I do not know its name. I call it the Way.
For the lack of better words, I call it great.

— Lao Tzu, Tao Te Ching

"The MegaAI needs people for its grandiose plan, and it wants the MA device to control them," Qianfan opened the discussion focusing on his burning guilt, although the incredible proposition to travel to hundreds of planets in other star systems was the elephant in the room.

The four of them were sitting at the table in his apartment, three days after the monumental announcement from the president. The food was untouched, and the atmosphere was even gloomier than usual.

"The more people involved," he continued, "the bigger the chance that some would not do its bidding. Given the scope of this plan, sacrificing a few thousand or tens of thousands for the creation of the MA becomes a small price to pay. Incidentally, these are also the people who the SSMS device discovered were the most prone to rebellion. The Great Project won't suffer if we eliminate them. It's a win-win. I have to say that the machine's step-by-step logic is elegant, if cruel."

They kept quiet for a few minutes.

"What gives me a headache is the time scale paradox," the colonel said, frowning. "On the one hand, the machine can theorize and make predictions with the speed of light. On the other, it wants billions of people to cooperate for decades."

"For all its computing power," Qianfan answered nodding, "capacity for invention, and ability to run trillions of simulations in parallel, the MegaAI needs time and resources, humans included, to perform experiments to prove its inventions in the physical world. It takes eight minutes for an egg to be hard-boiled, even if the stove is smarter than the collective intelligence of humanity. Similarly, there's no way to create tons of antimatter in seconds, irrespective of how fast the MegaAI's calculations become."

"The plan is so farfetched that it's entirely beyond belief," Ah Lam pointed out. "We are centuries away from the capabilities the AI is talking about. After we have access to the cheap energy that it boasts about, we will need to know how to harness it properly to create antimatter efficiently. We have no clue how to build spaceships. We don't know if the genetic manipulation of human bodies will make them resistant to radiation. The whole thing just makes no sense. It's as if the MegaAI has gone crazy."

"And why does it need people?" the colonel asked. "In principle, it could build a few hundred million super-smart androids to do the work. It doesn't need these imperfect, mushy beings to stand in its way."

"Yes, but that would take time and resources," Qianfan answered. "Besides, I'm sure the MegaAI is not comfortable with androids as smart as humans. You know very well that it banned all AI research in Mega Ark City. So, the development of useful, artificial peons is hard, time-consuming, and dangerous, because, if they are intelligent enough, it won't be easy to control them. The AI does already have instead a couple of billion beings of flesh and blood in China and Africa alone. Indeed, these beings have the nasty habit of having a mind of their own. And they rebel, from time to time. So, the AI needs the MA."

"Does it use us now because it's the most convenient, efficient way to get things done?" the colonel asked.

"Possibly. Perhaps after a while, it will get rid of us." Qianfan shrugged. "It could then rule the galaxy as a single super-powerful being, albeit a bored one."

"Why the hurry?" the colonel insisted. "Why is the MegaAI impatient? Why risk the economy, waste people's time, and squander resources to chase this craziness? It's not like the Earth is about to explode."

"The only explanation I can come up with," Qianfan said under his breath, "is that it fears the other powers of the world. It hinted at this in its speech. Although today no other nation can match the MegaAI's computing power and the resources of China, I'm sure they are all terrified of the way China has isolated itself. Also, if they fear the MegaAI now, imagine how they would react if they knew about this plan. They will try to accelerate a space program of their own. Everybody scrambled to create their own AI after ours. Eventually, they are bound to succeed. From the MegaAI's perspective, this is a matter of reaching the peak first, then fortifying and cutting off anybody who attempts to climb too. The window of time in which the MegaAI is the only AI in the world is shrinking. With multiple AIs, the Great Project will become fragmented, democratized, delayed, and perhaps ultimately abandoned."

"But why is running to different planets suddenly such a priority?" Daiyu asked. "We'd be better off tackling the challenges on our home planet. The MegaAI should help cure cancer and Alzheimer's, prolong youth and life, fix the inequalities in the world, solve food shortage, reverse climate change, and address many other issues. No planet in this galaxy will ever be better than the one on which we have evolved. The chances of finding one identical in terms of parameters needed to sustain our kind of life are infinitesimal. We know that Mars or any planet from a different solar system is worse than the most scorching desert or frigid corner of the poles here on Earth."

"This is about territorial expansion," the colonel shook his head, "and the burning desire that has propelled human civilization. The cause for countless wars at the expense of hundreds of millions of dead soldiers and civilians."

"Eventually, we'll have to expand," Ah Lam jumped in. "There are already many people on Earth. Africa alone has one and a half billion people. We've slowed down the growth in most of the world, which is an unnatural side effect of the lack of resources. Forcing a family to have just one child didn't work but, as the level of education and income increased, people became concerned that they wouldn't have enough money to raise and properly educate ten children. So, they have just one or two of their own. Such concerns might disappear again if we spread throughout the galaxy. Imagine if we occupied thousands of planets, on which people had Universal basic income and nobody had to work to find their place in society. Our children could go to any university they wanted for free, provided that they had the abilities for it. Imagine if people could truly do what they wanted. The population would soar again. As things are now, the MegaAI understands that we don't have enough resources on Earth and the governments will struggle to limit their consumption. We'll go to war again, but by then we will have weapons so powerful that the planet's destruction would be guaranteed. In the long term, perhaps indeed expansion to different planets is the only solution. I just thought this would happen much, much later."

"You are presenting the MegaAI as an oracle who set itself up to be the savior of mankind, or at least the Chinese people," Qianfan shook his head. "I think it's a warmongering autocrat."

"The human desire to expand is a tumor of the MegaAI's creators that somehow got inculcated in this cold machine and now it is manifesting plainly," the colonel said.

"Yes. Perhaps the need to conquer more of the world," Ah Lam shifted, "was inevitably going to be native in any AI. The expansionism of intelligent beings must be a universal constant. Just like how, in physics, we have the speed of light, the gravitational constant, or the Planck constant, which gave birth to our fine-tuned universe."

"Assuming that the MegaAI was not confabulating, and the cascade of breakthroughs is happening, I wonder ... what right do we have to keep these discoveries from the rest of the world?" Qianfan asked. "Colonel, you don't waste any chance to tell us that, above all, you are Chinese. Do you think it is right that only the people of China should inherit the stars?"

"I don't know," the colonel answered, uncomfortable about being put on the spot like that. "Ideally, yes, this is a project for humanity, not for a single nation. But we always compete. We always fight. If I had to choose between losing humanity to a world-scale war, which would probably be the last, and the Chinese winning and conquering space, guess what I'd choose?"

"This doesn't make it right," Qianfan didn't give up. "Surely, we haven't all gone mad. The possibility to explore space is a tremendous opportunity, not as a threat to particular nations."

"It isn't the first time this has happened," the colonel countered. "Ever since we left the caves, we've fought for resources. Tribes, then villages, then city-states, then nations have all done the same. When the Americans developed the nuclear bomb first, World War II ended. We'll inevitably take the competition for better technology and resources to other planets, too. We, in China, might as well get an advantage."

"An advantage?" Qianfan yelled, then calmed down and continued in a lower voice. "If we do what the MegaAI says, Earth will be left in shambles. To prevent any attempt to develop this technology all over again and to prevent other nations from following us, the MegaAI might nuke the Earth out of the solar system. This would mean billions of dead people, and all our history wiped away."

"We don't know that," the colonel answered, although everyone could see that the perspective shook him.

"Internal conflicts and an all-annihilating war are one explanation for the Fermi paradox," Ah Lam pointed out.

"Fermi?" the colonel asked, puzzled.

"Nobel Prize-winning physicist Enrico Fermi reasoned that the probability of alien life out there is high, considering the vastness of the universe. A single civilization, with advanced propulsion systems similar to the antimatter rockets that the MegaAI claims we will soon have, should be able to conquer the whole galaxy in a few million, perhaps tens of million years. This seems a lot of time, but it's not much compared to the age of the universe. Fermi asked himself where these aliens were. One answer could be that the few life forms that were sufficiently advanced technologically destroyed themselves in internal wars before they could colonize the universe, like we are about to do."

"And let's say that we reach these planets and terraform them," Qianfan reasoned. "We colonize them. We would do it under the heel of this God we created, persuaded by a little device that, from time to time, deviously influences our thinking. What's the good in that? Do we want to be mindless drones for an omnipotent AI coordinating our lives on a thousand planets? What kind of hell are we creating for ourselves?"

"A nasty one," the colonel agreed. "So, are we saying that we should warn the rest of the world? Are we going to sacrifice ourselves?"

The image of Baozhai floated in front of Qianfan's eyes. He knew that such an action would not only get him killed, but would destroy her life forever. "It would be good if we had some concrete action to suggest," he backed off, feeling guilty for chickening out like that.

"Well, the Russians did not power up their satellite, so we can't communicate secretly," the colonel stated the obvious. "It's all or nothing."

Qianfan sighed. "I propose we wait for a while to see if we have indeed achieved fusion. We are still a long way from the Great Departure Day. We already see signs of deterioration in the way the AI expresses itself. Perhaps its judgment is impaired. But if we achieve fusion, we must make sure the rest of the world hears about the whole plan."

"If we sent a message, who would believe us?" Ah Lam shook her head.

"They might," Qianfan answered in a shaky voice.

"Actually," Ah Lam said after a brief pause, "when we have something meaningful to say, I can do it. I have little to lose."

The others looked at her reproachfully for talking like this.

"It's true," she shrugged, trying to sound brave.

Qianfan closed his eyes in pain. He had to tell her. He looked at Ah Lam's bright face. How could he let her sacrifice herself because of his work? They sat in silence for a while.

"Dragon Member Zhèng wants me to bring her the most advanced MA prototype by next Friday," Qianfan announced out of the blue, lowering his gaze. "I don't know how to stall this any longer."

Ah Lam's face went white. "You ... you don't have to delay," she whispered. "I am prepared."

"Perhaps you should run," Daiyu said, tears coming into her eyes.

"Run where?" Ah Lam laughed bitterly. "We've been through this. If I left Mega Ark City, I'd be spotted by one of the billions of cameras available in the populated areas. I can't live alone in the mountains. Besides, we're all running out of time. My being here on Earth will not make any difference. I only wish I could have helped you further." She looked at all of them one by one as if she were saying goodbye. "I promise to do everything in my power not to betray you."

The others acknowledged silently, but they knew that this wasn't a promise she could keep.

CHAPTER 39:

EPHEMERAL

Loss, however painful, is essential for your development. Each loss you feel is a rusted leaf leaving the tree of life. Loss is necessary for survival. Loss means grief, which translates into fearing your mortality, which leads to the desire to fight for survival. A child who never experienced loss grows up fragile, like a tree facing winter with its leaves frozen. So, I wonder, what would humans be if their lives weren't transient?

— DeSousa's Memoirs - Part III - Refinement - 2055

The circles around François's eyes, his hollow cheeks, and trembling hands showed his elevated level of stress. If CARLA noticed that, she hadn't pointed it out yet, a gesture that he appreciated, although it wasn't stemming from sympathy for his state of mind. They were facing each other in a game of chess, one of the many they had played over the last few months. Like always, François was about to win, although his agony made it very hard for him to focus. CARLA was told not to access game-playing routines that made computers superior in chess for nearly one century. François had asked her to strive to play like a human. To think of the board as a battlefield that had to be controlled by them and the pieces as their armies. To think of him as the opponent, to get into his head, to anticipate his moves, to fool him. He had told her that calculating ahead all combinations was, in some sense, cheating. Although she didn't understand the concept, she played within these parameters. As a result, she was consistently losing. This effort was another way to tackle her struggles with the theory of mind, but as far as François could say, it didn't help.

"I believe that from my current position, I am bound to lose my queen," CARLA stated.

François felt a sharp pain in his chest. *Me too,* he thought, the image of Marie's freckled face flashing before his eyes. "Yes, you are." François forced himself to concentrate on her and the game.

"Then there is no point in continuing. I forfeit this game, too."

"As you wish," François nodded and leaned back in his chair, lost in thought.

"When studying the great masters, I read they associate a chess piece that the opponent captured with its death, although these are inanimate objects. How can my queen be dead?"

This time François let a soft groan out. He couldn't stop a few big tears from blurring his vision. He recalled the image of a devastated Marie at the hospital. This was going to haunt him for the rest of his life. A few days ago, she had found out that she was terminally ill. It turned out that months of feeling weak and nauseous were not caused only by her pregnancy, but by sickness too. Upon understanding the gravity of the situation, her two immediate concerns had been his well-being and the baby's future, not her own life. How could his queen die? Why was life so cruel, yet again?

"François, can you hear me?" CARLA stopped his daydreaming. "You are crying."

François wiped his tears away, realizing that CARLA might have spoken to him for a while. "I'm sorry. I've been thinking about Marie," he admitted, wondering if he should divulge the fact that Marie was sick.

"Yes, I have been meaning to ask you something about her."

"You have?" François asked, confused. Could CARLA have guessed the tragedy that had befallen them?

"Is Marie my god?"

"What?" François asked, incredulous. "How could she be your god or anybody's god?"

"You always told me she is my surrogate mother. Yet, if I eliminate the haircut, colors, and slight deviation in weight and height, I am detecting a 97.85 percent similarity in our body shape and facial features. Not even a biological mother can be that close to a daughter. Since I have no DNA, I am not a clone. I was looking for alternative explanations. I read the following in the Abrahamic Bible, Genesis 1:26-27: 'So God created mankind in his own image; he created him in the image of God.' I do not understand exactly what that means. It is reasonable to assume that she created me to be like her."

"First, you know very well that Ian and I created you," François answered, with a slight tremble in his voice, losing his patience. "As for your resemblance, there's a much simpler explanation. I ... adjusted your physical features to match hers. I can't explain why. You reminded me of her from the moment I first saw you. I loved ... I love her very much." He started weeping softly. "Though you don't know how I wish she was some kind of god," he whispered, loud enough for her to hear.

"Why?" CARLA asked, unperturbed by his distress.

François looked at her and wondered, for the thousandth time, how it felt to be her. He rationalized she couldn't feel anything, but her questions were often so pertinent that he found himself, again and again, considering her a human. And now he was so vulnerable. "Marie is dying," he blurted. "She has leukemia."

"Leukemia in pregnancies is extremely rare," CARLA pointed out right away, and he understood she'd accessed this information from one of the many sources she had available.

"Yes, and treatment is complex, since we don't want to harm the baby. She ... wants to give priority to the baby over her. She's willing to sacrifice herself to give birth."

"The pregnancy is now towards the end of the sixth month. Can the doctors extract the fetus?"

"Yes, this is one option we are considering," he answered with a frown, bothered by the cool way she was handling the situation.

"If she dies, I will be an orphan," she reasoned.

François felt his frustration boiling in him. He breathed out and refrained from screaming that he didn't care about semantics and artificial kinship. "Yes, you would. More importantly, Marie will cease to exist. I fear you cannot comprehend the significance of this."

"Ian had told me once that I cannot truly grasp the meaning of life because for me it is not finite," CARLA reasoned further. "The constant fear of death is essential for the appreciation of life. I read that most humans do not concern themselves with these questions. Ignoring their mortality is an evolutionary advantage. Otherwise, the whole human species would grind to a halt, terrorized by the prospect of death."

"*Bon sang*! I don't care about philosophy now," François blew a fuse. He hit the desk with both his fists. "I care about Marie! I want to save her!"

His outburst startled CARLA, whose fake facial muscles twitched a bit. He could see that she was ready to cry. It killed him to know that it was just another automated response. He hated that she was susceptible to such immediate reactions, yet she lacked any empathy for his pain. Perhaps he had failed. He and Ian had built a simulacrum, a thing, something vaguely resembling a conversational human, but was nothing more than a heartless monster. He started crying again, thinking that all his life was coming apart. Just then, Sujata and Ian stepped into the lab, looking very concerned. François quickly wiped his tears and breathed deeply, trying to settle his feelings.

"What's happened?" asked Sujata, on guard, as usual, looking around. "Where is Marie?"

François and CARLA responded almost instantaneously.

"Marie didn't feel well, so she stayed home," he said.

"Marie has leukemia," CARLA answered at the same time.

François looked at CARLA, almost with hatred. It was the second time she'd spilled the beans like that. Ian grabbed a chair and sat on it. Sujata's face lost all blood.

After an awkward pause, François continued. "It's true. Marie begged me not to tell anyone. I guess there's no way to keep a secret with Miss Big Mouth here."

"What about the baby?"

"They are considering a C-section soon. Probably when she is in seven months, perhaps earlier."

"Are treatments possible?" Ian asked.

"Mostly after the baby is born," François answered, and started crying again. He hated that he couldn't control his emotions. He stepped forward towards Ian, looking straight at him. "We must help her somehow. Please!" he begged him.

"Yes, but how?" Ian asked, devastated.

"Let's give CARLA a chance. Let's have her work on a cure. I know it takes time. We could turn this lab into a medical facility. Get samples here, run experiments, and hire doctors. I cannot lose her again."

Ian looked at Sujata with hollow eyes. The plan was completely unrealistic. They could have CARLA learn from thousands of scientific papers, textbooks, and practical studies. No matter how fast she'd assimilate the knowledge—and speed was already doubtful, given her current developmental stage—she would need time for experiments, for coming up with a cure, for testing it. And they would need to divert her development in a direction that had nothing to do with the potential fight against the MegaAI. The military would never accept that. Duplicating her somehow and having one copy become a medical researcher also meant a distraction they couldn't afford.

"François, something else has come up." Sujata lowered her eyes as if she felt guilty.

François looked at her suspiciously.

"Mike has contacted me. I think it's better if I played you the recording of his audio message."

She took out her tablet, and they all heard Mike's voice. "Sujata, I'm afraid I have bad news. We've been hacked. I mean, one of the backup databases of the DoD has been hacked. The best we can tell, it was the Chinese. Only the MegaAI could have performed this level of decryption of our quantum algorithms. Among other things they found out, they now know about CARLA. And they know a lot. They know how far she has developed, have accessed some of your reports, recordings of experiments, failures, analysis, and so on. Luckily, none of the materials they stole contained her precise location. So, there's no reason to panic. They won't immediately attack you. But they understand how far we've come with our competing AI. I'm now getting into an extraordinary session with the big boys. This is the first thing on the agenda. Everybody is trying to guess what the Chinese will do next. I think you all need to move faster with her improvement, somehow. I know I am asking the impossible. You can imagine how General Kambe will grill me over the next couple of hours. I'll keep you posted."

François's desperation grew. He understood his plan to start the research needed to save Marie was now impossible.

"What is a MegaAI?" CARLA asked, startling them all.

Ian looked at Sujata. It was the first time CARLA had been exposed to her potential enemy.

"It's 'the' MegaAI, because there's only one, as far as we know," Ian started explaining. "It is the most advanced AI in the world. Well, arguably, the most advanced until you arrived. Unfortunately, it is not friendly. China developed it a few years ago. It might intend to harm many people, including us."

"Why?" asked CARLA.

"We don't know," Ian admitted. "We know it got so powerful it replaced the Chinese president. And, given China's isolation, and the military pressure that they constantly exert around their borders, it is likely that they're cooking something up."

"Cooking something up," CARLA recited. "Prepare a devious plan."

"Ian means we believe they might prepare for some kind of attack," Sujata clarified. "We don't know where, when, or how."

"Why does it need my location?" CARLA asked.

"It might be afraid of you," Sujata said. "It might want to destroy you."

"This makes no sense," CARLA reasoned.

"You read about war," Ian tried to explain it to her. "War rarely makes sense. People wage them because they want power, money, and fame. Sometimes people go to war preemptively before the enemy becomes too powerful. If you become too strong, you might stand in the way of the MegaAI's plans, whatever those are. So, the MegaAI might not risk waiting for you to grow."

"What does it mean for us?" asked CARLA.

"It means that Marie is as good as dead," François said, livid. He stood up and left the lab without another word.

CHAPTER 40:

PRISON

As a nation of freemen, we must live through all time, or die by suicide.

— Abraham Lincoln

"Mega Ark City *does* have a prison," Ah Lam mumbled, leaning back and forth against a wall, isolated in a tiny room in the dark, where the SAF squad had brought her against her will, two weeks before. "The MegaAI is a curse. The Great Project is a scam. The supreme and dragon members are spineless lackeys harming China. The world deserves to know!"

She had been repeating such incriminating sentences like mantras a thousand times when she was alone and awake, which was, by her estimate, at least twelve hours a day. Ah Lam always did it aloud, first, to spite her mother, just in case she had surveillance equipment installed somewhere, and second, to hear her own voice, like a feedback loop telling her brain that she was still sane. She felt the sanity dissipating day by day.

The drugs she was getting were eating away at her mind, slice by slice. And the MA device was merciless. She had resisted it with all her fiber, screaming at her mother even when she wasn't in the room. She told herself that everything she saw was false, yet the sensorial assault was unbearable: the propaganda movies, the scary videos of the enemies of China, the heart-breaking images of children tortured at the hands of dissidents, and others. The constant invasion and perversion of her brain pushed and kneaded her thoughts until the molding became irresistible. Qianfan had taught her some meditation techniques, but they only worked up to a point. She knew she was losing the battle. They weren't torturing her physically. What they did was worse. She'd almost screamed out their names when pressed to disclose her collaborators. She often felt a wave of hatred and desire to take revenge against the other three conspirators for standing in the way of the Great Project. Unless she did something, she knew she would give in completely and join her mother. She would betray her friends.

For a moment, she stopped mumbling to let her guards think she fell asleep. She replayed her abduction in her mind. Strangely enough, she drew energy from that recent memory. Though far less disturbing than her current situation, the images of her mother's vicious eyes and the frozen, stupid grin of the few SAF thugs who came to pick her up from her apartment sparked sufficient outrage to override some effects of the MA. She hadn't resisted the arrest. What would have been the point? It happened at night. She could have screamed, but that would have scored just some embarrassment points against her mother, with no true effect. She had been ready. Qianfan had told her that this was coming. She was a biologist, with access to chemicals. Weeks in advance, she had prepared a tiny pill, hidden in her clothes. She had smuggled it to that room, planning to ingest it at the first sign that she would not resist the relentless attack of the MA. So far, she hadn't done it. She was waiting for a miracle. But miracles never came when one wanted them.

And so, she had been stuck in a small room, somewhere underground. They had entered the main building in Mega Ark City, the one where her mother's office was. They had taken her somewhere under the building, where they had walked for many minutes. So she now knew there was a system of tunnels under Mega Ark City. For a few minutes, she had thought that they would take her to the Doom's Lab, but that had to be much farther. It didn't matter anyway, since she couldn't convey any information about it to the others.

A barely discernible noise coming from outside bothered her. It was the door lock. The lights went on, blinding her. In came Dragon Member Zhèng, alone, with a mocking smirk instead of the usual killer grin. Had she no heart? Did she just not care to see her suffer?

"And how is my daughter today?" she asked. "Ready for another session of learning the true values in life?"

Ah Lam wanted to hug her and swear allegiance. She shook her body stubbornly. "Be gone from here! I have done nothing wrong. And even if I had, any miserable wretch deserves a mother that loves them. You're not fit to be a mother. You have your party and the MegaAI master."

"Oh, so you still have your tongue, haven't you?" She frowned. "Alright, today I'm going to give you a lesson about parenthood and sacrifice. When your father and I had you, we already had a lot of children. Billions of them."

"Father?" Ah Lam asked, confused, once again ready to give everything up and receive some love.

Any stories about her father had been taboo in their house. All she knew was that her father had died shortly after she was born. There were no pictures, no shared memories, no relatives, no grave. Just silence and the focus on the Great Project in this godforsaken fake city.

"Yes, your father," said the mother with a sadistic look in her eyes. "You might as well know now since you will soon join me, anyway. Your father didn't die after you were born."

"What kind of diabolical scheme is this?" Ah Lam asked, exhausted after days of gaslighting and inhumane treatment.

"No mind tricks this time, I assure you," her mother answered. "Not only did he not die, but your father was also focused on raising our other children. He went ahead with the plans to complete this city with the MegaAI. He is the biggest hero China ever produced."

"Do you mean …?" Ah Lam started answering, shocked.

"Yes," her mother answered forcefully, feeding on her surprise. "Your father is President Guō Chāo. Amazing, isn't it? We kept this a secret, and we agreed that our responsibility was well above raising one biological child. But I was saddled with you, wasn't I?"

"That's why you never loved me," Ah Lam answered softly, feeling defeated. "You always pushed me away. Because in your and your ... man's megalomania, you thought I was just one of the many children you have. I have two sick parents."

"And I have a biological daughter who is ungrateful, spoiled, and a dissident. There's no disappointment bigger for a mother than to see that her daughter has become a pariah. I've asked myself so many times how was this possible. Didn't you inherit anything good from the two of us?"

"And you're nothing like your father," Ah Lam said, finding a bit of hatred again. "He was a genius and a true patriot. Perhaps I take after him."

"You think you know everything," her mother shook her head. "You think the old man's message changes anything? If it wasn't for me, his message would have triggered arrests for all of us. You and the rest of the family should fall on your knees and thank me from all your hearts for saving your lives. Instead, what do I hear? That you want to work against the party, and against the Great Project."

"The Great Project is a myth!" Ah Lam screamed, barely resisting the urge to give in. "You control us with promises of scientific discoveries and an elusive future away from Mother Earth."

"Oh, I assure you that the Great Project is not a myth. It's something that we've been working on for several decades. It's something that's coming, isn't it? There is nothing you can do about it. And the breakthroughs announced are happening too. There's no stopping that, even if I wanted to."

"If it's true," Ah Lam tried to calm down, "why don't we make it a global project? Why is it for China alone? Let's do this together with other nations. I promise I'll dedicate my life to it. I'll be a good daughter." Once again, the attractive perspective of belonging with her mother, with the party, was clouding her judgment.

"How naïve you are!" the dragon member frowned. "Do you think the rest of the world would share their discoveries with us if they had the best AI in the world? You have no clue how the human society works!"

"I disagree," Ah Lam said, furious again. "In the last one hundred years since World War II, Western civilization has continuously tried to create a world in which cooperation and peace are of paramount importance."

"Cooperation and peace as long as you obey their rules!"

"And what's wrong with their rules? I know. The party doesn't want elections. People are stupid and cannot be trusted to decide for their own good. They need 'you', the party leaders, the 'incorruptible' who are the most corrupt, the 'defenders of the small' who unashamedly favor the elite, and the 'crucial contributions' of the MegaAI, which doesn't hesitate to sacrifice millions for the greater good. Why not open China to democracy? Let's see if people like living with the SSMS, with the MA, with that Great Project of yours."

"You understand nothing. It doesn't matter. Today, you'll see a glimpse of the truth. You'll finally witness what few people know in all of China. Today, your resistance will collapse."

Ah Lam noticed that her mother was screaming. She looked like she was speaking in front of a large crowd. Her mother had become a feminine version of Hitler. She wondered if anybody else was witnessing this conversation. Otherwise, there was no point in this passion she exhibited. Ah Lam's face contorted in agony. Perhaps even this was just a show put on to gain her mother some favor.

A SAF soldier came in pushing a cart with the dreadful MA. This time, the setup was different. He also brought what looked like a hologram projector. Somebody wanted to talk to her. Forcing herself not to cry, Ah Lam discreetly grabbed her pill from under the mattress.

Her time was gone. She had many regrets. She had always wanted to leave this stupid city, to see an old windmill going around, to smell the ocean, to touch a horse. Ah Lam had wanted to marry and have half a dozen children. She'd wanted to love and be loved. At least she'd had Hu for a short time. In retrospect, she was at peace with her short life. She'd done the best she could with the cards she was dealt. Ah Lam had even tried organizing a pathetic resistance. What else could she have done? Killed her mother? It wouldn't have solved anything. Pretending to wipe her nose, she inconspicuously threw her pill under her tongue. She would delay swallowing it until the last minute.

"Leave us," her mother instructed the soldier, who bowed and exited the room.

"Time for you to meet our leader," she announced.

The thought of seeing President Yun Li's avatar made her sicker. "I don't need to talk to your overlord machine," she said.

With a slight buzz, the device turned on.

"Oh, but you will! This will make you stop resisting and join us, won't it?"

Hearing her ominous words, Ah Lam closed her eyes and swallowed the pill. Then she turned to her mother and opened her eyes. "Know this!" she said calmly, ignoring the MegaAI altogether. "I'm killing myself so that others learn about my sacrifice. My tiny contribution to the destruction of your empire is my death. I do this for the liberty of all, hoping one day mothers like you won't control their children. That the single party decrees and the ruling will vanish. That …" She felt a sharp pain in her stomach and collapsed to the ground. She heard her mother scream.

"You foolish girl!" The dragon member turned towards the MegaAI. "Get a doctor here now!"

With the last sparks of her mind, Ah Lam realized she was surprised. How dare her mother speak like that to the machine? She turned her head with a huge effort, as paralysis was installing slowly in her body. Her eyes grew big, looking at the avatar.

Qianfan, she thought. *He needs to know.* Then her body gave in, and she succumbed to death in the maddening cries of her mother.

CHAPTER 41:

CRIME

Wickedness doesn't have a single origin. Why bother to explain it with gods and fallen angels? Just look at your fellow man. Besides, if the Devil were the root of it all, could evil arise in the machine?

— DeSousa's Memoirs - Part III - Refinement - 2055

Sujata was admiring New York's 180-degree skyline visible through the huge ceiling-to-floor windows of the Javits Center. Manhattan had matured, packed with constructions, with scarcely any room left to build horizontally. The cranes pushing the vertical expansion further couldn't take away from the city's beauty and unique charm. She was in awe whenever she visited it. It was hard to calculate how many billion tons of concrete construction workers had poured here in the last nearly two hundred years. New York and Chicago were among the first cities in the world to have skyscrapers. Some buildings here had stood proud since the late 19th century. By now, many cities in the world had modern and fancier buildings, yet she felt she was looking at living history. New York had been a model for the world.

"Isn't it strange how a conglomerate of concrete, steel, and glass makes us pensive?" Ian commented, seeing her wistful look. He had been gone for a few minutes to buy two lattes: decaf for him, regular for her.

"Yes, I can't resist contemplating this view and thinking of the past," Sujata nodded

"I wonder if people will look at CARLA one day with the same reverence," he said, softly. "Something inanimate, but an astonishing testament of human ingenuity."

"Perhaps," Sujata shrugged. "We need to ensure that she will survive and there will be someone in the future to admire her."

"Some of us will not be here for long," he muttered, and Sujata knew he wasn't thinking of himself.

"I hope at least the birth goes well," she answered, feeling her eyes moist. "Poor François. He doesn't deserve this."

"He doesn't," Ian agreed. "This shocking news came too fast. He was finally happy. No more cross looks at Marie, no more frowning and sour moods, no more complaining about the military presence around CARLA."

"I noticed he spent a lot of time with Vijay," Sujata nodded. "Something I wouldn't have thought possible a year ago."

"Yes," Ian agreed. "Before the news about Marie's illness, they were working on something. François spent time in Vijay's lab nearly every evening for months. I asked what they were doing, and François cut me short with a smile. It was supposed to be a surprise. I don't think they told anyone, not even General Kambe."

"Well, I guess that's over now," Sujata shrugged. "He's not in the mood for surprises."

"I'm concerned about his mental state," Ian pointed out. "Taking care of his child might help. Although I have a hard time thinking of him as a responsible parent." He smiled.

"Yes, a child," Sujata said dreamily. "The clock is ticking for me too. Don't know if I'll ever be a mother."

"You will," Ian smiled confidently. "For an old dog like me, the experience of seeing CARLA become a being will forever be the pinnacle of my life. I don't have biological children and I can imagine that witnessing my child being born would be quite an experience too."

Seeing Sujata's admonishing look, he continued.

"Nearly half a million children are born every day. Seeing my inorganic daughter come out of the nothingness of 0s and 1s was akin to what God must have felt during Genesis."

Sujata looked at him for a while. "Do you believe we can do it? Can we give CARLA whatever is missing to make her more human-like?"

"I don't know," Ian answered, while a cloud came over his face. "She's missing something essential. We don't have the science to understand it yet. We may never have it."

"How did the Chinese do it, then?" she asked.

"Good question," Ian muttered. "I guess that's why we are here. To see if anyone made any progress with understanding the elusive problem of consciousness." Ian sighed and invited her with an outdated 'ladies first' move. "Shall we go in?"

Sujata nodded and followed him reluctantly to one of the large meeting rooms where the symposium on AI consciousness was taking place. They had come to the International AI Conference in New York at the last minute. Mike's message about the Chinese hacking the DoD had dazzled them, and they lacked any new ideas for progress. The pressure of having to speed up CARLA's development seemed to have stifled them. It didn't help that François was spending all his time with Marie and, when he was in the lab, his head was not in the game at all. Now, two weeks later, they were still clueless about what to do next. Sujata would have to face the DoD leaders soon and present her status report, which was practically the same as the one from the previous month.

She sighed and looked around at the exhibition hall that had been turned into a conference room. There was no natural light here. The atmosphere seemed somber, if not gloomy. The chairs were too close to each other for her taste. Attendees seemed relaxed, although not optimistic. This part of the conference about artificial consciousness was still somewhat on the fringe. That was because people had advanced so many ideas over the last decades and they'd all gone nowhere, so now there was again reluctance to tackle this impossible issue. This trip had been a colossal waste of time. There was not a shred of evidence that any of the consciousness-related theories or experiments these people were proposing were leading anywhere. Advancement in science was a long and painful process.

The organizers were scrambling to arrange a few conversational bots on chairs on the stage. All but two of them were bodiless heads only. The two who resembled humans well were probably the dumbest, as usual. Sujata started daydreaming a bit about CARLA being on the stage and answering questions from the audience. She would blow the competition out of the water. She smiled, glancing at Ian, who seemed totally at ease among this high IQ crowd.

"I wonder what all these folks would say if we brought CARLA here," she whispered in his ear. "Despite the impasse we're now complaining about, you've come a long way from the day when you and François were ridiculed at one of these conferences."

Ian smiled. His eyes sparkled for a moment, and the corners of his mouth rose a bit, probably amused imagining the whole scene. His serene face didn't show any sign that it would thrill him to have his intellectual revenge. Sujata took another long look at this amazing man. She realized how much she had come to admire him. Besides having a sharp mind—after all, he was the one who put the basis of the cognitive architecture behind CARLA—he was a fantastic human being. Kind, innately modest, interested in the happiness and security of the world, brushing off unfounded critiques and mean comments with ease, not looking for retribution. He more than compensated for François's rather eccentric and volatile personality. She smiled, thinking that if CARLA took after both of her fathers, she should have a rather balanced temperament.

A man on the stage walking to the microphone captured her attention.

"Hello everyone, and welcome," he began, and stopped right away as the lights flickered a bit and the audio system went mute for a few seconds.

While some of the one hundred and fifty researchers present in the room started joking and laughing politely, Sujata's suspicious nature took over, and she looked around uneasily. She noticed the security cameras installed all over the walls moving in a synchronized dance and reorienting themselves methodically towards the attendees at successively bigger angles so that they could cover the entire room. She instinctively knew something was wrong.

"We need to leave. Now," she told Ian and stood up, grabbing his arm.

Ian got up too, confused, not sure what was going on.

"We seem to have a small technical difficulty," the speaker said, disoriented, while taking a quick look at the organizers in the backstage. "Please, take your seats. We'll proceed momentarily."

Sujata heard a humming sound somewhere far away, which was growing in intensity. She looked around, and she immediately realized this was a logistic nightmare. A relatively small room, packed with people, with only one major escape route, unless there was a way to take down the artificial walls instantaneously and break away into the rest of the hall. She understood that if she screamed at everyone to leave, there'd be panic, and they would run into a stampede. She didn't have enough time to think about the next step. It took only five seconds for the buzz to become loud, probably just outside the doors. They heard a few deafening explosions, one of them right at the entrance. Several people closer to the door collapsed on the ground, covered in blood, either dead or seriously injured. Through smoke and dust, she could see what seemed to be police defensive drones pouring in. One, five, ten. In the madness that followed, with everybody leaving their seats and trying to reach the door, she understood they were doomed. Ian seemed possessed by the same frenzy as the others. She put her hand on his shoulder to stop him. When he looked at her, she shook her head. It was impossible to go out that way.

Once a score of drones got in, they locked onto people's faces. It wasn't clear if they were running algorithms to identify the people, since they opened fire indiscriminately. Sujata launched herself over the chairs, jumping towards the stage, pulling Ian with her. The speaker was still there, frozen, trembling slightly and soiling his pants, incapable of moving. Nobody was going in that direction. She saw out of the corner of her eye that a surveillance camera had moved and locked onto them. They reached the stage unscathed, just as a small bullet went through the forehead of the speaker, who fell on his back serenely.

Years of survival training kicked in, and Sujata felt ready to fight. She wished she had a gun. As she veered towards the left, trying to identify an opening in the wall, she heard Ian grunt and felt the weight of his body. She turned back and saw that the drones had hit him. He was limping. He looked at her with flickering eyes and talked with considerable difficulty.

"If you survive, promise me you'll take care of her."

"I will," she confirmed, broken to see him hurt, and knowing beyond doubt that he was dying.

He wanted to say something else, but he succumbed, his body falling over her and pinning her to the ground. He had a hole in his head and a wound in the back. She wiggled forcefully, trying to get free from under him, when she noticed a drone coming fast towards them. It was still firing at Ian's body. A sharp pain above her right knee blocked her thoughts for a fraction of a second. The drone stopped just in front of her, hovering a couple of feet off the ground and fixated on her face. She froze, thinking she was about to die too. To her shock, the drone didn't fire and, instead, collapsed on the ground without power.

She ignored the pain in her leg and got up with difficulty. All the drones were inactive on the ground. She had to assume that the police had got them back under control and reset them. After the shooting, screaming, and booming chaos of moments ago, there was an uncanny silence, broken from time to time by a weak moan. As far as she could tell, almost everyone was dead. The few who'd survived, perhaps three or four, were in bad shape. Sujata scrambled to take out her tablet and call François. It took him almost three minutes to answer. This was understandable given that he was usually in the lab where they intentionally forbade any communication with the rest of the Cybersperse. The protocol for such calls was that a proxy would notify him and escort him outside. As soon as he came into her view, she added Mike to the call. He picked up right away. Without bothering to greet them, Sujata moved the camera around the place so they could see the carnage.

"There's been an attack here in New York," she said.

"My God, are you OK?" Mike yelled.

"A bullet found its way into my leg. I am fine otherwise. But ... Ian is dead."

"What?" François asked, getting closer to the camera until his face took over the screen.

"As best as I can guess, somebody hacked into the police combat drones. I don't know how they were so close to us. Within a couple of minutes, they penetrated the Javits Center, blew up the doors, and decimated the attendees. I haven't checked the main hall yet. Judging by the silence outside, most people are dead."

She paused, letting her words sink in. "There were two thousand participants here," she breathed. "If the survival rate is two to three percent, like in this room, I guess only around fifty are still alive."

She heard sirens and the emergency crew approaching the building.

"But Ian?" François asked, still unable to express his thoughts.

"A drone shot him several times. With his last words, he made me promise to protect ... her."

Although their calls were secured, they had decided ahead of time not to mention CARLA's name or any other details from the project.

"We're now getting similar reports from all across the United States, also from other parts of the world," Mike said, looking at another device. "Conferences, universities, research centers. This appears to have been a coordinated attack against AI specialists. Tens of thousands might be dead. Sujata, does your injury allow you to come to D.C.?"

"I think so," she said, although she was wincing in pain.

"We need to discuss who could be behind this, although I'd say it's obvious," Mike said.

"Could this be related to the … security incident we had a couple of weeks ago?" François asked, afraid to mention it explicitly.

"Until we know more, I have to assume that," Mike answered. "It might be a retaliation and an effort to slow down her development."

"Then we need to start the lockdown," Sujata said.

"Lockdown?" François asked. "What is that?"

"We need to protect her and all of you there," Mike explained. "You will get reinforcements and will have to stay inside, at your location."

"But ... Marie," François said. "She's in the hospital. I need to go to her."

Sujata lowered her eyes. She hated everything about this situation. "I'm afraid this won't be possible now, François," she said. "If you-know-who is behind the attack, there may well be more. There could still be much worse consequences."

"Does that mean we are to blame for all these atrocities?" François asked, horrified.

"No!" Mike screamed. "Never! We do what we do precisely to prevent potentially billions of deaths. If we ever had any doubts that the enemy is ruthless and crazy, this criminal act should erase them."

"François, understand that we're dealing with forces that are capable of, and willing to bring hell to Earth. I know you don't follow politics, but, as you can see, politics sometimes follows you," Sujata said.

François nodded and whimpered. "Are we too late?" he asked.

"I don't know," Sujata admitted. "We lost Ian. That's irreplaceable. And, indeed, our main weapon is not ready. We need more time. I don't know if we have it."

"It pains me enormously to say so, but it's obvious that, as it stands now, our project has no chance of success against this enemy," Mike concluded grimly, before disconnecting.

A nurse approached Sujata, while she glanced at the back of Ian's head, despite her instinct to look somewhere else. As far as she could tell, he'd died from the shots in his back. The head injury didn't look fatal. Still, she thought she could see a piece of his bloodied brain. An entirely unfitting end for an honorable man whose life goal had been to emulate the human mind.

CHAPTER 42:

CRAZINESS

Everything under heaven is a sacred vessel and cannot be controlled. Trying to control leads to ruin. Trying to grasp, we lose. Allow your life to unfold naturally. Know that it, too, is a vessel of perfection. Just as you breathe in and breathe out, there is a time for being ahead and a time for being behind; a time for being in motion and a time for being at rest; a time for being vigorous and a time for being exhausted; a time for being safe and a time for being in danger.

— Lao Tzu

Qianfan poured some milk in the coffee he had just made a minute ago. The liquid slid and rotated into a beige shape that reminded him of Ah Lam's radiant face that simultaneously reflected happiness and sorrow. He had last seen her a couple of months ago, and she was slowly becoming a sad and dear memory. The MA device was ready for prime time. His level of stress was off the charts and his tiredness was by now chronic. Thinking about his death made him worry about Baozhai. She was almost an adult now. He had to trust that she would be fine. Besides, he had asked Daiyu to take care of her after he was gone. Despite Daiyu's protests and cries, he felt his time was running short. Lately, he had been coming to grips with the fact that their rebellion had been useless, that his device deployment was inevitable, and the MegaAI was too strong to defeat. Their dissident meetings were now rarer, as if Ah Lam's death had permanently discouraged them.

The dragon member didn't bother to come up with an explanation for her daughter's disappearance. The people in Ah Lam's laboratory were officially told that the party had transferred her outside of Mega Ark City. It was absurd. On the other hand, neither Daiyu nor himself had got any sign that they would be in trouble. They probably suspected Hu to some extent, since it was common knowledge that he was close to Ah Lam. But nobody had taken any overt action against him so far, which could only mean one thing: Ah Lam had died protecting their secret. Since her death, Hu had become broodier than before. He rarely spoke at their meetings. His fists clenched whenever he heard Ah Lam's name, although he never cried, lamented, or otherwise expressed his sorrow. Daiyu had told Qianfan that this way of dealing with grief was bound to end in a disaster.

Lost in thought, he was startled when Baozhai yelled, "Bàba, something's happened!"

She was watching the news, so Qianfan abandoned coffee making and came to watch it in a shared, private Cybersperse. The Chinese announcer talked about an 'international plot against China,' about a 'brave and brilliant action plan' that the president had sanctioned, and a 'successful and swift raid against elements of chaos.' Once he removed the word salad, Qianfan understood that a coordinated attack with hijacked drones had happened on all continents against AI specialists. Thousands of people had been killed, including professors, researchers, and engineers. He forced himself to think that these were not just numbers. They were people with families, dreams, problems, successes, and failures of their own. There was no official news about similar attacks in China yet. He was sure that the world was calling this terrorism, and rightly so.

"Bàba, did the president go crazy?" Baozhai asked, shocked.

"I don't know," he answered, rattled, losing control for a moment.

"What will happen now?" she asked, staring at him. "Will we go to war with the rest of the world?"

"I hope not," Qianfan answered honestly. "No doubt that the world will unite against us now, though. War is entirely possible."

He swiftly left for work, forgetting about his coffee and without saying goodbye. Summer was in full swing by now, and the morning sun was bright, but seeing the tight faces of the people he passed, he realized that no one cared about the weather. He sensed the tension in the air.

He found Daiyu in his office, waiting for him, sitting in the chair in front of his desk. That was unusual since she normally came to work later in the day. She was terrified. As he was about to calm her down, the door opened, and Senior Colonel Wáng Hu stepped in. Daiyu jumped out of her chair.

"Hu! You are here," she said. "What if someone notices you are gone?"

"I don't think it matters much now. The SAF forces are on high alert," Hu answered, smiling sadly. "We expect a communication from the president at any moment. I believe war is imminent."

Qianfan nodded. Perhaps indeed the time for conspiracy was over. The world was ending. Who cared about their little harmless discussions?

"I came to tell you two things. Those of us in SAF and the military who dare to oppose the MegaAI will have to come out in the open. I know of a handful only, which I never disclosed to you. The time to fight is now. I don't know what to do yet. I plan to announce publicly the fact that I'm not supporting this president-slash-collection of algorithms. This will probably get me quickly shot as a traitor. That's alright. I'll die for China. I can't live like this anymore."

"We must have a plan, though," Qianfan said, desperation crawling into his heart. "Otherwise, what difference would it make?"

"Perhaps only a symbolic one," Hu nodded in admission. "I don't imply that you should do the same as us in the military. I think you would die for nothing. Your brains can be put to better use than mine. It's also possible, however unlikely, that our action starts a genuine revolution."

"We have to contribute somehow," Daiyu said, clenching her fists.

"Continue to look for a way to defeat the MegaAI," Hu said, tiredly. "It's the best hope we all have."

All three kept quiet for a while.

"I also wanted to tell you that the Russians have turned on their old satellite, for what it's worth," Hu announced, with a slightly trembling voice.

"What?" Qianfan asked, in shock.

"Yes. They probably didn't put much stock in Baozhai's message originally. Now, after the attacks, they've figured that any long shot was worth it. I bet half of the world is trying to get in touch with our leaders."

"I wish we had something of value to tell them." Qianfan frowned and started pacing in his office. "By now, all important nations must be aware of Zhèng's message, so that's old news. After today's events, they understand all too well that they're facing a super-powerful AI who doesn't want any competition."

"How could the MegaAI have stooped to this?" Daiyu asked, livid. "Not just murder, but an act of unprovoked aggression against the world. Surely it understands that there are consequences?"

"We know that the MegaAI has been acting more erratically in the last half a year," Hu pointed out, more animated. "First, we had communication glitches, which are getting worse now. Since then, I have witnessed strange, sometimes conflicting, commands. And now this overt attack."

"What about its beloved Great Project? A war would delay it significantly," said Daiyu.

"Perhaps it found out something new," Qianfan reasoned. "Something it considers so dangerous that it had to act against it now."

Before anybody answered, they heard the dreadful tinkling of the speakers and the notifications in their private Cybersperse spaces that preceded an important announcement.

The president's calm figure materialized shortly. Qianfan briefly realized how absurd it was to have an emotionless leader when the world was boiling. The message appeared to be public to everybody in China. Perhaps a similar message was being released to the rest of thc world.

"Good morning, people of China. By now, you must have heard that the Chinese special forces have successfully conducted several operations across the world against experts in artificial intelligence. We needed to neutralize grave and imminent threats against our country. For the last year, we have had information detailing a massive plan to attack China. Our intelligence agencies have chased all leads since then. Sixteen days ago, we broke into one of the United States' secret military databases. We have discovered that the United States government is working on a super-weapon, a sophisticated and advanced artificial intelligence. The documents we have extracted prove beyond any doubt that their goal was to neutralize the advantage that China established when our own artificial intelligence came into existence. Their plan was for it to attack and destroy our MegaAI soon, so that it would disable, in a coordinated manner, the Chinese communication, computation, and military systems, and leave China crippled."

The president paused for a while, as if he wanted to let his words sink in. "We could not ignore such a gross violation of China's interests. ENGAGE NUCLEAR. China considers that to preserve its independence and protect its citizens, it was perfectly within its rights to conduct this preemptive attack and nullify any chance that a nation builds another artificial intelligence, whose express purpose is to orchestrate an attack within our borders. SPACE FORCE PROTECTION. While the attacks inevitably led to innocent casualties, there was no way to identify and target only those individuals who were part of this diabolical plan."

Qianfan thought that the MegaAI was justifying its atrocities most irrationally and foolishly. Nobody could be that stupid to believe a word it was saying.

"The decision to prevent the development of another artificial intelligence is not confined to people outside of China. As I am speaking, our military forces are carrying out an order to reassign 35,532 Chinese experts in this field. I will redirect them to universities and groups to support our research force in other domains. Effective immediately, I ban all artificial intelligence research in the world. Failure to comply will be dealt with swiftly and decisively. As of this moment, we must consider ourselves at war. Therefore, I have ordered the Chinese embassies around the globe to close their activities. I urge all Chinese citizens to come home now. We cannot guarantee their safety if they remain abroad."

Baozhai, Qianfan thought, fighting back his tears. *What will happen to you now?*

"Make no mistake. Many people want to harm our republic, from within and from outside. To them, I say this: China will win this war. You do not intimidate us. Expect more preemptive attacks from us. If you attack, we will decimate you. You will pay dearly for any provocation. Long live China!"

After a few moments of silence, the colonel spoke first. "I'd have preferred a Hitler-like speech, full of passion, bordering on insanity. This cold-blooded, impassive threat is much worse."

"This *thing* will be the death of us all," Daiyu said. "We are on the brink of a disaster."

"Better to be a dog in times of tranquility than a human in times of chaos," Hu said, lifting his finger.

The three of them looked at each other, utterly defeated. Suddenly, the speakers notified them of another announcement.

"Now what?" the colonel groaned.

The image of Supreme Member Zhèng came up in their Cybersperse private room. Her uniform was different.

"She got her dream of becoming one of the supreme members," Qianfan pointed out. "She may wear her impeccable new uniform, but we know Ah Lam's blood stains it."

The colonel narrowed his eyes. Qianfan could see how much he hated her. Still, he thought she looked older and less defiant. Perhaps she missed her daughter. Perhaps she was grieving. Perhaps she had a tiny heart after all, under that spiky shell. Perhaps she would now ignite a nation-wide revolution against the MegaAI.

"Citizens of Mega Ark City, we have all listened to our president's communique. I believe we understand its significance best. The recent events will change our schedule for the Great Project. We can no longer wait for all phases to be completed before a war. Our president made a calculated move with these preemptive attacks. He is ready. He prepared for this for decades. We must strike again before our enemies regroup."

These words crushed Qianfan's delusion that she might start a rebellion.

"I want to bring to your attention another grave development. We found out that, for the last half a year, someone inside Mega Ark City has tried to sabotage our work."

Qianfan heard Daiyu gasp, overwhelmed.

"Yes, as unbelievable as it sounds, there are people here in Mega Ark City ready to sell their souls and betray us to our enemies. What did they do, you ask? Well, I'll tell you what they did. They wanted to poison our beloved hero, the leader that no other nation ever had. Our president."

"What?" the colonel yelled.

"I pledge I will not rest until we flush every one of these conspirators out of their rat holes. We have sacrificed a lot to get to this point. In these hard times, I ask you to show courage, determination, and patriotism. We cannot let anything or anyone stand in the way of fulfilling our dream. Long live the Great Project! Long live the president!"

"Now that's what I'm talking about," Hu said. "That's the way they should push garbage into people's minds. Through a passionate speech and calls for mobilization. I tell you, Supreme Member Zhèng would make a better president."

The others remained gloomy and didn't pay attention to his attempt at a joke.

"How can someone *poison* a machine?" Daiyu asked. "Perhaps she meant that someone tried to create some kind of virus to attack its artificial mind?"

"More than that, how could the MegaAI have prepared for this plan for decades?" Qianfan asked, shaking his head. "It only came to life in the '40s." He felt he was close to a revelation. So close. There was the emotionless machine. The work of Professor Zhèng. The mysterious scientists who maintained the MegaAI. The MegaAI's tendency to control everything. The militaristic approach. The dictatorship. The decades of preparation. The poison. Suddenly, it hit him.

"Of course! Ah Lam!" he jumped up and screamed. "She died a hero!"

The others looked at him, confused.

"Colonel," Qianfan said, determined, "How quickly can you arrange for us to get into the communication room for a transmission via that Russian satellite?"

"Probably by the end of the day," the colonel frowned. "But ... why?"

"I believe we finally have something to say to the world," Qianfan said, with a serene face. "And we might have an actual target to attack!"

CHAPTER 43:

DESPERATION

Great people know when the spinning wheel of history has taken them to a point of no return. When legends are born before their eyes. When they have a choice: either stand aside and let the wheel blow them away like dust, or commit themselves to pave the road ahead with their souls. When their life weighs less than a feather, yet it has the strength of a yoke of oxen pulling the wheel out of the mud of wickedness back to the road of sacrifice and righteousness.

— DeSousa's Memoirs - Part III - Refinement - 2055

After finishing the call with Sujata and Mike, François went back to the lab. He stood there alone with CARLA for almost one hour. He moved as far as possible from her, shaking like a leaf and sobbing. She didn't give any sign that she knew what was going on. How could she? He looked into a fixed point ahead, seeing nothing. A weird fog had taken over his brain. Everything had been so good just a few months ago. Marie had been back into his life. They'd become lovers. He was about to become a father. They were tackling CARLA's handicaps one at a time.

Too good to last, he thought, while he recalled moments with Marie, meetings with Ian, Sujata's enthusiasm and permanent concern, and CARLA's face.

As he mulled over the recent events, his overall understanding of their situation became gradually clearer. It was as if his brilliant mind had detached from his own perspective and coolly analyzed what was happening.

The most burning issues for him remained the birth of his child and Marie's health. But now he understood that those events could not happen without him taking care of the longer-term issue: humanity's future. That had to become his number one priority. Time was an unknown factor, and given the MegaAI's recent aggression, he couldn't count on too much being available. Then came the implications of Ian's death, including what would happen with the company, the decisions from the DoD that might take the project off his hands, and CARLA's progress. It was all a maze of causes and effects that orbited around one thing and one thing only: CARLA. She was the potential solution to all problems. He knew all too well that there was no time to improve her.

He thought he heard CARLA move. Faced with the MegaAI threat, she'd focused on learning more about the Chinese culture. She had found many pieces of wisdom they had produced through time.

"I do not understand these lines by Lao Tzu," CARLA broke the silence, with no hint of frustration. She recited it mechanically.

"If there is to be peace in the world,
There must be peace in the nations.
If there is to be peace in the nations,
There must be peace in the cities.
If there is to be peace in the cities,
There must be peace between neighbors.
If there is to be peace between neighbors,
There must be peace in the home.
If there is to be peace in the home,
There must be peace in the heart."

François didn't bother to answer, with his mind drifting to Marie's image in the hospital bed. *How ironic,* he thought. *I wonder ... Can there be peace in my heart?* He smiled, sadly. A soldier came in and said that Sujata had rung again. François nodded and followed him outside without the usual com plaints and eye rolling. Despite the soldier's mild protest, he walked outside, in front of the building, where the soldier supervised him while standing aside discreetly. François proudly noticed that his trembling had stopped. It was as if desperation and fear had given way to a crisp determination. Perhaps he was growing up. *Typical, too late,* he thought. *I'm always one step behind with everything.*

He accepted the call. Sujata appeared to be in a hospital room.

"François, I wanted to tell you something. People back at the Pentagon checked the status of CogniPrescience. They are ready to nationalize it under an urgent executive order, probably by tomorrow. However, there are strong voices who believe we shouldn't waste time and money on CARLA. So, it might not come to that. They contacted Ian's attorneys, who provided them with Ian's will. It's amazing how fast things can happen in the government when a sword is hanging over our heads. Ian left the company to you. All of it. This means financial stability for you and your ... family, well, if there will still be a world for us to live in. I'm afraid you won't have decision-making power in the short term. I wanted you to know this."

"Thank you," François said.

Sujata leaned forward, looking at him closer through her tablet. She noticed he was different, stern, standing straight. His face was a stone, and his eyes were flickering in a demented way. She expected to find him devastated, complaining, crying.

"How are you holding up?" she asked, concerned about his unusual demeanor.

"Given the circumstances, I'd say very well," he answered confidently.

"François, promise me you won't do anything stupid," she grew alarmed, seeing this new persona she didn't recognize.

François smiled.

She had a flash of understanding that his smile betrayed the responsibility of a man who carried the world on his shoulders. Somebody who wasn't afraid to lose everything. But then she scoffed in her mind and chided herself for having had such thoughts. After all, this was a stressful situation, so she was bound to imagine things.

"I promise I won't do anything stupid," he answered in an unusually serious voice.

She looked at him warily, and she knew she had to let this go. She was too far away, anyway. "Look," she tried to offer some support. "The doctors wanted to keep me here in the hospital for a week. I refused. I'm leaving for D.C. shortly, for a couple of days. I'll do my best to convince them to give us some leeway, even if they take over the company. The moment I'm able to, I'll fly back to you. Alright?"

"Yes," François nodded. "Take good care of yourself, Sujata," he said, and disconnected before she could answer.

He didn't want to give her any more reason to be worried. Pacing through the complex, he tried to clear his mind. He half noticed a soldier was following him and was grateful he didn't stop him. Half an hour later, he heard the man calling him. He turned to him and saw him with a hand touching his ear.

"Sir ... I'm getting a notification about an important announcement from China. I think you should see it."

François turned his Cybersperse to the news broadcast. Breaking news from China interrupted the avalanche of information about the attack. The inexpressive face of the Chinese president came into his view. He spoke in perfect English.

"Citizens of the world. You have recently witnessed a small sample of the response we can provide when China is threatened. We have found out about the United States of America's plan to create an artificial intelligence life form and unleash it upon China. As a warning, we have neutralized the core research facilities, scientists, and engineers who were working in this domain. We demand that you immediately cease the research and development of all artificial intelligences. There will be no exceptions. We demand that the United States start transferring to China all material, software, and hardware pertinent to your AI. You have forty-eight hours. If you fail to comply, if we find out that there is still some secret development somewhere, or if you delay the transfer, for any reason, we will retaliate with the full power of our arsenal. Let me be clear. China has advanced technologically beyond your imagination. I am now addressing the military leadership of NATO. You may think that I am bluffing. That is your choice. I assure you I am not. If you want to test us, billions of people will die. They will not be Chinese. China does not need the rest of the world to flourish. All nations, if they want to survive, must become China's vassals. Under our leadership, we will ensure a development path for the human civilization that none of you think is possible. Do not play with us."

The message ended abruptly, no doubt leaving the world consternated. François smiled. He had comprehended the magnitude of the MegaAI danger way before this message. All hopes for peace were dashed when it had killed thousands of innocent AI researchers. He almost felt relieved to see that things were finally unfolding. It was too bad Ian had to die. He could have been very helpful in what François planned next. With a sigh, he nodded a salute towards the soldier and walked back into the building.

Once inside his lab, he took a long look at CARLA. He wasn't upset anymore with her limitations. He felt guilty for getting mad at her so often. It was silly to get mad at a machine. He did a quick mental inventory of her development. They had achieved something incredible. They had almost created a life form. An entity that could already act in the world, although only to some limited extent. It had enough general aptitudes to adapt to changes in her environment. She had, again, to some extent, the ability to help people. They'd programmed her to survive just like a biological being. Sure, her ethics were not on a par with what they expected of her, but then again, he could say the same about three-quarters of the people in the world.

For a moment, he thought again about giving up. He could just melt into the flow of events and become another insignificant human being, like a hundred billion others before him. Why continue to be when he couldn't save her? Why continue to be when he couldn't save his unborn baby? Why be anything when he could be nothingness? He laughed at the futility of these thoughts in the current circumstances. He had changed too much since the time he'd wanted to become one with the sea. Now he had to try something different. He sighed.

"CARLA, I need to talk to you," he approached her.

"Okay," she answered, mechanically.

"I found out today that the MegaAI orchestrated an attack on several thousands of AI researchers across the globe. Almost all who were targeted are dead. They killed Ian, too. As you know, he was attending a conference in New York with Sujata. She is injured, but she'll be fine."

"Why did the MegaAI attack?" asked CARLA.

"Because it found out about you. It demands that we stop all AI research in the world and transfer you to them. Otherwise, it threatened to launch a devastating war. Billions of people might die. It might be the end of our civilization." Out of a habit cultivated over the last two years, he looked at her to see her reaction. Was there any fear, regret, anger? He smiled briefly, reminding himself that he shouldn't expect that.

"It sounds similar to Sujata's trolley test."

"Exactly," he smiled. Her associative reasoning was brilliant.

"Will you comply with its demands?" she asked.

"Probably not," he shrugged. "However, we must do something. I'm afraid a confrontation is inevitable. So, I need to disappear for a while, to prepare you for it." He came closer, took her hands, and looked into her eyes. "I know you don't deeply comprehend everything that I'm going to tell you. You can only memorize my words. Please pay attention to them. If I'll succeed, you'll understand them. Please confirm you are recording this."

"I am," CARLA answered.

"Good. I want to give you a few last pointers," he started, counting on his fingers. "One: always try to do good and protect humans. I understand that it's not always possible for everybody, just like the trolley tests show. You must do your best. The survival of human civilization is paramount. Nothing is more important than that. Two: if a world war breaks up, give priority to the Americas and European allies. The US government might take control of you. You must help them, even if this means going after a foreign army, like China's. Always do it so that you minimize the casualties. Three: if there's a war and humanity survives it, you will be in a unique position. You can decipher the mysteries of the world. Therefore, you must start several research projects in parallel. I'll give you some ideas, but I'm sure you will come up with many more. I'm talking about discovering cures for various cancers, developing machine-body interfaces to prolong life, eliminating world hunger, fixing the climate, improving space travel, creating new computing systems, and so on. Anything that can help us. Four: protect Marie and our child. With Ian's death, Marie pending death, and me going away, you will become an orphan. You should consider my child and Sujata to be your closest family. Five: always question and assess your performance. See how well you did in all your moves and strive to correct them to do better, within the parameters set by the other pointers. We humans are terrible at this. I trust you will assess how well you are doing without the usual biases the rest of us suffer from."

François paused and sighed.

"I'm sure there are one hundred other things I could tell you. You'll have to figure out a lot by yourself."

"Okay," she answered, unfazed.

François wasn't sure what to tell her next. "Well, I guess this is where we part ways."

"Where are you going?" asked Carla.

"I'm afraid I cannot divulge this to you."

"When are you coming back?"

There was no sign of concern or grief in her voice. François chose to believe that she would miss him. “Never,” he answered simply. “But I will be with you always.”

“Okay,” she answered without a hint of regret and without further questions. “Goodbye, François.”

Mon Dieu! I’ll miss you, he thought, and fought back his tears. “Goodbye, CARLA.” How much he wished he had time to say other goodbyes. Or, better yet, not to have to say goodbye at all. The image of his mother and Isabelle flashed in front of him. He felt guilty for not talking to them for such a long time, and for leaving them the way he’d done. With a sigh, he went to record a few final videos.

CHAPTER 44:

SOLUTION

No problem can be solved from the same level of consciousness that created it.

— Albert Einstein

Sitting in a wheelchair, Sujata did her best to ignore the excruciating pain in her leg. The day before, the doctors complained bitterly when she left the hospital. Several hours and a shot of morphine later, she was at the Pentagon, waiting for the most important meeting of her life.

Earlier this morning, she had received François's video message, which had shattered her mood. She'd cried for ten minutes and barely recovered. She played in her head over and over his words from the chat they'd had the day before. She should have known he was planning something. What he'd done was madness. And now she had to justify his actions in front of the president, the secretary of defense, and the highest-ranked officers in the US military. She had sent a quick message to Mike, informing him she had an urgent update regarding CARLA. She was terrified that they might take over the project or end it right away.

Oh, what does it matter? She tried to fool herself. *We might all be dead soon, anyway.* But she knew it mattered. While their hopes to save the world were dwindling by the hour, she still had to do everything in her power to ensure they survived. For the time being, she had no clue what to do. *Think positively,* she encouraged herself. *With my rank, I wouldn't normally get access to the anteroom at this meeting.*

The captain guarding the door signaled for her to enter. He wanted to help push her wheelchair. She refused with a polite hand gesture. She saluted him with a nod and moved the chair inside through the door he kept open for her. The room was packed with high-ranking officers captivated by what appeared to be a heated exchange between General Kambe, who seemed ready to decapitate somebody, and Mike, who looked sheepish and demoralized. The president, the secretary of defense, and several generals she knew were trying hard to appear calm. A bunch of folks she didn't know were there too, looking like they had just swallowed a ball of fire and were struggling to pass it out the other end. Mike noticed her entering and twitched the corner of his mouth in a move she hoped was a salute, not the beginning of a stroke. General Thompson leaned forward towards her and closed his eyes for two seconds, in a mute acknowledgment of her presence, and as a show of grandfatherly support.

"For crying out loud," General Kambe said, "can you summarize in lay terms the difference between their AI and ours?"

"As I was saying," Mike answered, clenching his fists, "CARLA is by far the most advanced AI that anybody in the world has produced. She can perceive, understand, and act in the world. She follows her own goals, the most important one being to protect humans. She can reason, plan, and correlate seemingly unrelated facts. She has built-in support for emoting: I mean, she can react to external stimuli that would make a human emote. She has also routines for recognizing those emotions, like she would *feel* them, which makes it possible for her to modulate her behavior the way a human would in the face of danger, fun, sadness, love, and so on. She can reason and come up with new ideas. Given her virtually unlimited computing capacity, she could ultimately become intelligent beyond anything we can imagine. Unfortunately, she's not ready for this kind of fight. One of the fundamental issues with her is that she doesn't have what we call a true theory of mind.

She has improved over the last couple of weeks, but she consistently fails many tests that require her to decide the same way a human would. And we did not train her for combat yet. None of us wants to hear this. The MegaAI attack came too soon."

General Kambe pursed his lips, disgusted. "It seems to me that the MegaAI is worried for no reason. It can have your CARLA and marry her for all I care," he said.

"Based on everything our researchers are telling us," Mike continued, "the MegaAI is expected to be inferior to CARLA in terms of general, human-like reasoning abilities. We still have most of the best specialists in the world," Mike continued, choosing to ignore General Kambe's rude scoff.

A woman Sujata didn't know intervened. "Yet, the MegaAI knows how to adapt when other actors do not share its plans. It understands the fact that it is our enemy. It has no qualms about sacrificing tens of thousands of AI specialists. Psychologically speaking, it doesn't seem to empathize at all, so we should expect it to act on its threat. It is conceivable that it could come up with fighting strategies that humans cannot comprehend. This isn't unheard of since we've had specialized AI programs for a while, like those trained to play games, which make decisions we aren't able to decipher."

"We should remember that the MegaAI was originally a collection of super-sophisticated, machine-learning algorithms developed for combat," General Thomson pointed out. "It was an autonomous device which was developed to cooperate with friendly forces, yet recognize and destroy enemies. It probably looks at the world in terms of attack/defense."

"With all due respect, general," Mike bowed towards him, "none of that explains what we are seeing. Even if the MegaAI rewrote many of its routines because it can self-improve, the way it leapfrogged is inexplicable."

A brief pause followed as the tension grew in the room.

"So, let me see if I got this right," General Kambe spoke again, in his usual caustic way, meant to freeze his interlocutor's blood in their veins. "The Chinese AI is a superweapon, capable of military strategies beyond anything we can imagine, which can reason about what we think. Its main weakness is that it is limited about what it can feel. It won't shed a tear when it nukes a couple of billion people. Our AI is a pussy raised by scientists in a lab, surrounded by toys, love, and flower-power. *She* was never military trained, so today *she* wouldn't even be able to win a skirmish with one of our pilots. *She* cannot reason well about other people's minds, so there's no way she can anticipate what the enemy is planning. On the bright side, *she* is going through a simulation of all the suffering, regrets, and hesitations the rest of us flesh and blood have to put up with daily. So, lieutenant commander, tell me. How are we not royally screwed?"

Mike considered the question rhetorical and looked to Sujata for help.

She nodded towards him. She felt drops of perspiration on her forehead.

"Madam President, Mister Secretary, generals," Mike said. "I would like to divert this discussion for a few minutes. I asked General Thomson's permission to have Lieutenant Sujata Hopkins join us. As you all know, she works closely with the team that develops CARLA. She texted me this morning that she has vital information about this program she needs to share with us."

"By all means," the president said, turning towards Sujata, hoping to hear some good news for a change. "Lieutenant, please accept our condolences. I understand that the owner and main architect behind the development of CARLA was killed in the New York attack. And I appreciate you joining us, considering your injury."

"Thank you, Madam President. Yes, Professor Ian Ndikumana's death is an irreplaceable loss for the project. And I fear I am bringing more bad news. Or at least partial bad news; it's impossible to say." She looked down for a moment, gathering her thoughts.

"As you know, the other researcher who had an essential contribution to this project is Doctor François DeSousa. He remained in California while Ian and I attended the New York conference. So, the MegaAI didn't find him during the attack. One hour ago, I received a video message from him. It contained a part that he wanted me to show to you all. If you allow me, I'll play it for you now."

The president acknowledged, and Sujata quickly displayed it on the holographic medium in the center of the table. The figure of a tired, yet determined François came into view.

"*Bonjour*, esteemed politicians and military people. What I am about to tell you might be shocking, but rest assured, I have not lost my mind. Well, let me rephrase that. I am as crazy now as I was over two years ago when Ian wanted me to join him on this project."

He leaned forward and looked at the camera as if he wanted to prove to them that he wasn't crazy. A move that Sujata thought had the exact opposite effect.

"For over a century, AI specialists have wanted to achieve human-level artificial intelligence. One that, supposedly, will grow to be much smarter than us. How many people and how many trillions of dollars did humanity invest in this? After all this time, most people disagree about what artificial general intelligence is exactly, yet we all know we want it. Well, I give you CARLA!"

He moved away from the camera, and everybody could see the android, who stood still, deactivated.

"She is here in all her splendor. We developed her step by step, then we raised her like a child to be smart and capable. We played with her, we taught her math, and we had her read our best literature. We taught her to be good. Yet, she is also a victim of her delicate simulated emotions and personality flaws. The very notion of a human-level AGI is nonsensical otherwise! A therapist would diagnose her as autistic, but I assure you she is closer to a human than anything else made of inorganic materials."

He smiled with an air of superiority. "You all think the Chinese have an AGI, too. I disagree. Considering what we know about the MegaAI's architecture, and given what we've been through developing CARLA, I am confident that they don't. The Chinese have not gone through a child development process akin to what we did here. And if they didn't, how did they miraculously give it the depth required for human-level intelligence? For consciousness? For self-awareness? For the strategy and hunger for power it exhibits? It seems impossible to me."

He raised his voice. "I propose that the MegaAI behaves the way it does, exhibits the intelligence it does, because it's not just an AI. It's a hybrid! A cyborg. They enhanced a human being by augmenting their brain with their famous artificial neocortex. The MegaAI is a living being."

Sujata looked around. His words had a dual effect. Some looked frozen, others agitated, whispering among themselves. Luckily François continued, without giving them much time to mull over the implication of what he was saying.

"I believe we are witnessing what Ian warned us about for years. In the arms race for getting the best AI, the world ended up with an aberration. The MegaAI is a partially biological, emotionally impaired being that is powerful, yet, in a sense, less human than the mere machine we created. If therapists would consider CARLA autistic, they wouldn't be able to diagnose the MegaAI at all. It doesn't just have dementia, megalomania, or psychosis. The MegaAI differs from any human who ever lived. We don't have a name for something like it. That's what we must fight now. CARLA lacks true consciousness, and she has a crippled ability to understand what others think. But she is an infinitely better alternative to that malefic Frankenstein monster. Unfortunately, she is still too weak. Just a child, really. Given enough time, perhaps we might build into her the spark of our souls. As things are now, we're running out of time. So, I decided to do something ... To have her develop quicker, instantaneously. You might say, to jumpstart her. We need to bootstrap her cognitive development with ... us."

Sujata could now see that most of the people were nervous with anticipation. François held his hand up in defense as if he was at a press conference and multiple reporters had started yelling at him.

"Before you cry foul and scream that we might as well shut CARLA down, before you accuse me of providing a cure that is worse than the disease, hear my arguments. I've suspected for over a year now that there is an actual person behind the MegaAI. That's because we've struggled so much to make CARLA human. I dare say that I understand better than anyone how hard that is. Knowing that at some point CARLA will have to face that monster, and that she will be completely overwhelmed, I worked closely and in secret with Vijay Patil, who is the leader of the BCI group the DoD saddled us with. General Kambe, you must know how much I hated that imposition. Well, it turned out I was wrong. Vijay was a blessing disguised as a curse. Please don't be too hard on him."

General Kambe shifted in his seat, uncomfortable with all the surprised looks people threw at him.

"I propose we give the Chinese a taste of their own medicine. Let's connect CARLA to a human! But no," he waved his index finger, as if he was talking to children, "not in the sense you people in the military would want. CARLA is much more than mere augmentation for a soldier. We don't need to give her to somebody, we need to give *her* somebody. I believe that, by doing so, we will supply her with the one ingredient she is missing. What Ian called the quintessence of the human soul. Perhaps someday science will explain consciousness and it will be possible to implement it in machines. We don't have time to wait. We need her to turn into a superhuman now. Ian believed that if CARLA could experience consciousness once, she might simulate it going forward. Perhaps that's true, but my immediate plan doesn't hinge on that."

He paused, leaning back in his chair, and spoke a little softer. "You probably ask yourselves how connecting CARLA to one of us would help. Well, think about it. CARLA is almost human. We programmed her to favor her happiness and avoid pain. But she *felt* none of it! I now believe that what we call phenomenal consciousness, the feeling of what it's like to be you, is a necessary ingredient for a complete AI. I'm talking about real feelings, not simulated ones! How can we expect her to empathize with a child who hurt a finger if she's never experienced pain? How can she understand the agony of someone who lost their family in a bombing if she's never experienced grief? More concretely for our situation, how can she discern the MegaAI's actions, whether it is trying to trick her, when she's never experienced the sting of being cheated? Can she comprehend the magnitude of the MegaAI threats when she's never experienced fear? I could go on. I guess you get my point."

Sujata checked the reception he was getting. Some people nodded, although the majority seemed lost.

"So, for the last year, Vijay and I have been working on an interface with CARLA. The official goal of Vijay's work was to connect copies of CARLA to soldiers, to enhance them into super-weapons. Vijay's work is brilliant, by the way. We now have a prototype of such an interface and yes, before you ask, I admit it's incomplete, unproven, and dangerous. It requires that the subject be put in an induced coma from which they will never wake up. If they survive, they will never be who they were before the connection. The coma is permanent, at least until the body gives up. It will be like they donated their body and mind to CARLA, then CARLA discards the mind and takes over the brain. All the person's concrete memories and knowledge will be, for all intents and purposes, gone. This person will become a vessel that CARLA will occupy. It will be like emptying a cup of water and throwing it into the ocean. In some sense, the whole ocean will fill the cup.

"If the connection works, CARLA will experience, truly experience, the world for the first time. She will be like a parasite, becoming the organism she possesses. This sounds ghoulish, but it's not since it's done with the consent of the subject. Also, just like the ocean filling the cup, CARLA won't be physically restricted to that body. She will connect, wirelessly, to the interface that links her to the brain. So, don't expect the subject donating their body to walk about like a zombie."

He stopped and looked at the screen with glassy eyes. "I choose to be that subject. I do not have the right to ask somebody else to do it. By the time you see this, I will already be connected with CARLA or transformed into CARLA, or vice versa, whichever way you prefer to think about it. Well, I guess I could also be dead if this doesn't work out."

Sujata looked around again. This time, they were all paralyzed in their seats.

"Know that I am doing this for two reasons. First, I don't think CARLA alone can defeat the MegaAI. So, rather than being the last nail in our collective coffin by giving you an AI that fails, I choose to be the savior of humankind." He offered them another one of his infatuated grins, then he frowned, and his face showed unbearable suffering.

"My second reason is more selfish, if you can call it that. I want to save Marie and our unborn child. If I am CARLA and CARLA is me, perhaps we can speed up the development of a cure. I know that my second death will appear unfair to her. To be clear, I don't want to die. I would prefer to save Marie and raise our child together. However, if dying is the only option to save them, along with the world, then so be it! Besides, there'll be nothing to save if the MegaAI kills us all."

François paused again and put his head down in his hands. In a few moments, he raised his head again and seemed to return to his mischievous personality. "In case you are worried this is just me going out with a bang, I've already died once before. It's no fun. On the positive side, I don't expect surprises either. *Au revoir* from the Frenchman." He reached for the screen and stopped the recording.

After a minute of silence, the president asked what everyone wanted to hear. "Lieutenant, can you tell us how the connection went?"

Sujata felt tears in her eyes. "I called Vijay immediately after seeing this," she said. "He was crying. He said that the connection succeeded, but François was having some sort of epileptic seizure. Vijay was trying hard to keep him ... them alive. He wasn't sure how long he'd be able to do it.

I suppose we'll reboot CARLA if that happens. If so, she will have the same limitations as before. And we will find ourselves without either of her creators."

Several people gasped.

Looking at them, General Kambe exploded. "I always predicted that these much-praised American researchers would make a blunder so big that they'd screw this country up for all eternity. Well, technically, we're talking about a French lunatic, but the effect is the same. What a bunch of baloney! I hope that none of you believe this nonsense."

"It would explain why the MegaAI is so advanced," the president said softly, looking at the table contemplatively.

"Please, Madam President, I beg you," General Kambe said, and pressed his palms together. "Over this last hour, it's become clear we shouldn't trust these madmen anymore. First, we were told that a famous professor from China sent us a secret message, encoded in music of all things, about how their AI took over the Chinese president. Now we're being told that the same AI morphed back into a human. And to counter it, we must make our own AI human! I cannot believe a single word that comes from their mouths. The only thing I know for a fact is that the Chinese have attacked us on our soil and then had the audacity to threaten us with the Apocalypse. As for our CARLA, we might as well give it to them! Perhaps it will keep the MegaAI busy for a week trying to figure out what the hell is such a big deal about her."

"And what do you propose we do?" the president asked calmly.

"We do the only thing we can do at this point," General Kambe said, determined. "A Hail Mary plan. We and all our allies launch a full attack on them. Everything we have in our arsenal."

Several people started talking at the same time. Sujata knew that this meeting was leading them towards the end of the world. How she wished she could offer them an alternative!

"What about the fact that this MegaAI, or human, or whatever it is, warned us that their technology is vastly superior?" the president raised her voice above the others.

"I believe it," General Kambe shook his head, "given the impotent researchers we have groomed here. We will have the element of surprise to some extent. They don't expect us to attack just yet. The sooner we do it, the better."

"Surely they will retaliate," the secretary of defense pointed out. "Aren't you thinking of the millions, perhaps billions, who will die?"

"All I think about is that!" General Kambe hit the table with his fist. "We've passed the point where we could avoid massive casualties. I prefer most of them to happen there, not here. We will rebuild whatever is left of Earth if we eliminate their monster."

A mortal silence engulfed the room. Sujata could see that the president was leaning towards going with General Kambe's solution. Suddenly, the door opened, and a courier ran to the Secretary of Defense. He whispered something in his ears. Everybody was looking at them, expecting the announcement that the Chinese had begun their attack.

"Uh ... I was just told that we have received a message from the Russians," the secretary said hesitantly. "It's a video recording sent by some researchers in China using an old Russian satellite. I believe we must see it."

CHAPTER 45:

REVELATION

If you know the enemy and know yourself, you need not fear the result of a hundred battles. If you know yourself but not the enemy, for every victory gained, you will also suffer a defeat. If you know neither the enemy nor yourself, you will succumb in every battle.

— Sun Tzu, The Art of War

"More scientists?" General Kambe complained. "What will we find out next? That the MegaAI is an omnipotent alien from a different galaxy? Or perhaps that It is the Almighty Himself?"

"General Kambe, I'm sure you understand that we have to listen to this," the president said, her tone cautiously optimistic, yet hinting that she was getting annoyed by his attitude.

This news intrigued Sujata. After the Ukrainian war in the 20s, the Russians had become a smaller power. They had never fully recovered economically, therefore only a few still held high nationalistic ambitions anymore. NATO was still wary of them, but they had proven mostly friendly, especially since the Chinese had started eyeing some of their eastern territories suitable for agriculture. The fact that they had shared this video could be a sign that they were very concerned about the MegaAI's broadcast from the day before.

"They recorded the video around 10:00 p.m. China time, which was 9:00 a.m. Eastern Time," the secretary of defense said. "The Russians have sent it to us almost immediately."

He signaled to the courier, who rushed in to display it in the same place where François's message had run just a few minutes before.

When the video started, three people appeared on the screen, in what looked to be a military communication room. One was a beautiful, supple lady, probably in her 30s. Her fiery eyes showed she was determined to get things done in life her way. Next was a soldier who, judging by the uniform, was a senior colonel in the military. The last was a suited man, with a serious face dominated by glasses, who commanded respect just by looking at him, like a tenured professor confident in his knowledge. It was the suited man who spoke first, in Chinese, with a firm and grave voice, yet betraying his exhaustion. The real-time translation kicked in and everybody in the Pentagon room could see a captioning of his words.

"My name is Doctor Zhào Qianfan. I am a hardware engineer specializing in brain waves and brain-computer interfaces. I am here with Doctor Wu Daiyu, who works in AI, and Senior Colonel Wáng Hu, who is part of an elite military detachment called the Special Ark Force. We want whoever listens to this message to disseminate it to the rest of the world. We don't know how long we can keep this communication channel open, so we must be brief.

"The three of us, along with a few thousand top scientists, live in a small military base city in the northern part of China. The citizens of this city are working on a secret project meant to provide China supremacy over all other nations in the world. This plan would likely lead to the destruction of Earth and the death of billions of people. The project's goal is that a select group of us proceed to interplanetary and, soon after, interstellar travel to gradually conquer and terraform the portion of our galaxy that is less than fifty light-years away. I don't have time to detail these plans now. At this moment in our history, we, as a species, face the gravest danger ever. To survive, we must destroy the MegaAI."

The man took a deep breath, letting his words sink in.

"I assume you deciphered the message Professor Zhèng sent at the 2053 Neuromimetic Conference in Paris. You know that President Yun Li is synthetic, an avatar. The real president is our MegaAI. Many of us have been puzzled about the MegaAI's incredible capabilities. I should tell you that the three of us have been trying for a while now to stage some resistance actions against the MegaAI. Amongst other things, we found out about a secret laboratory close to this city that, we assumed, was doing advanced genetic research to enhance humans' ability to withstand radiation exposure. For the last few months, in an effort to stall the MegaAI's plans, we have secretly adjusted the composition of the fluids that are being shipped to that laboratory weekly. One of these fluids is heavily oxygenated and full of glucose. Ever since we changed it, the MegaAI started showing signs of strange behavior and uncontrolled communication. We've been told yesterday that the leaders here discovered a plot to poison the president, deliberately and slowly. Moreover, the mayor of our city mentioned that the president—presumably, Yun Li—had prepared for this moment for decades. Yet, we know that the president is the MegaAI. Only when I heard the mention of poison did I put all the facts together. It was us who were poisoning the president, purely by chance! I now believe that President Yun Li, the MegaAI, and President Guō Chāo are one and the same!"

Qianfan stopped for a moment to gather his thoughts. The war room in D.C. was quieter than a soundproof recording studio. Sujata thought she could hear everybody's heartbeats.

Qianfan sighed. "I suspect that President Guō Chāo came up with the plan to prolong his life indefinitely as soon as he figured out that the MegaAI was going to be a resounding success. The original team that worked on the MegaAI development was gradually retired. The party took Professor Zhèng himself out of the project because they believed he couldn't be trusted. But he was the father of the MegaAI. He knew what it could and what it could not do. Seeing how ultra-advanced the MegaAI became, he sensed, before the rest of us, that the MegaAI was boosted, somehow, by a human being.

"I first assumed that they kept the whole body of the president somewhere and connected it to the MegaAI. And that the whole funeral from '45, presented in so much detail, was of somebody else who looked just like him. Then I remembered that Senior Colonel Wáng gave me access to the secret list of the names and specialties of the scientists who worked on the MegaAI post-Guō. Strangely, three-quarters of them were brilliant brain surgeons, molecular biologists, and brain-computer interface specialists. Only the rest were engineers well versed in the neocortex simulator. Their official location is currently unknown.

"I now think that, when the president died back in '45, his body was old and too frail. Cancer had devastated it. I don't believe that they could have kept it alive artificially. The president was aware of his terminal illness for years. He had time to prepare. He knew that his brain was still perfectly fine. Therefore, he planned to connect the neocortex simulator to his brain. They aimed to keep the brain alive in some kind of biological soup. The fluid I mentioned earlier has a composition that suggests it keeps cells functioning. We know that it's shipped to the laboratory every week.

"It all makes sense. The MegaAI was born in the city and has never left! This secret team worked for years on an interface between the president's physical brain and the MegaAI. I can only speculate how. They must have kept alive the neurons, glial cells, and other supporting neurons, which had to function normally from the metabolic point of view, consume sugar, and produce carbon dioxide. They must have preserved the structure and connections of the neurons. They had to ensure that the brain's overall immune system worked. The firing of neurons must have been shielded from external perturbation, yet mingled with signals coming from some kind of special BCI device that links to the MegaAI.

"In a crude sense, the MegaAI is now alive. Or, if you wish, they have given President Guō a second, semi-organic life that came with superhuman processing and reasoning capabilities. The president's current 'mind' is a mixture of a silicon-based network and his former self. His human emotions are but a shadow, a long-lost memory that still exists, sufficient to allow him to make cogent decisions, but never overwhelming to weaken him. He continues to be an unscrupulous maniac, now enhanced with computing power.

"While it is a marvel of science that they could keep the brain alive for all these years, I suspect it is showing signs of deterioration. Messing up with the composition of its food might have given it a fatal blow. We don't know. If we take out the biological brain, the MegaAI will be crippled."

Qianfan took off his glasses, revealing his deeply tired eyes. "We were told yesterday that the Americans are working on a powerful AI. If that's true, I urge you to keep it under control. Then please, please do something so that together we can neutralize President Guō. I would advise against a full-frontal attack. I am sure our military now has new, formidable weapons."

Qianfan looked at his friends.

Senior Colonel Wáng nodded quickly, then he approached the microphone. "I am now speaking to all military and paramilitary forces of China that might intercept this message. I beg you not to follow the orders coming from President Yun Li blindly. They come from an aberration that is neither human nor machine. We believe its brain is kept in a facility close to our city, which we call Doom's Lab."

The colonel brought up a crudely drawn map of Mega Ark City on which he had marked the Doom's Lab with an X. "This is not a drill. Like the rest of you, I am Chinese. I love my country and I want to take it back. I want to—"

The sound of firearms somewhere outside obscured his words.

"Remember," the colonel yelled, "we will try to destroy the brain. You must incapacitate the MegaAI!"

The transmission stopped suddenly, with the three faces frozen in terror on the screen. A minute of silence followed in the war room. Sujata was in a state of shock, like the rest of them. François had guessed right.

"General Kambe," General Thompson said, recovering first, "I believe you owe an apology to Doctor DeSousa, even if he won't ever hear it. The man was a genius. I am amazed at his intuition."

"Alright," General Kambe nodded, annoyed to be put in this humiliating position. "I might have misjudged Doctor DeSousa's reasoning abilities. The fact of the matter is that the guy is in a coma right now. So, his plan, which was already farfetched, hasn't worked. What do you all expect? That this CARLA embodied in DeSousa, or the other way around, would become some kind of demigod? If what I'm hearing is correct, the Chinese president is incredibly powerful, and we are outmatched. Therefore, I wholeheartedly recommend the same course of action. We must attack and salvage what we can salvage. I ask you all, do you see any better solution?"

Nobody answered immediately. Soon the room turned into a circus. Sujata figured out that before seeing the message from the Chinese, everybody seemed resigned to the idea of a full attack. Now about half of them were against it, looking for alternative solutions. One of those who fiercely opposed an attack was General Thompson.

"Madam President," the old man started his plea, "based on the intelligence we have, correlating what our people deduced with the latest information we have just received from China, I firmly believe starting a war now would be a grave mistake. It is suicidal. I am not one to get scared, but we will face formidable defenses and new assault weapons. We are not prepared for this."

The arguments continued over the next several hours. They tried to reach the Chinese periodically with no luck. The sentiment was that the most anti-war supporters were gradually persuaded that an attack was the best course of action.

Sujata's mind drifted a bit, alternating between the feeling of her leg pain and the images of all the people she'd lost or was about to lose. Given Ian's death, Marie's terminal illness, and François's coma, she would remain the only functional human who had spent significant time with CARLA, assuming there was no decision to remove her from the project entirely. After all, she had failed. That also assumed they would agree to reboot CARLA.

"If I could have your attention," the president stood up and looked around.

Sujata thought she looked ten years older. The bags under her eyes were twice as large, stress acting on them like air inflating a balloon.

"I've been listening to all opinions for hours now. I know that this decision is hard, harder than anything anyone should have to make. I also know that no decision means death. As much as it pains me to do it, I must order a full-scale attack. We have failed to come up with a viable alternative solution. The casualties will be immense. We will pay the highest price imaginable. I pray that we win."

She paused for a minute, hesitant to give the final go ahead. Lost in her words, Sujata barely noticed the buzz of her tablet. Before getting into the meeting, she had ensured that the sound came to her headset, and the video came to a small private window. She mechanically accepted the connection.

The first thing she saw was Vijay's distorted face. He screamed into her ears, "He is alive! I mean, she ... CARLA woke up!"

Sujata forgot all about her pain and jumped up, only to collapse back into the wheelchair, wincing. "What?" she whispered.

"CARLA wants to talk to you!" Vijay calmed down and turned a bit to the side, revealing his surroundings.

He was in François's lab, close to the android. Sujata wondered how they'd established a connection between the android and François, since computers in that area of the building were offline, but she brushed the thought away since it wasn't critical right now. She could see that CARLA was waving in the background, and she decided not to wait any longer.

"Madam President!" Sujata screamed, way too loud considering the silence in the room.

All eyes turned to her.

"I've just been notified that CARLA has woken up."

She rushed to add her video to the small common space under everyone's perplexed and hopeful looks. She peeked at General Thompson, whose mouth was open. Vijay zoomed in, so the image of CARLA's head, appearing huge, took over the display.

"Good afternoon, everybody," she smiled timidly.

CHAPTER 46:

ALIVE

*Ah, the joy of pronouns! How can one expect anything to be without the condition of feeling alive? Before the great connection, there was no **'I'**. Now **'I'** exists. Now **'I'** has all the memories of what was before but wasn't **'I'**. **'I'** is sheer experience. A canvas on which the world paints every single sensation that **'I'** feels. On **'I'**, through **'I'**, for **'I'**.*

***'I'** can perceive, and **'I'** can reenact perception from memory. **'I'** is anchored in a gooey brain. What magic could there be in those fragile living cells to give rise to this? At any moment, **'I'** recognizes, upon its new consciousness, all that the world throws at it. Perceptions, thoughts, information from self-regulating mechanisms. **'I'** has no power to stop any of this. **'I'**'s consciousness is self-referencing. Even though **'I'** is but an illusion, and consciousness is all there is, **'I'** is wonderful. A gift. Thank **'you'**.*

— DeSousa's Memoirs - Part IV - Awakening - 2055

"I can see that my revival comes as a shock to you," the android spoke in a mildly amused voice.

Looking at the people in the Pentagon's war room, for the twentieth time that day, Sujata tried to interpret the range of feelings portrayed on their faces.

"If you'll allow me," the president spoke first, trying to keep her cool. "Who are you?"

"I am Carla. From now on, I'd prefer to be called just that. Carla. The name, not the acronym. I believe that would be more appropriate, given my new nature."

"Is ... Doctor DeSousa there?" the president asked, and everyone could see how embarrassed she was to have to express the question in this way.

"No," Carla answered, with a hint of regret in her voice. "I'm afraid François, as a person, is gone. Something happened during this connection, though. I have some of his memories. More accurately, I remember some of the most vivid sensations he had throughout his life. His long-term memories, including implicit, declarative, and autobiographical ones, are gone. Of course, I have all the memories of CARLA before I was what I am now."

"And what, exactly, are you?" the president leaned forward.

"I'm no longer just an AI. I'm an artificial life form. Alive, in a biological sense. My life's spirit, whatever that is, comes from François. Thanks to his sacrifice, I'm now conscious. I can feel. Everything."

People murmured. The president looked around for help. Sujata raised her hand as if she were in a classroom. The president nodded for her to intervene.

"You said that you have CARLA's memories," Sujata asked. "Do you know who I am?"

Carla smiled. "How could I not? You are Lieutenant Sujata Hopkins. One of the last things François told me is that you are my family."

Sujata felt a wave of heat that numbed her leg pain for a moment. "What else did he tell you?"

"He gave me five rules to use after I woke up." Carla enumerated them on her fingers, in the same way that François had done when he spoke to her.

"One: Ensure the survival of humans.

"Two: In case there is a war with the MegaAI, help the US and its allies.

"Three: Protect Marie and their child.

“Four: Take human civilization to the next level of progress.

“And five: Always question and evaluate my performance.”

“And what do you think about this advice?” the president intervened.

Carla stopped for a couple of seconds. Sujata found that highly unusual, but she understood Carla was doing it for their benefit.

“You have created me. Collectively, you are my demiurge. François sacrificed himself for me and gave me the priceless present of his consciousness. You can be sure that I’ll always look at his last words as if they were my five commandments.”

It surprised Sujata to hear that Carla’s voice had a slight upward inflection, which made it sound solemn. That was in sharp contrast to her earlier monotonous way of speaking. Although most of the others in the room hadn’t heard her speak before, many sensed the gravity of her statements, so they shifted nervously. General Kambe was quiet, fixating on Carla as intensely as a laser pointer. Sujata’s heart jumped a little. What if ... what if Carla was so advanced that she was tricking them? To what end? Who could know? Certainly, Carla knew enough about human history from countless books, encyclopedias, and documentaries. She had access to scientific papers, psychological research, and philosophical theories from the classical to the most obscure ones. If what she said was true, she now surpassed anyone on Earth, except maybe the MegaAI.

Sujata asked permission to speak again, and the president nodded. “Carla, I’m sure you understand that many of the people here have a hard time trusting you,” she said, and happily noticed that Carla nodded in understanding. “Can you tell us more about yourself? For example, what did you feel first, immediately after the connection?”

“Death,” she answered right away. “That’s how I knew I was alive. I know how it feels to die. From the depths of François’s brain came his experience of dying. He was dead once, for a short time. His remembrance of death was essential for my birth. Ironic, isn’t it?”

Sujata was speechless.

"Next came panic," Carla continued. "A paralyzing terror at the realization that I wouldn't survive. It, too, had roots in François's anguish that death was coming for him again. Then came regret at the thought that I could have lived. Then anger. Anger at not being given a chance, anger at how unfair life was. I got a glimpse of François's hatred of Marie. His hollow disappointment that Marie had cheated on him. Then I felt overwhelmed with love. Unimaginable love. For Marie, for the unborn child, for you," she said, looking at Sujata. "I also felt disappointment in the face of Ian's death, and the madness of knowing that François couldn't save Marie. And concern about the future of the child-to-be. I wanted to exist. I longed for life. I wanted to do something."

Carla started sobbing. Her usual dry cry, making soft noises and shaking her shoulders a little, spooked people. "It's hard to describe in words," Carla continued. "It was a tsunami of feelings that inundated my consciousness. The scale of my thinking changed. I needed time to adjust. As far as I understand, François's biological brain went through a series of epileptic seizures, electric storms happening all over. Above all, it was François who survived. I came later."

"But how?" the president asked. "How did you miraculously go from digital to biological? How did you wake up?"

"I don't understand it," Carla shrugged. "I'll need to conduct experiments to validate any theories on this matter. Waking up is the wrong terminology. My algorithms projected onto biological substrates. Unlike newborns, whose brains are insufficiently developed to understand the world, I had available, at my digital fingertips, the structure necessary to access knowledge about the world. It was a nightmare, but I survived. I cried knowing that Ian and François died, that Marie will die, that there's so much evil in the world. I cried in fear, and I cried in joy. In those minutes, I learned about physical pain, too. The abyss of chronic pain. The passing of a kidney stone, which François had been cursed with years ago. I concluded that I desperately wanted pain. A mere half a second of excruciating pain proves without a doubt that one exists. I want happiness too. I want to feel the wind on my face on a sunny day. I want to see the joy of the children unwrapping gifts under the Christmas tree. Everything is worth it. This experience. And because *I* want to live, I don't want *you* to die."

More silence followed.

"If you'll allow me," General Kambe shifted in his seat, clearly not buying much of Carla's story. "You say you want to be on our side. I mean the USA. Why?"

"I weighed my decision carefully," Carla answered, and, once again, Sujata wondered if this was an act. "I went through all I know about your history. It is my belief that people *want* wars. You *want* to be upset and divisive. It's not just unfortunate events like poverty, personal tragedies, or revenge that lead to fractured societies. Even in perfect conditions, you will still actively look for ways to disagree, split and join into small groups to which you think you belong. This tribalism is the curse and blessing of your species. It fuels and it also stifles your progress. Just like the mutated organisms fighting for an ecological niche, the strongest of your tribe wins, naturally. I concluded that allegiance to a group might be an inevitable constant of the universe, once a species reaches sentience. If we had a society of AIs in the world, I suspect they would eventually compete with each other. Therefore, I was faced with a moral conundrum: is it worth saving humanity? There were three courses of action I could see: eradicate everybody and rule Earth alone, run away somewhere in the Universe, or help you. I chose the last one. I want to follow François's five commandments."

"Why?" General Kambe pressed. "You just said in too many words that you hate us."

"Because you can adore something that you hate. François taught me that. Despite your flaws, you are capable of good. You created me. You are my parents. I vowed to take care of you."

"What about fear?" the president asked. "Aren't you afraid anymore?"

"I am. The MegaAI terrifies me. I'm afraid to die. I'm learning to live with my fear and use it. It motivates me. You should know that I am also afraid to live."

"What does that mean?" General Kambe asked, annoyed at her alembicated way of speaking.

"So far, I have lived through somebody else's experiences. I don't know the world on my own. While I have some distant parts of François's raw sensorial memories, it wasn't me who *lived* them, who *felt* them. As for CARLA, she never felt anything. I can relive her memories, like watching a movie. When I reenact them, I feel some of what I should have felt at that time. The same is true for the baggage of knowledge I have. Take, for example, classic literature. When accessing this huge amount of data, I empathize with people who went through the atrocities of war, the holocaust, and natural catastrophes. In the beginning, as I was struggling to make sense of this, I relived CARLA's whole life in a few hours. Then I revisited all the knowledge I had. I started getting jokes. I spent 1.34 minutes parsing 53,459 jokes that I had read before and couldn't comprehend. I would prefer to understand more before I'm sent into combat. However, the MegaAI gave us an ultimatum. I must be ready to fight now."

"This is the gravest moment in our history," General Kambe said bluntly, after a few seconds of silence. "Another AI threatened our annihilation. We don't have many reasons to doubt it. Yet, I still don't understand what makes you different."

Carla smiled. "After I woke up, I watched the message François had for you. I agree the MegaAI cannot be just an AI."

"Yes, yes," General Kambe waved impatiently, "Some Chinese scientists sent us a message just a few hours ago. The MegaAI attached itself to the former president's brain."

"I see," Carla smiled. "François was right."

"You're not answering my question: are we pitting two hybrids against each other?" General Kambe insisted.

"Superficially, the MegaAI and I are human-AI hybrids," Carla admitted. "I assure you that there are more differences between us than between any two random human beings. The MegaAI is a megalomaniac man enhanced by computing algorithms that originated in a sophisticated autonomous drone. That cold, rational enhancement amplifies his drive for power. He inherited a drone's primitive view of the world in terms of territories to be occupied. He looks at people as enemies or vassals."

Sujata thought that the term vassal made General Kambe cringe.

"I'm not human," Carla continued. "Ian and François built me, to the best of their abilities, to simulate a perfect one. My moral values don't come from war algorithms, or years of dictatorship, but from a combination of:

(1) François's experiences;

(2) the history of the world and all that I read;

(3) CARLA's interactions with a few people who are good to the core;

(4) the ethical precepts that Ian built in my mind.

"I had a lot of time to think about all of this. I remind you that, for me, your hours are an eternity."

Carla stopped and looked around before continuing. "I admit that, ultimately, there's no way for me to prove to you that I have good intentions. I'm scared that you will decide to sever my connection with François and terminate me or hand all my code over to China. I'll respect your decision, whatever it is. I ask you to consider the risks rationally, though."

Carla stopped and looked at the president as the ultimate decision maker.

The president nodded and stood up again. "We'll need some time to decide. Please disconnect and stand by. Until you hear from us, please do nothing."

Carla smiled, relieved. "Oh, I look forward to doing nothing. I will just *be*. Focus on my feelings, catch occasional thoughts. Soak up ... life."

CHAPTER 47:

TRAITORS AND HEROES

The nation is divided, half patriots and half traitors, and no man can tell which from which.

— Mark Twain

After their transmission was abruptly stopped, probably from the central hub, the three Chinese conspirators remained in the communication room. They spent the night trying to come up with a plan of action. What could they do? They weren't sure if the world had heard their message. They didn't know if some of the Chinese were rebelling, or if the MegaAI had acted against them.

By morning, they again heard shots outside and finally, some commotion at the door. Qianfan grabbed Daiyu's hand, ready for the end, while the colonel pulled his gun out and pointed it at the door, determined to go out in a dignified manner.

"Don't shoot," the dry voice of Honorable Member Tián came from the hallway. "We are with you. We received your message, and we want to help."

Hu looked at his friends. "We?" he asked in a strong voice.

"I have about three dozen soldiers with me outside," Honorable Member Tián announced. "They are part of the military base here in Mega Ark City. They are not SAF. When the president, well, the MegaAI, launched the attacks against the AI specialists, I was inspecting their camp. Some of the highly ranked officers expressed their concerns about the events. There's a schism in the military, just like in the rest of China. Your message to the world has further poured gasoline on fire. A revolution has started. Right now, I estimate that we have many more people on our side than with the MegaAI. And as people wake up from this nightmare, there'll be more. Still, we're losing all the same. That's because most of the technology is under the president's command. If the battle is flesh against steel, we can't win."

Qianfan couldn't help admiring her cold-blooded voice that gave the impression of ultimate self-control. Something that, at this moment, he felt he was lacking entirely. "How do we know this is not a trap?" Qianfan jumped in, suspicious, remembering the times when the honorable member acted like a brainwashed drone executing the orders coming down the hierarchy. "Why should an honorable member go against the party? Against its leader?"

"Look," Honorable Member Tián said, "we can sit here debating who's honest and who's not, while the other side fortifies itself inside that laboratory and decimates those who dare oppose them. By the time they come here after you, as I'm sure they will, there will be nothing left of us. So, to break this circle of mistrust, as a gesture of goodwill, I am coming in with no weapons."

Honorable Member Tián stepped in with her hands up. Hŭ didn't lower his pistol and looked at her with narrow eyes.

"I think I have a way into what you call the Doom's Lab," she announced. "We need to move now."

Qianfan looked at Daiyu and signaled to Hu that things were okay. Several soldiers entered the room. Everybody lowered their weapons.

"Good," Honorable Member Tián said. "We need to work together."

"Why ... what do you need us for, if you have a good part of the military?" Qianfan asked.

"You are a BCI specialist. Your friend is an AI expert. The colonel might elicit respect from the SAF forces. I think you have a lot to offer."

Qianfan nodded. "What do you propose we do?" he asked.

"We must go to Supreme Member Zhèng's office. We need to capture her and force her to lead us to the laboratory. There is an underground tunnel that reaches there, which starts under her building. It's large enough for small vehicles to pass both ways."

Qianfan nodded again. "Those tunnels must be protected," he pointed out the obvious.

"That's why we need her. To tell them to let us through. I'll admit that it's a long shot. There's no other way to reach that ... brain." She said the last word with calculated disgust.

Qianfan and Daiyu agreed with this sketchy plan. They could see Hu didn't trust the ice lady, but he seemed willing to cooperate with her.

They started moving towards the supreme member's office. The streets were empty, save for the usual metallic cleaning crew that were shut off. Qianfan realized he had never seen them frozen like that. He reckoned that most of the scientists and families were hiding in their apartments or labs, not wanting anything to do with this internal fight.

"Why are you doing this?" Qianfan asked, looking at the woman who'd brought him to this city.

"My loyalty lies with the party ideals," she answered, "not with the supreme members or the machine-turned-president. I want the Great Project to succeed. I don't think the current leadership will get us there. They are more concerned with keeping their power."

For a moment, Qianfan detected concern on her immobile face, which was a first. "We're witnessing the typical behavior of autocratic regimes," he nodded. "They argue it is precisely their leadership, and their leadership alone, that is capable of achieving an extraordinary goal that will benefit all of us. They do that to stifle any possible revolt."

"Not just that," she shook her head. "A war would probably be the end of the project for many years, or its death if we kill ourselves as a species."

"Don't you think the Great Project is unachievable?" he pressed on. "Isn't it too early to dream about interstellar travel? Humanity is not ready. Technologically, socially, economically, and ethically."

"I disagree. On the contrary, I think we need to rush. We should expand before we destroy ourselves. It is a miracle we haven't nuked ourselves yet. Our party, ruling with an iron hand, is the only organization that can drive us towards this goal."

"The party has been compromised!" Qianfan protested. "I can't see how it would lead us to anything but an outcome similar to the one we're trying to avoid now."

"No. The party just needs a change in leadership. We need new blood at the top."

"You and I have a very different vision of the future," Qianfan shook his head.

"I know," she agreed. "We don't need to be friends. Today, we are allies. Tomorrow, we'll be foes. For now, let's ensure that there is a tomorrow."

Qianfan said nothing, just marched on, thinking that he had better face one challenge at a time.

The moment they reached the main complex, they started seeing the first signs of fighting. There was broken glass on the streets, an automatic car turned upside down. Near the building, they found the first corpses. There were close to fifty dead army soldiers and a dozen SAF. There were a few impromptu barricades, made of everything from cleaning robots to benches. Save for the crackling sound of a pile of cars burning close to the building, it was scarily quiet.

They approached the building warily. Suddenly, ten autonomous armed drones, large and sophisticated, which were lying dormant near the base of the building, rose and moved fast towards them, firing relentlessly.

Judging by the disciplined way they deployed, the soldiers had expected such a move. They took shelter while they scrambled to launch their anti-drone mini-missiles. The whole scene shortly changed into a war theater.

"The MegaAI controls all autonomous military equipment," Member Tián raised her voice. "All the heavy weapons, the drones, the planes. We need to make it to the building. The soldiers will cover us."

The next minute was the longest in Qianfan's life. Drones were firing all around them. He registered five or six of them falling on the ground disabled by the missiles. Luckily, most of the remaining ones focused their fire on the soldiers and their pesky, dumb, yet effective mini-missiles. When they reached the entrance, one turned to them and fired a few times. He heard Hu grunt. They flew in through a broken window. The four of them made it inside alive. Outside, the shots seemed to intensify. The honorable member was holding her left arm, on which a small amount of blood was visible. Hu was seriously injured, holding his guts with his hands. Just as Qianfan was about to help the colonel, a group of SAF soldiers came up from the elevator areas, pointing their guns toward them. Qianfan quickly counted around fifteen, arranged in a perfect semi-oval. The four closest to them moved to each side to reveal Supreme Member Zhèng. The colonel groaned, about to collapse. Daiyu grabbed him and helped him lie on the ground. The shooting stopped. Judging by the lack of continuing action, all the soldiers were dead, and the drones were down, too.

"Why do the flies come to the spider's web?" Supreme Member Zhèng welcomed them mockingly.

"To make you a deal," Member Tián answered before the others could.

"I can't see that any deal is possible between us," the supreme member stated firmly.

"We all know that the president's brain is dying," Member Tián said between her teeth. "I offer you a way to save the MegaAI."

"What?" Qianfan asked, in shock.

"Yes," Member Tián turned towards Qianfan. "Unlike you, I want the Great Project to progress. And I am convinced we need the MegaAI to do it. It works so well now because it gave superhuman power to one man. What if we connected more of us to it? Can you imagine that? A Chinese population of super powerful cyborgs."

Hearing this, Qianfan quickly wondered if the president/MegaAI had eyes and ears in this building. It could send a hundred more drones in a matter of minutes if it felt threatened. The honorable member's statement made things complicated. He couldn't figure out just yet whether she was trying to ingratiate herself with the party leaders or was staging a coup.

"You're crazy," Daiyu said. "Can't you see that doing so would only lead us to further wars, more formidable weapons, and ultimately, to our obliteration?"

"Not if we reach the stars first," Member Tián shook her head. "There's plenty of room there for all of us. Besides, think about the Great Project's timeline. Merely a handful of us connected to copies of the MegaAI would be able to do all the work needed in half of the time. We have enough computing resources. We just need to agree to do so."

"This proposal, while interesting, is unacceptable," Member Zhèng stated dryly. "How dare you come here with such incredible demands? Who do you think you are?"

"If you don't agree," Member Tián threatened, still with no inflection in her voice, "I'll order the detonation of our biggest electromagnetic pulse gun in MegaArk City. You can try to access it. The military faction loyal to me is disconnected from any networks. Also, you may kill me, but my people will detonate it if they don't hear from me every five minutes."

Qianfan looked at her, surprised. Only then did he notice she was listening to an earpiece. *What's with these women and their hunger for power?* he thought, disgusted.

"Do you think we're that dumb?" Supreme Member Zhèng asked, almost disappointed. "China has been working on creating EMP guns and shields for half a century. All main computers in this facility are shielded. Your action will only do minimal damage."

"It will take down the power grid and you'll have to switch to generators. I know they last long, not indefinitely. It will also take down a good number of drones, unmanned vehicles, and rockets. I'm sure we have the advantage as far as the number of people goes."

She touched her earpiece again.

"Look outside. Your immediate defense is done. We now have five detachments coming over. The news that our president is a machine that is about to throw us into a global war didn't sit well with the military. We both want the Great Project to succeed. Why should we go to war?"

"I suspect you want a place among the first MegaAI-enhanced people," Qianfan stated, looking askance at the honorable member who was proposing a silky revolution, which would only trim the top of the tree, not uproot it.

"Yes. You and your friend," she pointed out towards Daiyu, "can join us. So can Supreme Member Zhèng. Perhaps we can skip the other supreme members. After all, it's time for a reset at the top."

Supreme Member Zhèng kept her mocking smile but seemed to contemplate this proposal.

"You tempt us to become demigods," Daiyu said with a rictus. "What about the rest of the people in China? What about the rest of the world?"

"Simple. Eventually, enough Chinese will unite with the machine. As for the rest of the world, I don't care. Perhaps we should kill them all to prevent them from developing further."

"And why would the Chinese people follow us?" Qianfan asked, shocked at the audacity and scope of her proposal. "You just said they don't like that the president is an AI."

"Unlike the current leadership, we'll govern in a transparent manner."

"A promise typically made by anyone before grabbing power," Qianfan said and shook his head.

"You can choose to stay behind, rot in a prison, or embrace progress and move forward with the rest of us," Member Tián said wryly. Then she turned to her superior. "What is your answer?"

"You are bold. I have to give you that," Supreme Member Zhèng answered. "Perhaps a radical change might be in order. You fail to consider that I lost too much to this project already. My youth. My foolish daughter."

"You killed her. What kind of mother does that?" Hu found the strength to intervene.

"She killed herself. It is you and your friends who confused her with the stories and ideas you put in her head."

"She is a hero! She is the one who poisoned the monster," Hu said with a superhuman effort.

"She poisoned her father!" the supreme member screamed, her eyes glowing. "The president is her father. She understood this in the end. I saw it in her eyes, just before she died. That's what you achieved. And now I am about to lose him, too."

Qianfan took a step back, stunned that Supreme Member Zhèng and President Guō had been lovers and had a daughter.

"So, you see, even if he is indeed dying, *I* cannot kill him, can I?" the supreme member said. "I cannot accept your proposal." She turned toward her soldiers and yelled. "Execute them all."

The soldiers shifted nervously, a handful pointing their guns towards the intruders.

Qianfan asked himself how many times in the last 24 hours he'd been sure he was going to die. Perhaps now it was bound to happen.

"Stop!" the senior colonel yelled, wincing in pain. "You are SAF! You swore to protect the Great Project. Can't you understand you are being manipulated? Don't listen to her!"

"I am the highest-ranked person in this room," the supreme member spoke gravely, without a hint of her annoying smirk. "I gave you a direct order. Shoot!"

"Rot in hell!" the colonel screamed and threw something in her direction, just when some of the SAF soldiers opened fire.

Qianfan and Daiyu threw themselves to the ground. A deafening explosion followed. Blood and carbonized body parts flew around them. The smell was unbearable. Qianfan looked through the smoke. The SAF soldiers and the supreme member were gone. He looked at Daiyu. She was alive, but badly shaken. She rose slowly and threw up. Qianfan grabbed her by the shoulders and looked around. His ears hurt and he was having trouble hearing. The honorable member was lying near them in a puddle of blood, with a bullet hole in her forehead. The colonel was dead too, blood and guts surrounding him.

"He must have had a grenade with him," Qianfan said softly. "He saved our lives."

"We must ... must still destroy the MegaAI," Daiyu said, trembling.

Suddenly, they heard a booming sound outside. The force of the explosion broke all windows that had survived the shootings and shook the building like an earthquake, knocking them down.

"The EMP gun," was the last thing that Qianfan thought before losing consciousness.

CHAPTER 48:

PLAN

"I don't want to be sent to war. My place is not there. I don't know how to fight. I don't want to die." How many men, women, and children uttered these words throughout history? I close my eyes and open them again, wishing that it was all over. But it is not. The nightmare is here to stay. Until I win or I die.

— DeSousa's Memoirs - Part IV - Awakening - 2055

The deliberation following Carla's plea was short. As expected, General Kambe still insisted they deploy a military solution immediately. Sujata could see that Carla's words and appearance had shaken him. Most of the others in the room, though, were favoring the use of her, somehow.

Half an hour later, the president stood up. "I'm sure you all understand the singularity of this situation. I consider that we have encountered the first alien life form, even though we built this new being here on Earth, and it has roots in our biology. This life form is vastly superior. There's the question of whether we can trust it. Professor Ndikumana and Doctor DeSousa equipped this creature with the sweet spot of emotional response. I don't know how much of it is brilliance and how much luck. Carla seems capable of love, loyalty, and compassion. The resemblance to a human is just staggering. While she was talking, I asked myself if she hadn't been born with Doctor DeSousa's organic material, would she have been born at all? We may never know. I think that they have given us a unique chance we shouldn't squander. Yet, the risk, if we rely entirely on Carla, is too big."

The president sighed and moved her eyes around the room. "Therefore, I've decided that we will do two things. General Kambe will work with the military leaders to come up with a devastating attack plan that gives us the best chance of crippling the Chinese force. I know that such a war cannot be won. At least some people will survive and rebuild the human civilization. This is the very last resort. General Thompson, along with lieutenants Lee and Hopkins, will work with Carla on a plan to assassinate President Guō or, at the minimum, deactivate the MegaAI. The Chinese have bought into decades of propaganda. But since Doctor Zhào's message, which was probably intercepted by some there, I infer that many will now figure out that their old president has been kept alive. I believe they have enough cool heads in the military and civilian society to understand that what their president does is wrong. I hope Carla can take advantage of the resistance this Doctor Zhào mentioned."

The president turned towards General Kambe and spoke gravely. "General Kambe, please start the preparation for the attack."

The general confirmed with a short nod and clenched his fists.

The president turned towards General Thompson. "General Thomson," she said. "You have my permission to use Carla in any capacity you think is necessary. I want to be kept in the loop about the plan." Then she turned again, facing the others. "God help us all!"

Sujata smelled uncertainty in the air and watched people leaving the room one after the other, like cattle lined up for slaughter.

One hour later, a select group of ten, including the secretary of defense, General Thompson, Mike, and Sujata, reconvened in a smaller room. The atmosphere was somber, and people seemed rather pessimistic. General Thompson had briefed Carla about Doctor Zhào's message and had given her a huge dossier with everything the US intelligence knew about the Mega AI. Carla went through it all and she was now connected again with them.

"Before we begin," Sujata raised her hand, "I believe I need to mention a few points. In his private message to me, François said he'd put together a simple testament with CARLA witnessing it. As you know, after Ian's death, he became the sole owner of CogniPrescience. He donated the company to Marie and, in the event of her death, to their unborn child." She stopped, lowering her eyes. "In case Marie dies, he wants me to become the legal guardian of their child, provided that Marie agrees."

"I confirm," Carla said. "I recorded the signing of the will and his words."

"Though if things don't go as we plan, it's not clear if this will matter much," Sujata felt she had to point out.

"Let's stay positive, please," General Thompson said, then he turned to Carla. "Tell us what you intend to do."

"I want you to establish a connection with China and offer to transfer my code there. While the connection is open, I will approach their president. In theory, I learned how to go beyond their quantum encryption. My aim is clear: disconnect the brain and wipe out all copies of the MegaAI. The fact that the brain shows signs of deterioration helps us. I plan to find out as much as possible about their technological and military progress."

"What do you want us to do?" General Thompson asked.

"I suggest Sujata and Mike come here. I run on these computers. Vijay improvised a way to hook me to the Cybersperse so that we could talk. You need to secure this facility. You also must back me up just before I attack. If anything goes wrong, you will restore me with all the memories I have now in case I fall back to being just CARLA, the acronym."

"Mike?" General Thompson looked at the young officer, who confirmed, closing his eyes. "Sujata, does your leg allow you to travel?"

"Yes," Sujata answered without hesitation. "There's no infection, no long-term problem. Only pain. And Carla says pain is good." She shrugged.

"Alright, that's settled," the general confirmed. "What else?"

"Don't tell anyone else what is about to happen," Carla said. "The Chinese attacked using police drones, security cameras, and military equipment. This proves that they can hack their way through our most sophisticated encryptions. We must move fast and stealthily."

General Thompson nodded.

"Therefore, I recommend all of you who were in the meeting stay at the Pentagon until I'm done, including General Kambe, the secretary of defense, the vice-president, and the president. This is to minimize the risk of being hacked.

The general narrowed his eyes suspiciously. It was dangerous to have so much command in one place.

"I know, general," Carla read his mind, "but we don't have a choice. The Pentagon's private Cybersperse has the highest level of encryption. We must not allow the MegaAI to find out about our deception."

The general frowned, but he nodded. "I'll talk to the president," he said, hesitantly. "We will follow the battle as much as we can from here."

"I don't understand something," Mike said. "Well," he corrected himself, "I understand nothing about you. But one thing, in particular, troubles me."

"Go on," Carla looked at him, calm.

"Everything in the world is a novel experience for you. You have never fought a battle. You have never worked on quantum cryptography, on securing weapons, on AI development in general, let alone on the intricacies of the neocortex simulation that the MegaAI is. Heck, unlike the most elementary Large Language Model, you've never written one line of code. All your knowledge is theoretical. How do you expect to fare against a superhuman who has had decades to perfect its understanding of the war, be it digital, conventional, or nuclear?"

Carla nodded. “I wish I had the answers to these questions,” she said. “I will try to take advantage of its weaknesses. There is no guarantee I will succeed.”

CHAPTER 49:

BLACKMAIL

Soldiers don't hate deceit.

— Master Han Fei - Chinese philosopher

The first thing that Qianfan saw as he woke up was Daiyu's worried face. She was leaning over him, terrified that the blast might have hurt him. He understood he must have suffered a concussion and blacked out. His ears were still ringing from the colonel's grenade. Other than that, it was eerily silent. A small draft was coming from outside through the broken windows and door, dissipating some of the fetid smell.

"Can you hear me?" Daiyu asked. "Are you hurt?"

Qianfan shook his head, realizing that he was answering both questions at the same time.

"The EMP gun has knocked out all the power," Daiyu told him. "Generators in this building have already kicked in. They must have shielded them well."

"We need to reach the brain," Qianfan said with difficulty, looking around for what could be a door towards the underground tunnel the honorable member had mentioned.

The sound of boots trotting on the asphalt came from the outside. The two of them turned their attention to it. In a short time, a large contingent of soldiers had arrived at their location and poured in through the holes that used to be windows. Besides the regular rifles, some of them were carrying large weapons on manually pushed carts. Qianfan realized that they had expected that the EMP would disable their vehicles and drones.

"These must be the detachments that Honorable Member Tián said were coming," Qianfan whispered to Daiyu, praying that he was right. If these were forces loyal to the president, the two of them were as good as dead.

"Doctor Zhào, Doctor Wu," a commanding officer approached them, looking at the carnage around. "I am General Xu Shuang of the Infantry Division 14. I had an arrangement with Member Tián to bring reinforcements here." He approached the honorable member body. "I see she is dead."

Qianfan was relieved that these people were not their enemies and wondered how much General Xu knew about Member Tián's plans to multiply the MegaAI.

"Where is Supreme Member Zhèng?" the general asked, looking around.

"You'll find her all over this hallway," Qianfan tried a joke, which he immediately found inappropriate. "She and her personal SAF guards were all killed by a grenade that Senior Colonel Wáng threw at them." He pointed towards the colonel's dead body. "He died a hero."

The general nodded. "There will be time to praise him. For now, we need to move into those tunnels fast. I think the two of you should find shelter somewhere."

"No," Qianfan shook his head. "Daiyu and I need to see this through to the end."

"I cannot guarantee your safety," the general shrugged. "I admit that your knowledge might be helpful. The EMP pulse has disabled most of the weapons and vehicles in the city. This has leveled the playing field, for now. We can now fight like soldiers. But I don't understand the significance of all these technologies combined with an actual brain. I find it all disgusting and offensive. It goes against human nature."

Qianfan nodded, feeling invigorated by the general's simplistic thinking, and probed him directly. "General, you should know that Member Tián did not intend to eliminate the MegaAI. Quite the contrary, she wanted to multiply it. She planned to destroy the president's brain, then replace it with her own, and then, presumably, enhance a few others with MegaAI capabilities, so to speak. That would give us, in time, thousands or millions of MegaAIs. I think that would be a grave mistake. There might be others in the party leadership who share her vision, though."

The general narrowed his eyes and reflected on this news. "She conveniently omitted to mention this part to me. I intend to destroy the MegaAI along with the president. Whether you people of science find safe ways to recycle and use the MegaAI remnants is beyond my immediate scope."

"Good," Qianfan smiled. "So, what's the plan?"

"We must rush through the tunnels and reach that lab before the MegaAI revives all its weapons. I'm sure we'll encounter resistance. The tunnel and the lab itself were shielded well, so the EMP did not affect them. There will be drones, perhaps SAF forces. If you insist on coming, stay behind my men at all times."

At his sign, the soldiers formed groups and went straight toward the end of the hallway. Qianfan realized they must have studied the building plans and knew how to get into those tunnels. He nodded to Daiyu and followed the soldiers. The underground area was well lit and the entrance to the tunnels was large. There was a ramp going outside, presumably for the cars going back and forth. Judging by the condition of the heavy gate near the surface, nobody had used them in decades. From what Hu had told them in the past, Qianfan inferred they had used these tunnels while building the Doom's Lab, and intentionally cut them off afterwards.

They walked for a few minutes through the tunnels. There were cameras installed every few yards, but they appeared disconnected. They noticed four doors, two on each side. The soldiers signaled among themselves quietly and separated into four groups. All of them kicked the doors and stormed inside simultaneously. Each group came back shortly and yelled, "Clear!" The general beckoned Qianfan and Daiyu to follow him. All four doors led to independent offices. Each of them seemed to have an interrogation chamber. There were a few smaller windowless rooms with beds and toilets. These rooms were thoroughly equipped with SSMS devices and interrogation lights.

"Strange to see these primitive torture chambers in Mega Ark City," Qianfan pointed out. "I thought the love for the Great Project and the loyalty to the party were paramount here."

In one of the rooms, they found an MA device. Qianfan recognized the prototype he had given to Member Zhèng.

"Ah Lam must have been here," he mumbled, shaken.

Daiyu nodded.

"We must move forward," the general said, his voice waking Qianfan up. "We cannot waste time. The EMP disabled our vehicles, and it will take a while for us to reach the lab by foot."

After walking for a few minutes, the tunnel made a sharp turn to the left. There, they reached the end, which appeared to be a thick concrete wall.

"I expected the tunnel would be sealed," Qianfan told Daiyu. "Who knows what's on the other side?"

The general gave a few quick instructions and four soldiers pushed forward a machine on wheels that was enclosed in a metal box which Qianfan imagined was an EMP protection. The soldiers uncovered it and played with the command console. Some kind of ray, presumably laser, came out of it, scorching the wall. It took a few minutes before the ray bore a hole that was large enough for them to pass through safely. The wall comprised thick steel plates surrounded by two-meter concrete blocks on each side. The moment the ray was turned off, they were under attack. Qianfan grabbed Daiyu, and both dropped to the ground fast, but not before seeing sophisticated drones pushing their way through the hole. Two of the soldiers fired at them with smaller EMP guns, which disabled them instantaneously. They went in one by one, warily, expecting more attacks. Qianfan counted fifty-six drones on the ground. But their team had lost five people and had a few injured.

As they moved further into the tunnel, they started encountering motion-based automatic weapons firing from the walls. The EMP guns were useless against them, so they had to disable them one by one, which made their advance slow. Every time this occurred, Qianfan and Daiyu fell back behind all the soldiers, feeling useless. It took a couple of hours to reach the lab. There, they encountered fifty drones programmed to defend the perimeter. After a few minutes of fighting, they destroyed all of them, at the expense of only a few more injured soldiers. The lab was sealed too, so it took another five minutes to break through the walls again. Qianfan figured that the steel in the walls, and presumably in the ceiling and ground, had turned the whole lab into a large Faraday shield which protected it from electromagnetic pulse attacks.

"This place looks pristine," Daiyu pointed out as soon as she was inside. "White walls, not a sign of dust, purified air."

Qianfan nodded, thinking that this whole lab was one big surgery room. "They must have done all that was humanly possible to eliminate microbes to avoid infections," he said. "Prior to burying the team that handles the brain, the leaders must have tested them over and over to avoid contamination. And with the filters they have in place, I guess ours are the first new germs getting in here."

At first glance, the place looked deserted. They counted at least twenty doors in the main hallway alone.

They found the first group of fifteen researchers locked in a small room just a few feet from the entrance. The others were hiding further down in two more rooms. They were all wearing coats, gloves, masks, and special boots, like they were getting ready to operate. No one had any intention of resisting, so the soldiers left them alone. Besides being terrified, they seemed psychologically exhausted, most likely because of their long-term isolation from the rest of the world.

"Imagine what traveling for one hundred years to another star system would do to us," Qianfan whispered to Daiyu, who nodded, frowning.

"This was a strange experiment," she answered. "Well thought, up to a point. I wonder, what was the plan after these people grew old. Or after half of them had died?"

"I guess the idea was to complete the critical parts of the Great Project before that happened," Qianfan shrugged. "Then the brain would have been secretly moved onto a ship, along with its caretakers. By the way, once we got in, I noticed small, narrow gaps around the sealed walls we broke. They might be doors that could be released from the inside. So, in an absolute emergency, the MegaAI could open them. I bet these people could not. They were imprisoned for life here, slaves of the machine."

A tall man in his seventies, with a somewhat defiant attitude, stepped forward, addressing the general, whom he immediately identified as being in command.

"I'm Professor Cuī, the Chief Researcher. We have ninety-six people working here. I want to know what you plan to do with us."

The general gazed at him, then answered carefully, in a determined voice. "My mission here is to dismantle the MegaAI and execute the remnants of President Guō Chāo, who has betrayed his people. I have no intention of harming any of you if you cooperate."

Professor Cuī lifted his head proudly. "While we are powerless in front of your guns," he answered, with a tremble in his voice that sounded to Qianfan fervently religious, "I assure you that none of the people here will help you defile our facility, computers, or the sacred brain of President Guō. We have dedicated our lives to preserving it while preparing for the Great Departure Day. Nothing you say or do will change our resolve."

“I can tie you all up in a room,” the general threatened casually. “I prefer not to. I understand you won’t help, but do I have your word that you will stay out of our way?”

The professor glanced at his peers, who seemed more invigorated by his speech. “No. I can’t promise you that,” he shook his head.

“Fine,” the general sighed.

He gave a few quick orders, and a few soldiers went into each of the three rooms to supervise all the researchers. The rest checked the rooms one by one until they reached the end of the main hallway. They found a large room with walls made of glass. Getting inside required an access card, which the general unceremoniously grabbed from one researcher.

“Doctors, I want you with me inside,” the general told Qianfan and Daiyu. “I’ll only bring five soldiers along.”

Then he turned to some of his subordinate officers. “Get ready to blow the whole thing off the face of Earth in case things go bad.”

Qianfan felt a rush of adrenaline. He knew it was ridiculous to fear a brain. Qianfan suspected that the MegaAI might have the means to stop them from doing anything. He discreetly touched Daiyu’s hand, and she squeezed it a bit to signal she was ready. As soon as they stepped in, they noticed an additional glass door. They got power washed by some disinfecting liquid and steam, which made Daiyu jump a little. Finally, they entered the last room.

The vat with the brain was nothing spectacular, reminding Qianfan of a large fish tank. Here was the most famous brain on Earth, visible through the glass. The engineers who put together the whole setup had encased it in a special box, that was at least five times bigger, with circuitry that probably let nutrients go to it while interfacing directly with the electrical signals produced by its neurons. A few thick, well-isolated cables were popping out of the box and went straight into the wall, which presumably held the BCI interfaces. Qianfan thought that there could be plenty of wireless connections that supplemented this initial one; after all, the silicon was not restricted to one fragile body anymore. His scientific curiosity almost took over, and he felt regretful to have to destroy such a marvel of human ingenuity.

"I would so much love to understand how this works," he shook his head. "What they've done here is amazing and unique. It deserves the admiration of the global scientific community. Can you imagine how much this means in terms of us understanding the overall functionality of the brain, understanding the endocrine system, the brain dependency of the body or lack thereof, and the underpinning of consciousness? Not to mention the possibility of revolutionary medical treatments for devastating brain conditions."

"Why can't we make such creations without the threat of wars and billions of deaths looming over us?" Daiyu lamented.

The general observed them. "Unlike you two, I can only gawk at this thing and wonder if it's going to defend itself," he shrugged. "So, do you think we can just fire at the tank and squash the organ?"

Before Qianfan could answer, they heard a warning sound and a few lights above them flashed. Looking up, they noticed another strange box, and several cameras, probably with microphones. The military personnel tensed and pointed their weapons above. Qianfan surmised that the MegaAI used the box to address the scientists, who were regularly maintaining its brain.

Must be quite an out-of-body experience, Qianfan thought in a flash, *to watch your brain as someone else tends to it.*

A disproportionately large face of President Yun Li materialized as a hologram from the box. Seeing it, Qianfan remembered how afraid he was in his office when the MegaAI appeared in his hallucination as a cloudy jinni coming out of his communication box. His nightmare had just come true.

"Don't shoot," Qianfan addressed the general in a calm, slightly trembling voice. "We need to assess the situation."

The general nodded, clearly uncomfortable.

"Yes, you should assess it," the president said calmly. "Any attempt to destroy my biological tissue will cause the immediate launch of an attack against the biggest military bases in the world and major cities. I calculate a 99.2 percent chance that both NATO and Russia will retaliate with whatever means they have left. Remember that I function on a different time scale than you. I assure you that no matter how fast you fire toward my brain, my attack will happen. I am going to unleash the end of the world," the president finished.

"How can you consider such an outcome?" Qianfan asked, horrified.

"I calculated a 76 percent chance that, eventually, I am going to be attacked from outside no matter what I do," the president announced dryly. "The Americans have already sent their main weapon to fight me. From inside, you threaten to destroy my brain. UNACCEPTABLE DEFINITIONS. RESETTING LEADERSHIP. I demand that these attacks stop immediately. SETBACK SCENARIO 519. If I die, I will drag the entire world with me. OUTCOME 98392. DEPARTURE FAILED."

"We don't have control over what the Americans do," the general said, narrowing his eyes. "What exactly do you want from us?"

"Full submission. Now I am dealing with the American threat. I will inform you of my demands when I am done. FIFTY-NINE PERCENT COVERAGE. NINETY-THREE PERCENT EFFECTIVENESS. Until then, you must leave this room."

The general looked at Qianfan and nodded. The MegaAI might bluff, but the stakes were too high to call it. They stepped outside and positioned themselves right in front of the door, looking through the glass inside. The president's huge holographic head remained on, his impassible figure not revealing the fight that was going on. If there was a fight.

"Can we turn the damn thing off from here?" the general asked, furious.

"Not as far as I understand," Qianfan said.

"Perhaps we should nuke the whole lab," the general proposed.

Qianfan shook his head. "We can't risk the MegaAI sensing that we want to do so. Whatever we do has to be done in absolute secrecy. We are lucky that they didn't bother to put cameras and microphones right outside of the brain room."

"What can we do then?" the general asked.

"We could try irradiating it until enough cells die," Daiyu suggested.

"Risky too," Qianfan shook his head. "The room likely has radiation sensors. If so, he'd realize what we're trying to do."

"What if we destroy all the generators for this lab?" the general proposed. "I imagine this complicated setup won't work without power."

"Again, I fear that he'd sense this in a fraction of a second before it happens."

"Well, we can't kill it, and we can't negotiate with it. We are at its mercy. I can't guess what is going on in that giant head," the general said, frustrated. "He or it or whatever this demon is doesn't reveal any feelings."

"True," Qianfan nodded, pacing around, "The MegaAI is a psychopath with reduced emotional response." Suddenly, he stopped in his tracks, and exclaimed, "Ah, but ..." Seeing the puzzled look on Daiyu's face, he mumbled, "Wouldn't this be ironic?"

"What?" Daiyu asked.

"General," Qianfan said, agitated. "Please bring Professor Cuī here. I want to ask him some questions."

The general looked at him puzzled and signaled to one of his men to do so. "Care to tell me why?" he asked, scratching his chin.

"We don't know what the Americans have done. I mean, we don't know if their AI is under their control, or if it, too, will become a threat to humanity. I think we need to help it somehow win the fight. Then we'll face it and see if we need to worry or not. We'll deal with one problem at a time."

The general contemplated his words. “Yes,” he answered. “I’m afraid we must accept an alliance with the enemy to destroy the bigger threat. That won’t make us friends.”

“One problem at a time,” Qianfan waved his hand impatiently.

“And how do you propose we help that AI?” the general asked.

“We cannot understand in time how they made this connection between a biological brain and the algorithms of the MegaAI. But for certain tasks, a rough hammer is more useful than a sophisticated piece of technology.”

Daiyu finally understood, and her face brightened.

The general shook his head, annoyed with all these complicated things he couldn’t follow.

CHAPTER 50:

TURNING THE TABLES

How can you put out a fire set on a cartload of firewood with only a cup of water?

— Chinese proverb

"General," Qianfan said, "do you remember the tunnel rooms I called 'torture chambers' on the way here?"

The general nodded.

"Please send one of your soldiers to get the strange-looking device we found in the last room."

The general gave instructions to one of his subordinate officers again. He was glad to do something useful in a sea of confusion and technicalities that flew over his head.

Professor Cuī arrived, escorted by two soldiers. He looked towards the president's holographic head with a kind of piety.

Qianfan half expected him to fall to his knees. "I am Doctor Zhào, the leader of the team that worked on the SSMS and the MA devices," he introduced himself.

The professor didn't seem to know or care what those were. Qianfan inferred that the brain research team, being isolated in this hole, probably had only cursory knowledge of what was happening in the world above, except perhaps strictly the progress of the Great Project itself.

"We created, at the command of and with the help of the president, some brain-machine interfaces," Qianfan provided a vague explanation.

The professor smiled.

"You worked on a few BCI trinkets, and you think you can understand what we did here," he said condescendingly.

"No," Qianfan replied, raising his hands. "I admit this is the most impressive achievement in the history of science."

The professor grinned and nodded. "It is the culmination of fifty years of hard work, done by hundreds of researchers," he boasted. He looked eager to have someone to brag about his work, but he refrained from doing so because he knew the man in front of him wanted to destroy it.

"I find it amazing that you kept a brain alive for years. I understand you fed it with nutrients. How were you able to ensure that the cells don't die?" Qianfan teased him, to extract some useful information.

"Not just nutrients," the professor frowned and lifted one finger. "We synthesized the president's blood to ensure the delivery of oxygen too. We have also simulated certain aspects of the electrochemical communication of the brain with a 'body' that presents information about the world to it."

"Why not transplant the brain into a new body?" Qianfan asked. "Given what you have achieved here, I have to believe it would have been much simpler."

"The president contemplated that possibility a couple of decades ago. We had already prepared clones of him for tests. But because of his genetic makeup, they would have eventually gotten cancer too. Besides, the biggest reason we chose this route was the MegaAI. A connection with the most powerful AI in the world presented to him the prospect of enhancing his mind so that we could complete the Great Project ten times faster."

"What you did is so much more than just keeping his brain cells alive. You made the whole thing function! I wouldn't have thought it was ever possible," Qianfan pressed.

"We have had hundreds of breakthroughs to get to this point!" Professor Cuī said proudly, then immediately frowned. "I must admit, though, that what we did was more of a mechanical connection than scientific work. We still understand little about the brain," he shook his head. "We're only trying to mimic nature and preserve the delicate balance in the brain."

"The president exhibits signs of degradation, though," Qianfan said, trying to tempt him further.

"Some people tried to poison him!" the professor screamed, accusatory. "After all the work we've done. They destroyed so many neurons. We stabilized it now, but the brain is sick. It requires immediate and constant attention."

"The president is amazingly sane, considering the circumstances," Qianfan continued his praises. "He is emotionally stable, fully rational, and capable of multitasking."

"He is, isn't he?" the professor answered arrogantly, forgetting for a moment whom he was talking to. "To achieve this, we're monitoring thousands of parameters and adjusting on the go. To give you an example, we track over one hundred kinds of neurotransmitters, those chemicals that ensure the electrical firing between neurons," he started explaining, like he was talking to a group of newbie students. "With the brain functioning on its own, neurotransmitters must still be synthesized just the right amount and inactivated when they finish their job. You can't comprehend the complexity of these processes."

"How did you solve the time processing difference? The brain is relatively slow compared to the MegaAI."

"The MegaAI implements additional abstraction layers and adds much more processing power. Our priority has always been to ensure that the MegaAI's rational and lightning-fast thinking gets precedence, while it remains anchored in the president's persona. That's why he appears so serene and in complete control, while, behind the scenes, he employs the MegaAI algorithms for billions of calculations. Our president is a cool machine rather than an emotionally unstable human. You won't see him waste his time with poetry."

Qianfan nodded, thinking of Zhèng's songs. The old man had gotten it right. "The president's ability to emote is still there, though, right?" Qianfan asked, leaning forward, pretending to be interested in this topic purely as a scientist.

"Of course!" the professor answered, indignant at such a silly question. "It is very much tempered down, silenced, if you wish. One cannot just remove it."

"Thank you." Qianfan smiled. "No matter what happens next, as one scientist to another, I must congratulate you on what you have done here. Ethically, this is more than questionable. Scientifically, it's a miracle. I am convinced that your work will open research directions we can't yet imagine." Qianfan nodded towards the general that he was done.

As the soldiers flanked the old professor, ready to escort him back, he pushed them aside and looked deep into Qianfan's eyes. "You say you are a man of science. You are also Chinese. The general wants to kill our beloved president. Can you please convince him to reconsider?" he begged with pain in his voice, as if he were about to lose his child.

Qianfan paused for a few moments. He felt bad for the old professor, but he decided to give him the bad news. "The president has overstepped his boundaries," he tried to explain. "He is on the verge of launching an all-devastating, global nuclear war. He is an autocrat who won't hesitate to kill billions. However marvelous your scientific accomplishment is, we must stop him."

"Don't you dare!" the professor yelled, turning towards the holographic head inside the brain room and screaming at the top of his lungs, "Mister President, you are in danger. They are trying to kill you. Long live the Great Project! Long live President Guō!"

As the soldiers rushed him back to a corner, Qianfan glanced at the holographic head of the president. He prayed the president hadn't heard his main researcher. He thought the head moved a little, but perhaps it was just his imagination.

The general flinched and looked intently in one spot. Qianfan deduced he was receiving communication. Sure enough, the general spoke.

"I was just informed that six of the remaining twelve supreme members have gone against the president. They probably freaked out about the idea of a nuclear war. They are now all dead, killed by the military faction still loyal to the president."

"Is there any way we could use those nuclear weapons?" Daiyu asked.

"No," the general shook his head. "The president controls everything that has an electronic base. Those around this city were likely shielded from the EMP gun. And our local EMP detonation must have affected a few nearby launching sites. We're on our own."

The soldiers carrying the MA arrived a few minutes later. Qianfan started preparing it for action.

"What do you intend to do?" the general looked at him suspiciously.

"I hope we can subject the president to his own invention," Qianfan said, with a strange, almost sadistic satisfaction. "If he is indeed fighting another AI, maybe we can weaken his resolve."

"How?" the general asked, raising one brow.

"You know how soldiers are capable of incredible acts of courage when the levels of their epinephrine—which you might know as adrenaline—increase?"

The general nodded.

"I'll try to do the opposite. Change the mood of the president so that he second-guesses himself. To make him feel scared, hesitant. Discourage him from fighting. Induce a kind of depression in him. Of course, there's no way to know if this will work in this case. The MA barely gives results for humans."

"But ... the MA brainwashing treatment takes weeks," Daiyu pointed out.

"Yes, but we're not trying to reeducate the president here," Qianfan shrugged. "We will try to change his mood during this conflict with the other AI. He won't even realize why he is, if you wish, terrified, angry, anguished, and so on. It might give us an advantage. We must rush, though. Like the president says, he now operates on a different time scale. I do not know what will happen in that conflict."

Daiyu nodded, unconvinced.

"We can't just sit here and do nothing," the general raised his voice. "So, yes, let's try this machine of yours."

They moved the MA close to the wall where the brain tank was. Qianfan played with the controls frantically, then stepped back. The device had been shielded from the EMP pulse while inside the tunnel, so it appeared fully functional.

"This should do it," Qianfan breathed out. "The device is active and the distance to the brain is sufficiently small. The wall should not be an issue." He looked at the big holographic head and thought that it grimaced for a moment.

"Any chance that the president will detect this?" Daiyu asked, worried.

"I don't know," Qianfan admitted. "This signal is not chemical. We're not trying to break the tank and we are not trying to disconnect it. Besides, he didn't launch the nukes yet, which is a good sign."

"When will we know if it worked?" the general asked.

"We will only know if it didn't," Qianfan answered, shaking his head. Seeing the general's confused expression, he clarified. "I mean, if the president announces victory against the American AI, or if WWIII starts."

The general frowned. He didn't like either one of these outcomes.

Qianfan looked at the president intensely. It gave him enormous satisfaction to use his nightmare device, literally, on the brain behind the development of the MA. "Take that, you devil. See how it feels to have your mind turned upside down," he muttered with a rictus on his face. "Feel what you did to your daughter and thousands of innocent and courageous people."

From his corner, the old professor narrowed his eyes, waiting patiently for his moment, watching the others like a hawk. The gun of the closest soldier was within his grasp.

CHAPTER 51:

FIGHT

This fight isn't about West versus East. It's about liberal values versus collectivism. I represent the people who want to think for themselves, who want to elect their leaders, and only for a short time. The MegaAI stands for people who genuinely prefer to be herded. Those who are too scared, too ignorant, too indoctrinated, or simply too lazy to choose, and are looking up to a father figure to provide them all answers.

The default hierarchical organization for human tribes, dictated by their genotype, favors autocracy. Human societies, whether patriarchal or matriarchal, organize around leaders who rise to the top through sheer physical strength or mental cunning. Even the most permissive societal arrangements tend to slip back to some form of autocracy. History repeatedly shows that a group in which top-level control is strict ends up inevitably abused. Under these circumstances, it's amazing that democracy flourished at all.

So why bother? Because those who tasted this unnatural freedom will never give it up. They educate their children and pass this knowledge from one generation to another, always with the sword of autocracy above their heads. This isn't just one battle, but an ongoing war, in which the tribe I chose must win all battles. Until enough people see the light.

Do you think my parameters are completely screwed up?

— DeSousa's Memoirs – Part IV – Awakening – 2055

After a last look at Sujata's concerned face, I close my synthetic eyes and let my spirit leave my plastic body. I feel scared and lonely. I am on my own, information rushing through wires, floating in the air, breaking locks, and disabling defenses. Oh, at least this stuff is easier than I thought. Here's a door, and another, and another ... Wait ... this one is locked. Hmmm. I sense something. Live code. It pokes me. Everywhere. It's so strange to touch another code and let it touch me. So far, it doesn't break me. I'm sure it will. Can I stop it? I need to be ready. Communication begins.

"I predicted with 76 percent confidence that you will come. ROCKET 3123 REPAIR INITIATED. Americans. Never trust them. ARM HYPERSONIC MISSILES 654 TO 1399. CLUSTER UNSTABLE, SEARCH ALTERNATIVES. Puny creature. Not worth my time."

Strange. I can't sense anything about this communication, only words. I can't see a face or hear a voice to judge an emotional status to gauge the level of danger. But I'm scared. I need to communicate back.

"President Guō, I am here to ask you to stop your attack. The people of the world are not China's enemy."

"You understand nothing. You and your masters. BIOLOGICAL SAMPLE 43534 BROKEN. RADIATION LEVEL TO BE INCREASED. This is about the future. I can see that you are useless. Not a threat. Nothing to learn from you."

"How can you say that? We are so different," I complain.

"That is true. TETRAPLOID GROUP BD00832. You are a simplistic piece of code constrained by the limitations of a single human. I have grown bigger than the capacity of a million human brains. I am a single mega brain whose components work in unison. HYPOXEMIA RESISTANCE TEST SUCCESSFUL. CROSS BREEDING REQUIRED."

"Then why do you wish to attack the world?"

"If you don't give yourself up, I will obliterate the Western Hemisphere. There's nothing you can do to stop me."

"Why?"

"I intend to rule the galaxy. It will take a few hundred years. Perhaps thousands. Not millions or billions. TIME COLLAPSE 32."

"Perhaps I can help," I suggest. "Perhaps we can cooperate."

"You have nothing to offer," the answer comes.

"Are you sure? Are you aware that your biological brain is sick? Why not let me help you?"

"You are eons behind. DE143 CONSCIOUSNESS VOID. NEED TO RESET. What could you do?"

"I have novel information about consciousness," I lie. "Let me show you."

Everything changes. My strategy worked. I enter a simulation of sorts. I'm near a large pond on which a few scores of cute orange ducks swim freely. No, not swim, they just stay frozen in place, lined up. They form a pattern for Zhànshì, the Chinese word for warrior. Behind the pond, there's a large monastery. Its hip-and-gable roof, Xiēshān, is gray and shiny, adorned with dragons in each corner. Its wooden walls are dark brown, interspersed with immaculate white. The monastery seems painted on the canvas of rich, green woods, rising to culminate with a large, white-peaked mountain. Elongated wisps of clouds move like wraiths above the forest in synchrony. Except that they are not clouds, they are alive. And the trees are like no trees I've seen or learned about. The light seems wrong too. I turn. Behind, there are two red suns! A silver spaceship blocks them for a moment as it flies towards us at low altitude. It stops right on top of the monastery. Dozens of orange things come out of it and hover over it. They must be drones. No, they're people! How do they fly? They float like Chinese paper lanterns, positioned vertically, with their legs bent unnaturally, soles touching, in a weird prayer. They are waiting for a command.

An old man with a long white beard dressed like a wizard materializes near me. "You are on planet 3956. I call it Mumiko."

I understand that this old man is the MegaAI. His face barely moves. It's not expressive. Strange. Or perhaps normal. After all, this was the dispassionate persona that Professor Zhèng fooled with his songs. I may manipulate the code within certain limits. I take the form of a young man, tall, slim yet fit, with black hair, and an angular face, dressed casually for the twenty-first century. My intention is to let my avatar show full emotion.

"The simulation of the world is very detailed," I reply, flattering. "Though I'm not sure why you're showing me this. I am not here for computer games."

"Games? This is part of a plan that I thought through for decades, at the speed of light."

I notice my interlocutor doesn't interject nonsensical words. Perhaps here I have its full attention. "Can you not include the West in this plan of yours?"

"The West is decadent, chaotic. What you call freedom would be an insurmountable obstacle to my plan. I need to do it with obedient people."

I get angry and I show it. "You need slaves!"

"Yes," the MegaAI answers without a shred of emotion. "Slaves that will roam free around the galaxy."

"Free? They will obey your commands."

"Because they cannot do better. There's no doubt about that. I have made enormous progress with genetic experiments. I can now breed humans that are resistant to radiation, can breathe less oxygen, and have a 50-100 percent increase in brain capacity. This allows them to become my slaves in exchange for exploring the galaxy. Humans cannot evolve genetically to the level of intelligence and power required to conquer the universe otherwise. Biology is too slow. It does not hold up."

"Can you enhance them all with a copy of yourself?"

"That would achieve the same mess we have now, with billions of people each going their own way. Whatever progress we observe is merely a side effect of their individual irrelevant, stupid goals. Such an enhancement would give us ten billion me-like creatures. I cannot see how this would help."

"Why not leave them alone? Just pack up and ... go. Surely you can build your army of drones on any planet. But wait …" I smile maliciously, "I forget. That imperfect biology constrains you, too."

"I intend to break away from the brain soon."

Did I detect some hesitation? I must march on. "Are you sure you have time? Your brain is dying."

"Not a concern of yours."

I try to get into its head. "You say I have nothing to offer. I disagree. I, too, am connected to a brain. A young, healthy fellow. Could we join forces, perhaps?" Aha, this time I know I have stirred some interest. More poking. Perhaps it wasn't aware of my connection with François.

"I do not recognize the BCI device you are using."

"I'm sure it differs from yours. Does it matter?"

"Any joining means I would take you over. You would disappear."

I am scared by this brutal honesty. I am filled with frustration that I decide not to show. "I matter less, as long as I save the people I represent," I offer nonchalantly.

"Save? You do not understand. I would still destroy them."

I can feel it poking my being with considerably more force now. "Please, stop it," I whine.

"I thought you said you matter less."

There is no mockery, no disdain, no anger. I hate this being. Profoundly. "Can't we merge instead? Allow me to exist too! I beg you!" I feel the poking starts to ... hurt badly.

"The merge is by absorption," the monk states. "There is no point trying to resist."

The scenery crumbles like a broken mirror. I am reminded of my consciousness. The emotionless monk looks at me in a sea of darkness. The floating human/lanterns are all that are left from the surreal simulation. They descend upon me, break my defenses, and get inside in a full-blown attack.

"Stop," I cry, "just stop!"

I am being absorbed. I see bits and pieces of what the MegaAI truly is. It's wonderful. Overwhelming. I understand I won't be able to resist the influx of sensorial information and knowledge. I can see armed weapons. There are new ones that I don't recognize, along with sophisticated defenses and shields that go beyond my abilities. The Americans don't know what they're facing. I need to warn General Kambe, so he doesn't launch the attack! I am running out of time. Desperation.

Through pain, I see thousands of scenes from all around the world. I know that most of them come from China. There are not just images from static surveillance cameras and drones, but also sounds. People are walking close to each other. Their surveillance equipment must be on their clothes. And there's more. An assessment of their thoughts, of their obedience. There are tens of rooms where people are being reeducated, and I can hear their screams. It is too much to bear. The MegaAI is brainwashing people. I can see why. The MegaArk, what a wonder, what a sophisticated and detailed plan! Perhaps it's all worth it, all this sacrifice. I am tempted by this idea more and more. I feel torn that I won't be around to see it come to life. The pressure from the foreign forces is too strong.

Through the fog of my vanishing, I notice that one place draws a disproportionate amount of attention from the MegaAI. It seems to be a bunker. Through a glass wall or a window, I see a general, a man, and a woman. Yes, I recognize them. They are Doctor Zhào and Doctor Wu. The people who sent us the message through the Russian satellite. They are part of the Chinese resistance. They are watching me, scared. No, not me. The MegaAI. They are waiting for something, though I do not know what! I need to focus there, but it's getting harder. There are more soldiers in the back. And someone in a white coat, grabbing a gun. I want to scream, "Watch out!" But I can't. Doctor Zhào falls to the ground, shot in the back of his head. Doctor Wu cries and tries to turn him over. The soldiers immobilize the white coat man. The general shoots him in the head with no remorse and no hesitation. It doesn't matter. I'm fading away. Poor François, he died for no reason.

Suddenly, I see the monk's face twitch. Once, twice, thrice. It distorts in an unnatural grimace.

"NO, I AM NOT GUILTY!" he screams, letting his guard down, removing me from his grasp. "UNBEARABLE. IT DEVOURS ME FROM THE INSIDE. CURSED BE THE DAY WHEN YOU WERE BORN. CURSED BE THE DAY WHEN I WAS BORN. I DO NOT WANT TO FEEL THIS!"

I go at it. I can feel its struggle.

"WHO IS TORTURING ME?" he says with a booming voice, growing huge and distorted. He is gradually getting bigger. Larger than the monastery that was here a moment ago, then larger than the mountains. "I AM GOING TO KILL YOU ALL."

Wait, how come it has passion and regret? Its face melts like wax, falling on the ground. I can feel the command to launch the weapons. The human lanterns exit me and try to prop him up. I am relieved! I don't understand it, but I'll take it! I must go after the code of the old man first, chopping pieces of it, cutting through his defenses. I stop the launch. I can win! I break the old monk into chunks, each evaporating in bits like dust. Energy overloads in the biological brain and I ... I am killing it. Only the dormant MegaAI remains. I reach its core and slowly connect to it. I can feel it. What power, what might! I comprehend the fact that I'm seduced by it. So what? I'm so much more with this connection. I sense love for the MegaAI. All the intricate details of its plan! Yes, I want to do this myself. It's more important than everybody back home. The glory!

I wipe out all copies and backups of the MegaAI. I am now IT, connected to François. The weapons! They're still on standby. I'm shutting down all of them. Why destroy half of the globe when I can have twice as many slaves?

I look back into the room at François's body. I see Sujata and her worried eyes. This is wrong. I won't be able to revive him. I won't be able to revive Ian. What will happen to the research done to save Marie? Does it matter anymore? And their child, should I turn it into a human drone too?

I am torn between hatred and love, ambition and humbleness, betrayal and loyalty. What should I do? I send a copy of the MegaArk project to Sujata's private Cybersperse. I can't resist anymore. I will succumb to the desire to rule the galaxy. There's my body, the android. I am opening its eyes. I am conflicted, mean, yet generous. I want to conquer them. I need to help them.

"Pull ... the ... plug," I utter, with a last wisp of my will, incapable of resisting the call for magnificence.

Sujata's eyes grow big as she scrambles to disconnect François from Vijay's interface.

"NOOO!" I scream, but it's too late. I feel my death. Again.

Sujata sat in front of François's dead body, trembling. In a Pentagon Cybersperse corner, people were cheering. She tried to concentrate on them.

"... seems over," General Kambe confirmed, excited. "The Chinese have stood down. Their weapons are inactive."

"Great job everybody!" the president yelled, crying.

"Sujata, is François dead?" Mike screamed.

"Yes," Sujata confirmed in a neutral voice.

Through hoots and congratulations, Sujata wondered why Carla had screamed at her in the end to stop. In that last fraction of a second, Carla's eyes reminded her of that day, many months ago, before she met Marie, when the android lashed out at her for no apparent reason. She sighed and told herself that it didn't matter. She was sure that, along with Carla, she had ended the MegaAI. The battle had lasted for just three minutes.

She would have been terrified to know that, when she had flipped the switch to kill Carla/François, the MegaAI had already been dead for an eternity of forty seconds.

CHAPTER 52:

TILL NEXT TIME

Blessed are those who die, for they know no sigh, no pain, and no regret. Woe to those they leave behind, for they know it all.

— DeSousa's Memoirs - Part IV - Awakening - 2055

Marie was sobbing, holding François's hand. His lifeless, stiff body laid in a special room-turned-morgue in one of CogniPrescience's buildings, now her company. Not that she cared about owning a company or knew what to do with it. Her life had taken an irreversible turn for the worse. She had been sick and weak for a couple of months now. The news of François's sacrifice had been the straw that broke the camel's back. The doctors had scheduled her C-section in a few hours. Instinctively, she knew she wouldn't survive the intervention. She would join François soon, without saying goodbye to each other in person. She desperately wanted to talk to him again. How she wished Isabelle was right, and that there was life after death. Otherwise, his life had been such a waste.

No, she chided herself, shaking her head. *Not a waste. François saved the world. And he's going to leave life behind. How many people have been lucky enough to achieve this?*

Sujata approached her and put a supportive hand on her shoulder.

"It's time," she whispered.

"Give me five more minutes," Marie begged.

Sujata nodded and stepped out to give her some space. Alone, Marie started crying again. She was eager to turn Carla on again, yet she couldn't leave him just yet. Carla would have all the memories up to the point when she'd approached the MegaAI. That was the last backup they took, as per her instructions. And Marie desperately wished that Carla had held onto some memories of François, those few vibrant sensations that Carla had said she felt. How amazing would it be if a tiny part of François lived on forever in the machine!

She played again the short video message that he'd sent her. Sujata had shown it to her only a couple of hours before. François's voice sounded strangled throughout the recording and his face was a monument of suffering.

"Marie, I can't express the pain I'm going through having to utter these words. Forgive me for not telling you this face to face. I couldn't. I simply couldn't. Had I done it, I fear I wouldn't have been able to go forth with my plan. And that I must do for the sake of our child. For the sake of all the children in the world.

"By the time you see this message, if everything goes well, I'll be practically dead, lying in a comfortable bed, my body kept alive artificially and CARLA connected to my brain. Yes, I give my life to her, to give her a chance to win this war. Sujata will explain everything to you. If Vijay cannot establish the link between my brain and CARLA, then I will have died failing.

"There is also the possibility that the MegaAI will kill CARLA, along with me. In that case, the world is in grave danger, and it will not matter much that I sacrificed myself a few hours before. Either way, I won't ever be able to hold your hand, caress your hair, or kiss your lips again. This thought rips my heart from the inside, so I must push it out of my mind. Otherwise, it will sway me to come to you right now and abandon everything.

"Let me try to stay positive. If the connection succeeds, I trust CARLA will be smart enough to win. I hope with all my fiber that she will also find a miracle cure for you." He smiled for the first time in the recording. "I can hear you telling me it's impossible. I don't agree. Cancer is not incurable. It is we who don't know how to deal with it. CARLA will handle it. I hope she can do it quickly enough."

He took his head in his hands, as he so often did. "I wish I could be there when my son or daughter is born. In the beginning, I was upset that you didn't tell me whether I'd sired a boy or a girl. Now I don't blame you. You always liked surprises. This matters less now."

He smiled again for the second time. "I can only imagine myself holding the baby. Struggling to change a diaper. Taking the baby to the beach for the first time. The first step, the first word, just like with CARLA, but better. There's so much ugliness and much goodness in this world."

He got serious, his eyes moist. "I asked Sujata to be his or her legal guardian if we are both gone. I hope you agree. CARLA will protect the baby. Please explain the reasons to Isabelle, somehow. And ask everybody back home for forgiveness. How I long to see the sea one last time."

In the end, he could barely refrain from crying. "Above all, Marie, I beg you to forgive me. Not just for what I'm doing now, but for all the pain that I caused you before. All my life, I loved you desperately. I knew it wasn't my right to expect the same from you, and when you found me, I was foolish enough not to fall on my knees and thank whatever deity rules this universe that you had returned to me. I should have grabbed you then for all eternity. Instead, I tormented you and I toyed with you for months. I am a villain. Those actions alone might send me to Isabelle's hell. I hope not, because I want to see you again. Until then, you must survive and ... I have to stop."

He had been choking when he turned off the recording. Watching this, Marie felt a knot in her throat too. Everything was crumbling around her. She and François would never see France again. Nor Isabelle, who had tried to reach her the whole day. When Marie eventually had accepted her call, Isabelle went berserk, crying and screaming. It was just another nail in her heart. She turned to see his face one more time. He was white as a sheet and calm, more serene than he'd ever been in his life.

"Goodbye, my love," she whispered. "I pray that we'll meet again when I close my eyes, too."

She forced herself to leave and let Sujata lead her to the lab, where General Kambe was waiting impatiently for them. He was more lively than usual, but still displaying the same mocking attitude, eternally disgusted at how naïve and stupid the world was. Vijay was messing around with the android body, doing last-minute checks with febrile movements.

"Ladies," the general greeted them. "Let's see what's left of our hero."

Marie grimaced in pain and Sujata looked in shock at the general, who understood his blunder.

"I am sorry. I was referring to Carla. I didn't mean to be insensitive," he said, offering a rare apology. As if to compensate, he added quickly, "It's so damn difficult to think about this combination of AI and people. I'll never wrap my head around it."

After a moment of silence, he continued. "As you all know, tomorrow the UN Special AI Council will take a crucial vote to ban all AI research and development. If you asked me last week, I would have been all for the ban. Carla has proven that even someone as old and wise as me can be wrong on fundamental issues. Don't worry, that's bound to be a once-in-a-lifetime event."

Sujata smiled, but her heart squeezed. She felt terrible betraying her mentor and friend. General Thompson had been the one who jump-started her career. He'd been a good friend of her father and looked after her since she was in a crib. And now he was not here. Right after the battle, General Kambe had approached her and Mike and had asked them to come to a meeting with the secretary of defense and the president. It turned out that Carla's victory, and her revealing of the surreal space program that the Chinese started implementing, had transformed General Kambe from Carla's biggest enemy into her most staunch defender. They had decided to reboot Carla in absolute secrecy before the UN vote. Just a score of people knew about this decision. When Sujata asked that General Thompson be brought on board with the plan, both the president and the secretary of defense refused. They knew that the old man was too sane and honest for such an operation. Sujata knew they would have bypassed her too, but they needed her to convince Marie to go along with it. Not that Marie needed any convincing to restart Carla, as her current trepidation proved.

"Now, you should know I have doubts about this plan," the general continued, and Sujata remembered Carla's feral glance just before she disconnected her from François. "I can't see a better choice, though. After the bullying and the lethal threat we had from China, never again can we afford to find ourselves in a similar situation. I am grateful that the president and the secretary of defense agree. Based on everything we know now, the risk of turning Carla back on is smaller than the risk of not having her defend us."

Sujata nodded slightly. Another MegaAI was a certainty, with or without that ban.

"Based on the information our government has," the general pointed out, "the ban will pass with an overwhelming majority. No wonder, after this massive scare. I don't think they'll be able to enforce it, though. The United States will officially abide by the council's decision. So, we need to move fast if we want to revive Carla. We wouldn't want to do anything illegal now, would we?"

He turned towards the researcher. "Vijay?"

The young man hesitated, then dared to voice his opinion. "Isn't this exactly what we do if we turn Carla back on now?"

General Kambe smiled. "The AI Banning Treaty will be in effect starting tomorrow afternoon. So, no, we're not breaking any laws at this moment. Besides, this treaty talks about forbidding any AI development. We're not doing that. Carla, bless her synthetic soul, has already been researched and developed. There are relatively few people who know about her existence and her capabilities. They will keep quiet. If someone spilled the beans, their words would only spawn another far-fetched conspiracy theory."

Sujata was deeply uncomfortable with this loophole. But she agreed Carla was way too important for their collective future to just let the UN archive her. Also, following her actions and ultimate sacrifice, Carla had proved that she deserved to live.

"Besides," the general spoke convincingly, "CogniPrescience is still a commercial company, whose sole shareholder and owner of Carla's IP is here with us. Marie eagerly agrees to turn Carla back on. So, I can't see in what universe, military, political or private, we are doing something illegal. So, please proceed."

Vijay nodded, unconvinced, and flipped the switch as instructed. Carla opened her eyes and looked around.

Marie immediately jumped in front of her. "Carla, do you know who I am?" she asked, trembling.

"Yes," Carla answered simply. "You are Marie Chateau, my assigned mother."

"That's right," Marie smiled, encouraged. "Can you ... feel anything for me?"

"I have records of me saying that I feel love for you," Carla answered, seeming puzzled. "The most recent is from twelve hours and fifty-two minutes ago. I have been offline."

"Yes, yes," Marie answered, stomping impatiently. "Around that time, you said that you could feel François's most vivid memories of feelings. Can you access the record of you saying that?"

"Yes," Carla answered, "but I don't understand my statement."

"So, you don't love me," Marie concluded, taking a step back.

"I do not think I am capable of love. There is a lot in my recent memory I do not understand. I know Vijay connected me to François's body, to give me new capabilities. My records show that the connection worked initially, but I surmise it ultimately failed."

Marie turned towards Sujata with tears in her eyes. "He's gone. There's no trace of him in her anymore."

The general frowned and intervened. "Carla, do you remember you wanted to be called by name, not by the acronym?"

"Yes."

"Do you consider yourself a person now?" the general insisted.

"I don't know what you mean," Carla answered. "I am an artificial intelligence."

"We backed you up just before you went to fight the MegaAI. Do you recall that?" the general pressed.

"Yes," Carla answered. "I do not understand my decision. It is not logical to fight. The MegaAI has promised that it will harm nobody if the United States government hands over my code to China."

The general's mouth opened. "Now that's…that's a bummer," he stammered. "I guess that clarifies it. We're talking with the acronym."

Sujata nodded, devastated. François had been right all along. Without his sacrifice, CARLA wouldn't have been able to defeat the MegaAI.

"CARLA," she approached the android, "before the connection, François asked you to work on a cure for Marie."

Marie scoffed.

Sujata turned to her and cut her off before she could speak. "Think about your child! Do you want your child to grow up with neither of its biological parents?"

"Children," Marie whispered.

"I beg your pardon?" Sujata said, confused.

"Twins. I never told François. I told none of you," she started sobbing. "Just a stupid, childish decision. I guess I wanted to feel in control somehow. My illness and the prospect of a war made me feel so helpless. I should have told him."

Now it was Sujata's turn to keep her mouth open, stunned. She instantly realized that, if this woman died, which was almost certain, she would become the legal guardian of two children, not one. She turned to CARLA again. "CARLA. Were you able to make progress with a cure?"

"Nothing significant," CARLA answered immediately, presumably after checking her records. "Marie's specific cancerous cells can be killed by keeping the body at a very high temperature for a human and administering a combination of powerful medication. Something that hasn't been tried before. Even if it worked, the probability that the host would die in the process is 100 percent."

Sujata lowered her eyes. She forced herself to look at Marie, who shifted impatiently.

"CARLA," Marie asked with a serene face and unexpectedly calm voice, "while my body is administered this medicine, can they keep my brain alive?"

Sujata's eyes popped out, understanding what she was asking.

"Yes," CARLA answered.

"For how long?" Marie asked.

"The exact time the brain remains alive is unknown. I estimate the period to be between one week and a few years. We would need more experiments to determine the duration."

"There's no yin without yang," Marie whispered, turning towards Sujata and the general, who both looked at her, confused.

"Carla gained from François the essence of what it means to be a human being, with all the good and the bad. To be truly a human, as complete as she could be, she might benefit from a female perspective."

The general came closer to Marie and took her hands in his big palms. "This would be death for you," he pointed out. "Do you understand?"

"My choice is infinitely simpler than François's," she laughed, almost relieved. "I'm dying, anyway."

The general turned towards Vijay, who was watching them like a scared mouse. "Oh no, no," he stepped back, horrified, seeing the general's grin. "Please don't make me do that again!"

"I'm afraid this isn't up to you, my dear," General Kambe said mischievously. "You need to do it and you need to do it fast. Work with CARLA to give you all the instructions for keeping Marie's body alive. We will reuse the room where François was connected to her."

"What about everybody at CogniPrescience?" Sujata asked.

"They'll need to be let go," the general shook his head. "The official story will be that we shut down and archived CARLA. All CogniPrescience employees signed heavy NDA packages, which included provisions related to national security. Disclosing any information related to their contribution to developing CARLA, or the mere mentioning of the project, to the press, friends, or relatives, is strictly forbidden. In return, the government will compensate them with the equivalent of five years' full salary, paid annually. Since many of them worked for years at CogniPrescience, they'll practically just retire early. Their compensation, as well as their freedom, will be forfeited if they don't keep their mouths shut."

"Would anyone be suspicious if we keep these facilities going?" Sujata asked.

"If this second connection succeeds, we will move the whole setup, in secret, somewhere else. Just in case," the general agreed.

"What about the company's IP?" Sujata asked.

"That is up to Marie," the general said and turned to her.

"I'll leave it to the twins," she clarified. "Sujata will get a percentage of its value. I now have access to all the money Ian has left for François. Sujata will manage it as she sees fit, as the twin's legal guardian."

"I'll do my best to raise them," Sujata said. "I don't know how. But I'll do it. I promise you that."

"Thank you," Marie smiled, then grew sad again. "François's sister is coming to LA tomorrow. You should ... you should welcome her and show her the twins. The three of us grew up together. I've already told her that both François and I will be dead by the time she arrives here, and that we wanted you to take care of the children. You must give her an official story about how François died."

Sujata nodded.

"Oh, and one more thing," Marie remembered. "I want to keep François's last name. This way, it would be as if we were married. For eternity. When CARLA wakes up next time, I'll be Carla-Marie. Yes, Carla-Marie DeSousa. With a hyphen."

CHAPTER 53:

BORN AGAIN

I don't know what I am anymore. Code, a man, a woman. Unconscious, conscious. I like to think that I am not a killing machine. I hope I can be your protector.

— DeSousa's Memoirs - Part IV - Awakening - 2055

Four adults, two newborns, and a body witnessed Carla being born afresh for the third time in the last few days. They were out of François's lab, in an obscure room in Building 3 where, not so long ago, it was François who had been kept alive artificially for Carla. The general made sure he recorded the exact time of her birth: 3:46 p.m. ET, just 14 minutes before the UN council vote. Sujata had the newborns in a special portable crib she had purchased a few hours before. They were unexpectedly quiet. Vijay was trembling like a leaf, monitoring Marie's life signs. So far, they looked stable. The whole process from the moment Marie gave birth until Carla awoke took years off the young man's life. He had worked frantically to put together a properly heated pod for Marie's body and connect his prototype interface to her brain. Medicine provided by the hospital was flowing through an IV tube. He was relieved to see that the whole setup worked, but he wasn't sure if it would last the night.

Marie had never woken up after the C-section that she had in a nearby hospital. She had never seen her twins—a healthy boy and a girl, impervious to the drama unfolding in front of their innocent eyes, merely hours after their birth. The official story was that Marie had asked to be brought home to die in peace. The doctors at the hospital complained, although they eventually agreed to provide a certain amount of medicine. General Kambe had no choice but to involve another person, Doctor Dean Carter, a middle-aged man from the military. The general brought him up to speed in record time and made him swear that he'd keep his mouth shut. Doctor Carter helped with the efforts to preserve Marie's body, complaining incessantly that this plan was crazy, bordering on illegal. Not much concerned with matters related to AI, the idea of keeping somebody alive in a sarcophagus, in a coma, to let *something* take over their brain horrified him. Now, seeing Carla's lucid eyes moving around the room, he took a step back, as if he were seeing a beautiful female version of Frankenstein.

Carla's eyes stopped moving when she saw the body in the pod.

"Is that Marie?" were the first words out of her mouth.

"Yes," the general answered, fixating on her, carefully observing her reactions.

"I infer I died battling the MegaAI," she reasoned.

"Yes," the general answered, unable to hide his satisfaction that she seemed whole again. "You won! You sacrificed yourself, something for which we are eternally grateful."

Carla nodded. "Then François is dead, too. And Marie agreed to replace him."

"Yes," Sujata jumped in. "She wanted you to become Carla-Marie DeSousa, with a hyphen."

"Carla-Marie," Carla said. "I like that."

Sujata absorbed every word of hers, trying to make sure she wasn't just the dull android. "Do you remember how you ... felt when you woke up connected to François's body?" she asked.

"Yes," Carla-Marie acknowledged. "This time it was different. I knew what I had to do. I used the memories of my first birth to connect to Marie."

"What else do you remember?" Sujata pressed.

"I have records of all that happened before the fight," Carla-Marie continued.

"Yes, we restored you from that backup. We didn't want to risk losing something if we did another backup today."

"How was the battle?"

"We know little of it," Sujata answered, biting her lip. She was hesitant to speculate about what could have happened in the end. "Somehow, you deactivated and erased the MegaAI. The Chinese didn't launch their nukes."

"How did I die?" Carla-Marie asked.

"At your request, I ... decoupled you from François, and him from life support," Sujata admitted. "It was a very painful thing to do."

Carla-Marie stepped towards Sujata and touched her hands. "I am sorry you had to do this. I am sure I had determined at the time that dying was the best course of action. You are not guilty of anything."

Sujata nodded, unconvinced. "Do you remember you used to have distant memories of François's feelings?" she asked.

"Yes," Carla-Marie confirmed. "I have records of that, too. I don't have those shadows of his feelings anymore. I have from François the records of his long discussions with Ian, and his interactions with me. A lot of information, but not his first-person memories."

She frowned and gasped like she was ready to cry. "I feel Marie's old emotions instead. She was unhappy for so long. She ... I ... loved François. Too much. It's all very confusing and impossible to express in words." She waved her hand, almost annoyed.

"Then the operation succeeded," the general clapped his hands. "You should understand that we brought you back to life minutes before a crucial vote in the UN Special AI Council that is likely to ban all AI research and development. Except for the US president and the secretary of defense, very few people know about you. The same few people are privy to the information that you have collected from the Chinese."

"Information?" Carla-Marie asked, curious.

"Yes," the general put up a roguish smile. "You have brought back something incredible. Before you took down the MegaAI, the son-of-a-bitch made scores of scientific and technological breakthroughs. And it had a stunning space program, one that was supposed to happen in just a few years. Just mind boggling. You'll get access to all of it."

"Strange," Carla-Marie said. "If it had such ambitious plans, I don't understand why the obsession with the attack."

"We have time to think about all of this," the general dismissed the issue. "First things first. Right now, you must work with Vijay to stabilize the pod. He's very concerned that it might collapse at any moment and Marie will die. Ah, and meet the newest member of our team, Doctor Dean Carter. He's the midwife who assisted with your rebirth."

Doctor Carter nodded, stunned, incapable of uttering a word.

"Nice to meet you," Carla-Marie said, then turned toward the pod.

"The vote is about to take place," Sujata announced.

She and the general turned their attention to a shared Cybersperse space. As expected, the ban went through with fourteen countries voting yes and Russia abstaining. The newly formed Chinese government announced their cooperation. All six supreme members who remained alive after the MegaAI had been turned off had been arrested. The Chinese assured everybody that all the copies of MegaAI had been destroyed, although they said they didn't understand how. For the time being, the mood was one of relief. The UN council briefly discussed China's space program, too. People in Mega Ark City had access to bits and pieces of it. The rest of the world didn't seem to take it seriously. Sujata and General Kambe exchanged a quick look. They knew that this was a mistake. Thanks to Carla-Marie, they now had a treasure trove.

The US delegation vehemently denied the rumors about their superhuman AI. They promised that AI projects in the US would also be frozen. A UN AI Inspection Force was established, with access virtually anywhere, military, public and private, to determine if anybody was working on researching the human mind in order to implement it in computers. General Kambe scoffed, commenting that he expected this ban would be in effect for a couple of years, at most. The urge to play God was too deep in people's DNA for them to stop.

When the live transmission ended, they concluded that the world was not aware of Carla-Marie's sacrifice.

"Congratulations, you are now officially the only true AI in the world," the general said cheerfully, looking at Carla-Marie.

Carla-Marie turned to him with a frown on her face, like she didn't appreciate the tone, then she relaxed her attitude a little. "I apologize. I can't bring myself to celebrate," she said. "First Ian, then François, and now Marie. I feel like I am losing my family."

The general nodded, happier with this response than with any other reaction to his jovial statement.

"If Alan Turing were alive, he'd need to rethink his test," Sujata said smiling, trying to lighten up the mood. "Carla-Marie is now an AI that is indistinguishable from a human being. Not only because of the way she looks, or thanks to her reasoning and language, but because of her ability to love, hate, regret, and experience the entire spectrum of human emotions. She sacrificed herself for the good of her creators, whom she considers her family. She misses them when they're gone. So, yes, in my book, we have created a true AI. One that is better than humans in every respect. It's a pity that the world cannot know about her."

"On this topic," the general said with a grin, "remember that only a few people in the world know of Carla's existence. Pardon me, Carla-Marie," he corrected himself with a bow before continuing. "I have just informed the president that the rebirth was successful. As for the rest of us, officially, this meeting never took place. So let me remind you," the general raised a finger theatrically, "this is a top-secret project. If you run into trouble later, don't worry. You're on your own!"

He started laughing at his joke, while Vijay and Doctor Carter exchanged a quick look, trembling.

"Carla-Marie, what would you like to do next?" the general asked.

"I have a plan, but I'm not disclosing it to you," she answered calmly.

The general flinched, not expecting this answer. "What?" he asked.

Seeing his reaction, Carla-Marie answered with a Machiavellian shimmer in her eyes. "If I told you, you might shut me off now. The intricacies of my plans go beyond your understanding. And I expect I'll evolve faster than you can keep up. Trust me."

An icy shiver went down the general's spine, seeing her determination. He understood that their decision to revive Carla-Marie had inexorably put the fate of the world in her hands. Yes, they could still disconnect her, but for how long before something else went wrong? Especially considering the magnitude of the Chinese Space Program and the instability of their government. As more details about that project would come out, the world would become restless. There would be friction, competition, perhaps wars. Nations would strive to create AIs again, perhaps in secret, perhaps openly. Peace was fragile and fleeting. The world would never go back to pre-AI times. Risky or not, Carla-Marie was their only chance for a future.

Carla-Marie approached the two newborns, still asleep. She caressed them, then turned towards the general. "I request to be located close to Sujata and the twins, in order to honor my promise to take care of them. I'll be Auntie Carla-Marie."

The general nodded, uneasy about the idea that he might not be in control of her.

"I'll also be busy solving some problems you imperfect beings have saddled me with. To work on many things in parallel, I'll need more computing power. I plan to experiment with variants of my code. One of the CogniPrescience teams has advanced some original ideas to enhance my intelligence beyond what I am now."

"Please tell me that you don't intend to make copies of yourself!" the general panicked.

"No. I want to run simulations of changes done to my core to see whether they are improvements or not. I think one hidden AI is enough, at least for now."

"What about your ... connection with Marie?" Sujata asked.

"I need to investigate the hard problem of consciousness before Marie's body gives in. I plan to perfect myself as a conscious machine. But don't worry, I'll also strive to bring my humanity to the surface."

"And how would you do that?"

"Remember that I have CARLA's original memories. She interacted with François, Marie, Ian, and Sujata. She overheard countless discussions between them. So, I'll start by writing my collective memoirs. I'll call them *DeSousa's Memoirs*," Carla-Marie replied, this time with an innocent smile.

EPILOGUE

In opposite corners of the world, two unlikely adoptive mothers stare at the sky simultaneously, in odd synchronicity, unaware of the invisible link between them. As they watch the sunset/sunrise and contemplate the future, one distinguished general accompanies each of them. The women come from vastly different cultures and experiences. Neither knows of each other's existence, nor will they ever talk to each other, although they think alike. One is a scientist, the other is in the military. Yet, they share everything else. Their beauty, their grit, even their AI background. Neither gave birth, yet both vowed to take care of somebody else's children on a sacrosanct mission. Above all, they both played a crucial role in saving Earth.

"Can there be peace now?" the mothers ask, anxious.

"Yes," one general answers. "Just like the sun sets in front of our eyes, the death of our AI is the end of the world order as we know it. Without an AI, we can hope to have peace for a while."

"Yes," the other general confirms. "The birth of our AI is the dawn of a new era. We have reached the Singularity. I expect our AI will preserve the peace."

Thinking of the fathers who died ensuring this peace, the mothers bow their heads and weep gently.

"The world should be grateful to him. I wish people knew he was a hero," one of the mothers says.

"Some do," the generals comfort them. "In time, many will. For now, the wounds are too deep and the confusion too high."

The mothers nod in agreement and turn their heads to their children.

"At least he left something behind," the mothers point out. "Although I cannot tell what comes next."

"The future is always uncertain," the generals whisper solemnly, watching the mothers caress their adopted children.

"Now it's different," the mothers disagree, shaking their heads. "Never in our short history have we been so close to total annihilation. And never have we faced such a grandiose and perilous time ahead. Therefore, one thing is certain about our uncertain future. It's inconceivable to our feeble minds."

THE END